PERRY MASON

2 in 1

The Case of
the Drowsy Mosquito

The Case of
the Empty Tin

PUBLISHED BY POCKET BOOKS NEW YORK

PERRY MASON 2 IN 1

POCKET BOOK edition published April, 1976

The Case of the Drowsy Mosquito

William Morrow edition published 1943

POCKET BOOK edition published July, 1950

12th printing......................February, 1976

The Case of the Empty Tin

William Morrow edition published 1941

POCKET BOOK edition published October, 1969

19th printing......................February, 1976

This POCKET BOOK edition includes every word contained in
the original, higher-priced edition. It is printed from brand-
new plates made from completely reset, clear, easy-to-read type.
POCKET BOOK editions are published by
POCKET BOOKS,
a division of Simon & Schuster, Inc.,
A GULF+WESTERN COMPANY
630 Fifth Avenue,
New York, N.Y. 10020.
Trademarks registered in the United States
and other countries.

"Della, are you sick?"

Perry Mason asked, placing his hand over hers. She tried to smile. "Something I've eaten. There's a burning sensation in my throat—a metallic taste. I'm going to the bathroom."

Mason strode to the window and called to the nurse, Velma Starler, who ran in immediately. "Miss Street," he explained, "went to the bathroom. She had nausea and complained of a metallic taste—"

Without waiting for him to finish, Miss Starler grabbed the telephone and called Dr. Kenward. "He'll be over right away."

"What is it?" Mason asked.

"Arsenic poisoning. Mr. Mason, are *you* all right?"

"When Dr. Kenward comes," Mason said, collapsing into a chair, "tell him he has two patients!"

THE CASE OF THE DROWSY MOSQUITO and THE CASE OF THE EMPTY TIN were originally published by William Morrow & Company, Inc.

Two Complete Novels by
ERLE STANLEY GARDNER

The Case of
the Drowsy Mosquito

CAST OF CHARACTERS

Sun soaked the city streets, filtered through the office window so that the sign reading, PERRY MASON, ATTORNEY AT LAW, was thrown in reverse shadow where the sunlight splashed across the massive table loaded with law books.

It was a benign California sun that still held a touch of the growing greenery of spring. Later on in the season, this sun would burn down from the heavens with a fierce intensity that would dry the countryside to a baked brown, sucking every bit of moisture from the air, leaving a cloudless sky like that of the desert only a hundred and fifty miles to the east. Now it was a golden benediction.

Across the desk, Della Street held a fountain pen poised over the pages of a shorthand notebook. Mason, a pile of correspondence in front of him, skimmed through the letters, dropped some in the wastebasket, tossed others to Della Street with a few crisp comments. Only in cases of the greatest importance did he dictate the exact wording of his reply.

The pile represented accrued correspondence over a period of three months. Mason detested answering letters, and only tackled his mail when the pile had assumed threatening proportions despite the daily weeding of Della Street's skillful fingers.

The door from the outer office opened abruptly and the girl who operated the switchboard at the reception desk said, "You have two clients out there, Mr. Mason. They're very anxious to see you."

Mason looked at her reprovingly. "Gertie, a balmy sun beckons from a cloudless sky; a client, who owns a big cattle ranch, has asked me to inspect a boundary line that's in dispute. The ranch contains twenty-five thousand acres, and I have just asked Della how she would like to ride a horse with me over rolling cattle country. Think of it, Gertie, acres of green grass, live-oak trees with huge trunks and sturdy limbs. In the background, hills covered with sagebrush, chamise, and chaparral; and behind them, a glimpse of snow-capped mountains outlined sharply in the clear air of a blue back-drop. . . . Gertie, do you ride a horse?"

She grinned. "No, Mr. Mason. I have too much sympathy for the horse. The out-of-doors is a swell place on moonlight nights, but aside from that I like food and leisure. My idea of a perfect day is to sleep until noon, have coffee, toast and bacon in bed, and perhaps a dish of deep red strawberries swimming in thick yellow cream that melts the sugar when you pour it on. So don't try to tempt me with bouncing up and down on the hurricane deck of a cattle pony. I'd shorten his wheelbase and ruin his alignment, and he'd wreck my stance."

"Gertie, you're hopeless. As an assistant cowpuncher, you're a total loss. But how would you get along as a bouncer, a Mickey Finn chasing unwelcome clients out of the office? Tell them I'm busy. Tell them I have an important appointment—an appointment with a horse."

"They won't chase. They're insistent."

"What are they like?" Mason asked, glancing speculatively at the electric clock on the desk.

"One of them," she said, "is a typical picture of middle-aged prosperity. He looks like a banker or a state senator. The other is—well, the other is a tramp, and yet he's a dignified tramp."

"Any idea what they want?"

"One of them says it's about an automobile accident, and the other wants to see you about a question of corporation law."

Mason said, "That settles it, Gertie. The tramp's entitled to justice and may have trouble getting it. I'll see *him*. But the banker, with his question of corporation law, can go to some other attorney. I'm damned if I—"

Gertie said, "It's the tramp that wants to see you about the corporation law."

Mason sighed. "Gertie, you're hopeless! Your mind is steeped in strawberries swimming in cream, hot coffee-cake, and sleep. A tramp comes to my office to consult me on corporation law, and you treat it as a purely routine affair! Della, go out and chase the banker away. Treat the tramp as an honored guest. We'll put off our horseback riding until tomorrow."

Della Street followed Gertie through the door to the reception room. She was back in a matter of five minutes.

"Well?" Mason asked.

"He's not a tramp."

"Oh," and Mason's tone showed disappointment.

"I don't quite make him out," Della said. "His clothes are not exactly shabby, but they're well worn and sun-bleached. I place him more as a man who has lived outdoors for some definite purpose, and he's taciturn and suspicious. He won't tell me a thing about his business."

"Let him get sore and leave then," Mason said irritably.

"And he won't do that. He's waiting with the patience of a—of a burro. Chief, I've got it! The man must be a prospector. I should have realized it sooner. He has the stamp of the desert on him, the patience acquired from associating with burros. He's here to see you, and he's *going* to see you—today, tomorrow, or next week. Someone told him to see Perry Mason, and he's going to see Perry Mason."

Mason's eyes twinkled. "Bring him in, Della. What's his name?"

"Bowers. He didn't give me any first name or initials."

"And his residence?"

"He says just a blanket roll."

"Splendid! Let's have a look at him."

Della smiled knowingly, withdrew and returned with the client.

Bowers, standing in the doorway, surveyed Mason with an appraisal which held just a trace of anxiety. He was neither deferential nor affable. There was about the man an aura of simple dignity. The sun-bleached work-shirt was scrupulously clean, although it had been laundered so many times it had gone limp and frayed around the collar. The leather jacket was evidently made of buckskin, and it definitely was not clean. It had been worn until various incrustations of dirt had brought to it a certain polish, like the glaze on pottery. The overalls were patched and faded—but clean. The boots had acquired a pastel shade from long miles of plodding travel. The broad-brimmed hat had seen years of service. Perspiration had left deep permanent stains around the hatband. The brim had curled up into a distinctive swirl.

The man's face dominated his clothing. Behind that face, a simple, unpretentious soul peered out at a world that was largely foreign. Yet the eyes held no bewildered expression. They were hard, determined and self-reliant.

"Good morning," Mason said. "Your name is Bowers?"

"That's right. You're Mason?"

"Yes."

Bowers walked across the office, sat down across from Mason and glanced at Della Street.

"That's all right," Mason said. "She's my secretary. She keeps notes on my cases. I have no secrets from her, and you can trust her discretion."

Bowers clasped the brim of his hat between bronzed fingers, rested his forearms on his knees, let the hat swing back and forth.

"Just go ahead and tell me your troubles, Mr. Bowers."

"If it's all the same with you, call me Salty. I don't like this Mister stuff."

"Why 'Salty'?" Mason asked.

"Well, I used to hang around the salt beds in Death Valley quite a bit and they got to calling me that. That was when I was a lot younger, before I teamed up with Banning."

"And who's Banning?"

"Banning Clarke. He's my partner," Salty said with simple faith.

"A mining partner?"

"That's right."

"And you're having trouble with him over a mine?" Mason asked.

"Trouble with *him?*"

"Yes."

"My gosh!" Salty exploded. "I told you he was my *partner*. You don't have trouble with a partner."

"I see."

"I'm protecting him. It's a crooked corporation—a crooked president."

"Well, just go ahead and tell me about it," Mason invited.

Salty shook his head.

Mason regarded the man curiously.

"You see it's this way," Salty explained. "I ain't smart like Banning. He's got education. He can tell you about it."

"All right," Mason said crisply. "I'll make an appointment with him for—"

Salty interrupted. "He can't come. That's why I had to come."

"Why can't he come?"

"The doc's got him chained down."

"In bed?"

5

"No, not in bed, but he can't climb stairs and he can't travel. He has to stay put."

"His heart?"

"That's right. Banning made the mistake of housing-up. A man that's lived out in the open can't house-up. I tried to tell him that before he got married, but his wife had sort of highfalutin' ideas. Once Banning got rich—and I mean stinking rich—she got the idea he had to get high hat. Well, I shouldn't say anything against her. She's dead now. What I'm telling you is that a desert man can't house-up."

"Well," Mason said good-naturedly, "I guess we'll have to go and see Banning."

"How far from here does he live?" Della Street asked with sudden inspiration.

"About a hundred miles," Salty announced casually. Mason's eyes twinkled. "Put a notebook in a brief case, Della. We're going to see Banning. I'm interested in the miner who housed-up."

"He ain't housed-up now," Salty said hastily. "I fixed that as soon as I got there."

"But I thought you said he was," Della said.

"No, ma'am. The doctors say he can't leave the place, but he ain't housed-up."

"Where is he then?" Mason asked.

"I'll have to show you. It'd take too long to explain, an' when I got done, you wouldn't believe me, anyway."

2

At thirty miles an hour, Perry Mason turned right at the city limits of San Roberto, trailing along behind the battered, unpainted 1930 pickup in which Salty Bowers was leading the way.

The car ahead turned sharply and began to climb.

"It looks as though he's going to give us a whirl through the exclusive residential district," Della Street said.

Mason nodded, took his eyes from the road long enough to glance at the ocean far below—a blue, limpid ocean with a fringe of lazy surf, a border of dazzling white sand outlining the fronds of palm trees.

The driveway skirted the crest of sun-drenched hills, spotted with country estates of the wealthy. In a small amphitheater below, less than a mile away, Mason could see the dazzling white of the little city of San Roberto.

"Why do you suppose he's taking us up here?" Della Street asked. "He certainly can't—" She broke off as the dilapidated car ahead, wheezing and knocking, rattling and banging, yet covering the ground with dogged efficiency, swung abruptly to a halt by the side of a white stucco wall.

Mason grinned. "By George, he lives here. He's opening the gate."

Della Street watched as Salty's key clicked back the lock on a big gate of ornamental grillwork.

Salty Bowers returned to his automobile and wheezed it through the gates, and Mason followed.

There were a good six acres in the place, a location where real estate was valued by the inch.

7

The spacious Spanish-style house with white stucco and red tile had been designed to fit into its surroundings. It sat back high up on the sloping ground, as if it had simply settled itself to enjoy the view. The terraced grounds had been so skillfully landscaped that it seemed as if Nature herself had done most of the work, and man had only added an occasional path, a few stone benches and a fish pond.

The high stucco wall wrapped an air of privacy about the estate, and, at the far corner, outlined sharply the weird forms of desert growth, cacti, creosote and even the gawky arms of a cactus palm.

Della Street all but gasped at the view which swept out before them in a vista of blues, dazzling whites and restful greens.

"Is *this* Banning Clarke's house?" Mason asked Salty when the latter had moved up to his running board.

"Yep. This is her."

"A beautiful house."

"He don't live there."

"I thought you said he did."

"He don't."

"Pardon me. I misunderstood you. I asked if this was his place."

"It's his place. He don't live in the house. I pulled him out of that. We're camped out down there in the cactus. See that little column of smoke going up? Looks like he's cooking up a bite to eat. It's just like I told you. He housed-up. That put his pump on the blink. So I sort of took over. He's too weak to go gallivantin' around the desert yet. The doc says he can't even climb stairs. I'm gettin' him back in shape. He's better now than he was last week—better last week than he was last month."

"You're eating and sleeping out there in the grounds?"

"Uh-huh. That's right."

"Then who's living in the house?"

"People."

"Who?"

"I'll let Banning tell you about that. Come on. Let's go see him."

They walked down a trail into the sandy corner devoted to a cactus garden. Here prickly pear grew in ominous clumps. Cholla cactus seemed delicate and lace-like. Only those who were acquainted with the desert would realize the wicked strength of those barbed points or the danger that lurked in the little balls of spine-covered growth which dropped to the ground from the parent plant. Here also were spineless cacti growing to a height of some ten feet, furnishing a protective screen as well as a windbreak for the rest of the garden.

A six-foot wall of varicolored rocks skirted the cactus garden. "All rocks from desert mines," Salty explained. "Banning built that wall in his spare time before his heart went bad. I hauled in the rocks."

Mason let his eye run over the highly colored rocks. "You kept the rocks from each mine separate?" he asked.

"Nope. Just hauled 'em in and dumped 'em. They're just color rocks. Banning arranged 'em."

The little trail twisted and turned, detouring the cactus patches, making it seem as if they were walking through the desert itself.

In a little cove in the cacti, a very small fire was burning in a rock fireplace on top of which had been placed a couple of strips of iron. Straddling these iron strips, a fire-blackened agateware stewpan emitted little puffs of steam as the boiling contents elevated the lid in spasmodic jerks.

Beside the fire, squatting on his heels, watching the flame with an intensity of concentration, was a man of perhaps fifty-five. And despite the fact that he was thin, he seemed to have gone soft. The flesh had sagged under his eyes, dropped down on cheeks and chin. In repose, the lips seemed flabby and a little blue. Only when he looked up and his visitors caught the steel-gray impact of his eyes was it apparent that while the body had gone soft the soul within the man was hard as nails.

He straightened up. A smile lighted his face, his pearl-gray cowboy hat came off in a sweeping bow.

Salty Bowers said succinctly, "This is him," and then after a moment, "The girl's the secretary. . . . I'll watch the beans."

Salty moved over to the fire and assumed a squatting position, sitting on the heels of his boots looking as though he could be comfortable in the position for hours. His attitude was that of a man whose duty has been done.

Mason shook hands.

"You're just in time for a little bite of lunch—in case you can eat plain prospector's grub," Banning announced, glancing surreptitiously at Della Street.

"I'd love it," she said.

"There aren't any chairs, but you don't need to scrape away the sand to make certain there isn't a sidewinder in the place where you're going to sit. Just sit down."

"You seem to have quite a little desert of your own here," Mason said by way of making conversation.

Clarke grinned. "You haven't seen it all, yet. How about taking a look around my little domain before you sit down?"

Mason nodded.

Clarke led them around a large clump of cactus into another little cactus-enclosed alcove. Here, two burros stood with heads lowered, long ears drooping forward. A couple of worn packsaddles were on the ground, together with a litter of pack boxes, ropes, a tarpaulin, a pick, shovel and gold pan.

"Surely," Mason said, "you don't use these here?"

"Well," Clarke said, "we do and we don't. The outfit belongs to Salty. He couldn't be happy away from his burros and I don't think they'd be happy away from him.

And somehow you wake up feeling better if a burro bugles you awake than when you just sleep yourself out. Now, over here—right over around this trail, if you will, please. Now over here we have—"

Banning Clarke abruptly ceased talking, whirled to face Mason and Della Street, lowered his voice almost to a whisper, spoke with swift rapidity. "Don't ever mention this in front of Salty. They've set a trap for him—a woman. Once this woman marries him, she'll live with him a couple of months, sue him for a divorce, and either grab his stock or tie it up in litigation. He's absolutely loyal. He'll do anything I ask him. I've told him I want him to pool his stock in a certain mining company with mine. The minute that woman finds out she can't get control of the stock, she'll never marry him. He doesn't know this—why I'm doing it. He doesn't understand what's back of all this, but once this woman realizes that stock has been tied up so she can't get her hands on it she'd no more think of marrying him than she would of jumping into a hot furnace. Don't say anything about this."

Almost immediately Clarke raised his voice and said, "And this is our bedroom."

He indicated another little sanded alcove. Two bedrolls were neatly spread out in the shade of a big cactus.

"Some day I'm going to move out of here and back into the real desert. It won't be today, tomorrow, or the next day, but I'm starved for the desert. I don't suppose I can explain it so you'll understand."

"Salty gave us a pretty good explanation," Mason said.

"Salty isn't much on using words."

"He's pretty good at conveying ideas, though," Mason observed.

"Ever hear of the Louie-Legs Mine?" Clarke asked abruptly.

"I don't believe I have. Rather an unusual name, isn't it?"

"It's the name of that burro over there. We named the mine after him. It was a good strike. Salty sold out his interest to a syndicate, got fifty thousand and blew it all in. A few months later he woke up one morning stony broke."

"Oh," Della Street exclaimed sympathetically.

There was a twinkle in Banning Clarke's gray eyes as he shifted them to Della. "That," he announced, "was the sensible thing to do. That's what *I* should have done."

Mason chuckled.

"You see," Clarke went on, "we get a warped perspective on money. Money isn't worth a thing except to use in buying something. And money can't buy anything better than the life of a prospector. There's something back in a prospector's subconscious mind that realizes this. That's why so many of them try to get rid of money as quickly as possible. I hung onto my money. It was a mistake."

"Go on," Mason said, "you're beginning to say something."

"I kept my interest in the mine," Clarke said. "I should have thrown it away. That mine kept getting richer the more we developed it. The syndicate that had purchased Salty's share tried to freeze me out. We had litigation. Then one of the members of the syndicate died. I picked up his stock. That gave me control. After that I got the other shares. I called Salty in one day and told him I'd bought his stock back for him. I told him I'd give him some and hold the rest in trust. He almost cried with gratitude. For a month he lived here with me and everything was fine. Then he went on a bat again and came back broke. This time he was so ashamed he couldn't face me. He disappeared into the desert.

"Then I saw a chance to make some more money. I organized the Come-Back Mining Syndicate, started buying up old mines, developing them and bringing them back. It was a hectic life. My wife had social aspirations. I found myself living in a huge house, attending functions for which I cared nothing, eating heavy meals of rich food— Oh well, there's no need to go into that.

"I'd been a plunger all my life, but I'd made good on my gambles. My wife disapproved of the wild chances I took, so I put virtually all of my property in her name. Then I wanted to go hunt up Salty and go back into the desert. The fact that I even thought of such a thing shocked and hurt her. She wasn't well at the time. I stayed on. She died. Her will left all of her separate property to her mother, Lillian Bradisson, and to her brother, James Bradisson. I don't think she had ever anticipated the effect of that will. Because I was the producer she thought I was rich. She didn't realize that inasmuch as that stock had been a gift, she had left me broke. I went to court, claiming that the stock was really community property, kept in my wife's name for her protection."

"And you want me to represent you in that case?" Mason asked with an obvious lack of enthusiasm.

"No," Clarke said. "The case was settled. The judge who tried it suggested it would be a good thing if we'd quit fighting and split the stock sixty-forty. We did that. There'd been hard feelings engendered over the litigation. Jim Bradisson, my brother-in-law, thinks he's a business genius. He'd never amounted to anything, but always claimed it was because he'd been hounded by bad luck. My wife was a lot younger than I. He's only thirty-five, cocksure of himself, conceited. You know the type."

Mason nodded.

"My wife's death, the life I'd been leading, the worries, and then that litigation coming on top of everything else was too much for me. I broke all at once. My heart went bad. My nerves went to pieces. Salty heard I was sick, and showed up. Then a peculiar thing developed.

13

It turned out that the stock I'd set aside for Salty, holding it in trust for him, represented the controlling interest in the company.

"Salty was shocked to find how ill I was. He started to bring me back out of it. I think he's going to do it. I turned the stock over to him so he could vote it. Between us, we keep Jim Bradisson from going absolutely hog-wild. And then Salty had to go and fall in love. I think Mrs. Bradisson engineered it. He's going to marry. His wife will get that stock just as sure as I'm standing here. I want you to draw up a pooling agreement and—"

He broke off just as the sound made by beating on the bottom of the frying pan with a big spoon announced that Salty had lunch ready.

"I'm going to have Salty sign a pooling agreement by which he votes his stock with mine," Clarke went on quickly, as the lunch call subsided. "I wanted you to know why I was doing it so you wouldn't ask too many embarrassing questions. If Salty thought I doubted the woman he's going to marry, it would hurt him."

"I see," Mason said. "That's all you wanted?"

"No. There's one other thing, but I can talk that over with you in front of Salty."

"What is it?"

"It's a fraud case. I want to hire you to represent the defendant. You're going to lose the lawsuit. You haven't a leg to stand on."

"Who's the plaintiff?"

"The corporation."

Mason said, "Just a minute. Are you trying to retain me so you can control both sides of the litigation and—"

"No, no. Don't misunderstand," Clarke said. "Win it if you can, but you can't. You're licked before you start."

"Then why go to court?"

For a moment Clarke seemed on the point of giving Mason his full confidence. Then the beating of the frying pan was resumed and Salty's voice called out, "Come and get it or I'll throw it out."

Clarke said abruptly, "I can't tell you all of the ramifications."

"And I don't think I'll handle the case," Mason said.

Clarke grinned. "Well, anyway we can eat some lunch and talk it over. I think you'll handle it when you know more about it. And after a while there'll be another matter—a mystery you'll have to solve. And in the meantime Jim Bradisson is buying mines by the dozen from Hayward Small, and I think it's a situation that stinks. But by all means let's eat."

3

They sat around the little cooking fire over which a kettle of dishwater was now steaming. Salty, moving with a certain awkward efficiency, seemed to do everything without appreciable effort. There were well-cooked frijoles, a dish made of jerked venison chopped up and cooked with tomatoes, onions and peppers, cold bannock, thick sirup, and big agateware cups of hot tea.

Banning Clarke attacked the meal with relish, cleaning out his plate and passing it over for a second helping.

Salty's eyes twinkled. "Couple o' months ago," he said, "he was toying with his grub—couldn't eat."

"That's right," Clarke agreed. "My heart started going bad and kept getting worse. The doctors had me taking medicine, then keeping perfectly still. Finally, they had me in bed. Salty showed up and made his own diagnosis. He said I had to get back out in the open. The doctor said it would kill me. So Salty fixed up this little camp out here in the cactus garden and moved me out here. I've been eating and sleeping out in the open, living on the sort of grub I'm accustomed to, and I can feel myself getting better every day now."

"Your heart's a muscle just like any other kind of muscle," Salty said positively. "You get to living soft, and your muscles *all* get soft. The main thing is fresh air and sunshine. I don't mind telling you, though, this air sorta gets me down. It ain't like the desert. It's nice all right, but when fog comes in from the ocean—*b-r-r-r!*" Salty shivered at the very thought.

"Won't be long until we'll be getting out of here," Clarke promised. "Miss Street has brought a portable typewriter, Salty. Mason can dictate an agreement pooling our stock. We can sign it and get it over with so Mr. Mason won't have to make another trip."

"Suits me."

"What about this fraud suit?" Mason asked.

Clarke said, "I'll have to tell you a little something about how I'm situated here so you'll get the picture. I have a nurse who lives in the house and keeps an eye on me, Velma Starler. I have an eccentric housekeeper, Nell Sims. She kept a restaurant out in Mojave. Salty and I used to eat there whenever we were in that section of the country. After my wife died she sort of moved in."

"There is perhaps some bond of affection?" Mason asked.

Clarke laughed. "Not in that way. She's married and has a daughter by a former marriage around twenty years old. She's really a character. Her husband, Pete Sims, is just as much of a character in his way as she is in hers. Pete's a claim-salter, a bunco artist, and a periodic drunkard with an aversion for work. Hayward Small, a mining broker and promoter who has been dabbling around in psychology and the power of mental suggestion, told Pete, a year or so ago, about split personalities— and ever since then Pete has had a secondary personality for a scapegoat. It's absolutely ludicrous, but he seems naïvely sincere about it. He claims Small asked permission to use him as a subject in conducting some hypnotic experiments, and that almost as soon as he became hypnotized this secondary personality began to make its appearance. What makes it so utterly ridiculous is that Pete hasn't a sufficient idea of split personalities to make his stories even slightly plausible. He just goes ahead with his drinking and swindling and then blames all of his lapses on this secondary personality, a mysterious entity whom he calls 'Bob.' "

"Makes it handy," Mason said, and then added, "for Pete."

"Very."

"Does *anybody* believe him?"

"Sometimes I think his wife does. You never know just what Nell believes and what she doesn't believe. She has a peculiar philosophy of her own and is given to garbling proverbs. People used to flock to her restaurant just to hear her garbled proverbs. She's great for interpolating short comments. However, you'll meet her."

"They're all living at the house?"

"Yes."

"Also Mrs. Bradisson and James Bradisson?"

"That's right."

"Anyone else?"

"This Hayward Small I was telling you about. He's a mining broker. I think if we could uncover the actual relationship between Small and Bradisson we'd have something."

"In what way?"

"Since I became ill, Bradisson has become president of the company. The company is spending money right and left buying new mining claims. Nearly all of them are handled through Hayward Small. Of course, on the face of it it's all right, but I think Bradisson is getting some sort of kickback from Small. I haven't been able to prove anything."

"And this fraud action?"

Clarke chuckled. "Nell Sims had a string of mining claims that she'd taken in on a board bill. Everybody considered they were pretty worthless. They are. Pete Sims sold the claims to the corporation. They're the Shooting Star group. He swindled Jim Bradisson into buying them. The corporation claims Pete salted the mines and juggled samples so that he gave the properties an entirely fictitious value."

"Can they prove any of that?" Mason asked.

"I'm afraid they can prove every bit of it. But I want you to fight the case for Mrs. Sims. *And I want everyone to know that I have retained you to do so.*"

18

"And you expect I'll lose it?"

"I'm sure you will. When Pete showed up on one of his occasional homecomings and found Nell ensconced in a house where a tenderfoot had money to spend for mines, the temptation proved too much for him. He proceeded to take Bradisson to the cleaners. Pete's an innocent-appearing chap, but he pulls some mighty fast ones. He's a terrible liar, a whimsical crook who readily admits his own trickery, only blaming everything on his secondary personality, the unscrupulous 'Bob' who takes over every so often."

"And why do you want to have it known you've retained me to fight the fraud?" Mason asked.

"That," Clarke said, "is something I can't tell you. I—Oh, here's Miss Starler now."

Mason turned to watch the woman who came swinging along the sandy path—a woman in her early thirties, Mason judged, with finespun hair that glinted gold in the sunlight, slate-gray eyes that seemed just a little wistful, and a mouth that could smile easily.

Clarke said hastily in a low voice, "My doctor says she's too sympathetic to be on general duty. He likes to get her out on chronic cases where— Decided to check up on me, eh? Come on over and meet the company."

Clarke performed introductions. Velma Starler said, "Remember, you're supposed to lie down for half an hour after eating. Stretch out over there in the shade and relax."

She turned to Mason with a laugh. "He's rather an obstreperous patient. Now that Salty has entered the picture, I have my hands full trying to make him behave."

Clarke said, "Just a little business to do today, Velma. We'll have it over with in half an hour. Then I'll rest."

She frowned slightly, said, "I promised Dr. Kenward I would make you rest every day.

"And Nell Sims," Velma went on, "wants to know if

you won't please come in and have a bite of *civilized* grub."

"Civilized grub!" Salty growled. "A lot of spiced-up lettuce leaves and green vegetables. He ain't used to that stuff. He's used to good plain grub, and that's what he's getting out here."

Velma's laughter was easy and spontaneous. It made the others want to laugh too. And Mason could see the nerve tension which had gripped Banning Clarke as he recited his business troubles relax under her easy good-natured affability.

"The trouble with you men," she said, "is that you've been partners too long. Mr. Clarke thinks that anything Salty cooks is all right. It's like Nell Sims says: 'The real way to a man's stomach is through his heart.'"

Mason said, smiling, "Well, that's a novel way of quoting an old proverb."

"Wait until you meet Nell Sims," she said. "She's full of those things. Well, I'll be running back to the house. I'm very glad to have seen you, and I hope you get things cleaned up so Mr. Clarke doesn't worry about them." Her glance at Mason was significant.

"We'll try," the lawyer promised.

Della Street said, "I'll go get my portable typewriter out of the car and—"

"I'll get it," Salty said. "I know right where it is. I saw you put it in."

Velma Starler said, "Well, I'll be running along. I— Oh, oh—here comes Nell Sims with your fruit juice."

She turned to Perry Mason, said jokingly, "There seem to be three dietitians on the job. Dr. Kenward tries to work out a balanced diet, but Nell Sims thinks he needs more fruits and salads, and Salty Bowers thinks he needs more of what he calls plain victuals."

The woman who had rounded the patch of cactus carrying a tray on which was a big glass of tomato juice stopped abruptly.

"It's all right, Nell," Banning Clarke said. "This is Miss Street and Mr. Mason—Mr. Perry Mason, the noted lawyer. He's going to represent you in that fraud case."

"Oh he is, is he?"

"Yes."

"Who's going to pay him?"

"I am."

"How much?"

"Never you mind."

She said inclusively to Della Street and Perry Mason, "How do you do," and added abruptly, *I'm* not going to pay you anything. My husband sold that mine, I didn't."

Nell Sims was somewhere in the fifties, a strong woman whose shoulders had been stooped by hard toil, a competent big-boned worker who had never shirked a job in her life. Her eyes, black and inscrutable, had receded back of heavy dark eyebrows, to peer out at the world over heavy pouches; but she gave an impression of robust strength, of two-fisted competency.

"Nell insists that I don't get the proper vitamins in my camp cooking," Clarke explained. "She's always following me around with fruit juice."

"Better get fruit juice from Nature than bills from doctors," Nell said. "I'm always telling him that a stitch in time is worth a pound of cure. I've got some nice lunch up at the house if you folks would like to eat."

"Thanks. We've just had lunch," Mason said.

Nell Sims surveyed the empty plates piled on the sand, and all but sniffed. "That Salty's going to be the death of you yet," she said to Banning Clarke. " 'Ptomaine Stew' they used to call the stuff he cooked up when he was cooking out at the Desert Mesa Mine. I've known him for thirty-five years. He ain't never—"

Salty came around the big cactus clump carrying Della Street's portable typewriter and her brief case. "What's that you're saying about me?"

"Drat this cactus," Nell exclaimed irritably. "You can't see around the stuff and it don't give you no privacy. Land sakes, you can't even talk about a body without him sticking his ears in on the conversation. Well, it just serves you right, Salty Bowers. They say an eavesdropper never gathers no moss."

Salty grinned good-naturedly. "Professional jealousy," he explained to Perry Mason.

"Jealousy nothing," Nell said. "That slum you cook would kill a horse."

"*I've* always thrived on it."

"Yes, you have!—You used to come sneaking into my restaurant so as to get some decent home-cooked food. The trouble with you, Salty Bowers, is that you ain't scientific. You don't know nothing about these here vitamins, and you cook everything in grease. Taking that stuff into the system is just loading it up with so much poison."

Salty grinned and let it go at that.

"Nell has just so much sputtering to do," Clarke explained, "but she's fond of Salty, aren't you, Nell?"

"Crazy about him," she said sarcastically. "He's without an equal in his field—so's sandpaper. As a cook I think he's one of the best burro packers in the business. Well, give me that empty glass and I'll be getting out of here. Don't want me to take those dishes up to the house and give them a decent wash, do you?"

Salty pulled a brier pipe from his pocket, tamped tobacco into it, grinned up at Nell and shook his head. "You get 'em all soapy."

"Know what he does to dishes?" Nell asked Della Street. "Spreads them out on the ground, rubs sand in them until the sand comes out dry, then he scalds them off with about a cupful of water."

"Only way on earth to get dishes really clean," Salty said, puffing contentedly at his pipe. "Out in the desert you have to wash 'em that way because you haven't much water; but if you come right down to it, that cleans 'em. You take good clean sand and scour 'em out, and then wash the sand out, and you've got a clean dish."

"Clean!" Nell sputtered.

"And I mean *good* and clean."

"Just plain poison," Nell insisted. "I don't know what bad influence brought you back to poison Banning. You'd ought to be up at the house cooking for that brother-in-law of his. A little poisoning would do that man good."

Salty twisted his mouth into a smile. Little puffs of white smoke emerged at regular, contented intervals. "Why don't *you* poison him, Nell?"

Of a sudden, her face became utterly wooden in its lack of expression. She took the empty glass from Banning Clarke, started away, then turned and said meaningly to Salty, "Many a time in jest we cast pearls of wisdom before swine," and marched away.

Mason, grinning broadly, opened his cigarette case, passed it to Della Street, offered one to Banning Clarke. "I'd say," he announced, "she's quite a character. Where does she get the garbled proverbs?"

"No one knows," Clarke said. "Sometimes I think she twists them unintentionally; and then again, I think she's done it deliberately to make them conform to a philosophy of her own. At any rate, she's made a lot out of her stuff. The boys around Mojave used to come in to hear her talk as much as to eat her grub. Can you fix up that agreement here?"

Della Street opened the portable typewriter, balanced it on her lap, opened her brief case, fed in paper and carbons. "I've never typed out a pooling agreement in an imitation desert in the millionaire row of San Roberto," she said, "but I can certainly try. It may not be a very neat job."

"We don't care what it looks like," Banning Clarke said, "just so it's binding."

Mason nodded, asked a few questions, and started

dictating the agreement to Della Street. When he had finished, he handed a copy to Clarke and one to Salty Bowers.

Clarke studied the paper carefully. Bowers didn't even bother to read his copy.

"You've got to read it," Mason told him.

"Why?"

"It might not be legal unless you did."

Bowers picked up his copy, laboriously read through it, his lips moving as he silently pronounced the words.

"All right?" Mason asked.

Banning Clarke whipped out his fountain pen, scrawled a signature across the agreement, handed the fountain pen to Salty Bowers.

Bowers signed both agreements, gravely handed the pen back to Banning Clarke, picked up his pipe, started to put it back in his mouth, then changed his mind, let his eyes bore into those of his partner. "She's going to fool you," he said.

"What do you mean?" Clarke asked with that quick nervousness which showed embarrassment.

"You know what I mean," Salty said, and then put the pipe to his lips and scraped a match into flame. He paused with the flaming match held over the bowl of the pipe, shifted his eyes once more to Banning Clarke.

"She'll stick," he announced, and then sucked flame down into the crusted brier bowl of the pipe.

■ 4 ■

Velma Starler, R.N., had been troubled of late with insomnia. Nurselike, she fought against taking drugs, particularly as she realized that her sleeplessness was due to an inner conflict.

She knew what "Rinkey" would say. Rinkey was her brother, a year younger, supercharged with the spirit of adventure, his head filled with a lot of definite ideas—new, unconventional ideas about people, about property, and about human rights. Rinkey would think she was wasting her time being tied by a golden chain to a pampered millionaire whose life was of no great importance. Rinkey was flying a plane somewhere in the South Seas. The Army needed nurses. Why didn't Velma get in where she could do some good, he kept writing.

That was one side of the picture. The other was Velma's mother. Her mother said, "Velma, you aren't like Rinkey. He's restless. He can't stay still for a minute. He'll always be in danger. He loves it. That's his nature. I wouldn't change it, even if I could. I've known ever since he was a boy that I must prepare myself for the shock, that some day they'd come to break the news to me—perhaps bluntly, or perhaps stumbling around trying to break it easy. A speeding automobile and a blown-out tire. Trying some new stunt in that airplane of his. I always knew it would be something swift and sudden; and that's the way he would want it, and that's the way I would want it. But you're different, Velma. I can depend on you. You're steady. You look ahead. You have a sense of responsibility. . . . Oh, *please* don't go, darling. After all, one in the family's enough. I couldn't stand to be left all alone. The world's in such a hurry, it pushes you to one side and rushes on past you if you haven't some anchor to hold you to the current of life."

Then there was Dr. Kenward, tired, patient, over-worked, knowing that he was no longer physically robust enough to stand the strain of night calls. Day after day he coped with an endless procession of sick people constantly crowding his office, with the same old symptoms, with the same old ailments, only the patients being new. Dr. Kenward had said, "Velma, you're the only one I can depend on. The good ones have all gone. You won't have to do much, just be there with the hypodermic in case he needs it. But don't think what you are doing won't be important. Keep him quiet, let him build himself up, and he'll snap out of this. But the trouble with him is that the minute he begins to get well he'll think he's cured. He'll crowd too much strain on that tired muscle, and then—well, that's when you're going to have to be there with the hypodermic—and minutes will be important. The way things are now, they won't be able to get me in time. You'll have to be on the job. A man of a different type could go to a hospital or a sanitarium. With him, it would be fatal. Remember, Velma, I'm counting on you to stand by me."

And so Velma Starler lived in the big red-tiled house, had a spacious room which looked out over the ocean, her professional duties being virtually nil, more psychological than physical. Her patient had moved out of the house, sleeping under the stars, eating an unbalanced diet, scorning advice—and thriving on the treatment.

The one concession he had consented to make was to have the push-button call bell wired to an extension so that a mere pressure of his thumb would summon Velma at any hour of the day or night.

Velma fought against a desire to turn over in the bed. Once give way to that twisting and turning and the cause was lost. She also knew better than to *try* to go to sleep. Trying to sleep was a mental effort. Sleep won't

26

come when it's summoned; only when one is indifferent and completely relaxed. . . . There was a mosquito somewhere in the room. . . . Velma frowned annoyance.

A part of her mind was trying to concentrate on restful relaxation, another part was definitely irritated at the intermittent buzzing of that mosquito. She tried to locate the sound—apparently over in that far corner—. Well, she'd have to get up, turn on the light and kill him. She simply couldn't sleep with a mosquito in the room, not the way her nerves were now.

She reached up and switched on the bed lamp over the head of the bed.

Almost instantly the mosquito ceased buzzing. Velma thrust her legs out of the side of the bed, kicked her delicate pink feet into sturdy slippers, and frowned at the corner of the room. She had known it would be like that. Turn on the light and the dratted mosquito would play possum somewhere—hiding in the shadows behind one of the pictures, probably. By the time she found him, she'd be wide awake for the rest of the night. . . . Oh well, she was awake now anyway.

Velma picked up a fly swatter from the table near the bed, the table on which various articles were arrayed with professional efficiency. A little alcohol lamp for boiling the water, the hypodermic, the five-cell flashlight, a little notebook in which she kept track of the activities of the patient—a supervision which Banning Clarke would have bitterly resented had he known of it.

The mosquito simply wouldn't start again. Velma switched out the light, sat on the edge of the bed waiting.

Still the mosquito wouldn't buzz.

Knuckles sounded gently at her door.

"What is it?" Velma asked.

Velma could never hear the sound of a knock on her door at night without having a thoroughly professional reaction. What was it this time? Had a spell hit Banning Clarke so suddenly that he couldn't even give that one convulsive press to the call button—? "What is it?" she called, again.

The voice of Nell Sims, sounding almost surreptitious, asked, "Are you all right, Miss Starler?"

"Why yes, of course. Why?"

"Nothing. I saw your light go on and I just wondered. Jim Bradisson and his mother are sick."

Velma was throwing a robe around her. "Come in. What's wrong with them?"

Nell opened the door. Attired in a somewhat dilapidated dressing gown, and broad shapeless slippers, her stringy, colorless hair wrapped in curlers, her eyes swollen with sleep, she came shuffling across the room, dragging her feet. *"They* say it's something they ate."

"Are any of the others sick?"

"That's what I wanted to find out. I saw your light go on. You sure you're all right?"

"Why, yes, of course. What are the symptoms?"

"Just ordinary symptoms—nausea, burning sensation. Something they ate! Bosh! That's all stuff and nonsense. They ate too much. Look at Mrs. Bradisson—keeps talking about her weight, never does a lick of work, picks out all the rich things to eat, can't ever pass up dessert, usually has a second helping if she can get it. Know what I said to her just the other day when she was struggling with her dress?"

Velma was hardly listening. She was debating whether to let the situation rectify itself, or to see what could be done. One thing was definitely certain: she mustn't let them get alarmed and call Dr. Kenward at this hour of the night.

"Know what I said to her?" Nell Sims repeated.

"What?" Velma asked, her mind far away.

Nell chuckled. "I spoke right up to her. I says, 'You've got to remember, Mrs. Bradisson, you can't eat your cake without having it too.' "

"How long has she been ill?"

28

"I don't know. I imagine about half an hour, from what she said."

Velma said, "I guess I'd better see if there's anything I can do."

Velma followed Nell Sims down the long hallway to her suite of rooms in the north wing, where Lillian Bradisson and her son James had a private sitting-room with bedrooms opening off from it.

Velma could hear the sound of retching, followed by groaning. The door to Mrs. Bradisson's room was open, and Velma, walking in with professional competence, said, "They told me you were ill, Mrs. Bradisson. Is there something I can do?"

Mrs. Bradisson, weakened by her retching, dropped back against the pillows, regarding the nurse with blood-shot, watering eyes. "I've been poisoned. I'm going to die. I'm simply burning up." She stretched forth a trembling hand to a glass about a third filled with water, drained it eagerly, said, "Would you mind filling that for me again?"

Nell Sims took the glass to the bathroom, held it under the tap. "Nonsense," she said. "It wasn't what you ate. It was how much you ate. No one else in the house is sick."

"My son and I have both been poisoned."

"Nonsense!"

Mrs. Bradisson said, "I'm so glad you came down, Miss Starler. I just telephoned Dr. Kenward. He said to have you look in, and if you thought it necessary, he'd come right over. I think you'd better get him here."

"Oh, I think we'll do all right," Velma said cheerfully. "Whatever it is that's causing the gastric upset, you're getting rid of it, and you should be feeling all right within fifteen or twenty minutes. Perhaps we can find something that will sort of settle that stomach. I understand your son is ill?"

"He isn't as bad as I am. He— He—" Her face

29

twisted with pain for a moment. Then she lay back limply against the pillows, utterly exhausted.

Velma said, "I'll look in on Jim and see how he is."

Jim Bradisson was apparently having the same symptoms as his mother, but he was stronger and more lucid. "Look, Velma," he said, "I think you'd better get Dr. Kenward up here right away."

"He's so overworked now," Velma explained, "I don't like to bother him with night calls unless it's very urgent. Quite frequently a person gets acute digestive upsets from food poisoning."

Jim Bradisson lowered his voice. "I've had food poisoning before. This isn't food poisoning. This is some other form of poison. My mouth seems to be full of metal filings—and I'm burning with thirst. It's a terrible burning thirst, which doesn't seem right to me, and my stomach and abdomen are sore. I can hardly touch them. I—I tell you, Velma, I think we've been poisoned."

Velma tried to make her voice sound casual. "Any cramping of the muscles?" she asked.

Bradisson showed surprise. "Why yes, now that you speak of it, I've had cramps in the calves of my legs—but that wouldn't have anything to do with this other. I suppose I walked a little too much this afternoon. You know, Mother and I climbed up around the hills. She's really determined to take off some weight."

Bradisson smiled. Keenly devoted to his mother, he recognized, nevertheless, the utter futility of her sporadic attempts to take off weight. "About all she did," he said, "was to work up a terrific appetite, and, of course, she gave me one too. It was a lot of exercise. And then Nell Sims had fried chicken. Mother and I certainly went to town on that fried chicken. I'm afraid I'm going to have another spell. Good Lord! This is worse than seasickness."

Velma said, "Well, I'll telephone Dr. Kenward. Perhaps he'd better run over."

Bradisson dashed in the direction of the bathroom. Velma went downstairs to telephone Dr. Kenward. "I'm afraid you're going to have to come," she told him.

"The ordinary gastric disturbance in a violent form?" he asked over the telephone.

She placed her lips close to the mouthpiece. "The symptoms of arsenic poisoning, completely typical cases even down to the muscular cramps in the calves of the legs."

Velma always marveled at the way Dr. Kenward would seem half asleep over the telephone, and then suddenly, when confronted with an emergency, could become as wide awake as though he had been fully dressed and waiting for this particular call. "It will take me about twelve minutes," he said. "Watch the symptoms. I don't suppose you have any dialyzed iron?"

"No I haven't."

"All right. Give stomach washes, and stand by. I'll be there."

Dr. Kenward made it in just a little better than ten minutes, and for the next forty minutes Velma was as busy as she had ever been in her life. Dr. Kenward wasted no time in conversation. He simply went to work with stomach washing, the introduction of iron oxide to form the sparingly soluble ferric arsenite, and then washing out the iron compounds. The patients responded rather quickly to treatment. By two o'clock they were resting easily, and Dr. Kenward, with an all but imperceptible jerk of his head, summoned Velma Starler to a conference in her room.

Velma sat on the edge of the bed, giving Dr. Kenward the comfortable chair, saying nothing until he had settled back with the first deeply relaxing drag of cigarette smoke, exhaling it with what was almost a sigh.

It was a tense period of waiting, similar to that which she had shared with Dr. Kenward on innumerable nocturnal vigils. He had, for the moment, done everything

31

that medical science could do. But before going home, he waited for the turn of the tide, for the treatment to develop its full efficiency. During such periods, he was relaxed in the sense that a pugilist is relaxed between rounds. His mind, keyed up to racing efficiency, could not relax, but he could somewhat lessen the nerve strain by stretching out in a chair and relaxing his muscles as much as possible.

"There was fried chicken?" Dr. Kenward asked abruptly.

"Yes."

"Mrs. Sims has some sort of contract by which the people are boarded?"

"That's right. I don't know just what the arrangement is. I think Mr. Clarke makes up whatever deficit remains after she collects the board allowance from the various people. It's a peculiar arrangement, but the whole household is peculiar."

"There was plenty of fried chicken?"

"Plenty."

"All on one platter?"

"No. There were two platters."

"One at the end of the table where Mrs. Bradisson and her son were seated?"

"Yes."

Dr. Kenward said thoughtfully, "The fried chicken probably accounts for it."

"You mean the poisoning?"

"No. The length of time after the ingestion of the poison and before the development of symptoms. Greasy food delays the appearance of symptoms. Now the question is, *how* could the food have been poisoned without poison being administered to others at the table. You're certain the plates weren't served individually with food on them?"

"No. Everything was taken from dishes which were passed around."

32

Dr. Kenward said, "They're both insisting they didn't eat a thing after dinner. It must have been administered in some liquid, then."

"It's arsenic?"

"Undoubtedly. Mrs. Sims checked up on all the others. No one else was sick. Therefore, it must have—You checked up on Banning, didn't you?" Kenward's voice was sharp with anxiety.

"Yes. I tiptoed out to the cactus garden. He and Salty were snoring peacefully away in their sleeping bags."

"They ate dinner at the table?"

"No, they didn't. They eat out there about half the time. Salty is quite a camp cook."

Dr. Kenward said, "Not exactly the sort of treatment you'd prescribe, and yet it seems to be doing the work, which is all one can ask of any treatment. I give it my frowning disapproval, which makes the pair of them feel something like a couple of schoolboys who have sneaked out for an adventure. That's half of the battle—gives them that mental stimulus which comes of doing something they shouldn't be doing. Now, is there any possible way that you can think of—" He broke off at the sudden flash of expression which crossed her face. "Yes? What is it, Velma?"

"The salt shaker."

"What about it?"

The words were coming quickly now, rushing from the tip of her tongue as she suddenly realized the full import of the idea which had occurred to her.

"The salt shaker—Jim and his mother are both great salt eaters. They've developed such a taste for it that they pile salt on everything in sight, and Mrs. Sims finally gave them a special salt shaker. Every piece of chicken they ate they salted liberally, and I'll bet they're the only ones at the table that put salt on it. It was seasoned just right as it was."

Dr. Kenward ground out the half-smoked cigarette,

was on his feet. "Let's go take a quiet look at that salt shaker."

They tiptoed through the corridors of the big, silent house, down the stairs, and into the dining-room. Velma finally located the saltcellar on the huge sideboard. Dr. Kenward spilled out some of the salt in the palm of his hand, took a small magnifying glass from his pocket, inspected it carefully, rubbed the salt around in his hand, then abruptly slipped the saltcellar into his pocket. "I think that does it," he said. "It will take an analysis to make certain. You had a bright idea there, Velma. It was the saltcellar—an easy way to eliminate the others. Don't say anything about it for the moment. I suppose we've got to go to the District Attorney with this, and I'd like to find out just a little more about it before I notify him. Of course, Jim Bradisson will accuse Banning Clarke of trying to administer poison.—How do these two rate with the others here?"

"Jim is all right," Velma said somewhat dubiously. "He has a repertoire of nineteen-thirty-four jokes. The polite ones are insipid, the impolite ones are strained, heavy—just aren't clever. But on the whole, he tries to be affable and agreeable, and if it weren't for that assumption of infallible superiority, he'd be popular."

"How about his mother?"

Velma shook her head. "She's vain, selfish, and so completely enraptured with that son of hers that she's absolutely impossible. She's full of little tricks—cheating on herself, announcing what she's going to do in regard to diet, what she's going to eat and what she isn't going to eat; then pretending that she's forgotten all about it until after she's taken the second helping. Or surreptitiously taking a second piece of cake when she thinks *we're* not looking—as though that, somehow, would make it less fattening. She's over fifty, admitting thirty-eight, pretending twenty-eight."

"Enemies?"

"I suppose so."

"But mostly, the situation revolves around this mining proposition?"

"Yes. And that fraud suit."

"What do you know about that?"

"Nothing much. Naturally, they don't discuss their business matters before me. There's friction. Pete Sims salted a claim and sold the string of mines to Jim Bradisson. I guess he really salted them. He's an old reprobate, a periodical drunkard. Does things and tries to blame them on a split personality. Then there's some trouble over control in the corporation. It's not at all a happy household, but they try to keep up appearances—in front of me, at any rate."

"How about this mining man?"

"Hayward Small? He's a live wire all right, but I wouldn't trust him. He's personally magnetic—a good salesman. Incidentally, he's paying a lot of attention to Nell Sims' daughter, Dorina—and he must be twelve or fifteen years older than she is."

"He has some sort of business hookup with Bradisson?"

"He's been scouting mines for the corporation."

Dr. Kenward said, "Well, I've got to notify the authorities. I think I'll wait until morning and get in touch with the District Attorney personally. In the meantime, you keep an eye on things. I'll take this salt shaker with me as evidence. I'll leave it to you to see that the patients eat absolutely nothing until I advise you. And that will be after the District Attorney has been notified—perhaps around eight o'clock."

When Dr. Kenward had left, Velma looked in on the patients to make certain they were resting easily, and then went back to her room and stretched out on her bed. Almost immediately she became drowsy. "Strange," she reflected; try to sleep and she couldn't. But once let her get hold of a case where she might have to take her sleep in little cat naps and she could stretch out on the bed and almost instantly start dozing—sleeping with one eye open—senses alert underneath a veneer of relaxation. No trouble now to drift off to sleep. . . . Only thing to guard against was too deep a slumber. . . . Just drift halfway into unconsciousness then stop, resting, but ready at the slightest . . . noise . . . noise. . . . Not a noise connected with a patient, just a mosquito noise. That was it. Neglected to find that mosquito. . . . Somewhere in the room . . . peculiar mosquito . . . doesn't come closer . . . buzzes for a second or two, then seems to light . . . there he goes again . . . perhaps the mosquito's sleepy too. . . . Do mosquitoes sleep? . . . Why not? . . . But this mosquito is drowsy . . . tired. . . .

Abruptly Velma wakened. Definitely, she was going to put that annoying mosquito out of the room. She reached for her flashlight, waited to hear the mosquito once more.

She heard the peculiar buzz and snapped on the flashlight. The low-pitched buzzing noise abruptly ceased.

Velma was up out of bed with a start. That mosquito was acting peculiarly. Mosquitoes usually buzzed around in concentric circles, coming closer. This one didn't seem to like light. Perhaps she could locate him again if she switched out the light and waited in the dark.

Velma turned off the flashlight, walked over to stand at the window.

It would be daylight within an hour or two. A big moon hung low in the west, suspended over the reflecting surface of the calm ocean—a moon that was just past the full, shining in Velma's face, making a golden path to Fairyland along the ocean, flooding the grounds of the estate with a light that radiated tranquillity. Somewhere across that ocean Rinkey would be flying. Not a breath of air was stirring—just the calm, limpid moonlight, the glassy surface of the ocean far below, the dark splash of shadows where. . . . Something moved down in the yard.

Velma's eyes hardened into searching scrutiny of a dark patch of shadow that wasn't a shadow. It was an object. It had moved. It—it was a man crouched over, motionless now, apparently trying to escape attention by making it seem he was merely one of the dark shadows. But there was nothing at that spot to cast such a shadow.

The window was open. Almost without thinking, Velma released the catch on the screen, flung it back, swung her five-cell flashlight into position and pressed the button.

The beam of the light was a vivid white against the soft gold of mellow moonlight. Concentrated by the big lens into a spot of brilliance, the pencil of light just missed the crouching man. Velma swung it toward him.

Two orange spots of light centered with bluish brilliance winked at her from the darkness. Two crisp, businesslike explosions rudely ripped apart the moonlit tranquillity. Two bullets crashed through the window just over Velma's head.

Involuntarily, Velma jumped back. The instinctive realization that the flashlight made her a perfect target caused her to thumb back the catch as a purely reflex action.

The man was running now—across the strip of white moonlight into the shadows, down the hedge, around by the end of the stone wall. . . .

Two thoughts flashed through Velma Starler's mind. One was concern for the safety of her patient. The man was running toward the cactus gardens. If he came on Banning Clarke, the shock wouldn't do Clarke's heart any good. The other thought was definite annoyance that her hair was full of the glass splinters which had rained down on her head when the bullets had crashed through the window above her.

Velma could hear sounds in the house now—bare feet thudding on the floor, voices raised in question. She'd have to get down to reassure Lillian Bradisson and her son. . . . Just a minute more. . . .

Banning Clarke's voice, high-pitched and querulous, yelled, "Hey!"

From the shadows down near the lower gate came another spurt of orange flame, the sound of another shot.

Almost instantly there were two answering flashes from the cactus gardens. The *pow-w-w-ie . . . pow-w-w-ie* of a big-caliber gun. That would be Clarke's forty-five.

Velma saw the skinny figure of Banning Clarke, attired in long underwear and nothing else, running awkwardly out of the cactus gardens toward the place where the fugitive had disappeared.

Instantly she forgot her fright. Her professional instincts came at once to the surface. "You stop that running," she called authoritatively. "That's dangerous. Go back to bed. I'll call the police. Where's Salty?"

Banning Clarke looked up at her. "What's happened? Some son-of-a-gun took a shot at me."

"He shot at me, too—shot twice—a prowler. Where's Salty?"

"Here," Salty Bowers said, emerging into the moonlight, struggling with the belt on his overalls. "Better get dressed, Banning."

For the first time, Banning became conscious of his wearing apparel, such as it was. "Oh, my *gosh!*" he said, and scuttled off into the cactus like a startled rabbit.

"Quit running," Velma shouted, her voice sharp with exasperation. "I've seen underwear before."

38

■ 5 ■

The cattle ranch was a huge, sprawling anachronism which continued to exist within a hundred miles of Los Angeles much as it had seventy-five years ago, a tract of many thousands of acres of rolling plateau country garnished with picturesque live-oaks, canyons green with sycamore, and peaks covered with chaparral and greasewood, watched over by brooding, snow-capped mountains in the purple distance.

The cat-footed cattle horses came winding in single file down from the rugged back country, following a rough cattle trail which was all but obliterated in places. Down below, ranch headquarters rested in a little tree-studded valley. There was still a faint trace of green in the grass, but for the most part it had turned to a parched brown, tribute to the dry air, the cloudless skies, and the blazing sunlight.

Della Street, the notebook in her right saddlebag well filled with data concerning old corners, witness trees, abandoned roads, and burned fences, rode with that easy rhythm which absorbs the motion of the saddle and is so easy on both horse and rider.

"Tired?" Mason asked.

"No. I think it's delightful."

Harvey Brady, the owner of the ranch, half turned in the saddle and grinned. "Think you've got it all straight now?" he asked. "Otherwise, we can go back."

"I think," Della Street laughed, "I'll settle for something to eat instead."

The cattleman tilted the sweat-stained sombrero back on his head and looked out over his vast domain with shrewd sun-bleached eyes that saw everything. The little cavalcade hit a more traveled trail now. A cloud of reddish-gold dust enveloped them, a dust cloud heavy enough to cast a shadow in the sunlight. Fine particles of dust settled on the riders. The horses, their sides incrusted with the salt of dried perspiration, increased their rapid walk.

Down far below, a horse was standing in three-legged relaxation, head drooped forward. The reins casually dropped to the ground held him as motionless as though he'd been tied, a sure sign of the trained cattle horse.

Harvey Brady said, "Don't know what they've got that horse out there for—standing in the sun. Must be waiting to pick up our dust. . . . That's right, here comes one of the men."

A cowpuncher, running awkwardly in black leather chaps and high-heeled boots, emerged from the ranch house, picked up the reins, tossed them back over the horse's neck and grasped the horn of the saddle. Instantly all awkwardness left him. The man swung into the saddle, the whirl of the horse circling him into a firm seat. Thereupon, horse and rider became merged into a streak of motion which dust-spurted across the little amphitheater of valley at a gallop, and then started climbing the zigzag trail.

The cattleman pushed his horse into swifter motion. "Looks like something's gone wrong," he said.

The courier met them within a matter of minutes, a bronzed, slim-waisted cowpuncher who reined back to the side of the trail, the horse balanced precariously on the edge of the steep slope, moving restlessly, apparently in danger of losing his footing at any moment and precipitating both himself and his rider down the sharp declivity.

The cowpuncher sat easily in the saddle, his body swaying with the motions of the horse, paying no attention to the sharp drop behind him, holding the sensitive-mouthed animal with a light hand on the reins.

"Long-distance Los Angeles operator's been trying to get Perry Mason all day. They really began burning up the wires about twenty minutes ago. They say the call's terribly important. He's to take it just as soon as he can."

"Thanks, Joe. We'll be moving right on," the cattleman said.

Della Street exclaimed, "Oh, do be careful. That horse is going to lose his balance and —"

White teeth flashed a contrast against the bronze skin. "Don't worry, ma'am. He knows that slope's there just as well as I do."

Harvey Brady spurred his horse into motion.

"Take it easy," Mason called. "All clients have a way of thinking their particular business is terribly important. But thanks for letting me know, Joe."

The cowpuncher grinned an acknowledgement. As the horses moved on past, his mount, eager to get in the lead, threw back his head, showed the whites of rolling eyes, distended red nostrils. "Thought I'd better let you know," the rider said, and then fell into place behind the little cavalcade.

The slope became less abrupt. The trail ceased to zigzag. The cattleman ahead, setting the pace, broke into a full gallop; the horses lunging up the short climbs, scurrying down the slopes, leaning far over to one side and then the other as they followed the winding turns of the cattle trail.

Mason, swinging from the saddle, seemed stiff and awkward beside the easy grace of the professional cattlemen. They clumped across a porch, opened a door marked OFFICE and entered a room with an unpainted floor splintered from the pounding of many heels. A counter ran two thirds of the length of the room. A stove made out of a fifty-gallon gasoline drum reposed in the center of the room. A girl working over some books at a desk smiled at Perry Mason. "There's the telephone, Mr. Mason."

Mason nodded thanks, walked across to the telephone, picked up the receiver and asked for the Los Angeles operator.

Della Street saw the morning newspaper which had just been brought in with the mail. And, while waiting for the call to come through, she turned to the "Vital Statistics."

"Looking for corpses?" Mason asked, smiling.

She said, "You have no romance in your soul. You wouldn't—Oh, here it is."

"Here what is?"

"The notice of intention."

Della Street folded back the paper, circled the item in the Vital Statistics with a pencil and read: "Bowers—Brunn, Prentice C., 42, 619 Skyline, San Roberto; Lucille M., 33, 704 6th Street, San Roberto." She smiled across at Perry Mason. "I'm glad they're going ahead with it. Somehow I had an idea that romance might have hit a legal snag. There was so much—"

The telephone rang. Mason picked up the receiver.

Banning Clarke's voice, shrill with excitement, said, "This you, Mason?"

"That's right. Mason talking."

"Been trying to get you all day. They said you were just out on the ranch somewhere, so I kept thinking you'd call any minute. How big *is* that ranch, anyway?"

Mason laughed. "You could ride all day getting to one boundary fence and back."

"Heck, I thought it was just a ranch. Told 'em to *get* you about half an hour ago—couldn't wait any longer."

"So I understand. What's wrong?"

"I'm in a mess. Got to see you just as soon as you can get here."

"That may be some time the latter part of the week. I—"

"No, no. I mean right now—today—as soon as you can drive up here. They've dug up the old by-laws. Seems

42

as though there's a regular annual stockholders' meeting due for today. They've been kind of slipping one over on me. They've got some smart lawyer coming up to put me in a jack pot."

"I'm sorry," Mason said firmly. "I've been out ever since daylight looking over a disputed boundary line and—"

"And last night somebody poisoned my mother-in-law and Jim Bradisson. Then somebody took a couple of shots at my nurse. That, and the arsenic in the food. . . ."

Mason's face twisted into a grin. "The shooting does it. I'll be up just as soon as I can get there."

"Be sure to come to the back door," Clarke said. "I want to see you before any of the others know you're here."

Mason hung up and turned to Della Street. "Want to take a fast ride?" he asked.

"On a horse?"

"Definitely not on a horse."

"That," she announced, "is *quite* different."

The cattleman's voice was dry. "Try to get away from here without a drink and something to eat, and I'll show you what shooting *really* is."

The back door of the big house was opened by Nell
Sims almost as soon as Mason knocked.

"You alone?" she asked suspiciously.

"Miss Street, my secretary, is the only one with me."

"That's fine. Come in. The boss is anxious to see
you. He told me to let him know just as soon as you
came."

"Where is he, in the cactus garden?"

"Yes."

"And still batching?" Mason asked jovially.

"He eats one square meal every other day here," Nell
Sims snapped. "That keeps him from starving to death.
The rest of the time, he eats that awful slum that he and
Salty cook up.—I guess this has been a hard day for you,
hasn't it?"

Della Street and Mason followed her into the
kitchen. Mason said cheerfully, "Oh, well, there's no rest
for the wicked."

"That's right," Nell Sims said, regarding him in serious
contemplation, "but blessed be the pure in heart, for they
shall multiply as the grains of sand."

Della Street glanced mischievously at Mason. Mason
regarded Nell Sims with a coldly suspicious eye, but she
met his gaze with bland innocence. "Do you," she asked,
"want something to eat?"

"Got anything without arsenic in it?" Mason asked.

"It's a little bit early to tell, yet. Land sakes, I certainly
had trouble enough getting them to eat a thing this noon.
And it was even worse than that for dinner."

"What do *you* know about the poisoning?" Mason
asked.

"Absolutely nothing."

"But surely you know in general what happened."

"Where ignorance is bliss, a little learning is a dangerous thing," Nell Sims proclaimed. "I don't know anything about it, and I don't intend to know anything about it. The police have been traipsing all over the house. As far as I'm concerned, let 'em. . . ."

The back door opened and Banning Clarke grinned with relief when he saw Mason. "Been sort of keeping an ear to the ground," he said. "Thought I heard you come in. Good evening, Miss Street."

Della smiled a greeting. Mason shook hands.

"How about some dinner?" Banning Clarke asked.

"Maybe he's afraid of arsenic," Nell Sims suggested. "Everybody else seems to be. People barely touched their dinners."

Mason laughed. "We'll take a chance. We've only had a few sandwiches. Bring out your arsenic."

Nell Sims said, "There's lots of fried rabbit left. It's a case of one man's poison being another's meat."

Banning Clarke drew up a chair and sat down, jerking his thumb toward the front of the house. "They're having a regular stockholders' meeting in there. I want your advice. Should I burst in and take part in it, or should I not take part in it?"

"What do you have to gain by attending?" Mason asked.

"Nothing. Under that pooling agreement Salty can vote my stock."

"What have you to lose if you don't attend?"

"That," Clarke confessed, "is something that's been worrying me."

"I'm afraid I don't follow you."

Mrs. Sims opened the oven, took out a big pan of fried rabbit, placed tea in a teapot, poured on boiling water. "My boarders would hardly touch a thing tonight," she snorted indignantly.

45

Clarke said, "I'll have a cup of tea, Nell, and that's all. You folks go ahead and eat, and I'll talk while you're eating."

Della Street said, "I'm so hungry I could eat the enamel right off the plate. I hope you don't mind an unladylike exhibition of hunger."

"*Why* are you worried about not attending the meeting?" Mason pressed for an answer. "And what about the shooting?"

"The shooting is a mystery. Some prowler was in the yard. He shot twice at Miss Starler when she directed the beam of a flashlight toward him—the bullets struck the upper window, only about three inches apart, perhaps two feet above her head. The shots wakened me and I grabbed my old forty-five and ran out into the moonlight. He was down by the gate then. He took a shot at me, and I fired at the flash of his gun. Didn't hit him, but must have come close. This morning I found where my bullet had struck the wall, right by the lower gate—a gate that's always kept locked, by the way."

"And the poisoning?" Mason asked.

"Someone put arsenic in the saltcellar Mrs. Bradisson and her son use. A prompt diagnosis enabled the doctor to pull them through. We have Velma Starler to thank for that."

"All right," Mason said with a smile. "*Now* we'll come back to the original question. Why are you afraid not to attend that meeting?"

"Because . . . well, I. . . . Mason, I'm going to tell you something I haven't told any other living soul, although I think Salty Bowers suspects it."

"Want me to leave?" Nell Sims asked.

"No. Stick around, Nell. I know I can trust you."

"Go ahead," Mason said, passing the rabbit to Della Street and then filling his own plate.

"Know anything about any of the famous lost mines of California?" Clarke asked.

"Only a little."

"Ever hear of the Goler Placer Diggings?"

Mason, his mouth full of rabbit, shook his head.

"Lost mines," Nell Sims interpolated. "Lots of 'em in the desert."

Clarke put sugar in his tea, stirred the beverage, took a little blue paper-covered book from his coat pocket.

"What's that?" Mason asked.

"The Miners' Guide, compiled by Horace J. West. West collected a lot of information about the famous lost mines of California. This book was published in 1929. You'll find there are several versions of the famous lost mines— some of them sound plausible, some of them won't hold water. West went out and examined records, talked with old-time miners, compiled his history some twenty years ago, and made it as accurate as was possible."

"All right," Mason said. "What about the Goler Lost Mine?"

"Around 1886," Clarke said, "if we take West's account, three men who had been prospecting in the Panamint Range that borders Death Valley emerged from a pass in the Panamints and headed toward San Bernardino. These men were well mounted on good horses, had ample packs and ten-gallon water canteens. And they rode out into the desert filled with confidence.

"About the second day, there was a dispute as to the best way to go, and the dispute warmed up into a pretty good quarrel. Frank Goler, one of the party, thought they were heading too far to the south and west. He claimed they should keep on a more easterly course. After the quarrel, he pulled away from the others and headed pretty much east. No one knows what happened to the other two. They may have been lost in the desert. They may have come through to some destination. They may even have reached San Bernardino. So far as history is concerned, they just disappeared."

47

Nell Sims said briefly, "Two men get along. Three fight."

Della Street, her eyes shining with interest, paused in her eating, watching Banning Clarke. Perry Mason kept on eating rabbit.

"Want your tea now?" Nell Sims asked.

"Please," Mason said.

As she poured tea into their cups, Banning Clarke went on, "By noon two days later, Goler, pretty well spent and badly frightened, reached some low hills that sprawled out exactly in his path. He crossed them, and on the far side discovered a canyon that actually had vegetation and a little stream of water—and he reached it just in time. He was almost delirious. He flung himself down on the bank of the stream and started drinking, soaking up the water in the shade cast by a big cottonwood that was directly behind him. While he was drinking, a little wind stirred the branches of the cottonwood and let a shaft of sunlight through that struck directly on something yellow in the stream just a few inches beyond Goler's face.

"Goler finished drinking, plunged his arm into the stream and picked up the yellow object. It was a big gold nugget, weighing several ounces. There were quite a few more lying near it on a bedrock formation in the stream. Goler picked these nuggets up and shoved them inside his shirt."

"I'd have got a sackful," Nell Sims said.

"Struck it rich, eh?" Mason asked.

"Struck it rich all right," Clarke said. "But until you've been out in the desert you haven't any idea what you're up against when you're at the mercy of the bleak, barren waste. Goler had gold, but he couldn't eat gold and he couldn't drink gold. He was a long way from civilization. His horse was tired and hungry. He himself was weak from lack of food; and suddenly the realization dawned on him that his gold wasn't worth anything whatever except in civilization. Out in the desert it was merely that much extra weight for Goler's tired horse to pack. The several gold nuggets Goler had picked up would actually lessen his chances of getting through to civilization.

"With that realization, Goler had a touch of panic. He decided to compensate for the extra weight of gold by lessening his weight as much as possible. He unbelted his six-shooter, tossed it into the brush, and spurred his horse to action. As so frequently happens with people when they're fatigued, he didn't pay too much attention to his exact location. What's more, he'd been lost—he was still lost—and that does strange things to a man's mind.

"He rode on down this canyon, then came out to more level country and saw what apparently had been the place where a big lake had evaporated and left a smooth, dry plain. Then was when he began to take his bearings. He saw that Mt. San Antonio was just about due west—we call it Old Baldy now—and that was his first landmark. There was a little mining town at the foot of an arrowhead mountain in the general direction of that peak. Goler headed for that town.

"He reached Arrowhead, and fell sick. The nuggets rubbing inside his shirt had chafed his skin raw, the wounds had become infected. His resistance to infection was low, and he lay in bed for three weeks before he could even think of getting started back to locate his claim. Three weeks can be a long time when your mind keeps constantly dwelling on one subject. After a while, your memory begins to play tricks on you."

"Certainly does," Nell Sims said, throwing the comment over her shoulder as she took more rabbit from the oven.

Clarke went on. "Well, naturally, he didn't go alone. A lot of prospectors trailed along behind, hoping to locate claims of their own in a new bonanza. The party straggled around the desert for quite some spell. Then the prospectors got disgusted and began to drift back. It was

49

all too plain to them that Goler, somewhere, somehow, had lost his bearings, and was wandering blind.

"Goler himself came back after about a month, rested up, got more provisions and started out again. He never did get back to that canyon—couldn't even locate the range of those hills.

"Now then, that's pretty well authenticated history. Most of it is right here in West's book. Some of it I've gleaned from other sources—about the gun, for instance. I learned that from finding a letter Goler wrote. It's in a rare collection in a library in Pasadena."

"It hardly seems possible a man could lose himself so completely," Della Street said.

"It's perfectly possible," Clarke said. "You can get lost in the desert very easily. Just think of the people who go out on hunting trips, leaving camp in the morning determined to remember exactly where it is so that they can get back at night. And when it comes to finding the camp, after a few hours' walk, they can't come close enough to locate any familiar landmarks."

Mason nodded. "That," he asked, "is the end of the Goler Mines?"

An enigmatic smile twisted Banning Clarke's lips. "Well," he said, "let's go back to Horace West's account. This, mind you, was 1886. Now, a few years later, in 1891, there was a two-fisted old prospector by the name of Hen Moss who hung out around San Bernardino and made little periodic prospecting trips out into the desert.

"Moss was making one of his regular trips, when a new burro he had bought and was taking on its first trip decided to wander away from the rest of the outfit. You can figure how exasperated Moss was. The burro had a pack containing a lot of stuff that Moss simply had to have for his prospecting trip, and that burro just calmly took off across the desert. Moss couldn't head him off and he couldn't catch him. All he could do was trail along behind with the rest of the outfit, cussing and sputtering. That suited the burro fine. He had suddenly become the leader of the whole outfit. Well, Hen Moss tailed along behind that burro, cussing him, occasionally chasing him, then trying to wheedle him back. But a burro is a peculiar sort of customer. He gets an idea in his head and that idea is there for keeps. This burro was heading toward a barren stretch of country that Hen Moss had never been in before. No prospector had ever looked around very much in it because it was a wicked-looking, waterless country far removed from any base of supplies. In those days, such places in the desert were sure death.

"However, Hen Moss simply couldn't afford to lose the stuff that was on that burro, and he hated to lose the burro. He kept on, thinking all the time that if he couldn't catch him within the next mile, he'd turn back and let the burro go. Then, just as he was about to give up, he found that the burro was headed toward water.—Take a burro out in the desert that way and when he begins to head toward water you can tell it every time. However, the other animals smelled the water too, and they all began to move right along. So Moss just trailed along behind, and his burro led him right down into a canyon filled with water and rich with gold.

"As soon as Hen Moss found that gold he went completely crazy. He filled up his pockets and went delirious with joy. He ran around in circles, whooping and shouting, and then started back to San Bernardino to have the time of his life. He was about halfway back before he suddenly realized he'd been so wildly excited he hadn't even staked out a claim. For a while he hesitated about going back, but the thought of the big celebration he was going to have in San Bernardino was the determining factor. He decided to move right on into town and have one good spree, then go back to the canyon, locate his claims and do some serious mining."

51

"Men always make good resolutions when they're going to get drunk—and right afterwards," Nell Sims said.

Clarke smiled. "What he hadn't counted on was the reaction in San Bernardino. The town went crazy as soon as it saw Moss's gold nuggets. They knew old Hen Moss had struck it rich. And they knew that pretty soon he was going to have to go back and get more gold. So they poured liquor into him, and watched him and *kept* watching him.

"Finally old Hen got down to the bottom of his gold and couldn't buy any more booze. He began to sober up, and then realized what he was up against. He started back to his diggings, and the minute he pulled out of town, just about half of San Bernardino pulled out along with him, all of them on good horses, and packs all provisioned for a long stay in the desert.

"Hen wandered around the desert trying to throw them off his trail. He tried to pretend he'd lost the mine, tried to steal marches at night, and do about everything he could to shake them; but there was no chance. They followed along right behind—"

Banning Clarke broke off to say, "This isn't boring you, is it?"

"Exciting," Mrs. Sims remarked.

"It's remarkably interesting. I take it this is all vouched for," Mason said.

Banning Clarke tapped the little blue book. "I'm giving you history," he said; "and so there won't be any chance of getting it wrong, I'm checking up as I go along, although I know the story by heart. But this was back fifty years ago when the desert was full of gold, and before there was any fast transportation."

"I understand," Mason said. "Go on. What happened to Hen Moss? Did he manage to shake his pursuers?"

"No. He finally doubled on back to San Bernardino pretty much sore and disgusted. He was stony broke, yet he knew where he could go and in a few hours pick up enough gold to make him the king of the saloons and the dancehalls. But he couldn't move two feet out of town without all of San Bernardino moving right along with him. He tried to find some way of getting out of town without anyone knowing it. He was licked before he started. It would have been suicide to go out in the desert without packs, and San Bernardino was keeping too close a watch on him to enable him to cache some pack burros somewhere to be picked up later."

"And this mine he'd discovered was the lost Goler claim?" Mason asked.

"I'm coming to that in a minute," Clarke said, and then after a moment added, "It's been generally conceded that what he discovered was the Goler claim."

Mason became thoughtful. "I'm interested in poor old Hen Moss and his predicament. It hardly seems possible that all this could have happened in San Bernardino. Why, we go whizzing out there in an automobile, perhaps stop long enough to buy gas, and then are on our way. It seems to be just an ordinary bustling little community, modern and up to date—just a regular city."

"There was lots that happened in San Bernardino," Clarke said, "but the automobile blots out history. It used to be a real mining town."

Nell Sims, standing over by the electric stove, said, "It's a good thing those times have passed. Think of the poor people who had to run restaurants out in that country, with no ice, no electric refrigerators, no transportation."

"They got along somehow," Clarke said.

Mrs. Sims wagged her head dolefully. "I don't see how. Food preservation is the first law of nature."

"Self-preservation," Clarke corrected.

"Well, don't that mean food? You can't live without food."

Clarke winked at Mason. "The more you try to argue with her, the deeper you get."

"That's because I'm right," Mrs. Sims announced with the calm finality of one who is sure of her position and doesn't have to bother about the impression she makes on others.

"But we're leaving Hen Moss right out in the middle of the desert," Della Street prompted.

"Right in the middle of San Bernardino," Clarke reminded her, "and a mighty disgusted, disillusioned Hen Moss he was. But the old chap was something of a philosopher. So one day he whimsically observed to just about everyone in town, 'Well, I can't seem to get away without taking you with me, so all get packed up. We're going to start, and this time we're going right to the diggings. The more the merrier. If I can't get rid of you, I'll save a lot of time and energy just taking everyone along and not making any detours.'"

"Wore him down," Nell Sims observed.

"And he actually meant it?" Della asked.

"Sure he meant it. Old Hen was a man of his word. He got his outfit together and waited on the outskirts of San Bernardino to make certain that everyone was along who wanted to come. Then he started out for his mine. . . . They had characters in those days."

"Then what happened? Were there enough claims to go around?"

Clarke smiled. "That," he said, "is the pathetic part of it. Old Hen Moss was a good scout, generous to a fault. He'd live out in the desert for weeks at a time on the scantiest provisions imaginable, having a poorly balanced diet, absolutely alone, without anyone to talk to. And then he'd come into town and squander every cent he'd been able to scrape up. And that's what he'd done just before he returned to his mine. As a result, the horse he was riding wasn't the best, and Hen Moss probably wasn't the best rider in the outfit.

"About the time the procession, after several days in the desert, got within a reasonable distance of this watered canyon, the smart ones suddenly realized that this was the end of the road. So they spurred their horses into a gallop and started ahead. Hen Moss clapped spurs into his own horse. That started the stampede. And it must have been some sight—pack horses left behind, a big cloud of desert dust rising up to the heavens, the sun beating down out of a cloudless sky, and these horsemen frantically spurring into a wild gallop over rough desert country, tearing headlong down a steep rocky slope and into a canyon! And poor old Hen Moss was just about at the tail end of the procession.

"The stampede reached the canyon. They found no claims had been staked, and men scurried madly about staking out claims. Those were the days when men had the power of quick decision, and there wasn't any fumbling around. A man picked what he considered the best available claim, took possession, and held possession. By the time Hen Moss finally got his jaded horse down into the canyon, just about the whole creek had been staked out. Hen Moss heaved himself off his staggering horse and looked around, to see his bonanza in the possession of intruders. Eighty claims had been located ahead of him. The one that Hen Moss finally located was just about the poorest of the whole outfit."

"The law of retribution," Nell Sims said.

"And that was the Goler Placer?" Mason asked, realizing by this time that no one ever paid the slightest attention to Nell Sims' chirping interpolations.

"That was *considered* to be the Goler Placer. Mining men looked the territory over, remembered the story Goler had told, and decided it was the Goler claim."

"And it was?" Mason asked.

"It was not."

Della Street ceased eating to watch Clarke.

"Goler," Clarke went on, "wasn't quite as simple as he seemed to be. The story that he told of the location of his bonanza didn't quite fit the actual facts. The description

55

of the location was doctored just enough so it would fool anyone who wanted to go trailing along behind him, and keep him from being outdistanced at the last by younger men on fresher horses, the way Hen Moss was. Goler was smarter than Moss. He deliberately fabricated the description of the country in which his mine was located."

"How," Mason asked, "do you know?"

"Fair question," Mrs. Sims chirped.

Banning Clarke looked furtively around the kitchen.

"It's all right," Nell Sims reassured him. "They're all in that meeting. Hayward Small nearly always comes in for a cup of tea this time of night, but he won't be in as long as that meeting's going."

Clarke opened his coat, hitched a holster into sight which had once been black but was now faded to a dark brown and polished with much wear. "I want to keep this pretty much out of sight."

His hand dropped to the holster, snaked out the weapon and placed it on the table.

Mason, Della Street and Mrs. Sims bent over it.

It was a worn, badly rusted single-action Colt revolver. Whatever the finish had originally been, it was now buried under the deep incrustations of rust which had formed a deep shell over barrel, cylinder, and trigger. The yellowed ivory handle alone had completely resisted the elements. And etched in that ivory handle was the word *Goler,* and, below that, a date, 1882.

Mason gave a low whistle.

"I found that," Clarke said, "purely by accident near a little trickling spring beneath some cottonwoods in the desert. The man who was with me had gone off to do some climbing. It was before my heart got as bad as it became later, but even then I was troubled with shortness of breath and was trying to take things easy. I stretched out in the shade of the cottonwood. About three inches of the barrel of this gun was protruding from the ground by the side of the spring. I saw that it was part of a gun barrel and dug it out, looked at it curiously for a minute, then saw the name Goler and the date—and then knew what I'd found."

"What did you do?" Della Street asked, her eyes big and shining with excitement.

"I didn't have any tools or equipment with me," Clarke said, "but I grubbed around in the bottom of the stream a bit with just my bare hand. There was a little pocket right next to the bedrock, and I scooped out gravel that was thick with gold."

"But how does it happen no one has ever heard about this?" Mason asked.

"That," Clarke said, "is the rub. The ground on which that spring was located was part of a quartz claim on which some poor befuddled prospector was starving to death, trying to find rock that would be worth mining. The idea of placer gold on the place had apparently never occurred to anyone. Hang it, the Come-Back Mining Syndicate has an interest in that claim right now, thinking that it holds only a quartz mine of problematical value. Only one of hundreds of similar mining propositions that it's bought up. And I'm not going to pour any more money into the laps of Mrs. Bradisson and her infallible son, James."

"Anyone any idea you know about the location of this mine?" Mason asked.

"I think Bradisson does."

Mason raised his eyebrows.

"Out there in Salty's camp I have no place to keep anything of this nature, so I left the gun in a drawer in my desk—left it with the side of the handle that had Goler's name etched on it turned *down*. Well, a week or so ago, I found that side turned *up*. I don't often get up to my room now—it's a job for me to climb the stairs. I have to take it mighty easy when I go up, resting for a minute or two every second or third step. You see, I have—"

The swinging door creaked on its hinges. Banning Clarke's hand shot out to the old rust-covered six-shooter, jerked it back out of sight and into the holster.

The door opened. A girl of somewhere around twenty, a lithe girl in a sweater who knew she looked well in a sweater, drew back as she saw the compact little group around the table. "Am I intruding?"

Banning Clarke said, "Not at all, Dorina. Come in. This is Mr. Mason and Miss Della Street, his secretary.— And this is Dorina Crofton, Mrs. Sims' daughter by her former marriage.—I was just explaining something to Mr. Mason, Dorina, but it's all right now."

Clarke turned to the lawyer. "So you see the peculiar position in which I find myself—particularly with reference to the corporation."

"Do they," Mason asked, "have any suspicion of the true facts?"

"I think they have."

"I mean the legal title—the ownership of the property that is—er—involved?"

"Yes."

Mason's eyes narrowed. "You say they have an attorney at that meeting?"

"Yes. Chap named Moffgat. You may know him. He was my wife's lawyer. He handled her estate. Then Bradisson started going to him. Moffgat represented their side in the litigation over the stock. I don't think he cherishes any great love for me—and I know I don't for him."

"He's attending that directors' meeting?" Mason asked.

"Oh, yes. He has a finger in every pie the corporation cooks these days."

"Look here," Mason said suddenly, "when you resigned as president did you resign as a director also?"

Clarke nodded.

Mason said, with a trace of irritation in his voice, "You should have told me this before I drew up that pooling agreement."

"Why? What's that got to do with it?"

"Suppose," Mason said, "they put you up as a director in the corporation. Salty is in there, voting your stock under that pooling agreement. That would be the same as though you voted for yourself. Once you become a director you're acting in a fiduciary capacity. If you have knowledge affecting the value of corporate assets and fail to give the corporation the benefit of that knowledge— Get Salty out of that meeting before they can do anything about—"

"The meeting's all finished, Mr. Mason," Dorina said. "I heard the chairs scraping back just as I came by the room."

Clarke looked at Mason. "Isn't there some way I can beat that?"

Mason shook his head. "The minute you become a qualified director, even if it's only for a few minutes, you're licked. You can't withhold this information and then subsequently. . . . Wait a minute—under the by-laws does a director have to be a stockholder?"

"I believe he does," Clarke said.

"What's your stock worth?"

"Three or four hundred thousand, anyway, and perhaps more. Why?"

"I want to buy it," Mason said, and added with a grin, "for five dollars. I'll have a private understanding with you that I'll sell it back to you for five dollars and five cents day after tomorrow, but no one is to know of that agreement."

"I can't hurry up those stairs," Clarke said. "It's up in my desk on the second floor, in the third pigeonhole from the right."

"Desk locked?" Mason asked, getting to his feet.

"No. There's a lock, but it won't work. I've been intending to have it fixed. A key broke off in it. Suppose you could find—Dorina, how about showing Mr. Mason the way to my room? You can go up the back stairs."

Dorina, standing by the table, seemed for the moment not to have heard him.

Mrs. Sims said, "Dorina, honey, wake up. Look out —don't upset the sugar! Mr. Clarke wants you to take Mr. Mason up to his room."

"Oh, yes. Certainly." She smiled with the vague expression of a person waking from a sound sleep. "Will you come this way, please, Mr. Mason?"

Mason said, "Here's your five dollars, Clarke. Consider the sale completed."

Clarke lowered his voice. "If you hear the meeting breaking up, Mason, and find you can't possibly make it, you know what to do."

Mason held up his right hand, made a signing motion and raised his eyebrows.

Clarke nodded.

"That," Mason said, "would make complications."

"I know, but we can't afford to let them catch us in that trap."

Mason caught Dorina by the arm. "Come on, young lady," he said.

Dorina Crofton led the way up a flight of back stairs. Wordlessly she hurried down the corridor.

"You seem to be a young woman of deep thoughts," Mason said.

She gave him the smile which politeness demanded, said after a moment, "I guess I'm rather quiet today. This is Mr. Clarke's room."

Mason, who had been prepared for a sumptuous master's bedroom, found himself surprised at the small room on the north side of the house. It contained a plain single bed, a bureau, a chest of drawers, a somewhat battered table, an old-fashioned roll-top desk, and a dozen or so

60

framed photographic enlargements. A couple of coiled rawhide ropes hung on the wall. A pair of big roweled Mexican spurs hung between the two ropes. From the other wall, a worn rifle scabbard, still holding a gun, was suspended at an angle from a peg placed in the wall. A glass-enclosed gun cabinet held an assortment of rifles and shotguns. The skin of a big mountain lion was stretched along the third wall. At one time the room had evidently been an intimate part of a man's personality, but now it had not been lived in enough to keep the atmosphere of warm friendliness and human occupancy which should have been a part of such a room. It had been kept scrupulously clean, yet it was a stiffly starched cleanliness that seemed divorced from the swirling currents of everyday activity.

Mason crossed over to the desk, pulled out the papers in the pigeonhole Banning Clarke had mentioned. He found the envelope containing the stock certificate, took it out, looked at it, saw that it was in order, and was just starting for the door when, from the lower floor, there came the sudden sound of several people talking at once, of footsteps gravitating toward the back part of the house, and that general bustle of activity which attends the breaking up of a meeting.

Mason stood still frowning at the stock certificate.

"What's the matter?" Dorina Crofton asked.

Mason said, "The sale is completed, the certificate should have been signed before that meeting broke up."

"Will it make any difference?" Dorina asked.

"It may make a lot of difference. Do you suppose there's any way you could rush this certificate down to him before they get to the kitchen and—"

"They're headed out that way now. I think they're looking for him."

Mason abruptly sat down at the desk, whipped out his fountain pen, pulled papers out of the pigeonholes until he found one bearing the signature of Banning Clarke.

61

He flashed a quick glance over his shoulder at Dorina Crofton.

She seemed completely unaware of what was going on, her mind apparently entirely occupied with some personal problem which absorbed her entire attention.

Mason spread the stock certificate out, placed the paper containing Banning Clarke's signature just above it. For a moment he studied the signature; then, with a swift, sure touch, made a somewhat amateurish job of signing Banning Clarke's name to an endorsement transferring the stock.

He replaced the paper from which he had copied Clarke's signature, folded the stock certificate, pushed it down into his pocket and screwed the cap on his fountain pen.

"All ready," he said.

Dorina moved silently out into the corridor. Mason felt certain that she had been so completely absorbed in what she was thinking that the significance of his act had not dawned on her.

They were all in the kitchen by the time Mason got there—Lillian Bradisson, who carried a little too much flesh and used just a bit too much make-up; Jim Bradisson, outwardly affable and good-natured in his friendliness; Moffgat the lawyer, stocky, well tailored, with hair that had been combed back so that every strand, glistening with hairdressing, was held in just the right position; Hayward Small, a wiry chap with quick, restless eyes; and Salty Bowers, seeming completely detached from the others.

Mason gave them the benefit of a lightning survey and had them catalogued in his mind even before they became aware of his scrutiny.

Banning Clarke performed perfunctory introductions, and it seemed to Mason that the others were almost effusive in their cordiality. Moffgat particularly went out of his way to be friendly, although retaining somewhat of a careful reserve.

"I have just learned," Moffgat said, "that you are to represent Mr. and Mrs. Sims in that fraud action. It will indeed be an honor to have such a famous opponent, Mr. Mason. I've seen you in court several times. I'm not certain that you place me—Moffgat & Steele, attorneys in the Brokaw Building." He gravely tendered Mason a card.

Mason slipped the card into his pocket and said, "I haven't had time to familiarize myself with the issues involved in that fraud action."

"No hurry, no hurry," Moffgat said. "I think as soon as you hear the evidence, Mr. Mason, you'll decide not to contest the action. In the meantime, Mr. Clarke, we have some good news for *you.*"

"What is it?" Clarke asked, his voice and manner coldly impersonal.

"It has occurred to us," Moffgat said, "that because of various litigation and other things, the corporation has really done you an injustice. You aren't physically able to go out on the properties and take an active part in their operation, but you do have certain highly specialized knowledge; and the company feels that it owes you a debt of gratitude for the work you have done in developing the mining property. In short, Mr. Clarke, we have elected you to a place on the board of directors, and have employed you as supervising manager at a salary of twenty-five thousand dollars a year and all incidental expenses."

Clarke looked surprised.

Mason said, "I'm sorry, Moffgat, but it's no go."

"What do you mean?"

"Exactly what I said. It's a cleverly baited trap, but it won't work."

Moffgat said angrily, "I don't know what right you

have to make any such statement. We are trying to bury the hatchet, that's all."

Mason smiled at him. "I'll tell you something else, Counselor. The election of Clarke to the board of directors is invalid."

"What do you mean?"

"Directors have to be stockholders in the corporation."

"Banning Clarke is a very large stockholder, Mr. Mason."

"He *was*," Mason said. "It happens that he's sold his stock."

"The books of the corporation don't show it."

"They will when the stock is presented for transfer."

"But on the books of the corporation he's still a stockholder. He—"

Mason pulled Banning Clarke's stock certificate from his pocket, spread it out on the table.

"The question," he said, "is whether Banning Clarke actually is a stockholder, and I think this answers the question. Gentlemen, *I* have bought Clarke's stock."

Moffgat became angry. "That stock purchase," he said, "is just a subterfuge."

Mason grinned. "Would you like to go to court and ask to have the transfer set aside on the grounds that you engineered a trap for Clarke, hoping that he would walk into it, and that he avoided it by selling his stock?"

"It wasn't a trap, I tell you. We were trying to extend an olive branch."

Nell Sims said in the peculiarly chirping tone of voice which she reserved for interpolations, "Fear the Greeks when they bear olive branches."

Mason said suavely, "Well, perhaps I have been a little hasty."

"I think you have."

"Would you," Mason asked, "make that contract of employment on an annual basis—provide that the contract couldn't be terminated by the corporation except on twelve months' notice?"

Moffgat flushed. "Certainly not."

"Why?"

"Well, there are . . . there are reasons."

Mason nodded to Banning Clarke. "There you are," he said.

Clarke said, "I'm satisfied to leave the entire matter in your hands, Mason."

Mason folded the stock certificate and put it in his pocket.

"May I ask what you paid for that?" Moffgat asked.

"Certainly," Mason observed.

Moffgat waited for a further reply.

"You are at liberty to *ask*," Mason said, smiling.

James Bradisson injected himself into the conversation. "Come, come. Let's not have any hard feelings about it. As far as I'm concerned I don't want Banning Clarke to feel there's any personal animosity. Frankly, Moffgat said that if we'd elect him to a position on the board of directors and give him this contract we could jockey him into a situation where either he'd have to disclose everything he knew about the company property, or—if he ever exploited or developed it in his own name and for his own benefit—we could go to court and establish that he was acting as an involuntary trustee for the company. Come on, Moffgat, you've had your fling and you came out second best. Mason anticipated what you were up to and beat you to it. And I, for one, am just as well pleased. I'm tired of lawsuits. Now let's forget our business differences and be friends.—Banning, I don't suppose there's any chance of reaching an agreement and getting you to give us certain information that you have, is there?"

"What information?"

"You know what I mean."

Banning gained time by extending his teacup for Mrs. Sims to fill. "So it *was* a trap?" he asked.

"Sure it was," Bradisson said, as Moffgat, taking a quick breath, apparently started to deny it. "Now then, let's talk of something else."

Mrs. Sims, carrying the teapot around the table to refill the teacups of Della Street and Perry Mason, asked, "What about *my* case?"

Moffgat, in a cold rage, said, "I'm glad you mentioned it. It's one of the things I wanted to discuss. But it probably would be better to discuss it in the absence of your client, Mr. Mason."

"Why in my absence?" Mrs. Sims asked.

Moffgat said, shortly, "You might get angry."

"Not me," Mrs. Sims said. "*I* didn't have a thing to do with it. All I want to know is where I stand."

Mason said, "I left instructions to have a demurrer filed this afternoon in that case."

Mrs. Bradisson, who had kept in the background, said, "James, I suppose we've discharged our obligations as directors and can go now."

Bradisson seemed somewhat reluctant to leave.

Dorina Crofton walked around the table, stood by the corner, then impulsively crossed over to the place near the stove where her mother was standing, and kissed her.

"What's that for?" Mrs. Sims asked.

"For luck," Dorina said, laughing.

There was a moment of general confusion with people moving around the big kitchen, Bradisson holding the door open for his mother, Mason on his feet bowing and expressing his pleasure at having met the others.

As the swinging door to the kitchen closed on the parting directors, Moffgat said, "I have a stipulation I'd like you to sign, Mason. I've left my brief case in the other room. If you'll pardon me a moment. . . ."

"Watch him," Clarke said tersely when Moffgat had left the room. "He's full of tricks. He's putting something up to Jim right now. That business of leaving his brief case was just a stall."

Mason said in a low, hurried voice, "That stipulation probably means he wants to take the deposition of Pete Sims. He *may* want to take yours."

"Why?"

Mason smiled. "A general fishing expedition. Once he gets you before a notary public, he'll start asking questions designed to trap you in connection with this other matter. Sorry I had to do what I did with reference to that stock, but we were working against minutes."

"Quite all right," Clarke said, laughing.

"You see," Mason said, "I didn't have time to explain it to you, but the law in regard to corporation directors is rather obscure. It isn't like being elected to some office where you have to qualify by taking an oath of office. Under the pooling agreement your shares were voted by Salty. Naturally, Salty thought they were doing you a favor putting you on the board of directors."

Salty Bowers said sheepishly, "They were so doggone nice about it, I thought they were really and truly trying to patch up all the differences. I feel like kicking myself."

"No need to feel that way," Mason said. "It was a clever legal trap."

"Darn clever," Banning Clarke said. "But I suppose if they ever get to checking up on the time element there was a period of five or ten minutes during which I actually was a director and therefore—"

Mason frowned, glanced warningly toward Nell Sims.

Banning Clarke laughed. "She's all right. I'd trust her and Dorina with my life."

Mason said, "Well, just to make this thing legal and get me out of a mess in case there should be an investigation, take your pen and trace over the signature on this stock certificate. I want you to do it in the presence of witnesses. I'd particularly like to have Dorina Crofton here to see you do it because she was with me when—"

"I'm afraid she's left," Nell Sims interrupted. "That's the way with youngsters these days—go streaking out just as soon as they get an opportunity. Time was, when I was a girl, that you wouldn't think of going out without getting your parents' permission."

"She's a mighty good girl," Banning Clarke said with feeling.

"She's all right, the way girls go nowadays," Mrs. Sims announced; "but she's too independent."

Mason said, "It's a good thing for children to be independent. Gives them a chance to develop individualities."

"Not too independent," Nell Sims sniffed. "Children overdo it. As the twig is bent, so the branch is broken."

Banning Clarke grinned at Mason and took out his fountain pen, and Mason unfolded the stock certificate.

"When Moffgat comes back," Mason said, "if it looks as though he has any papers to serve on you, I'll cough twice. When I do, make some excuse to get out, and then keep under cover so he can't serve you with a subpoena. I distrust that man and—"

The swinging door pushed open. Moffgat was talking almost as he entered the room. "Well, Mr. Mason, I am hoping our adverse interests as counsel won't interfere with our friendly relations." He was smiling affably now, and his manner had undergone a complete change, as though Jim Bradisson had given him definite instructions to try a new approach.

Mason whipped the stock certificate out from under Banning Clarke's hand before the pen had a chance to touch the paper. Under cover of reaching across the table for the teapot, he folded the stock certificate and slipped it in the inside pocket of his coat.

Moffgat noticed the fountain pen in Banning Clarke's

hand, frowned with concentration, but said suavely enough, "I have here a stipulation, Mr. Mason, for the taking of the deposition of Peter Sims, one of the defendants in that fraud case. I'd like to take the deposition tomorrow if that isn't too short notice. I think it's vitally important to have a clarification of the issues." Moffgat pulled a cardboard filing jacket from his brief case, opened it, and handed Mason a blue-backed legal document.

Della Street, sitting at Mason's side, glanced toward the filing jacket and nudged Mason's elbow.

Mason coughed twice.

Banning Clarke pushed back his chair, said, "Excuse me. I'll get a drink of water."

He moved over toward the sink, glanced toward the table, saw that Mason was reading the stipulation with the greatest care, that Moffgat was watching him with slightly narrowed eyes.

Quietly, Banning Clarke slipped out through the back door.

Mason said, "If we're going to take the deposition of Pete Sims as one party to the controversy, I'd like to take the deposition of James Bradisson at the same time."

"Why do you want his deposition?"

"He's the president of the corporation, isn't he?"

"Yes."

"And the one with whom Pete Sims had his dealings shortly prior to the execution of the contract which is now claimed to be fraudulent?"

"Yes."

"I want his deposition," Mason said. "If you're going to take the deposition of one party, I want the deposition of the other."

Moffgat yielded the point reluctantly. "Interline it in pen and ink," he said. "And while you're doing it, put in the name Banning Clarke."

"He's not a party to the controversy. You have no right to take his deposition," Mason said.

Moffgat's smile was crafty. "He is in poor health. I have a right to take a deposition to perpetuate his testimony. He's a material witness."

"To what?"

"To something connected with this controversy."

"What?"

"I'll disclose that at the proper time."

"Then I won't include his name in the stipulation," Mason said.

Moffgat said, "You don't have to. I have anticipated your refusal and secured a court order and a subpoena. Under those circumstances, since it will save your client the annoyance and embarrassment of having the subpoena served on him, you'd better have his name included in the deposition."

Mason merely inserted in pen and ink the words, "Also the deposition of James Bradisson, at the same time and place."

Moffgat seemed definitely annoyed. "I warn you, Mr. Mason, that I shall serve that subpoena at the first available opportunity without regard for the convenience of Banning Clarke."

"That," Mason announced, slipping his fountain pen back into his pocket, "is your privilege."

Moffgat blotted Mason's signature, signed his own name, handed Mason a copy of the stipulation, returned the filing jacket to his brief case.

"And now," he said, "if you'll pardon me, I'll join the Bradissons. I'll see you tomorrow, Counselor."

He had no sooner left the room than Mrs. Sims, walking over to the icebox, said, "I've got something in here to take the taste of that lawyer out of your mouth. I wasn't going to bring it out while he was here because he'd be wanting a piece."

She took out a lemon pie. The dark gold of the

browned top was dotted with little amber-colored globules.

Mason glanced at Della Street, then smiled contentedly. "If I were a cat," he said to Mrs. Sims, "I'd stretch out in front of the fireplace and start purring."

Salty looked at his watch. "Gee, I'm sorry I walked into that trap, Mr. Mason."

"You don't need to be. It was cleverly baited. Look here, Salty—Moffgat is going to slip out there and try to serve that subpoena on Banning Clarke. Do you suppose Banning can keep out of his way?"

Salty chuckled. "Give him ten seconds' head start out there in the dark and the Devil himself couldn't find him!"

When Mason and Della Street had finished their pie, Mason said, "Well, I guess we'd better go have a talk with Banning Clarke. Hope he didn't get too excited."

Salty Bowers fidgeted uneasily, suddenly blurted, "I wish you'd wait for just a minute."

Mason elevated his eyebrows in a silent question.

"The woman I'm going to marry is coming in—Lucille Brunn. I told her to be here by eight-thirty, and she'll be right on the dot. I—well, I'd like to have you meet her."

Mrs. Sims, clearing off the table, said, "Trouble with Banning Clarke is he's always been active and he can't slow down. If he'd just take life real easy for a while, he could get well; but about the time he gets half cured, he goes and tears himself down again. Gets right back to where he started."

"He's coming along all right," Salty said defensively.

"I ain't so certain. He looked bad tonight. And if Miss Brunn is coming here, Salty Bowers, you get out of my kitchen so I can get my work done. It's a wonder," she went on, sputtering as she attacked the stacked dishes with swift competence, "that I get any work done at all, what with people using my kitchen for directors' meetings and what not. Police find poison in the food and ask *me* how it got there. How should I know, with everyone traipsing around the kitchen? And that slick promoter— whisks my daughter right out of the kitchen and leaves her Ma with all the dishes. Now that boy friend she had who went in the Army, Jerry Coslet, wouldn't ever do anything like that. Girls used to do the dishes before they'd go out, back when there was some consideration shown to parents. . . ."

Salty Bowers grinned across at Mason. "We may as well go into the living-room. She'll go on and on like this. . . ."

"Seems like men don't have no consideration for women nowadays," Nell Sims went on. "They just don't stop to think. Lucille wants to make a good impression on your lawyer friend, and you bring her into a kitchen!— Land sakes! What's this?"

Mrs. Sims picked up the sugar bowl, and under it a folded paper began slowly straightening out as the weight of the bowl was removed from it.

"Looks like a note," Della Street said.

Mrs. Sims spread it open, held it out at arm's length, and squinted her eyes. "There," she said, "I've gone and forgotten my glasses again. Something's written on it all right, but I can't read it without my specs." She handed it to Della Street. "You've got young eyes. Suppose *you* read it."

Della Street glanced through it hastily. "It's from your daughter, Mrs. Sims. Do you want me to read it out loud or—"

"Certainly I do. What's the idea of Dorina slipping notes under the sugar bowl? Why didn't she come right out and say anything she had to tell me?"

Della Street said, "The note says: 'Dear Mom— Hayward has been after me to go to Las Vegas and get married. I've been trying to make up my mind all day. I still don't know the answer. But if I'm not home by midnight, you'll know what's happened. If you don't like it, don't try to stop us, because you can't. Love—.' And it's signed with just the initial D."

Mrs. Sims slowly dried her hands on the dish towel. "Can you beat that!" she demanded.

Salty Bowers said, "Well, if she's in love with him, and—"

73

Nell Sims sputtered. *"If* she's in love with him! The idea of a girl leaving a note like that when she's going away to get married. Land sakes! If she'd been in love with him, she'd tear the house down getting started. Been thinking it over all day and can't make up her mind! It's a wonder she wouldn't ask her Ma for a little advice. I could have told her. Looks good to her now because all of the younger men are in the Army. These birds that are left look like picture actors to the girls, because the girls ain't seen any young men in civilian clothes for so long they've forgotten what they look like. You wait until these young men start coming back. Why, land sakes, when Jerry Coslet gets back, this Hayward Small will look like an old dodo to Dorina.—That's the way with girls these days, won't ask their mothers for any advice. Think they know everything. Soak up a little sophisticated patter and think they can brush life off to one side with wisecracks."

Mason said, "Your daughter seems to be a very level-headed young woman, Mrs. Sims. Perhaps she's been taking all of these things into consideration."

"She's a good girl," Mrs. Sims said positively. "A mighty good girl, and she'll be all right. You just can't make a sow's ear out of a silk purse, no matter how hard you try."

"That's right," Mason observed, smiling.

Salty Bowers, standing awkwardly ill at ease, said, "Lucille is just about due and. . . ."

"You get out of my kitchen," Nell Sims said. "Go on, all of you now. Get out of the kitchen."

Della Street said, "Let me help with the dishes, Mrs. Sims. There's quite a stack here, and after all, *I'm* not trying to make any romantic impression."

Nell Sims' black eyes swung to Della Street. "Well, if you're not, you should be," she snapped. "Land sakes! The way some educated people are so blind they can't see. . . . Go on, all of you. Get out of my kitchen."

"She means it," Salty grinned.

Della Street flashed her a quick smile. "It was a very nice dinner, Mrs. Sims. And I'm quite certain your daughter will be all right."

"Of course she'll be all right. I just wish you could have seen Jerry Coslet the day. . . . That's the worst of it, she hasn't seen her friends. Been hanging around the kitchen too much. Just a case of absence making the heart grow fonder of the bird in hand.—Wait until I see that Hayward Small. I'll give him a piece of my mind. Son-in-law or no son-in-law, I'll tell him.—Go on now. Get out, all of you. Lucille Brunn's going to come any minute and if she gets into this kitchen she—go on, get out of here."

In the living-room, Mason grinned at Salty Bowers. "She even shook her apron at us," he said, "shooing us out of the kitchen as if we were a bunch of chickens."

"She's a character," Salty grinned. "Out in Mojave the boys used to come in and egg her on just to hear her talk. She—"

He broke off as the doorbell sounded.

Salty Bowers excused himself, hurried to the door, returned with an air of beaming pride. "Lucille, this is Mr. Mason," then suddenly realizing that he should have introduced Della Street first, corrected himself hastily, "Miss Street *and* Mr. Mason."

Lucille Brunn had a small face, dark, intense eyes and a quick, nervous manner. She tactfully turned to acknowledge the introduction to Della Street first, then gave Mason her hand.

Bowers said, "We're getting married day after tomorrow and going to head out into the desert for a honeymoon."

"You've lived in the desert?" Della Street asked Miss Brunn.

"No. I'm getting acquainted with it through Salty," she laughed.

"The desert," Salty announced, "is the best mother a

75

man ever had. You do what she wants you to and she's kind to you. She trains you to do your thinking for yourself, too, and that's good; but just you forget about her laws, and you've got trouble on your hands—lots of trouble. A man don't make a mistake only once in the desert."

It was a long speech for Salty, and showed the depth of his feeling.

Della Street said politely to Lucille Brunn, "I hope you'll be happy out in Salty's desert. He makes it sound very tempting."

"I'm certain I will," and then, with a quick, nervous laugh, "I'll be happy anywhere with Salty."

The door from the hallway opened and Velma Starler, hurriedly entering the room, brought up to a sharp stop at sight of Perry Mason and Della Street.

"Oh, hello. I didn't know you were planning to be here. It isn't. . . . I mean my patient hasn't had any trouble?"

"None whatever," Mason said. "He simply asked me to come up on a business matter."

"Oh! I'm relieved. Dr. Kenward insisted I should take an afternoon off. He said he'd send out another nurse for the day, but Mr. Clarke made such a to-do about it that the doctor let it go. You see," she went on to explain, "we had a rather hectic night. But how about you folks? You've been at the beach?"

"Riding," Mason said. "That accounts for the sunburn. We were in the saddle all day."

"I love to ride," Velma said, and then, turning to Lucille, "Been here long, Lucille?"

"Just arrived."

"What's happened? Anything new?"

"I haven't heard of anything. Try and get Salty to tell you anything, even if he knows it." She laughed. "When it comes to information, he's a one-way street."

Mason said, "It seems that this was the date for the regular stockholders' meeting of the mining corporation. They brought up their attorney and tried to use an olive branch as cover for a little scheme."

"Moffgat?" she asked.

Mason lit a cigarette, nodded. "Rather an energetic schemer."

"I'm afraid of him," Lucille Brunn said, in a low voice to Salty.

"Why?"

"I don't like his eyes."

Mason cleared his throat, ground out his cigarette in the ash tray, said nothing.

"Well, I'll run along and take a look at my patient," Velma said cheerfully, "before I change my clothes—just make certain that he's all right. I'll have to run up and get a flashlight."

"Nice girl," Salty remarked when she had left. "Well, Lucille and I will be on our way—be seeing you folks again."

Della Street watched them out of the door, said musingly, "He certainly is terribly in love with her."

"You'd think she was the only woman on earth to watch him," Mason agreed. "His eyes keep feasting on her."

"She is, as far as he's concerned," Della said. "It must be nice to be loved like that."

Mason smiled. "They say all the world loves a lover. I'd say that all the feminine part of it does. Show a woman a romance and her eyes begin to sparkle."

Della laughed. "I wonder what Mrs. Sims would do to that proverb to twist it around and still make sense. I wasn't aware my eyes were shining. As a matter of fact, I'm feeling low, terribly low. While you're driving me home I'm going to—" She broke off to clear her throat.

"Probably you've had too much exertion," Mason said. "That long horseback ride and. . . ."

"No, it isn't that type of fatigue. I—Is your throat all right?"

"Yes, why?"

"There's a peculiar burning sensation in mine—a metallic taste."

Mason, suddenly solicitous, said, "Whoa! Wait a minute. You're not letting your mind play tricks on you, are you?"

"I don't think so."

Mason looked at her face, stepped forward and placed his hand over hers.

"Della, you *are* sick!"

She tried to smile. "Something I've eaten has most certainly disagreed with me. I'm—I'm a little nauseated. I wonder where they keep the bathrooms in this house."

Mason strode across to the plate-glass window, pulled back the drapes, looked out into the shadowy darkness of the big yard. The little spot made by a flashlight bobbing along marked the place where Velma Starler was walking. She had not as yet quite reached the stone wall of varicolored rock.

Mason flung up a side window. "Oh, Miss Starler," he called.

The beam of the flashlight stopped abruptly.

"As soon as it's convenient can you take a look at Miss Street?" Mason asked.

"What's the matter?" she called.

"She's been taken suddenly ill."

For a moment the flashlight hesitated, then became a spot of brilliance as the nurse whirled in her tracks and started running toward the house.

A few moments later, breathless and plainly alarmed, she was in the dining-room. "Where is she? What's the matter?"

"She went in search of a bathroom. She had nausea and was complaining of a metallic taste—"

Velma Starler dashed from the room without waiting for Mason to finish.

It was a good ten minutes before she returned. Her face was grave. "I've telephoned for Dr. Kenward. He'll be over right away."

"What is it?" Mason asked.

She said gravely, "I'm afraid it's serious, Mr. Mason. It has all of the symptoms of arsenic poisoning. She—But, Mr. Mason, you're looking. . . . Are *you* all right?"

"Do the symptoms of arsenic poison," Mason asked with calm dignity, "include a burning sensation, nausea, griping pains in the abdomen, and a metallic taste in the throat?"

"Yes. Are you—"

Mason said, "When Dr. Kenward comes, tell him he has two patients," and collapsed into a chair.

■ 8 ■

Dr. Kenward, by an almost imperceptible motion of his head, indicated he wished Velma to join him for a conference, and then moved toward the dining-room.

Velma Starler joined him after a few seconds, finding him seated in a chair at the dining-room table, leaning forward, his elbows on his knees, gazing somewhat dejectedly at the carpet.

No longer was Dr. Kenward the cool, efficient master of the sickroom, the quickly decisive, perfectly poised medical man whose calm professional competence could not be shattered by emergencies, the hysteria of patients, or those diabolical coincidences of fate when everything seems to go wrong at once.

The man who sat on the edge of the dining-room chair, his elbows propped on his knees, his body sagging with weariness, was merely a very tired, very much overworked, and somewhat distraught mortal who had reached the limit of his endurance. He looked up as Velma entered the room, and she was shocked as some trick of lighting threw into undue prominence the dark circles of weariness under his eyes.

Recognizing that this was not a case where the nurse should remain standing in the presence of the doctor, but a matter of two tired human beings bound together by a common interest, Velma drew up a chair and seated herself at his side.

For the space of nearly a minute he was silent. Velma, waiting for him to speak, later on realized that he had no desire to talk for the moment, but was drawing a certain amount of strength from her presence.

She offered him her package of cigarettes.

Silently, he took one. And she was the one to strike the match and hold the flame cupped in her hands to light both cigarettes.

The silence was not in any way strained, nor was it embarrassing. It was as though a cloak of wordless understanding had thrown itself about them, shutting off, for the moment, cares and worries of the outside world.

It was Dr. Kenward who at length broke the silence. "Thanks to the fact that you had the antidote on hand, I don't think it will be serious."

"Arsenic?" she asked.

"Undoubtedly. Perhaps not a very large dose, but nevertheless arsenic."

Several seconds later he sighed wearily, then said, "I'm afraid what you told me about Banning Clarke didn't completely register—all the little details. Would you mind very much repeating what you told me?"

"Not at all," she said.

He sucked in a deep drag from the cigarette, then placed his head back against the chair, exhaled slowly, and closed his eyes.

Velma said, "I was on my way to see Banning Clarke when Mr. Mason called. I telephoned you and then washed out the stomachs and administered the ferric solution. Then I dashed out to see how Mr. Clarke was getting along.

"You know how the pathway runs along the side of that rock wall, then swerves around the big clump of cactus and winds in and out through the sand around the cactus patches.—I was running just as fast as I dared—so fast that for a moment I couldn't realize the significance of what I saw . . . or rather, what I failed to see."

She paused and peered at him sharply as though wondering whether the closed eyes and relaxed muscles indicated he'd drifted off into the slumber of physical exhaustion.

"Proceed," he said without so much as flickering his eyes.

"You know how they slept—Salty Bowers on the north side of the little sand cove, and Banning Clarke down to the south near the wall. Well, I had actually run past the fireplace before I suddenly realized what was the matter. Neither sleeping bag was there."

"And there was no sign of Clarke?" he asked.

"None whatever. Both sleeping bags were gone, the cooking utensils were gone, the jalopy that they used to drive around with is missing, and there's no sign of Banning Clarke or Salty Bowers."

"Any indications in the sand, any tracks?" Dr. Kenward asked.

"I didn't look for that."

"Are the burros gone?"

"No. They're there."

Dr. Kenward pushed the end of his cigarette down hard in the ash tray. "Let's go look the place over. You have a flashlight?"

"Yes."

"Look in on the patients," he said. "Tell them you may be out for five or ten minutes. Where's that housekeeper, by the way?"

"I don't know. It seems as though people cleared out of the house by magic. Mrs. Sims simply isn't here. Her daughter went out with Hayward. I understand she left a note saying they were going to Las Vegas to be married. Mrs. Sims was pretty much upset over it. She left the dishes in the sink and dashed out."

"Upset? Why?"

"She doesn't like him."

"Where are the others?"

"I don't know. It seems they'd been having a stockholders' meeting. Moffgat, the lawyer, was here. He tried some of his clever tricks and they didn't pan out, thanks to Mr. Mason. Then everyone went out. I'm a little

82

surprised that Mrs. Bradisson and her son went, because they should still be feeling weak from the effects of the poison. At least, one would think so. They were terribly sick last night."

Dr. Kenward said, "They seem to have made a very satisfactory recovery. However, that doesn't need to concern us. We've got to notify the police again. But before they take over, I want to see what's happened to Banning Clarke. I want to make sure that he isn't on the grounds, or anywhere around the house. If he needs medical attention, I want to see that he gets it before the officers start another inquisition."

Velma Starler looked in on her patients, advised Dr. Kenward, "They're resting quietly. Shall we go now?"

He nodded.

They walked out through the back door, around the flagstone walk, down stone steps, and then followed the beam of the flashlight through the terraced slope which had been so skillfully landscaped. To their left was the rock wall, ahead of them and to their right was the cactus garden. A moon, but slightly past the full, hung in limpid brilliance in the eastern heavens, sending shafts of silvery light, creating splotches of inky shadows.

"Just like being out in the middle of the Mojave Desert," Dr. Kenward said. "It gives me a creepy feeling every time I come out here. Not creepy exactly, either; it's as though you had suddenly walked out of the present into the past."

"I know exactly how you feel," she said. "It's such a complete change.—Over here is where they had their camp. There's the fireplace, you see, and here's where their sleeping bags were."

"Let's see the flashlight for a moment," Dr. Kenward said. "Ah, I thought so."

"What?"

"That peculiar oblong section of sand. Notice how

83

those marks lead up to that little smooth section—slightly concave as though a cylinder had been pressed down."

"Why, yes. I hadn't noticed it before. What causes it?"

"That is where Banning Clarke's sleeping bag was spread out. That sleeping bag has been neatly rolled up. You can see where someone started rolling and pushing, moving forward on his knees, rolling the sleeping bag into a tight roll. See those peculiar marks? They're made by knees pressing into the sand as the sleeping bag was rolled as tightly as possible. Then, when the bag had been rolled into a compact bundle, it was picked up for roping. The last pressure on the bag shoved it down into the sand and left that little rectangular, slightly concave space."

"I see—but is that particularly important?"

"I think so."

"I'm afraid I don't see just what you're driving at."

"A camper," Dr. Kenward said, "no matter how great the rush, would roll up a sleeping bag and carry it rolled—unless he were going to put it on a horse, in which event he might fold it double. A tenderfoot, however, hurriedly trying to remove a sleeping bag as evidence, would rush in and pick it up any old way and dash out with it."

"So you think this sleeping bag was rolled by someone who had done a great deal of camping?"

He nodded.

"Banning Clarke?"

"Either Clarke or Salty Bowers."

"And what does that mean?"

"One of the possibilities is that Salty Bowers and Banning Clarke are playing some deep game. I'm afraid that out on the road somewhere, at a point affording no immediate medical attention, Clarke will develop symptoms of arsenic poisoning, and the retching and nausea will overtax his heart even if the poison is not fatal."

Silently they moved toward the house, soaking up the night tranquillity. Velma had switched off the flashlight. The light of the moon was sufficient to guide them through the weird cacti, the stone wall casting a sinister shadow, the ocean far below—a misty sheet of mystery from which could be heard the low pulsing of booming surf.

Abruptly Dr. Kenward stopped, his back against the wall. "Let's take ten minutes," he said. "Surely we're entitled to that much. Our patients are coming along all right, and if the police aren't notified for ten minutes, no great harm will be done."

"You're tired, aren't you?"

"I've been going pretty steadily," he admitted. "It seems so calm out here, so utterly peaceful. You're away from the jangle of the telephone, the neurotics, the hypochondriacs.—Sometimes, since I've met Salty Bowers, I've wondered about life in the desert, being out with a burro somewhere in the big open spaces, rolling out a sleeping bag, stretching out to slumber with the vast silence reaching down from interstellar spaces to wrap you in a blanket of oblivion. It must be a wonderful sensation."

"Look, Bruce," she said abruptly, almost unconsciously using his first name, "you can't keep this up day in and day out, month in and month out, year in and year out. Why don't you prescribe for yourself the same treatment you would prescribe for a patient? Take a month off and get away from everything, simply drop the whole business."

"I can't."

"The argument you would use for the patient is that if you had a nervous breakdown, or if you fell over dead, things would go on without you."

The moonlight softened the harshness of the smile that twisted his lips. "Quite true," he admitted. "That, however, is something I could not control. But if I left now, it would mean that my practice would simply fall on other shoulders that were already overburdened with troubles of their own. The only thing to do is to keep plugging.

There are only a few of us, relatively, to carry on. But we *are* entitled to a ten-minute recess once in a while."

Abruptly he took her arm, walked back down to the place where Banning Clarke and Salty Bowers had had their camp. He seated himself and drew her down beside him in the sand.

"Now then," he observed, "we are a couple of prospectors sitting out in the desert. There's nothing we can do till daylight; we're absorbing the regenerating peace and tranquillity which comes only to those who live close to Nature, in the open air."

Velma Starler, a catch in her throat, pointed her finger out toward the vague blue of the moonlit mountains. "Tomorrow," she said, trying to mimic the slow drawl of Salty Bowers, "we'll head up through that pass and prospect around that outcropping. Meantime, guess there ain't anything to do except drop off to sleep."

"That's the spirit," Bruce Kenward applauded. He clasped his hands behind his head, lay back on the sand, his face turned toward the sky. "Strange how many stars there are, even when the moon's almost full. I guess we don't really see the heavens in the city. Salty Bowers was trying to tell me about how you could lie on your back in the desert and look up at the heavens blazing with myriads of brilliant stars whose existence you never even suspected until you got out away from the cities into the clear dry air of the desert."

"They're exceptionally clear tonight," she said, "even with the moon. There are dozens of stars visible."

"Dozens," he said musingly. "I wonder how many stars are visible in the desert—on a moonlit night. I wonder if we couldn't play hookey some evening and drive out into the desert just to see.—I wonder just how many there are visible now. Let's see, there are five . . . ten . . . fifteen . . . twenty . . . twenty-five . . . thirty . . . thirty-one . . . thirty-two . . . thirty-three . . . I wonder if I counted that one. . . ."

She didn't say anything when he lapsed into silence. A few seconds later she heard the even, regular breathing of an exhausted man dropping off into the deep contentment of much-needed slumber.

Noiselessly, she raised herself to her feet, moved as silently as she could through the soft sand until she was half a dozen steps away, then she turned to look back at him, a wistful tenderness in her eyes as she saw the moonlight caressing the careworn features relaxed in sleep.

For a moment she stood looking down at him, then she turned and walked quietly toward the big house which had always been so distasteful to its owner. She invaded a guest room, folded a couple of heavy blankets over her arm, returned to the cactus garden, tiptoed up to the sleeping physician and very gently placed the blankets over him, using the deft skill of a trained nurse so that no pressure would rouse him.

Then she hurried back to the house, looked in on Perry Mason, then on Della Street. Then, going into the library, she dialed Operator and said, "Police Headquarters, please. I wish to report an attempted homicide."

■ 9 ■

Lieutenant Tragg of the Metropolitan Police Force seated himself on the edge of Perry Mason's bed. The motion of the bedsprings, due to his weight, caused Mason to open his eyes.

"Hello," Mason said. "What the devil are you doing here?"

Tragg grinned at him. "Believe it or not, I'm on my vacation."

"It's optional with me?" Mason asked, his voice showing weakness.

"What is?"

"Whether I believe it or not."

Tragg laughed outright. "It happens to be the truth, Mason. My brother-in-law's the sheriff here. I've been on a fishing trip, dropped in on my way back to leave a few trout with my sister—and the telephone call came in about the poisoning. Sam Greggory, my brother-in-law, wanted me to take a hand. I told him nothing doing. I have enough of that sort of stuff in my own bailiwick without trying to borrow trouble. Then he explained to me that his latest victims were from my home town, Perry Mason and Miss Della Street, his secretary. You can imagine my reaction. I couldn't miss a set-up like that."

Mason's eyelids fluttered. He tried a grin, but it was only a grimace. "I'm a little groggy. I think they've given me a hypodermic. Tell me the truth now, Tragg, are you real, or are you just part of the drug-induced nightmare?"

"I'm part of the nightmare."

"That's what I thought. It's a big relief."

"How does it seem to be the victim, for once?"

"Terrible."

"Well, you've had it coming to you for a long while. You've been sticking up for criminals and now you can see the other side of the picture."

Mason roused himself. "Not 'sticking up for criminals,'" he protested indignantly. "I have never stuck up for any criminal. I have merely asked for the orderly administration of an impartial justice."

"Taking advantage of all the technicalities, of course," Tragg said.

Mason's voice was blurred as that of a man who talks in his sleep, but there was no fumbling over words. "Why not? The law is technical. Any man-made rule is technical. You make a line of demarcation between what is prescribed and what is prohibited, and you will always have borderline cases that seem so close to each other as to be absurd. And furthermore, Lieutenant—furthermore, . . . I'll thank you to remember that my clients are not criminals until they've been convicted by juries—and so far, that hasn't happened. . . . Guess I just had that hypo . . . I'm shaking it off."

Tragg said curiously, "I suppose you'll be telling me next that the person who slipped that poison into your sugar is entitled to the benefit of all the safeguards of the law."

"Why not?"

"Don't you feel any resentment?"

"I couldn't feel enough resentment against anyone to ask that due legal process be disregarded. Due legal process is my own safeguard against being convicted unjustly. To my mind, that's government. It's law and order. Damn it, Tragg, can you understand what I'm saying?"

"Sure."

"My mind is clear," Mason said, "but my tongue seems a foot thick. You've cleared the fuzz out of my brain, but the words seem to get garbled as my tongue wrestles with them. However, I'm getting better and stronger every minute. How's Della?"

"Doing fine."

"What time is it?"

"Around midnight."

"Where's Banning Clarke? How is he?"

"No one knows. He isn't here. Now let's finish this question of ethics. Would you be able to pocket your individual resentment enough to defend whoever my brother-in-law arrests for putting poison in the sugar?"

"Why not?"

"Even if you thought that person guilty?"

Mason said, somewhat wearily, "The law guarantees a person a trial by *jury*, Tragg. If I should refuse to defend someone because I thought him guilty, that would be a trial by Perry Mason, not a trial by ·jury. Of course, the accused wouldn't want me to represent him. Why do you say the poison was in the sugar? Is that just a guess?"

"No. We've found white arsenic in the sugar bowl."

"All through the sugar?"

"No. Apparently some had been scattered on the top of the sugar bowl. Looks as if the poisoner hadn't had time to mix it in with the contents of the bowl, but had just dumped it on top."

Mason struggled up to a sitting position in the bed. His eyes were clear now, his words crisp. "Look here, Tragg, that can't be right."

"What can't be?"

"The sugar."

"What about it?"

"It happens that Della Street and I both take sugar in our tea. So does Banning Clarke. Now Clarke had already eaten his dinner. He said he'd have a cup of tea with us and the housekeeper served him his tea first. He took two big teaspoonfuls from the top of the sugar bowl, then Della and I both had sugar when our tea was served. After that, Nell Sims helped herself to a cup of tea and I distinctly remember she put two full spoonfuls of sugar in it. Then, as I remember it, there were several more cups all around. At least Della, Banning Clarke and I had a couple of refills. If arsenic had been put in the *top* of the sugar bowl and hadn't been mixed with the sugar lower down, I doubt if you could have recovered very much from what sugar was left in the sugar bowl."

"Well, we did. We—" Tragg broke off suddenly. He looked up, grinned, said, "Come on in, Sam. I want you to meet my own particular thorn in the flesh. Sam, this is Perry Mason, the noted lawyer, the man who has upset my apple cart several times."

Sam Greggory, a powerful, thick-set man with a good-natured grin and steel-hard eyes, crossed the room to shake hands with Perry Mason. "I've always wanted to meet you," he admitted.

"Now don't tell him that you've followed his cases with such great interest," Tragg said. "That sort of talk spoils him."

"Not at all," Greggory said. "My interest has been purely one of family connection. I've always wanted to see the man who could get the Lieutenant's goat and keep it the way you've done."

"Ouch," Tragg said. "I should have known better than to lead with my chin on that one."

"What," Mason asked, "does the housekeeper say, and is she poisoned?"

"The housekeeper, so far, has said nothing," Tragg said, "and we don't know whether she's poisoned for the simple reason that we haven't been able to find her. Apparently her daughter's out getting married, and it's my hunch Mamma is on the long-distance telephone somewhere trying to stop it. Mrs. Bradisson and her son James evidently went out with an attorney by the name of Moffgat. They're having a conference somewhere. Apparently they're afraid you might have a dictograph concealed in the walls here."

"How long have you been here?" Mason asked.

"A little over an hour. Lucky thing that nurse was here and had an antidote for arsenic poisoning where she could put her hand on it. She knocked the poison out of your system almost as soon as the symptoms showed up. She's a wonder. Only thing we have against her is that she didn't notify us at once. Seems that she gave you the proper treatment, telephoned the doctor, and didn't report the case at that time because she wanted the doctor's diagnosis. Can't blame her for that. After she got that diagnosis, she was too busy with treatment for a while— or so she says. My own idea is that she's got the doctor hidden out somewhere where we can't question *him* until morning. We've been unable to raise him on the telephone. He reports to a central agency when he goes out on calls, and they insist he's on a call here."

Tragg grinned at Mason. "Women certainly are loyal. I don't blame her too much if she did stall things along until the doctor could get away. But it makes Sam mad. I guess the doctor's all in, and Sam would have been throwing questions at him for an hour. Women in jobs certainly do give their bosses a loyalty. Take Della Street, for instance. She's made being your secretary her life's work. Lord knows all the things she's had to put up with, too. I imagine that with your nervous temperament you're not the easiest man in the world to get along with. I used to think it was a loyalty to you personally that kept her at it, but now I guess it's a loyalty to the job and what it stands for."

Mason nodded. "It's something that's bigger and finer than you realize at first. They dedicate themselves to a job and—Say, wait a minute! If we pulled through because of getting such prompt treatment, what will happen to Banning Clarke and the housekeeper, with the amount of sugar *they* consumed?"

92

Sheriff Greggory said, "That's what's bothering us. We're making every effort to find them. Apparently Clarke and Bowers started out in that old rattletrap car they drive, and we've broadcast a description of it. It should be picked up any minute now."

A man thrust his head in the door, said, "Sheriff, can I speak to you a moment, please?"

"What is it?" the sheriff asked.

"Mrs. Sims has returned."

"Has she been ill?"

"Apparently not. I didn't tell her anything about the poisoning. She's gone up to her room to get ready for bed."

"Go get her and bring her in," Greggory said, arranging the light so she would be unable to see Mason's features. "I want to ask her a couple of questions."

When the man had left, Tragg said to Greggory, "Wise me up to her. What sort is she? You've been questioning her on that Bradisson poisoning."

Greggory laughed. "She's a rugged individual, all right. As I get the story, Banning Clarke sent for her in January of 'forty-two right after his wife died. She was running a restaurant in Mojave, but he made it worth her while to come down here and take over the house. He evidently hated this house—probably had reason for doing so, too. His wife went in for entertainment and bridge parties, late hours, heavy meals and somewhat steady drinking. Those prospectors go on terrific sprees, but in between times they're out in the desert living and sleeping in the open air. There's a lot of difference between that and—"

The door opened. Mrs. Sims said tonelessly, "Did you want me? Land sakes, can't a person even get to sleep without being called in for more questions? I thought you'd combed the place from cellar to attic and—"

"This," the sheriff interrupted, "is a new development. You served a late dinner in your kitchen tonight, didn't you?"

"Well, if that has anything to do with you, yes I did. I told Mr. Clarke the kitchen was no place to serve dinner to a famous lawyer, but he didn't want the others to know he was here, and said it had to be in the kitchen. Goodness knows it's a big enough kitchen, with a table—"

"And you served tea with the meal?"

"I did. You just can't dish out coffee any more whenever—"

"And you yourself drank some tea?"

"I did. And if it's bothering you, I'll—"

"And you take sugar in your tea, don't you?"

"I most certainly do—and as far as that goes—"

"You got your sugar out of the sugar bowl that was on the table, didn't you?"

"Yes. I've almost quit scooping it up off the floor. It took a lot of will power to break myself of the habit, but—"

"And you felt no ill effects?"

"From the tea, or the sugar, or your questions?"

"Never mind the sarcasm. Just answer my question, please. You felt no ill effects?"

"Certainly not."

"Others did."

"What do you mean?"

"I mean that Perry Mason and his secretary were both poisoned."

Mrs. Sims said, "I suppose this is some sort of third-degree?"

"We're simply questioning you, that's all."

"Then why tell me all this pack of lies? Why not ask what you want?"

"We're telling you the truth. Mason and his secretary were poisoned."

She seemed bewildered as incredulity gave way to belief. "Why . . . why— Did they die?"

"No. Thanks to the fact that the nurse was on the job with proper treatment and antidotes, they're coming along very nicely. The point is, however, that we found large quantities of white arsenic mixed in with the sugar in the sugar bowl."

"Why, goodness sake! *I* had sugar out of that sugar bowl tonight myself!"

"And you felt no disagreeable after-effects?"

"Certainly not."

"You're certain the sugar came out of that same sugar bowl—the white one with the round knob on the top?"

"Certainly. There was only one sugar bowl on the table. That's the sugar bowl I keep for the kitchen."

"Where do you keep it?"

"In the pantry on the lower shelf."

"And I suppose anyone in the house would have access to it?"

"Naturally. Look here, Mr. Clarke had sugar out of that bowl. How is *he?*"

"We don't know. We can't find him."

"You mean he's gone?"

"Yes."

Sheriff Greggory said, "I think you must realize, Mrs. Sims, that since this is the second time food that you have served has been poisoned, you are placed in a rather peculiar position."

"I don't understand what you're getting at."

"You'll have to give a most detailed account of everything you've done."

"What do you want to know?"

"You've been out?"

"Yes."

"Where?"

"That's my business."

"We want to know. I told you you'd have to give an account."

"I don't see how that concerns you in any way."

"It may be important."

"Well, if it's any of your business, my daughter ran

away with that mining promoter, Hayward Small. They're going to Las Vegas to be married. Well, Jerry Coslet is in an Army camp near Kingman, Arizona. He'd given Dorina the name of a man who runs a sort of poolroom in Kingman. He said that this man could always get word to him in case she ever wanted to call him. Some boys from the camp would always be there. Well, I called that poolroom, and it happened Jerry was there himself. I told him what was happening. I told him Dorina was a good girl, but that slick mining salesman was handing her a line, and he hadn't been having enough competition."

"What did Jerry say?"

"He didn't say anything much."

"Did you ask him to do anything about it?"

"No. I just told him. If he's the kind of man he should be, he'll do something about it all right."

"And you've been telephoning all this time?"

"I'll say I have. Try to put in a telephone call and they stall you along for an hour and then tell you the circuits are busy for two hours. This war certainly has increased the production of talk."

Tragg grinned. "Talk is cheap."

"Not to Kingman, Arizona, it isn't. Not when you're a working woman."

"How," Tragg asked, "do you account for the fact that you took sugar from that bowl, and felt no ill effects, when two other people who took sugar from the same bowl developed prompt symptoms of arsenic poisoning?"

"I don't 'account' for it," Nell Sims snapped. "It's up to you to 'account' for it. That's your business."

"You don't think your daughter is in love with Hayward Small?"

"He's glib. He's just naturally slick and he's been going around with her, keeping her out late—later and later. I don't like it. He's too old for her. And he's always giving you that steady eye—pretending he's working his psychology on you. A girl Dorina's age don't want psychology. She wants romance. He isn't the type, and he's been married. He told me that himself. You know as well as I do it isn't right for a married man to go traipsing around with a girl Dorina's age, even if he has been divorced. It ain't right."

"You think—that is—you think there's been anything wrong in the relationship, Mrs. Sims?"

Mrs. Sims glared at both of them. "Let him," she proclaimed, "who is without stones among you cast the first sin. My daughter is a good girl."

"I know. I understand. But I'm merely trying to find out exactly what you meant when—"

"I meant what I said. There ain't no good going to come of a thing like that. And now I've told you all I know, and I'm going to bed."

She turned and stalked out of the room.

Tragg turned out the light, which had been shining so brightly in her eyes that she couldn't see Mason on the bed. "How you feeling, Mason? Has the hypo sneaked up on you again?"

There was no answer. Mason was breathing regularly, eyes closed.

"Drugged," Tragg said, "and I guess he's pretty weak. The nurse says he's okay. Wish she'd kept Dr. Kenward here so we could have questioned him. Well, Sam, figure that one out. Either she's lying, or she took sugar from a bowl that had a lot of arsenic in it and felt no ill effects."

"She might be lying about the sugar."

"No. Perry Mason says she had sugar in her tea."

"That's right. . . . I'm playing with a thought that worries me."

"What?"

"Suppose that instead of taking sugar out of that bowl she was putting arsenic in. It would be easy to dip in with

97

a spoon and then, after lifting it out, while replacing the cover, drop in the poison."

Tragg said, "I've had the same idea. The last person to take sugar out of that bowl without being poisoned is the most logical suspect. Let's have a smoke, Sam. We aren't getting anywhere right now. Our next step is to check all the possible suspects, and then see if we can't find arsenic in the possession of one of them—or find where someone has been buying arsenic."

They scraped matches into flame, smoked for a while in silence. Sam Greggory stretched out his big arms, yawned. "Well, I'm going to bed. I—"

A staccato explosion coming from the direction of the gardens spatted against their eardrums, caused the sheriff to bite down abruptly on an unfinished sentence, turn his head, listening. Two more explosions made the silence which followed seem sinister.

Somewhere on the floor above them feet thudded to the floor, then raced to the stairs, came rushing down them.

The side door that opened out to the garden was jerked open so hard that it banged against the wall.

Sam Greggory tugged a big revolver from a holster that had worn shiny with much usage. "I guess," he observed grimly, "this is it. . . . From the southeast corner of the grounds?"

"I think so," Tragg said. "Let's go."

They ran out of the room. The sheriff, in the lead, called out, "In case we—"

He was interrupted by the sound of Velma Starler screaming.

Two more shots sounded from the cactus garden.

■ 10 ■

Sam Greggory and Lieutenant Tragg, racing ahead, had some trouble orienting themselves in the moonlit grounds. There was no longer any sound of screams to guide them. A spurious peace had descended upon the shadow-splotched grounds. Everything seemed calm and peaceful as the two officers, weapons in hand, moved cautiously forward.

Abruptly, Tragg clasped the sheriff's shoulder. "Voices," he whispered, and then added, "Steps—over here."

They listened. The sheriff, stocky and carrying a little too much weight, was breathing heavily, making it difficult to listen—but after a moment they could hear the crunch of sand as steps came toward them.

The sounds were coming from the other side of a large, circular patch of spineless cactus. Tragg took one side, the sheriff the other, circling swiftly.

Velma Starler was walking slowly toward them. Dr. Kenward was leaning heavily on her shoulder. The nurse's face showed white and apprehensive in the moon-light as she saw the two men converging on her. Then she recognized the officers, said, "Dr. Kenward has been shot."

The doctor's professional fingers were exploring the injury even as he walked. He said, calmly, "A perforation of the adductor magnus, possibly a perforation of the muscular branch of the profunda artery. Rather more extensive hemorrhage than would otherwise be expected. I think we'll be able to control it all right. We'll go on to the house if you don't mind, gentlemen."

He resumed his hobbling.

"How did you happen to get shot?" Greggory asked.

"Who did the shooting? Did you fire any shots? What were you doing out there?"

Velma Starler said almost angrily, "He fell asleep when we were out here, and I let him stay there, hoping he'd get a little much-needed rest. Night calls have been wrecking his health. He doesn't have the faintest idea who fired the shots."

Lieutenant Tragg picked up Dr. Kenward's left arm, flung it over his neck and shoulder so as to give the doctor more support.

Dr. Kenward said in his even, unemotional voice, "I was asleep, gentlemen. I am not certain, but I believe it was a shot that roused me; yet I cannot definitely identify the thing that awakened me as being a shot. However, I do know there were at least two shots fired during the interval that it took me to regain my senses as I awakened from deep slumber. I had some difficulty remembering where I was—and then I realized that projectiles were thudding into the sand and that they were intended for me.

"I jumped to my feet and started to run.

"Apparently the person who was doing the shooting must have been partially concealed. As I ran, I evidently placed a clump of cactus between us. My assailant thereupon detoured around this cactus, stalked me in the moonlight, saw me again in time to fire more shots. It was the second of these shots that took effect."

"I saw him fall," Velma Starler explained, "at the last shot. I knew, as soon as I saw him running toward me, that someone had been shooting at him."

"You never saw your assailant?" Greggory asked.

"No."

"Saw no flashes of gunfire?"

"No."

"I did," Velma Starler said. "I saw the flashes from the last two shots. They were over behind that big barrel cactus. That's about fifty or sixty feet from where Dr. Kenward had been lying."

"You can make it from here on all right, Doctor?" Lieutenant Tragg asked.

"With Velma's help, yes. I'm somewhat alarmed about the apparent extent of the hemorrhage, but we can quite possibly control that. Let us hope so. I should dislike to disturb another physician."

Tragg released the doctor's arm, nodded to Greggory.

The two men turned back toward the cactus gardens, separated slightly, revolvers drawn.

"Take it easy," Tragg said to his brother-in-law. "He's apt to shoot from ambush."

Sheriff Greggory detoured still farther to the right. "Shoot first," he said. "Ask questions afterwards. Don't take any chances."

They were walking slowly now, clinging to the shadows, darting swiftly across the moonlit strips of sand, working together like well-trained bird dogs moving through cover, keeping just about the same distance apart, spaced in such a way that any person concealing himself from one could not avoid the other's angle of vision.

And at the end of their stalk they came to the gleaming whiteness of the stuccoed wall that surrounded the grounds. They had seen and heard nothing. The garden had been tranquil in the moonlight, filled with deep silence, punctuated at rhythmic intervals by the undertone of booming surf softened by distance to a vague rumble. Only the sinister red trail left by the wounded man bore witness to the deadly menace of the moonlit silence.

"Let's go back," Tragg said, "to where the man was lying and see if we can find the place from which the shots were fired. Then we'll look for tracks."

They located the rock fireplace covered with a sheet of iron which had served the prospectors as an outdoor stove and to which the smell of stale wood smoke still clung. They found the crumpled blankets at the place where Dr. Kenward had stretched out and gone to sleep, and the furrowed indentations which marked where at least two of the bullets had plowed into the sand. Converging on the huge barrel cactus some thirty yards away, the two men caught the glitter of an empty brass cartridge case as it reflected back the moonlight.

Lieutenant Tragg picked it up. "Thirty-eight caliber automatic," he said, briefly.

There were tracks here behind the cactus. Sam Greggory, wise in the ways of the cattle country, lowered his flashlight and held it close to the ground so that the tracks would be made more distinct by an oblique illumination. By patience, he read the story of what had happened, although it took him some twenty minutes to satisfy himself.

Someone had stalked the sleeping doctor as a hunter would have stalked a deer, starting first at a point behind the wall, then emerging into the moonlight, crawling along on hands and knees through the sand, then at length lying down flat and hitching along an inch or two at a time. Then three shots had been fired. The person who fired those shots had then jumped up, leaving deep footprints in the soft sand, had rushed around to another cactus fifty yards away, and had fired two more shots. Then the tracks showed a headlong sprint toward the white stucco wall.—That much the sand told plainly and distinctly, but for the rest the record was blurred. The sand was so soft and dried that it had flowed back into the tracks, leaving it impossible to tell much about them save that the tracks seemed rather small.

Lieutenant Tragg moved off to one side, took half a dozen running steps in order to compare the indentations made in the sand by his own feet with those that had been left by their quarry.

"Small feet," he said.

Greggory wasn't so certain. "Ever notice the tracks made by high-heeled cowboy boots?" he asked.

"Can't say that I have," Tragg admitted.

"I have. It's just a guess that these tracks might have been made by high-heeled cowboy riding boots."

"Or by a woman?" Tragg asked.

Greggory gave that suggestion thoughtful consideration. "Per*haps* by a woman," he admitted, somewhat reluctantly. "Let's go back to the house."

The telephone was ringing by the time they reached the house, but no one paid the slightest attention to it. Velma Starler was working on Dr. Kenward's leg. And the physician, sitting back with an air of professional detachment, was giving her directions.

Sheriff Greggory went to the telephone, picked up the receiver, said, "Yes, what is it?"

"This the sheriff?"

"Yes."

"Headquarters in San Roberto. A radio prowl car has just reported in over two-way radio to get in touch with you and tell you that a case of arsenic poisoning that occurred up in the Skyline district is being pushed to the Haven of Mercy Hospital."

"Can you give me any details?" Greggory asked.

"An old battered pickup loaded with camp stuff carrying a house trailer on behind went through a boulevard stop. The prowl car pulled alongside. Man at the wheel says his name is Bowers and his partner in the trailer is dying with arsenic poisoning. He had driven to the residence of Dr. Kenward, but the doctor wasn't home and he was rushing to a hospital. The prowl car is clearing the way with a siren. Bowers said it tied in with another poisoning case, and to notify you. There are two men in that prowl car. One of them made the report while the other was driving. I can reach them within a couple of seconds. Do you want me to contact the car and deliver any message?"

"Yes," Sheriff Greggory said. "Tell them that I'll meet them at the Haven of Mercy Hospital."

He slammed up the telephone, turned to Tragg. "Banning Clarke," he said, "in a house trailer. Car driven by Salty Bowers. Clarke's dying with arsenic poisoning. Rushing to the Haven of Mercy Hospital. Want to go? We'll leave the deputy here."

Tragg started for the door. "Let's go."

They raced down the reception hallway, their feet pounding loudly on the waxed tiles awakening echoes from the somber walls of the silent house. They dashed through the front door and into the sheriff's automobile. Greggory slammed the car into gear, shot out of the graveled driveway, skidded into the winding concrete boulevard and turned on the siren.

"After all," Tragg protested, bracing himself between the back of the front seat and the instrument board of the car, "there *are* four wheels on this automobile, Sammy, my lad. You might as well use all of them at once instead of just two at a time."

The sheriff grinned, whipped the car around another curve, still gathering speed. "When I'm down in the city, you scare the pants off of me driving like hell through traffic, so I'm glad our open roads make you nervous. It's just a question of what you become accustomed to. We have curves. You have traffic."

"But after all, a half a minute isn't going to make too much difference in the case," Tragg pointed out.

"The report is that Banning Clarke's dying. I want to get a dying statement from him."

"He won't know who poisoned him."

"You might be surprised." There was no further discussion. The sheriff whipped and skidded around turns, hit the straightaway at the foot of the grade, and, with siren screaming, tore through the slumbering residential outskirts of San Roberto, slammed on the brakes and skidded into the ambulance entrance of the huge hospital which was located well outside of the congested district.

The sheriff's blood-red spotlight threw the back of a house trailer into wine-colored brilliance. A little group of men was standing around the door of this trailer, and as the sheriff slid his car to a stop and jerked the door open, a nurse, accompanying a doctor who was wearing a white coat and carrying a stethoscope in his hand, emerged from the house trailer.

The sheriff pushed forward. "What are his chances, Doctor?"

The man in the white coat said quietly, "He hasn't any."

"You mean he's—"

"Dead."

Sam Greggory let out his breath in a weary sigh. "Arsenic poisoning?" he asked in the voice of one propounding a routine question merely for the purpose of establishing a foregone conclusion.

"Apparently," the doctor said dryly, "it was a thirty-eight caliber bullet fired almost directly into the heart at short range. There are evidences that at some time before the shooting the man had ingested a considerable quantity of arsenic, and, in view of the cardiac history given me by his friend, Mr. Bowers, there is every reason to assume that the symptoms had progressed too far for remedial treatment to have been of the slightest benefit. The bullet, therefore, merely hastened the end by a matter of minutes."

Tragg turned to the sheriff. "And with Perry Mason in the case, is *that* a sweet legal situation! When you see your District Attorney, give him my sympathy."

105

Perry Mason awakened from a sleep of utter exhaustion. His head was clear now. A dim light at the far corner of the room furnished enough illumination to enable him to see the face of his watch. It was three-fifteen.

Mason sat up for a few moments on the edge of the bed, then put on his clothes. His stomach and abdomen felt as sore as though someone had been beating him with a club. He was weak and groggy, but the metallic burning sensation had left his mouth and throat. He felt mentally alert.

There was in the back of his mind a vague recollection that finally crystallized into clarity. Some time during the night, Velma Starler had wakened him taking his pulse, had told him to go back to sleep, informed him Banning Clarke was dead, that Dr. Kenward was resting easily, and that Della Street had been sleeping peacefully since shortly after eleven. At the time, Mason had been too exhausted to care about anything except that Della was out of danger. The rest of what Velma Starler had said had been merely words which had meaning but no significance.

Now, Mason was mentally alert once more. He felt rested, although weak as a wet kitten. His mind was already beginning to correlate various facts into a composite whole.

He started out to search for Velma Starler.

The big house seemed ominously dormant. It retained an atmosphere of having been lived in, yet somehow conveyed the impression of having, for the moment, lost its tenants. The long, dimly lit hallway seemed a sepulchral passage rather than part of a residence. The huge room into which Perry Mason glanced might have been a section of a museum, after the doors had been closed and spectators turned away.

Mason wished to avoid disturbing anyone who was sleeping. He hoped he'd find Velma Starler cat-napping in some room with the door open. He didn't know where Della Street was located. Velma could tell him. He had been put to bed in a downstairs room, probably one designed for occupancy by a maid. He knew generally that Della Street was somewhere on the second floor, but didn't know where.

A reading lamp in the library cast a shielded circle of illumination which served to emphasize the deep shadows in the far corners of the big room. Almost directly under the reading lamp was a smoking stand on which reposed a telephone, a long extension cord running back to a plug in the wall. A huge chair was drawn up near by.

Mason was tiptoeing past when, seized with an idea, he turned back, dropped into the depths of the soft cushioned chair, picked up the receiver, dialed long distance, and said, "I want to talk with Paul Drake, of the Drake Detective Agency in Los Angeles. Reverse the charges. Don't call on the regular number. Use this unlisted number, Rexmount 6985. I'll wait on the line."

Mason realized once more how weak he was as his head welcomed the support of the cushions at the back of the chair while he was waiting for the call to be put through.

At length he heard Paul Drake's voice, thick with sleep, saying, "Hello—hello. Yes." The connection abruptly clicked off while the operator asked his okay on the long-distance call. Then a moment later Drake was back on the line. "Hello, Perry. What the hell's wrong with you? Haven't you got money enough to pay for a telephone call?"

Mason kept his voice low. "I'm calling from Banning

107

Clarke's residence in San Roberto, Paul. I want you to get started on a job right away."

"You always *do* want something in the middle of the night," Drake said irritably. "What is it this time?"

"I want you to become a prospector, Paul."

"A what!" Drake exclaimed incredulously.

"A prospector. A seedy old miner."

"You're kidding."

"No. I mean it."

"What's the idea?"

"Now listen," Mason said, keeping his lips close to the mouthpiece of the telephone and his voice low. "Get these instructions straight. I won't have a chance to repeat them. Harvey Brady, who has the big cattle ranch down below Las Alisas, is a client of mine and a pretty good egg to boot. He'll give you a hand in putting this across."

"I know where the ranch is," Drake said. "What do I do?"

"Do you know some newspaper reporter who would give you a good break if he got a nice human-interest story out of it?"

Drake said, "I know reporters who would cut their grandmothers' throats to get a good human-interest story."

"Even if the story weren't true?"

"They like their stuff true, Perry."

"All right. Make it true for them then."

"Go ahead. What's the gag?"

"You're a prospector," Mason said. "You were a little down on your luck. Harvey Brady picked you up in the desert. You struck him for a grubstake. He'd been interested in some of the famous lost mines of California. He told you he'd grubstake you to find one of those lost mines if you'd set about locating it his way. He had a theory about how it could be found."

"Which lost mine?" Drake asked.

"You'll be mysterious about that and keep it very

108

much under your hat, but you'll let the information slip some way that it's really the famous Lost Goler Diggings. You'll be mysterious and secretive about the whole business. Harvey Brady will be jubilant.—Now listen, Paul, you've got to get hold of some gold—quite a bunch of gold, so you can make it sound convincing. Think you could do that?"

"I can do it," Drake grumbled, "but I can't do it at three o'clock in the morning. Have a heart, Perry."

Mason said, "This story has got to break before noon. You'll have to pick yourself up a couple of burros, a gold pan, a pick and shovel, a sweat-stained sombrero, some old patched overalls, and all the rest of it."

"Okay. I'll work it out some way. Then what do I do?"

"Then," Mason said, "you proceed to make whoopee."

"On an expense account?"

"On an expense account."

Drake's voice showed more enthusiasm. "This may not be so bad. You're a hard taskmaster, Perry, but you do have your good points."

"When you get properly jingled," Mason said, "you let it slip that the mine you've found is on patented property, and for that reason you'll have to keep it a secret until your backer, Harvey Brady, can buy up the property. And then Harvey Brady claims you're talking too much and grabs you and whisks you into oblivion."

"How much of an oblivion?"

"I'll engineer that," Mason said. "I'll be on the job by that time. But the main thing is to get started on this thing right away."

Drake said, "All right. I'll see what I can do. You *do* ask the damnedest things, Perry."

"What's wrong with this?" Mason asked with well-simulated surprise.

"Oh nothing," Drake said. "Only some time, when you get a little bored with life, try rolling out of bed at three-thirty in the morning with an assignment to have a couple of burros and a prospecting outfit picked up by daylight, then in addition, to get several hundred dollars in placer gold. Then throw in a sweat-stained sombrero that looks convincing, some worn overalls and. . . . Oh, it's all right, Perry. I guess I'm just getting a little crabby. It sounded bad when you were talking about it, but now that I list over the things I have to do it sounds easy. You're sure there isn't anything else you want?"

"Never mind the sarcasm," Mason said, and hung up before Drake could think of something else to say.

For a few moments Mason rested in the chair, getting his thoughts in order. Then as he checked back over his conversation with Paul Drake, he suddenly frowned with annoyance, picked up the telephone again and said to the long-distance operator, "I was just talking with Paul Drake in Los Angeles at Rexmount 6985. There was something that I forgot to tell him. Can you get him back on the line right away? It's *very* important."

Mason held the line. Within a matter of seconds, he heard Drake's voice again. "Hello, Perry. Something else you forgot to tell me, I suppose."

"Yes," Mason said.

"What is it—do you want me to be riding a white elephant when I have my picture taken, or something like that?"

"After you've completed your build-up," Mason said, "be very careful what you eat and drink."

"What do you mean?"

"I mean that someone will try to slip you a big dose of arsenic. And it's not a particularly pleasant experience. It starts with a burning, metallic taste in your throat. Della and I are just recovering."

And Mason dropped the receiver back into place before the astonished Paul Drake could think up any reply.

110

■ 12 ■

It was a good three minutes before Mason could get himself up out of the depths of the chair and resume his search for Velma Starler.

He passed through heavy drapes and entered the reception hallway, tiptoeing his way along the waxed tiles. The wide sweep of the curved staircase with its wrought iron balustrades stretched gracefully upward. Somewhere a wall clock was ticking monotonously. Aside from that, there was no sign of life in the house.

Mason climbed the wide staircase, oblivious alike of architectural beauty and painstaking construction. To him the stairway was only a painfully laborious means of enabling his wobbling legs to reach the second floor.

In the upper corridor, Mason tiptoed down the long passageway looking for an open door. He felt certain that Velma Starler would be dozing fitfully, her clothes on, ears tuned for the slightest sound from her patients, a skillful nurse making intermittent rounds to see that her patients were all right, catching little catnaps in between.

Mason passed a long file of closed doors, then came to one that was open. He glanced inside.

He saw a sumptuous bedroom elaborately appointed. A bed had been slept in, the covers thrown down. It was quite evidently the bedroom of a woman. But even with the standard of luxury prevailing throughout the entire establishment, Mason had some difficulty realizing that this must be the bedroom of Velma Starler.

As he stood in the doorway, another door slightly ajar caught his eye; and feeling certain that this would be far more apt to be the room he wanted, Mason moved with swiftly silent steps down to this partially opened door, gently pushed it farther open. Then, as the door swung on silent hinges so that he could see into the room, Mason abruptly caught himself. This was Banning Clarke's room.

A woman clad in a negligee was seated at the roll-top desk in the far corner. For the moment Mason could not recognize her, but the back of the head, the lines of the neck, and the slant of the shoulders hardly indicated Velma Starler. They were a little too heavy—a little too. . . .

The woman half turned her head as though some faint sound had caught her ears.

Mason had no trouble in recognizing the profile. It was that of Lillian Bradisson, and the illumination from the green-shaded desk lamp on the top of the roll-top desk etched the lines of expression on her face—lines of cunning greed, an avarice which had become unchained and had wiped all of the carefully cultivated smirk from her face. In that moment, Mrs. Bradisson's emotions had lost their protective covering and stood unpleasantly naked for his inspection.

Whatever slight noise had caused her to raise her head and listen was apparently dismissed as being of no consequence after a few seconds of motionless waiting. Her head swung back so that Mason could no longer see the face. Her shoulders moved slightly. Mason could not see her hands, but, after a moment, realized she was skillfully and thoroughly searching through the pigeonholes in the desk.

Mason stood silently in the doorway.

The woman at the desk was now too completely engrossed in what she was doing to listen for suspicious sounds. She was running through papers taken from each pigeonhole before pushing them back, then pulling out the contents of the next pigeonhole.

As Mason watched her, she found that for which she

had evidently been searching—an oblong, folded document, which she unfolded and read. As she read, she turned to get the light on the page, so that Mason could once more see her face, could watch her expression of curiosity change to one of angry determination.

Mrs. Bradisson reached down through the opening in her negligee, took out another folded paper, so similar to the first at that distance as to be indistinguishable. She placed this paper back in the pigeonhole of the desk. Mason watched her push back the creaky, dilapidated swivel chair preparatory to rising, transfer the folded paper to her left hand, her right reaching toward the switch on the green-shaded desk lamp.

Quietly, Mason tiptoed down the corridor, picked the first door on the left and tried the knob. The door was unlocked.

Mason stepped far enough into the room to be invisible, in case Mrs. Bradisson should take occasion to look back down the corridor.

Someone was sleeping in this room, and Mason could hear the sound of gentle, rhythmic breathing.

The partially opened door caused a current of air to blow briskly through the room, billowing the curtains and sweeping directly across the bed; and Mason, fearing that this current of air might arouse the sleeper, pulled the door almost shut, peering impatiently down the corridor, waiting for Mrs. Bradisson to emerge.

But Mrs. Bradisson didn't make her appearance. After almost two minutes, Mason heard a peculiar intermittent *thump—thump—thump* from the room where Mrs. Bradisson had been going through the contents of the roll-top desk. A moment later there was another series of pounding sounds.

Exasperated, Mason realized the predicament into which he had betrayed himself. If he started once more toward the room to see what Mrs. Bradisson was doing, he was apt to meet her face to face as she emerged. If he remained where he was, he would be in complete ignorance of what was going on.

The sleeper stirred restlessly in the bed.

Mason resolved to take a chance. He stepped out into the corridor. At that moment, Mrs. Bradisson emerged from the room. Mason, caught between two fires, hastily stepped back into the bedroom.

Bedsprings creaked suddenly, a figure sat up in bed.

"Who is it?"

Mason, his hand on the knob of the door, standing poised on the threshold, grinned as he recognized Della Street's voice. He closed the door, said, "How do you feel, Della?"

"Oh, it's you! I woke up and saw someone standing there—there was something stealthy about—Is everything all right, Chief?"

"Everything's okay if *you're* feeling all right."

"I'm better," she said. "My gosh, wasn't that the most awful experience?—What time is it?"

"Getting along toward four o'clock," Mason said, switching on the light.

"I've been sleeping quite a little while. I remember the nurse was in here. She gave me a hypodermic. Are you feeling okay?"

"I'm wobbly," Mason admitted. "You knew that Banning Clarke was dead?"

"Yes. Miss Starler told me they'd found him—but he wasn't poisoned. As I understand it, he'd been killed by a bullet."

"An interesting legal situation," Mason said, sitting down on the edge of her bed. "Want a cigarette?"

"No, thanks. My mouth still has a peculiar taste. I don't think I'd enjoy it.—What about the legal situation?"

"Suppose," Mason said, "I should give you a dose of poison and you should die. That would be murder, wouldn't it?"

She laughed. "Sometimes when I've made mistakes

114

I think it would be justifiable homicide. But go on. What's the idea?"

"But," Mason went on, "suppose that before the poison had quite resulted in death, someone came along, whipped out a gun, fired a fatal shot, and made his escape.—Who is guilty of murder?"

Della Street frowned. "Both of them," she ventured.

Mason shook his head. "Not unless there's a joint venture, or a conspiracy. In the absence of any joint effort, or any conspiracy, only one could be convicted of murder."

"Which one?"

"Figure it out."

"I can't. You mean that the victim would have enough poison so that he'd surely die?"

"That's right."

"And was actually dying?"

"Yes. Only be a matter of minutes—perhaps seconds."

Della Street said, "Well, in any event, I'm not going to bother about it now. I have other things to think of. *You* should wake me up at four o'clock in the morning to propound legal puzzles! Get out of here and let me dress. I take it you want to leave?"

Mason got up off the bed. "We," he announced, "have work to do."

"What sort of work?"

"I think," he told her, "that what I am about to do is something that would be very irritating to Sam Greggory."

Mason paused in the doorway of the bedroom. "You're sure you're feeling well enough to travel?"

"Yes. I'm all right now. I felt, for a while, like a dishrag that had been tied in knots."

"Tell you what I want you to do, Della. Cover me while I go into this room down the hall, will you?"

"What do I do?"

"Stand here in the doorway. If you hear anyone coming, act as though you were just on the point of stepping out in the hall, start a conversation and—"

"But suppose that person goes into that room?"

"That's a chance I'll have to take. I can't avoid that. What I want to prevent is having anyone see me entering Banning Clarke's room or emerging from it."

"Okay. It doesn't make any difference who it is, you don't want *anyone* to know you're in there?"

"That's right."

"If Lieutenant Tragg should come back, I'll have trouble. He'll want to know just where you are."

"Yes," Mason said. "All we can do is pray. Raise your voice and greet whoever it is by name so I'll have a chance to know just what I'm up against. All ready?"

"Give me a few minutes to get my clothes on."

"No. I can't wait. I'm going to pop in that door now. Cover me. You can dress while you're keeping an eye on the corridor. All ready. Here I go."

Mason left the doorway, moved quietly down the corridor until he came abreast of the bedroom in which he had seen Mrs. Bradisson sitting at the desk. The door of this room was closed now. Mason opened it abruptly, darted into the room, closing the door behind him, and waiting for a moment, listening to see if Della Street gave any signal.

When he heard nothing, Mason clicked on the light switch near the door, flooding the room with brilliance, and went over to the roll-top desk. He had no difficulty finding the legal paper which Mrs. Bradisson had placed in the pigeonhole.

Mason unfolded it. It was a will dated the twelfth day of July, 1941, apparently entirely in the handwriting of Banning Clarke. The will left everything to his beloved wife, Elvira, or "in the event she should predecease me, then to her lawful heirs at law—excluding, however, James Bradisson from any share in my said estate."

Mason wasted only a few seconds on the will. He hastily glanced through it, returned it to the pigeonhole in the desk, and then set himself to the task of finding what had caused the pounding noises he had heard after he had left the room.

Mason first gave the carpet a careful scrutiny. There was nothing to indicate that it had been lifted and then replaced. He tried all of the edges, carefully inspected the corners. There were half a dozen framed photographs in the room. Mason moved them out from the walls, scrutinized the backs of the picture frames to see if the brads which held the cardboard in place had been removed and then replaced.

At the end of his search he could find no indication that any of the pictures had been tampered with.

There was no evidence that any nails or any tacks had been pounded into the walls. Mason turned chairs upside down, looked on the bottoms, looked also on the bottom of the table. He then lay down on the floor, flat on his back, and ran his hand along the under side of the drawer containers in the roll-top desk. When he found nothing here, he pulled out the drawers, one by one, taking them entirely out of the desk and tilting them enough so he could see the bottom part of each drawer.

117

It was on the bottom of the lower drawer on the left-hand side that Mason found what he was looking for.

This was an old-fashioned desk made of the finest materials throughout, and the bottoms of the desk drawers were of a hard wood, which had made it necessary for Mrs. Bradisson to pound the thumbtacks in order to make certain they were driven in to the heads. This, Mason realized, accounted for the pounding noises he had heard.

It took Mason a few moments to empty the drawer of its contents, then turn the drawer bottom side up and inspect the document which had been laid out flat, and, in that position, fastened to the bottom of the drawer.

It was a will dated the preceding day. It was entirely in handwriting—an angular, somewhat cramped hand.

Mason opened the blade of his pocketknife, started to pry off the thumbtacks, then paused long enough to read the will.

The will read:

I, Banning Clarke, realizing, not only because of precarious health, but also because of certain sinister influences at work around me, that I may die suddenly and with no opportunity to pass on vital information to those whom I cherish, make this my last will and testament in words and figures as follows, to-wit:

First: I revoke all previous wills made by me.

Second: I give, devise and bequeath to Perry Mason the sum of two thousand five hundred dollars, which I trust will be accepted by the said Perry Mason in the nature of a fee to see that my wishes are carried out, and I leave it to his shrewd judgment and understanding to determine what these wishes are.

Third: I give, devise and bequeath to my nurse,

Velma Starler, the sum of two thousand five hundred dollars.

Fourth: I give, devise and bequeath all of the rest, residue and remainder of my property to P. C. (Salty) Bowers, my friend and for years my partner.

There is one other person for whom I wish to provide, but I am unable to do so because any attempt to put a proper provision in my will would defeat its own purpose. I am leaving it to the perspicacity of my executor to understand what I have in mind. And as the only clue which I dare to give, I warn my executor that there is danger of the drowsy mosquito robbing of a valuable heritage the person I wish to benefit.

I nominate Perry Mason executor of this, my last will and testament, to serve without bond. I direct his attention to that which he will find in the right-hand small drawer in the upper pigeonhole compartment of the desk. It is the only clue I have so far been able to find, but it is highly significant.

Entirely written, dated, and signed in the hand of the undersigned testator,

Banning Clarke.

Mason opened the little drawer described in the will. The drawer contained only a small glass phial. A few fine flakes of gold still adhered to the bottom of this bottle. But the thing that arrested Mason's attention was the only other thing in that bottle—a mosquito.

Even as the lawyer turned the bottle, the mosquito moved its legs slowly, gave a series of spasmodic kicks, then became motionless.

Mason unscrewed the top of the little phial, prodded the mosquito with the point of a pocket pencil.

The mosquito was dead.

Suddenly Mason's thoughtful contemplation was disturbed by Della Street's voice saying, "Oh, *hello, Lieutenant Tragg!* I was starting out to look for you. Can you tell me where Mr. Mason is?"

Mason heard Tragg say, "He's in the downstairs bedroom at the northwest corner. You'll find him there."

For a moment only, Della Street hesitated, then, keeping her voice at the same high pitch, said, "Oh, so you and the sheriff weren't looking for *him,* then?"

It was Sheriff Greggory who rose to the bait. "We're going to take a look through Banning Clarke's room," he said. "We're trying to find out the motive for his murder."

Mason, working against time prying at the heads of the tacks with his knife blade, heard Della Street say in a desperate attempt to get the men away from there, "Oh, but he's not in *that* downstairs bedroom. I've looked there already. You don't suppose anything could have happened to *him?*"

Sheriff Greggory seemed somewhat concerned. "You're sure he's not in the bedroom?"

"Why, yes. I looked down there about ten or fifteen minutes ago."

Mason dropped the tacks into the drawer. He folded the will and thrust it into the inside pocket of his coat. He then pushed things back into the desk drawer striving desperately for speed, yet daring to make no sound. The little phial went into his vest pocket.

Outside he heard the conversation going on, Greggory saying, "After all, I suppose we should have. . . . Oh well, he's all right—probably out looking for evidence of some sort."

"Without even coming up here to see how *I* was getting along?"

"Well, he may have looked in—or had a report from the nurse."

"He'd have come up here," Della Street asserted positively, "unless," she added, "something has happened to *him*."

The momentary silence which ensued indicated that there was a possibility Della might win a respite, but in the end it was Tragg who determined the matter. "We can just take a look in here, Sam. It'll only take a minute. We can look up Mason later."

"It would only take us a minute to look in on Mason." Tragg's voice was weary. "For the last three years, Sam, I've been hoping I could get on a murder case where that guy was on the other side and at least have an even break. He's always beating me to the punches. This time he's laid up with a dose of poison and I intend to make my hay while the sun is shining. Come on, Sam, let's take a look . . . right now."

Mason replaced the desk drawer, settled back in the swivel chair, put his feet up on the desk, dropped his chin on his chest and remained motionless with his eyes closed, breathing deeply.

He heard the doorknob open, heard Sam Greggory say in surprise, "The light's on here." Then Tragg, "Well, for the love of Mike! Look who's *here!*"

Mason kept his head on his chest, his eyes closed, his breathing slow and regular.

Greggory said to Della Street, "Well, here he is, Miss Street."

Della's exclamation of surprise was, Mason thought, superbly done.

Tragg said, "Well, here we go again. The same old run-around. I suppose that if there *were* any clues in the place he's got them by this time."

Greggory said, "He doesn't get away with that in *this* county. If he's so much as touched anything in this room he'll find out he can't pull that stuff in this county and get away with it."

Mason kept his face absolutely devoid of expression, his lids closed, his breathing deep.

Tragg said, "It's a good stall, Mason, but not good enough. You may as well go through with it, however. Put on the rest of the act. Go on, wake up in startled surprise, blink your eyes, rub them with your knuckles, ask, 'What's going on?', pretend you don't know where you are for a minute. I've seen it done often enough to know the whole routine. . . . I've even tried it myself on occasion."

Mason's breathing did not vary in the slightest.

"I think you forget," Della Street said with dignity, "that both of us have had hypodermics. I'm still groggy myself. I could hardly get awake."

Sheriff Greggory said, "That's right. You *did* have hypodermics, didn't you? Are you feeling all right now?"

"Only groggy," Della said. "I don't dare close my eyes or I'd drop right off to sleep. I guess it's all right for us to go now. The doctor didn't say anything about how long we were to stay here."

Mrs. Bradisson's voice said from the doorway, *"What* is it, please? What's going on here?"

"We were just looking around," Greggory said. His voice held that deferential tone a county official reserves for an influential taxpayer.

"Well, I must say that's rather an unusual way of doing things, isn't it? To come walking right into my house and—"

"You see, we haven't much time to waste," Lieutenant Tragg interposed. "We're doing this to protect you, Mrs. Bradisson. You and your son. We want to catch this murderer before he can strike again."

"Oh, I see. Well, I can appreciate your point—yes."

Mason heard Nell Sims' voice coming from down the corridor. "What is it, another one?" she asked.

"It's all right, Nell. You can go back to bed," Mrs. Bradisson said.

Della Street reached forward, grabbed Mason's shoul-

122

der and shook him. "Come on, Chief," she said. "Snap out of it. Wake up."

Mason mumbled indistinguishable words in a thick voice.

"It's that hypodermic," Della said, shaking him harder than ever. "Come on, Chief. Are you all right? Perhaps we'd better get that nurse. Oh, I hope he hasn't had a relapse. He *must* have gotten that poison out of his system!"

Mason pushed his tongue into extra thickness against his teeth, made more sounds that could hardly be interpreted into words, then rolling his eyes toward the top of his head, raised his lids for a few brief flickers, closed them and slumped even lower in the chair.

Della Street kept shaking him, gently slapped his face. "Wake up, Chief," she said. "Wake up. Tell me, are you all right?"

She dropped to her knees by his side, took his hand. Her voice was edged with anxiety. "Tell me, are you all right?—Are you all right?—Get that nurse someone, please. He's sick."

It was, Mason decided, a superb job of acting. Even he would have sworn there was almost a note of hysteria in the increasing anxiety manifested in Della Street's voice.

He opened his eyes wider this time, gave Della Street a groggy smile, said thickly, " 'S all right. Le'me sleep."

She was on her feet at his side again now, shaking him. "Chief, you've got to wake up. You've got to snap out of it. You've—"

Mason yawned prodigiously, opened his eyes, looked at her. "Full of drugs," he announced, running the ends of his words together. "You all right?"

"Yes, yes. I'm all right. What are you doing in here?"

Mason, apparently shaking off the chains of slumber, looked around at the other occupants of the room in

123

bewildered surprise. "What's the matter? Has something happened?"

"No, no, everything's all right. But how did you get in here? What are *you* doing here, Chief?"

He appreciated the quick-witted technique by which Della was giving him the opportunity to make explanations in advance of questions. "Came up to see how you were getting along," he said. "You certainly were sleeping. I spoke to you but you didn't even hear me, so I decided to wait until you awakened to tell you we'd start driving back as soon as you felt up to it.—I left your door open and sat down in the hall for a while. It was drafty there. I saw this door was open. It looked like an office so I came in and sat down in the swivel chair so I could hear you as soon as you moved. Guess I still have some of that drug in my system.—What's new, Tragg?"

Tragg turned to his brother-in-law, made a little gesture with the palms of his hands. "There you are, Sam," he said. "It's always like that. You never can tell whether he's thrown one across the center of the plate for a strike so fast that you can't see it come, or whether he's just winding up for practice."

Greggory said ominously, "We don't like to have fast ones pitched at us here in this county. When that happens we disqualify the pitcher."

Mason yawned once more. "I don't blame you, Sheriff. I'd feel that way myself. Well, come on, Della. If you feel like traveling, we'll get started back. What's the excitement here? Did someone think I'd passed out?"

"No," Sheriff Greggory said. "We are taking steps to see that there are no more murders committed."

Nell Sims, from the outskirts of the group, chirped almost impersonally, "Locking up the horse after the stable has been stolen."

From outside came the raucous bray of a lonely burro.

Mason took Della Street's arm. His eyes met those of Mrs. Bradisson. She alone knew and could prove, if she

124

chose, the falsity of Mason's story. To betray him, however, would of necessity force her to admit her own nocturnal intrusion into the room of the dead man.

"*Good* morning, Mrs. Bradisson," Mason said, bowing.

"Good morning!" she snapped.

■ 14 ■

Lieutenant Tragg made himself at home in Mason's private office. "How you feeling?" he asked, his eyes hard and shrewd as he surveyed the lawyer.

"A little wobbly," Mason admitted, "but we're all right. I've got to take some depositions this afternoon. How's the doctor?"

"Coming along all right."

"How's the case?"

Tragg grinned. *"That's* out of my jurisdiction. That's up to brother-in-law, Sammy. However, Sammy's asking for assistance down here, and if he gets it the Chief will probably put me on the job."

"It has some local angle?" Mason asked, curiously.

Tragg nodded.

"Can you tell me what it is?"

"Not now."

"What have you found out about the murder of Clarke?"

"It's one of those things," Tragg said. "The story told by Salty Bowers is a weird procession of coincidences. And yet, it *may* be true."

"What's the story?" Mason asked.

"Clarke had told him a situation might arise where they'd have to take a quick trip to the desert. He swore he was feeling well enough to make such a trip if Salty would get everything all packed and ready to go as soon as he gave him a signal."

"And he gave him a signal last night?"

"Apparently so. Salty started out with his girl. He never even took her home. He dropped her down at the foot of the hill and told her she'd have to take a bus home.

126

He doubled back and then packed everything into that old jalopy. And he made a quick job of rolling up the bedrolls, putting the pots and pans into the pack boxes. I guess he's done it often enough. He knows how to go about it. Claims it only took ten minutes."

"And the burros?"

"For a while," Tragg said, "they apparently figured on taking the burros, in a trailer. Then Clarke got afraid he might find the trip a little too much for him. So Salty investigated the possibilities of a house trailer, found Clarke could simply crawl aboard and go to bed just as though he were on a yacht. So it was arranged that Salty would make two trips, first to take Clarke out in a house trailer, and then come back, pick up the horse trailer, load in the burros and take them."

"What started all of this, anyway?" Mason asked.

"That's what I wanted to see you about. You did!"

"Me!" Mason raised his eyebrows in a gesture of elaborate surprise.

"Salty says that you gave Clarke some signal to get out, and Clarke tipped him off that now was the time to start."

Mason grinned. "I guess it was over that subpoena."

"What subpoena?"

"This lawyer, Moffgat, started talking about taking depositions, and I had an idea from the way he was beating around the bush he was going to make an excuse to take Clarke's deposition, apparently only in connection with that fraud case, and then go on a general fishing expedition to see if he couldn't dig out some information about an entirely different matter."

"What matter?"

Mason merely grinned.

"How did *you* know about this plan of Moffgat's?"

"Well, Della caught a glimpse of a subpoena in his brief case when he pulled out a stipulation to take the deposition of Pete Sims."

"That deposition you're going to take this afternoon?"

"Yes."

"Why don't you have it postponed?" Tragg asked solicitously. "You're not feeling well and. . . ."

"Thanks very much indeed for your consideration—I may say your *rare* consideration—of my health," Mason grinned. "But I'd like to have the deposition taken and get it over with. The longer Moffgat waits, the more questions he'll think of. I seem to have done quite a bit of passing out—what with sickness and drugs. Where was everyone during the course of the evening?"

"Various places," Tragg said evasively. "We're checking on them."

"Apparently Salty is the only one you want to talk about."

"I think he's the only one you can assist me on."

"What do you want to know?"

"The exact reason Clarke started for the desert."

"What does Salty say?"

"Simply that you tipped him off."

Mason shook his head. "I'm afraid he misunderstood my signal."

Tragg regarded the lawyer speculatively.

"Also," Tragg went on, "what you were doing in Clarke's room when Sam and I came in."

"Waiting for Della Street," Mason replied innocently enough, and then added with a prodigious yawn, "It makes me sleepy every time I think about it."

Tragg said dryly, "It makes me a little tired myself. Did you know Clarke had left a will in that desk?"

"Did he, indeed?"

Tragg made as if to go. "I guess I'm just an incurable optimist," he announced. "I always kid myself into believing you *might* say something you didn't intend to, some day."

"Just what happened to Clarke?" Mason asked. "Exactly how did he die?"

128

"Just about the way it's in the papers," Tragg said. "They started for the desert. Salty was up in front driving. Clarke was stretched out on the bed in this house trailer apparently sleeping. It was something of a novel experiment for both of them. They'd neglected to provide any means of communication by which Clarke could get in touch with Salty up in front. And that pickup made such a choice assortment of noises Salty couldn't have heard a clap of thunder, let alone a shout.

"Salty stopped, after they got out a way on their trip, to see how his passenger was making it. He found him very ill and weak, with the same symptoms of arsenic poisoning that the Bradissons had shown. Salty jumped back into the pickup, turned around, and drove like mad back to San Roberto. He rushed to Dr. Kenward's house. Dr. Kenward wasn't there. Salty went down to a drugstore that was open all night, telephoned the hospital, said he had a poisoned man and was coming right out. He went through a boulevard stop. A radio prowl car picked him up. He kept right on driving, shouting fragmentary explanations to the officers. They went ahead with the siren clearing the way, and reported to headquarters. And that, as the radio commentators say, is all the news right up to this moment. That is—all that I'm going to tell you."

"It was the bullet that killed him?" Mason asked.

"The bullet killed him," Tragg admitted.

"But he was dying of poison?"

"Well. . . ." Tragg hesitated.

"What does the post-mortem show?" Mason asked.

Tragg smiled. "I think I'll save that."

15

George V. Moffgat was full of eager efficiency and impatience to get on with the matter in hand. But he went through the motions of being politely solicitous. "You're certain you feel like going ahead with these depositions, Counselor?"

"I think I can make it all right," Mason said.

"Why don't you wait a day or two?"

"Oh, it's all right. I'll go ahead. I'm feeling a little wobbly, that's all."

Jim Bradisson said, "Any time will suit me. Don't bother about inconveniencing me, Mr. Mason. I appreciate the circumstances and I'll be glad to. . . ."

"No. It's all right," Mason told him.

Moffgat turned to the notary public with the alert eagerness that characterizes a Boston bull pup about to pounce on a ball as soon as it is tossed by his master.

Moffgat announced, "This is the time and place heretofore fixed for taking the deposition of Peter G. Sims, one of the defendants in the action of Come-Back Mining Syndicate versus Sims et al., and of James Bradisson, the president of that mining company. The defendants are represented by Mr. Perry Mason. I represent the plaintiff. The witnesses are both present ready to be sworn."

The notary public said, "This deposition is being taken pursuant to stipulation, gentlemen?"

"That's right," Mason said.

"Correct," Moffgat announced.

"The witness, Sims, will be sworn," the notary public said.

Pete Sims looked inquiringly at Perry Mason.

"Stand up," Mason said.

Sims, a gaunt man in the fifties, with the whimsically woebegone facial expression of a man who has wrestled with life and been worsted in the fight, stood up.

"Hold up your right hand."

Sims raised his right hand.

The notary public made something of a ceremony of administering the oath. "Do you solemnly swear that the testimony you are about to give in the case of Come-Back Mining Syndicate versus Sims et al., will be the truth, the whole truth, and nothing but the truth, so help you God?"

There was awed solemnity in Pete Sims' voice. "I do," he promised, then sat down, crossed his legs, and looked with cherubic innocence at George Moffgat.

Moffgat opened the brief case, jerked out a file of papers, hitched a small suitcase into position near his right hand, glanced at the court stenographer who had been selected to take down everything that was said, then turned to the witness. "Your name is Peter Sims. You are the husband of Nell Sims. You are familiar with the mining claims known as the Shooting Star Group?"

"That's right," Pete agreed in a drawl of disarming frankness.

"Some six months ago, Mr. Sims, you had a conversation with Mr. James Bradisson, did you not?"

"I'm talking with him all the time," Pete said, and then added, "off and on."

"But about six months ago you had a specific conversation in which you told him about discovering certain ore on the Shooting Star claims, didn't you?"

"Well, now," Sims drawled, "I just can't remember."

"You mean you can't remember a conversation you had ninety days ago?"

Sims said, "I guess I'll have to explain."

"I guess you will," Moffgat said sarcastically.

"Well," Pete said, "it's like this. I've got one of these here split personalities you read about. Most of the time

131

I'm me, but every so often Bob takes charge—and then I just ain't me."

Moffgat snapped, "You're under oath, Mr. Sims."

"Sure I'm under oath," Mr. Sims said.

There was gloating triumph in Moffgat's voice. "Go right ahead, Mr. Sims," he said. "Remember you're under oath. Tell us about your split personality and why you can't remember your conversation with Mr. James Bradisson."

"Well, it's like this," Pete explained, glancing guilelessly at the somewhat startled notary public. "Personally, I'm a pretty good sort of a fellow. I can take a drink or I can leave it alone. I'm ambitious and I want to get ahead, and I'm truthful. I'm in love with my wife and I think I'm a pretty good husband."

Mason said, "Make your answer responsive to the question, Mr. Sims."

Moffgat snapped, "He considers it responsive and so do I. Go right ahead, Mr. Sims. I want you to explain about this split personality. Remembering, of course, that you are now under oath."

"That's right," Sims said. "Well, I call this other personality Bob. He may have some other name. I don't know what it is. To me, he's just Bob.—Well, I'll be getting along all right, and all of a sudden Bob will come and take possession of me. And when that happens, I just pass out. I just don't know what Bob does while he's sort of in charge of things."

"Do you," Moffgat asked triumphantly, "have any preliminary warning when this secondary personality is about to take possession of you?"

"Only a sort of a thirst," Sims said. "I'll get this awful thirst and sort of head toward some place where there's a cool drink of beer, and about the time I get that beer ordered, Bob will take charge.—Now I was going to tell you about the difference between me and Bob."

132

"Go right ahead," Moffgat said. "That's what I want to hear."

"Well, Bob can't leave booze alone. He's an awful drunkard. That's what makes it so annoying to me. Bob will be sort of runnin' things and take me out and get me awful drunk. Then when I wake up with a headache, Bob is gone. It wouldn't be so bad if Bob would stick around to wrestle with the hangover, but he never does that. He pushes me out and has all the fun of doing the drinking, and then goes away and leaves me to handle the headache that comes the next day."

"I see," Moffgat said. "Now getting back to this sale of the mine to Mr. Bradisson who was acting on behalf of the plaintiff in the action. You have no recollection of what you told him about that mine?"

"I only know I was talking to him about mining property, and then all of a sudden I felt that funny thirst, and Bob must have come in then because the next I remember was waking up with an awful hangover about two days later, and a lot of money in my pocket."

"And," Moffgat said, "you gave him certain samples of ore which you told him you'd personally taken from the Shooting Star Mine, didn't you?"

"Well, now, I can't remember about that."

"Would you say that you did, or that you did not?"

"Well, I think there's a pretty good chance that he might have got the ore from me while Bob was in the driver's seat."

"Now then," Moffgat went on, "that ore had not been obtained from the Shooting Star Mining Group. That ore consisted of some samples that had been taken by you from specimens Mr. Banning Clarke was keeping in the lower drawer of a roll-top desk in his room, isn't that right?"

"I'm not saying anything about those samples because I can't remember a thing in the world about them."

"Now this secondary personality which you call Bob

133

didn't assume charge until after you had started talking with Mr. Bradisson about the Shooting Star Group?"

"Well, I can't remember exactly. We started talking about mining claims—and of course, since my wife owned this mining property, I *may* have said something about it. That is, before Bob came. After that, I don't know what happened."

Moffgat's voice became silky. "I understand your position exactly, Mr. Sims. You, yourself, under no circumstances would be guilty of any fraudulent representation, but there are times when you are not exactly responsible, times when this secondary personality takes over and you are placed in the embarrassing position of being held responsible for things which were done without your knowledge and entirely without your volition."

"That's right," Sims agreed. And then, after a moment's thought, added with great emphasis, "That's *right!*" He beamed at the lawyer with that warm friendliness which is inspired by perfect understanding.

"Now then," Moffgat resumed, "on this day in question, *you* certainly had no idea, when you started out, that this impish secondary personality would lead you to defraud Mr. James Bradisson, did you?"

"I most certainly didn't. Mr. Bradisson is my friend and I wouldn't do a thing in the world to harm him. I just wouldn't harm a hair of his head."

Bradisson rubbed a well-manicured hand over his practically bald dome, and let his eyes soften into a twinkle.

Moffgat went on suavely, "You yourself had no intention, not even the most remote intention, of trying to sell any mining claims to James Bradisson that day, did you?"

"Absolutely not."

"Now, had Bob been in possession of your personality at any time shortly prior to this conversation you had with Bradisson?"

"You mean that same day?"

134

"Oh, that day or within a day or two of that time," Moffgat said carelessly.

"No, he hadn't. He'd been letting me alone pretty much. And *that* should have been a warning to me too, because Bob only stays away about so long, then the thirst catches him and he comes in and takes charge."

"I understand. But Bob definitely hadn't been in what you refer to as 'the driver's seat' during any time within three or four days prior to your conversation with Bradisson?"

"That's right."

"Then," Moffgat sneered, dropping his suave manner, and appearing suddenly belligerent, *"how* do you account for the fact that you went to that conference with Mr. Bradisson with your pockets loaded with samples of ore that you had filched from the lower drawer in Banning Clarke's roll-top desk?"

Expression popped into Sims' face. His complacency was suddenly jarred as the full impact of that question dawned on him. He shifted his position uneasily in the chair.

"Go ahead, answer that question," Moffgat stormed at the dismayed witness.

"Well, now. . . . Now wait a minute. You ain't sure those rocks came from Clarke's desk."

Moffgat triumphantly produced a small suitcase, opened it, thrust a rock out in front of the witness. "You see that specimen of ore?"

"I do," Sims said without touching it.

"And you see this one which is marked with a little cross which has been chiseled into the surface of the rock. Isn't this marked rock one of the specimens you gave James Bradisson, and isn't that rock absolutely identical with this other specimen which came from Banning Clarke's group of mines—the ones that are known as the Sky High Group?"

135

Sims fidgeted for a moment more, then suddenly blurted, "I never gave that rock to Bradisson."

"You mean you didn't give him this rock with the cross chiseled on it—the rock I am now showing to you?"

"No, I didn't," Sims said positively. "It's his word against mine. I didn't give it to him."

"At no time during the conversation, or during the negotiations leading up to the signing of this contract with James Bradisson, did you give him this rock and tell him that it had been taken by you from this Shooting Star mining group, and represented a new strike you had made in that group of mines?"

"No, sir, I didn't." Sims' manner was now dogged and stubborn.

"You're certain of that?"

"Absolutely."

"How can you be certain?" Moffgat asked, smiling triumphantly down at the witness. "You don't remember a thing of that conversation. Your split personality was in charge at that time—Bob, as I believe you have mentioned, was 'in the driver's seat.'"

The witness ran his left hand up along his head, scratched at the hair over his left temple. "Well, now," he said, "my memory's beginning to come back mighty clear on that. Maybe it *wasn't* because Bob had taken over. Maybe it was just because I'd got a little drunk and couldn't remember things very clearly."

"During the time that you were discussing this mine with Mr. Bradisson, you had been drinking?"

"That's right."

"And couldn't remember things very clearly?"

"That's right."

"Then how can you testify positively that you didn't give Mr. Bradisson this rock, together with certain other rocks, and tell him that these were specimens of a body of ore you had just uncovered in your wife's claims— the Shooting Star mining group?"

"Well," Sims said, squirming uncomfortably, "I'm beginning to remember it a lot clearer now."

"Would you say that your memory was clear on the subject?"

"Well, pretty clear."

"Then this secondary personality that you have referred to as Bob wasn't in charge at all. He didn't enter into the picture?"

"Well, I—I don't *think* he did. Not the way things look now."

Moffgat sarcastically slammed his file of papers closed, popped it into his brief case and slid the zipper in a dramatic gesture. "That," he announced, "is *all!*"

He turned to Mason and said, "Well, Counselor, you certainly aren't going to contest this case any further, in view of the circumstances. Are you?"

Mason said gravely, "I don't know. I'll give the matter some thought."

"Humph!" Moffgat said. "It's so dead open and shut that there's nothing to it."

"Don't forget," Mason said as Moffgat started to get up, "there's another deposition to be taken—that of James Bradisson."

"But surely, Mr. Mason, you don't want to take Bradisson's deposition *now.*"

"Why not?"

"Because the deposition just taken is completely determinative of the case. You can't possibly avoid the charge of fraud now. Your own witness has virtually admitted it. If you went into court you wouldn't have a leg to stand on."

"But," Mason insisted, "I would like to take Bradisson's deposition. Even without a leg to stand on, I can still talk."

"Well, I don't see what for," Moffgat snapped testily. "I'm not aware of any rule of law that says you can avoid fraud after that fraud has once been established, by browbeating the defrauded party."

Mason said, "I want to take his deposition—and I intend to do it."

"Stand up," Moffgat said irritably to Bradisson. "Hold up your right hand and be sworn. If Mr. Mason is going to derive any comfort from questioning you, I suppose we'll have to let him."

Bradisson rose, held up his right hand, listened to the oath, said, "I do," and then grinned at Perry Mason. "Go right ahead, Mr. Mason. Although I don't think I have anything to add to what Pete Sims has said."

"You're an officer of the Come-Back Mining Syndicate?"

"President."

"And have been such for how long?"

"Oh, about a year or so."

"You inherited a substantial block of stock from your sister, Mrs. Banning Clarke?"

"Yes."

"And as president of the corporation, you determine its policies?"

"Isn't that what a president is for?"

"I'm merely trying to get the facts in the record," Mason said.

"Well, I'm no stuffed ornament. I was elected by the directors to run the company, and I'm trying to do so— to the best of my ability," he added virtuously.

"Exactly. You're acquainted with Nell Sims, the wife of Pete Sims, the witness who just testified?"

"That's right."

"How long have you known her?"

"Oh, I don't know. A year or so, perhaps a few months longer than that. I met her originally in Mojave."

"Where she was running a restaurant?"

"Yes."

"And you also met Pete Sims up there?"

"I think so. I may have."

"And for the last year you have been more or less intimately associated with them. They've been living in the same house. She has been acting in the capacity of general cook and housekeeper?"

"That's right."

Moffgat said, "I object to all this waste of time. You can't change the fact of fraud if you question this man until Doomsday."

Mason paid no attention to the interruption, went on in a conversational, intimate tone with his examination.

"And during that time you've had occasion to see Pete Sims rather frequently?"

"Quite frequently. That is—what I might say was in between intervals."

"What intervals?"

"When he isn't on a spree. I suppose he would express it as 'when Bob isn't in the saddle.'"

"So you've known about Bob for some time?"

"Oh, yes."

"Now about six months ago, Mr. Sims returned from the desert and told you about a strike he had made?"

"Yes. He said he'd been doing some assessment work on his wife's claims and had made this strike. He thought the ore was very rich indeed. He showed me the ore. I thought it was very good ore. I told him that the syndicate might be willing to take the claims over at a fair price."

"And you subsequently agreed on a price?"

"We bought the claims, yes."

"And how much of the price has been paid?"

"We paid the original cash payment and then filed this suit to rescind the contract on the ground of fraud and be relieved of any further liability on payment of purchase price."

"When did you first learn that you had been defrauded?"

"Well, the report of the assayer came in and then, weeks later, it came to my attention that the peculiar combination of minerals in the ore was exactly the same and in exactly the same amounts as appeared in another claim that was a part of the corporation properties—claims we had optioned from Banning Clarke."

Mason said, "Had you had much mining experience when you became president of the corporation?"

"I hadn't had much experience on the ground, but I knew a great deal about mining, and I had a natural aptitude for it. I picked up the practical points rather quickly—unusually fast, to be more truthful than modest."

"So that you consider yourself thoroughly competent to be the president of a mining corporation having rather extensive interests?"

"If I hadn't, I never would have accepted the presidency. I have made a detailed study of all forms of mining, Mr. Mason, and particularly of the properties of the Come-Back Mining Syndicate and of the problems pertaining to those properties."

"And you're a fair judge of character, Mr. Bradisson?"

"What do you mean by that?"

"I mean that after you had an opportunity to see and study Mr. Sims, you had a pretty good idea of his general character?"

"Well, yes—if you want to go into that."

"You yourself went out and looked over his mining properties before the deal was closed?"

"Naturally. I would hardly obligate my stockholders to pay out a large sum of cash for something I hadn't looked at personally."

"You went down in the little shaft?"

"It isn't so little. It's down some fifty feet, and then it runs on a drift back about one hundred and thirty-five or forty feet."

"You inspected the ore in that shaft?"

"Certainly."

140

"Before you signed up the agreement to buy?"

"Of course. The rich samples I found were planted."

"You've heard about Mr. Sims' mischievous second personality, the inscrutable Bob, who forces Pete's unwilling body to depart from the narrow path of rectitude and into the ways of inebriation?" Mason asked.

Bradisson laughed. "I certainly have, Mr. Mason. You'll pardon me if I laugh, but I thought you expressed that rather neatly."

"Thank you. And you've had an opportunity to hear many of these stories of what Bob has done when he's taken over the control of Mr. Sims' body?"

"Oh, yes."

"And I take it you've formed something of an opinion of Bob?"

Bradisson said, "Let's not misunderstand each other, Mr. Mason. This so-called Bob has absolutely no existence whatever. Pete Sims simply uses him as a scapegoat. He's an alibi. Whenever Pete gets a little out of line or does something he shouldn't, he claims that he has no memory of what occurred, and that this secondary personality has taken over. This so-called Bob is merely his way of making excuses to his wife. She may or may not believe him. At any rate, she does nothing to discourage his prevarications. Because of that, Pete Sims has developed a rather childish, immature attitude. His wife swallows his falsehoods with such ease and apparent gullibility that the man doesn't even bother his brain to think up good lies.—Just by way of illustration, you can see how easily Mr. Moffgat trapped him today—although I don't want to take any of the credit from Mr. Moffgat for a brilliant piece of cross-examination. However, the fact remains that Sims has a childish faith in the efficacy of his own falsehoods that keeps him from using ordinary care in thinking them up. This business of a secondary personality has been too easy for him."

Mason's face and voice both showed surprise. "You

mean that he has deliberately built up the fiction of this secondary personality?"

"Of course," Bradisson said, his voice and manner showing some disdain for Mason's attempt at acting. "Surely, Mr. Mason, you didn't expect to establish that there actualy *was* any such secondary personality."

"Of course I haven't had the benefit of such an intimate acquaintance as you. I have merely met the man, but he seemed sincere enough when he told me about his secondary personality. I was hoping you could confirm his statements."

"Don't insult my intelligence, Mr. Mason."

"And you mean that Mr. Sims deliberately lies about this?"

"Of course."

"How long have you known this?" Mason asked.

"Almost ever since I first met him. It should be apparent to anyone of discernment. He is a thoroughly disreputable old reprobate, and an awful liar. Remember that you asked for this, Mr. Mason. There's a certain likable streak in him, but he's just a periodic drunkard and a congenital liar as well as being basically dishonest. He tries to account for his shortcomings by telling falsehoods even a child wouldn't believe.

"Understand me, Mr. Mason, you're the one who brought this up. But since you've brought it up, I don't mind telling you frankly that I wouldn't trust him, to use a colloquial expression, as far as I could throw a bull by the tail. He's a crooked old reprobate with no conscience, and only a limited intelligence.

"He's clever in just one thing, and that's his ability to apparently get drunk, pretend there's some information he's trying to keep from spilling, and then let you pry it out of him in an unguarded moment that he's struck it rich. In other words, he's a very, very good actor, and that's all. He can act a lie infinitely better than he can tell one."

"Thank you," Mason said. "That's all."

"That's all?" Moffgat asked in some surprise.

"Yes."

Moffgat's face was crafty. "You understand, Mr. Mason, that I have a right to cross-examine this witness?"

"Naturally."

"Despite the fact that he is my client."

"I understand."

"Upon *any* matter concerning which you have examined him in direct examination."

"That's my understanding of the law."

"And you yourself, Counselor, have opened the door."

Mason merely made a little bow.

"Now then," Moffgat said, turning to Bradisson with a smirk, "I will ask you, Mr. Bradisson, if you are familiar with the reputation for truth and veracity of this Mr. Peter Sims."

"I am."

"What is it?"

"It's terrible."

"He isn't considered trustworthy among those who know him?"

"Absolutely not."

"Would you believe his testimony under oath?"

"Definitely not."

"That's all," Moffgat announced triumphantly.

Mason said, "I guess that completes our depositions." He rose, stretched and yawned.

"And you're seriously going to proceed with the contest of this action?" Moffgat asked him.

Mason turned on him. "Go back to your office and read up on the law of fraud, Counselor. You'll find that it takes a lot more than a fraudulent representation to give a person a cause of action for fraud. The representation must be believed. It must be acted upon. It must be relied upon. Your own client has now stated that he considers Pete Sims an awful liar; that he wouldn't trust him as far as he could throw a bull by the tail; that he wouldn't place any reliance in anything he said; that he himself is a mining expert; that he himself made an examination of that mine before he purchased it. Therefore, it is obvious that the thing he relied upon was his own judgment, his faith in his own infallibility.—There are times Counselor, when it pays dividends to have a poor reputation.—After you've read the law of fraud once more, see whether you want to go ahead with *your* side of the case."

Bradisson turned to regard Moffgat. It needed only one look at the sudden consternation he saw on his lawyer's face to make him realize the deadly accuracy of Mason's statement.

"But my client hasn't said that he relied on his own judgment," Moffgat said. "That is, he didn't specifically so state."

"Wait until a jury hears that deposition read," Mason grinned. "The man with the natural aptitude for absorbing mining knowledge; who was thoroughly capable of directing the destinies of a big mining corporation before he permitted himself to become president; who didn't need to call in any mining engineer to help him; who made his *own* inspection and *then* went ahead and closed the deal before the reports of assay had been returned.—Don't argue with me. Save your argument for a jury. And incidentally, Counselor, you aren't convincing your own client and you aren't convincing yourself."

Moffgat said, "I think you misunderstood the witness's statement in regard to the investigation he himself had made of the property, Mr. Mason. The witness will have an opportunity, of course, to read through his deposition and sign it before it's filed. I happen to know the facts of the case myself, and I know that Mr. Bradisson's investigation was *not* of the kind that would prevent him rescinding the contract on the ground of fraud."

144

And Moffgat flashed his client a warning glance to make certain that Bradisson remained silent.

Mason smiled. "Read the case of Beckley versus Archer, 74 Cal. App. 489, which holds that even where one didn't make an independent investigation, where he fully disbelieved the representations made by the seller as to the character of the property, he still can't rely upon fraud, no matter how flagrant the fraud may have been. Bear in mind that your client stated that he wouldn't trust Pete Sims as far as he could throw a bull by the tail."

Moffgat combed his mind for an answer and could find none. Abruptly he turned on Mason and said, "I'll discuss that angle of the case with you in court, Mr. Mason. In the meantime, there's another matter that I wish to take up with you."

"What is it?"

"You hold the stock which Banning Clarke held in the Come-Back Mining Syndicate."

"That's right. I do."

"I take it that you know a will has been discovered."

"Has it indeed?"

"A will dated some time ago leaving all of his property to his wife, or in the event of his wife's death, to her heirs at law, excluding, however, Mr. James Bradisson."

"Indeed," Mason commented noncommittally.

"I am sorry," Moffgat went on punctiliously, "that Mr. Clarke felt it necessary to put that proviso in his will. It is a direct, unnecessary and entirely unwarranted slap in the face—a gratuitous disparagement of a man who has always tried to be his friend."

Bradisson looked properly virtuous.

"However," Moffgat went on, "be that as it may, Mrs. Bradisson is the sole heir at law, and, as such, will inherit the property. She is filing the will for probate. Now, naturally, Mr. Mason, you won't try to keep that stock, but will turn it over without any delay to the executrix."

"Why should I?" Mason asked.

"Because we know that sale was not an actual sale at all."

"Who says it wasn't?"

"Will you claim that any consideration was actually paid for the transfer?"

"Certainly."

"Would you mind telling me what that consideration was?"

"I see no reason for doing so."

"I think you are aware, Mr. Mason, that as an attorney you were acting in a fiduciary capacity, that any contract you made with your client would be presumed fraudulent, that any undue advantage you took of your client would be a very serious matter—might possibly become grounds for an accusation of unprofessional conduct."

"That sounds like a threat, Moffgat."

"Perhaps it is—and *I* don't make idle threats."

"I'm glad to hear it."

"And do I understand that, despite my demand, you refuse to surrender this stock?"

"That's it in a nutshell."

"That, Mr. Mason, is going to make things very, very unpleasant. It will create a certain amount of personal friction between us."

"Oh, well," Mason said, "differences of opinion make horse races and lawsuits."

"But this is more than a mere piece of litigation. It will be necessary for me to contest the ethics of your actions. The controversy will become personal and bitter."

"That's fine! I like combat. I like the acrimonious personalities of a grudge fight.—And now, if you'll excuse me, I'll return to my office."

And Mason walked out of the office without so much as a backward glance from the doorway.

16

Della Street spread the afternoon newspaper on Mason's desk. "Look at our friend, Paul Drake," she said.

Mason regarded the picture with an approving eye—a photograph of Paul Drake clad in tattered shirt, patched overalls, wearing a big battered Stetson, leading a burro that had on its back a canvas-covered pack. A pick, shovel and gold pan were roped to the outside of the pack. The entire picture carried an air of authenticity. Paul Drake had managed to get just the proper expression of good-natured sincerity on his face. In the photograph he seemed lean and brown and hard, toughened by years of clean living in the desert. His extended right hand held a buckskin sack.

Underneath the photograph was the legend: "P. C. Drake, Who Claims To Have Rediscovered Famous Lost Mine. In the photo Drake is shown handing a sack of gold nuggets to Harvey Brady, wealthy Las Alisas cattleman. Story on page six."

The newspaper account was in a position of prominence on page six. Headlines read: "PROSPECTOR LOCATES LOST BONANZA. Southern California cattle king shares clue with penniless prospector."

Mason read the story with a great deal of interest. Harvey Brady, prominent cattleman of Las Alisas, had, it seemed, always wanted to be a prospector, but Fate decreed that he should go into the cattle business on a small scale, make money, invest in more cattle, and then become one of the Southland's leading cattle barons. But always in the back of his mind was the desire to prospect.

Because his extensive business interests prevented his

going into the desert personally, Brady began reading about mines and mining, and, in particular, about the famous lost mines of the Southwest. Painstakingly, laboriously, he devoured every scrap of information that was available, gradually built up one of the most complete reference libraries in the Southwest.

Fearing ridicule, Brady kept his hobby from even his closest friends and associates. Men who had known the cattle king for years never entertained the slightest suspicion that he was interested in lost mines and through intensive research work had developed certain theories by which some of these lost mines might be relocated.

So it was that when some six months ago Brady was motoring through the desert, Fate, which had decreed that Brady should become a cattle king instead of a prospector, apparently decided to reward Brady for his continued interest. At the exact moment when Harvey Brady was driving across the desert to Las Vegas, Nevada, to attend an important livestock conference, P. C. Drake, a typical desert prospector, was sadly shuffling along the hot stretch of desert pavement between Yermo and Windmill Station, lamenting the fact that his burro had died in the desert, and that the only part of his worldly belongings Drake could salvage were the things he could carry on his own back.

Drake, plodding along the highway, heard the sound of brakes and looked up to see the friendly grin of the cattleman. A few moments later Drake, with his heavy pack thrown into the trunk of Harvey Brady's automobile, was being speeded along the highway toward Windmill Station.

In the conversation which ensued, it appeared that Drake was familiar with a section of the desert in which Harvey Brady had concluded one of the famous lost mines was probably located.

Drake didn't stop at Windmill Station. He went on to Las Vegas as the guest of Harvey Brady. All during the cattlemen's convention, Drake stayed in Brady's hotel. Whenever the cattleman could get a minute to spare, he would be in Drake's room getting better acquainted, sizing up his man.

Then, on the last day of the convention, Brady made his proposition. He would grubstake Drake. Drake would cease prospecting for just any good body of ore and become, instead, a desert detective tracking down a certain route which Brady deduced must have been followed by one of the men who had located, and subsequently lost, one of the richest mines in the entire Southwest.

The newspaper went on: "Naturally, both parties are secretive as to the detailed conversation which ensued, but an agreement was reached. That agreement culminated yesterday afternoon when Brady, who had all but forgotten the penniless prospector he picked up in the desert, received the welcome news that his powers of deduction had resulted in once more locating one of the most fabulously rich lost mines of the desert.

"And as Fate rang down the curtain on this little drama of casting bread upon the waters, prospector Drake was in the act of handing to Harvey Brady a buckskin sack containing several hundred dollars worth of placer gold which had been picked up in less than twenty-five minutes. It had been found at what must have been the exact spot where two-thirds of a century ago a man went so delirious with joy over the discovery of great wealth that he was unable even to find the place again."

Mason chuckled. "I'll hand it to Paul Drake," he said. "He did a good job."

"And to Harvey Brady," Della Street said. "He certainly was a good sport to tag along."

"He was for a fact. His friends will probably give him an unmerciful ribbing when the blowoff takes place. But, in the meantime, Brady certainly has dressed the thing up for us."

Della Street's eyes twinkled. "Somehow I think he got an awful kick out of doing it, too. He has that whimsical sense of humor that makes him so refreshing."

"And a loyalty to his friends which makes him so dependable," Mason said. "We haven't heard anything from Paul Drake?"

"Not a word."

"I told him to do a little celebrating," Mason said.

"Drake would enjoy celebrating on an expense account."

"And how! Let's see if we can get Brady on the phone, Della."

Della Street moved over to the telephone on her secretarial desk, gave instructions to Gertie at the switchboard, and within a few minutes had the cattleman on the line.

Mason said, "Sorry I had to ask so much of you on such short notice, Brady. I'll explain as soon as I see you."

"Never explain," Brady said. "A friend who needs explanations isn't worth keeping. Whenever you ask a cattleman to do something for you, he either tells you to go to hell or he does it and is tickled to death. Is there anything else I can do for you?"

"Not a thing right now," Mason told him.

"Your man Drake is getting stinko. Is it all right?"

"It's all right."

"He said you wanted him stinko in public so he could make inopportune statements. However, he was just a little under the weather when he made that statement, so I've played it safe by keeping him shut up."

"Isn't that quite a job?" Mason asked.

"Not so much. He got away once and started running, but I brought him back on the end of a riata and he's been more tractable since."

"Is he in any condition to drive a car?" Mason asked.

"Hell, no."

"Do you have someone who could take him up to Mojave and turn him loose?"

"In his present condition?"

"Yes."

"Sure. I'll drive him up myself. If you want to see a couple of real old-time prospectors on the loose, come to Mojave and watch Paul Drake and Harvey Brady celebrating their great strike."

"I may at that," Mason said, laughing. "Only don't—"

Mason heard over the phone the crash of what was evidently breaking glass.

Brady said, "Shucks, that locoed maverick's jumped through the window." Then Mason heard the noise as the receiver was dropped, followed by a series of regular rhythmic thumps as the receiver swung back and forth, striking the wall at the end of each pendulum-like swing. He heard Harvey Brady shouting. "Don't get on that horse!—He bucks!" Then the line went dead.

Mason sighed, hung up the receiver, said to Della, "Were you listening in on that call?"

She nodded. "Sounds as though Paul Drake were learning to be a cowboy."

"The hard way," Mason agreed.

Della said, "I'll see what I can find out about the others."

Fifteen minutes later she brought him the information. Salty Bowers had been questioned and released by the police. His house trailer was being held by the police, so Salty had simply substituted the horse trailer, loaded in the burros, and departed for parts unknown.

Dr. Kenward, suffering from shock, with some slight danger of subsequent infection from the wound, had gone out into the desert somewhere in search of quiet. Velma Starler was with him.

Mason said, "Get hold of the detective agency. Let's see if we can pick up Salty Bowers' trail somewhere."

Della went down the hall to the office of the Drake

Detective Agency, returned to report they had men on the job. "How did you come out with your depositions?" she asked.

"Think I cracked their fraud case wide open."

"I'll bet that made Moffgat furious."

Mason nodded.

"You'd better watch him. If you best him twice in a row he'll be trying to get something on you."

"That's just it," Mason admitted. "He's on the trail of something."

"What?"

"That stock certificate. He's not certain of his ground yet, but he's thinking. You see I signed Clarke's name to that certificate. I had to. If Clarke had simply traced over the signature it would have authenticated it. If he'd lived, it wouldn't have made any difference one way or the other because he knew and approved what I had done. But with Clarke dead, I find myself between the devil and the deep sea. They could call that forgery, you see— an attempt on my part to get a quarter of a million dollars' worth of stock for myself by forging the name of a dead client."

"And Moffgat suspects?"

"Yes, I think so. . . . Moffgat is only fishing around so far. He made a tentative pass at it by trying to threaten me. I won't try to hold the stock, of course, yet I don't dare to surrender the certificate."

"What did you do?"

"Stopped him in his tracks by calling him cold."

"Chief, do be careful."

He grinned. "It's too late for that—I never liked being careful, anyway."

It was four o'clock in the afternoon when Drake's agency reported. Banning Clarke owned some claims up in the Walker Pass country. They were known as the Sky High Group and were under option to the Come-Back Mining Syndicate. The option would expire at midnight. Apparently Salty Bowers had gone up to these claims. Dr. Kenward and Velma Starler had accompanied him, the physician seeking some place where he could have a change from hospital background, and complete quiet.

Mason made note of the exact location of Banning Clarke's Sky High claims, then smiled at Della Street. "Della, haven't we a couple of sleeping bags stored with the janitor?"

She nodded. "Ones we used on that camping trip last fall. I'm not too certain about the air mattresses."

"We'll take a chance," Mason said. "Tell the janitor to drag them out. Go out to your apartment and put on some clothes that will stand the gaff. Take along a portable typewriter, a brief case with some stationery and carbon paper, see that your fountain pen is filled, and be sure to bring a shorthand notebook."

"Where," she asked, "are we going?"

Mason's smile became a broad grin. "Prospecting—for a lost murderer—and dodging a forgery charge."

■ 17 ■

For miles now, the dirt road had wound and twisted. The weird Joshua palms standing as silhouetted sentries gave somehow the impression of warning travelers back with outstretched arms. An occasional kangaroo rat scurried across the white ribbon of roadway. Clumps of prickly pear furnished spine-covered sanctuary for frightened rabbits. Cholla cacti, catching the headlights, seemed shrouded with a delicate transparency of silken fringe, the most deceptively deadly cactus on the desert. An occasional barrel cactus, standing straight and chunky, served as a reminder of stories of prospectors who, trapped in the desert without water, had chopped off the top of the big cactus, scooped out the pithy interior, waited for the watery sap to collect, and so assuaged the pangs of thirst.

Della Street sat with the little penciled map she had made spread across her knees. She held her small flashlight shielded by her cupped hand so that it would not interfere with Mason's driving. Frequently now, she looked at the speedometer.

"Two-tenths of a mile and the road turns off," she said.

Mason slowed the car, searched the left-hand side of the road for the turnoff, finally found it, little more than two faint ruts in the desert.

Della Street snapped off the flashlight, folded the map and put it back in her purse. "It's three and six-tenths miles from here. We just stay on this road."

The road climbed to an elevated plateau which rimmed the lower desert.

"I caught a flicker of light," Della said.

"Car coming?"

"It was rather reddish. Now, there it is off to the right. It's a campfire."

The road twisted around a jutting promontory in an abrupt turn and debouched on a little shelf where a blob of red light resolved itself into a small campfire.

"See anyone?" Mason asked.

"Not a soul," she said.

Mason slowed the car to a stop at a place where wheel tracks fanned out. The headlights showed a late-model sedan parked near Salty Bowers' old jalopy, the trailer in which the burros had been carried.

Mason shut off the motor, switched off the headlights.

There was complete silence, save for the little crackling noises which emanated from under the hood of his car as the motor started cooling off—noises which, under ordinary circumstances, would have been inaudible, but in the desert silence sounded like a distant naval bombardment.

Against this background of silence, the deserted campfire seemed utterly incongruous, an attempt at artificial cheer that was as out of place as a wisecrack at an execution.

"Br-r-r-r!" Della Street said. "I feel all creepy."

Mason opened the door of the car.

A voice from the darkness some fifteen feet away from them said in a slow drawl, "Oh! It's you!" Then Salty Bowers raised his voice. "All right, folks, it's the lawyer."

Almost immediately the camp bustled into activity. But not until Dr. Kenward, hobbling along on crutches, came out of the darkness which rimmed the circle of illumination around the campfire, and Velma Starler's trim figure silhouetted itself against the orange-red glow, did Salty Bowers emerge from the blackness which marked the location of a clump of desert juniper.

"Can't be too careful," he explained, "not with what's been going on. People around a campfire are the best targets in the world. Saw your car coming and decided

155

we'd just better be on the safe side. What's the matter, something new happen?"

"Nothing new. We're hiding out for a while. Have you got room for a couple more campers?"

Salty grinned, swept his arm in a wide sweep. "All the room in the world. Come on over to the fire. I'll brew a cup of tea."

"We've got the car loaded with camp equipment," Mason explained.

"Take it out later," Salty said. "Come on over and sit a while."

The three of them moved over to the campfire. Mason and Della shook hands with Dr. Kenward and the nurse, then settled down around the little blaze. Salty produced a fire-blackened graniteware coffee pot, poured water in it from a canteen, put it over the flames, said, "I use this one only for tea. Have another one for coffee. —Guess you understand, Mr. Mason, I warn't running away from anything; but around the city, people just don't seem to understand the feeling a man's got for a partner. Banning's death busted me all up. Folks wanted to *talk* about it—just talk—talk—talk. All of a sudden I got so I was hungry for the desert just like a man gets when he's been wanting something and don't know exactly what it is—and then the smell of frying bacon and coffee happens to hit him and he knows he's just plain damned hungry."

"And I," Dr. Kenward explained, "decided that I needed to really rest. I think Velma was the go-between who fixed it up with Salty. I'm certainly indebted to him for taking me along."

"This is Banning Clarke's claim?" Mason asked.

"It is now," Salty said; then, looking at his watch, amended, "It will be at midnight. That's when the option expires."

"Of course," Mason pointed out, "they *could* exercise that option between now and midnight."

156

"They could," Salty observed dryly.

Dr. Kenward said abruptly, "I'm going to say something about that murder, and then, if it's all the same to you, I think it would be a fine idea to quit talking about it."

"That," Salty announced with feeling, "suits me."

"What was it you wanted to say?" Mason asked.

Dr. Kenward said, "While the police haven't taken me into their confidence, I assume it's their theory someone tried to shoot me under the mistaken impression that I was Banning Clarke."

"So I gather," Mason said. "But the police don't exactly confide in me, either."

"Of course, it's an obvious conclusion. I had wandered out to the place where Banning Clarke would have been camped if he hadn't pulled out. I was visible in the moonlight only as a sleeping figure swathed in blankets. Quite obviously any person who didn't know that Clarke had left for the desert, and who wanted to kill him, would have assumed that I was Clarke."

Mason nodded.

"But," Dr. Kenward went on, "I have been wondering whether such was actually the case."

"You mean someone tried to kill you *knowing who you were?*"

"It's a possibility."

"And the motive?" Mason asked.

Dr. Kenward hesitated. "Come on," Mason prompted. "There could be only one motive—certain information that you possess. What is it?"

"I hadn't intended to go *quite* that far when I started talking about it," Dr. Kenward said.

"Well, we've gone that far now," Mason told him. "I should say, Doctor, that it was some bit of medical information you had uncovered—something about the poisoning, perhaps. And I think it's only fair to all concerned, including yourself, that you should tell us."

Dr. Kenward laughed. "You have all but deduced what it is. Purely as a matter of routine, I saved some of the stomach contents on the occasion of that first poisoning. That, you will remember, was the occasion when we found arsenic in the private saltcellar used only by the Bradissons."

"And what," Mason asked, "did you find?"

"A report on the analysis of the stomach content," Dr. Kenward said, "reached me just before I left town. It was, of course, given to me over the telephone but the analysis shows that there was no trace of arsenic."

"Then what," Mason asked, "induced the symptoms?"

"Apparently ipecac."

"And what," Mason pressed, "would be the object of taking ipecac?"

"To induce certain symptoms of arsenic poisoning."

"And what would be the object of inducing those symptoms, Doctor?"

Dr. Kenward said dryly, "That is a question, Mr. Mason, which comes within *your* department. I am reporting only the medical facts."

"But how about the metallic taste in the throat, the cramps, the general soreness?"

"I have questioned Velma about that very carefully," he said. "As nearly as she can recollect now, she *may* have been the one to suggest those symptoms. I have asked her particularly whether, when she first began to suspect the possibility of arsenic poisoning, she didn't ask the patients if they were suffering from cramps, general abdominal pain, a metallic burning sensation in the back of the mouth, and cramps in the legs. She can't remember now whether she asked that question of the patients, or whether they told her they were experiencing such symptoms."

"Does it make a great deal of difference?" Mason asked.

"A very great deal. Whenever a patient becomes violently ill, there is usually a certain element of depression, quite frequently a receptivity to suggestion, occasionally definite symptoms of hysteria. Under those circumstances a person normally experiencing a part of the symptoms which accompany a certain disease, and learning of other symptoms which are supposed to go hand in hand, will immediately develop those other symptoms."

"You're certain it was arsenic in the saltcellar?" Mason asked.

"There can be no doubt of that. The analysis shows it."

"Then *why* was the arsenic placed in the saltcellar?"

"That also is a question which is in your department rather than mine. But there are obviously two alternatives. One is that the arsenic was put in the saltcellar by someone who knew that the Bradissons were suffering from a poisoning, the symptoms of which resembled arsenic poisoning, and for some reason wanted to make it appear arsenic poisoning had been attempted."

"And the other alternative?" Mason asked.

"Is that someone actually tried to poison the Bradissons, that the poison was intended to take effect some time during the next day when the Bradissons would use the saltcellar, that through some peculiar coincidence, and from an undisclosed source, the Bradissons ingested a sufficient quantity of ipecac to produce violent illness."

Mason said, "I will ask you this, Doctor. Have you considered the possibility that the ipecac was taken by the Bradissons themselves with the deliberate intention of simulating the symptoms of arsenic poisoning?"

"Purely as a man of science trying to explore all possibilities which would account for all of the symptoms I encountered, I *have* taken that into consideration."

"Is there any evidence to support it?"

"None."

"It is a logical explanation?"

"There is no evidence against it."

"And you feel someone tried to murder you because you had this information?"

"It is a possibility."

They were silent for nearly a minute, then Mason said, "I want to think that over. In the meantime, I'm going to get my sleeping bag spread out."

Mason walked over to the car, pulled out the sleeping bags, fitted the power pump to the motor, inflated the air mattresses, and looked up to find Salty Bowers at his side.

"Have you," Mason asked, "staked out any particular sleeping quarters?"

"We've got a tent," Salty said. "The girls can use it for a dressing-room. They won't want to sleep in it. It's better to sleep out under the stars."

"Then let's put Miss Street's sleeping bag over by the tent," Mason said. "Where are you sleeping?"

Salty lowered his voice. "I'm not too easy in my mind about what's been going on. I've pulled my blankets down the trail a piece where I can sort of keep watch in case anybody should come pussyfooting along.—You pick up that end of the sleeping bag, I'll pick up this end and we'll carry it over. And when we get done, the tea will be just about ready to drink."

When the sleeping bags had been placed in position and the duffel bags brought out of Mason's car, the little group gathered once more around the fire. Salty put an armful of sagebrush on the fire, which promptly crackled into brilliance, a circle of illumination chasing back the encroaching shadows.

Salty poured tea, said, "The air's different out here somehow."

"It most certainly is," Mason said. "Dry and clear."

"A few months ago I developed a sinus condition," Dr. Kenward said. "It's clearing up out here with great rapidity. I am most encouraged."

"How's the wound?" Mason asked.

"Nothing serious at all. I have to watch for certain complications and nip them in the bud if they arise. I

160

naturally have to be quiet. Believe it or not, this is a great boon to me. It's an enforced vacation, but a very welcome one."

"What's Nell Sims doing?" Mason asked. "Staying in the house?"

"Staying in the house nothing," Salty said. "She headed back to Mojave, says she's going to open up her old restaurant. I guess," he added wistfully, "the desert has a way of reclaiming its own."

"It's marvelous out here," Della said.

"Lots of people hate the desert," Salty explained. "That's because they're really afraid of it. They're afraid of being left alone with themselves. There's lots of people you could put down in the middle of the desert, go away and leave 'em for a week, and come back and find them completely crazy. I've seen it happen. Man sprained his ankle once, couldn't travel. The party he was with had to go right on, but they left him with lots of water and food, plenty of matches, lots of wood. All he had to do was to just keep quiet for three or four days until he got so he could travel. He showed up in civilization just about half crazy. His ankle was all inflamed, said he'd rather have lost the whole leg than to have stayed on in that desert for another ten minutes."

"*I* think it's beautiful," Velma Starler said.

"Sure it's beautiful," Salty agreed. "People get scared of it because out here they're alone with their Maker. Some people can't stand that.—How about some more tea?"

The sagebrush finished its preliminary crackling, got down to a steady burning.

"How," Mason asked, "do you go about prospecting? Do you just wander around and look the desert over?"

"Gosh, no. You have to know a little something about how the ground was formed. You've got to figure out your formations, and then you've got to know what to look for. Lots of prospectors have picked up rock that

161

would have made them rich, and thrown it away.—Here, let me show you something."

Salty put down his teacup, got up and walked over to the pickup. He rummaged around for a few moments, then produced a boxlike affair.

"What's that?" Mason asked.

"Black light. Ever seen it work?"

"I've seen it used in connection with the detection of forgeries."

"If you ain't seen it in the desert, you just ain't seen anything. We've got to have it where it's dark. Come on, walk around behind this rock outcropping and I'll show you."

"I'll plead my crippled condition and stay here," Dr. Kenward said. "I don't want too much getting up and down."

They moved around behind the big rock outcropping. Here the light of the fire was shut out, and the stars, blazing with steady brilliance, seemed interested spectators regarding with a steady scrutiny the vague figures that moved over the desert.

Salty noticed them looking at the stars. "They say stars twinkle when air is mixed up with dust and stuff, and different air currents make 'em twinkle. I don't know anything about it. Maybe some of you folks do. All I know is that they don't twinkle out here."

Salty clicked a switch. A low humming sound came from the interior of the machine.

"Sort of induction coil," Salty explained. "Steps the current up from six volts to a hundred and fifteen. There's a two-watt bulb in here. It's on now."

The darkness assumed a peculiar color. It was hardly an illumination, was as though the darkness had turned a deep, almost black, violet.

"Now," Salty said, "I'll turn this beam of invisible light over toward this rock outcropping and you see what happens."

162

He swung toward the outcropping, turning the boxlike arrangement with his body as he pivoted.

Almost immediately it seemed that a thousand different colored lights had been turned on in the rocky outcropping. Some of the lights were blue, some a yellowish green, some a bright green. The lights varied in size from small pin points to great blobs of illumination the size of a baseball.

Della Street caught her breath. Velma Starler exclaimed out loud. Mason was silent, fascinated by the spectacle.

"What is it?" Della Street asked.

"I don't know too much about it. They call it fluorescent light," Salty said. "We use it in prospecting. You can tell different minerals by the different colors. I'll admit that I sort of fixed up the face of that rock outcropping a little bit, putting in some float I picked up in other parts of the desert that didn't rightly belong there.

"You were asking me about prospecting. We do a lot of it at night now. Lug around one of these outfits and spot minerals with it. Rocks that you'd pass over by day without a second glance will show you they've got valuable mineral in 'em when you turn this black light on 'em.—Well, let's go back to the fire. I don't want the Doc to think we ran away and left him. I just wanted to show you."

Salty switched off the mechanism which made the black light.

"Well," Dr. Kenward asked as they returned to the campfire, "how about it? Did it work?"

"Wonderfully," Mason said.

"It was the most awe-inspiring, the most beautiful sight I've ever seen," Velma Starler said enthusiastically. "Do you know how it works?"

"Generally. A bulb filled with argon and having a very low current consumption, usually about a two-watt-current rating, emits ultraviolet light. Our eyes aren't adjusted so we can see this light, but when it impinges upon various minerals, the wave length is changed back to that of visible light. The result is that these minerals have the appearance of actually emitting rays of light of various colors as independent sources of illumination."

"You've used those machines?" Mason asked him.

"I—Ouch! A twinge of pain in that leg. It's all right, Velma . . . nothing to be done."

"More tea here," Salty announced, and filled the teacups.

The sagebrush on the fire sputtered into a last flicker of flame. There was a lull in the conversation and, in that momentary lull, the silence of the desert made itself so apparent that it seemed to dominate the senses— a silence so intense that the lull in the conversation became a blanket of silence.

The last wavering flame flickered bravely, then vanished, leaving only a bed of glowing coals. Almost instantly the circle of darkness, which had been waiting just outside the campfire, moved in with a rush. The stars overhead brightened into added brilliance. A vagrant breeze coming down from off the higher ridges behind the camp fanned the coals into deep red for a moment. Over all, the brooding silence of the desert cast its spell.

Wordlessly, Salty got up, walked out into the darkness. Long experience in moving around at night without artificial illumination had made him as sure of himself as a blind man moving about through familiar surroundings.

"Well, guess I'll be turning in. Good night."

Dr. Kenward tried to get to his feet without asking Velma Starler for assistance, but she was at his side helping him up within less than a second. "Why didn't you tell me you wanted to get up?" she asked chidingly.

"I don't want to be so dependent."

"You've got to get over that some time. You have to depend on other people some. Are you going to bed?"

"I think so. If you'll help me with my shoes. . . . That's fine! I don't want to bend that leg. . . . Thanks."

Mason and Della Street sat by the dying fire, sharing the desert silence, looking into the red circle of coals.

Behind them the range of high mountains was a black silhouette against the western stars. Ahead and to the east the country dropped sharply into mysterious nebulous darkness which they knew held the level expanse of desert. Directly in front of them, the little circle of glowing coals gradually faded into a mere pool of pastel color which the night winds no longer had the power to fan into brilliance.

Mason's hand moved over, found Della Street's hand, took possession of it and held it in quiet understanding.

In the east, a faint band of nebulous illumination as vague and indistinct as the first flickers of Northern Lights paled the brilliance of the stars. Then, after a few minutes, the eastern range of mountains far out on the other side of the desert showed as a threadlike, sawtoothed strip outlined against a yellow illumination. This illumination grew in intensity until the slightly lopsided moon rose majestically to pour light over the surface far beneath them, bringing out ridges which were tinged with gold above pools of black shadow, pools that kept shrinking.

For more than two hours Mason and Della Street sat there watching the ever-changing spectacle, surrounded by the vast spell of silence.

Mason was awakened from deep slumber by the bugling of a burro. Almost immediately the other burro joined in the chorus, and Mason was grinning even as he opened his eyes.

The dawn was crisp and cool. One or two of the bright stars were still visible. There was not enough moisture in the sky to form even the faintest wisp of cloud, nor was there any trace of dew on the outside of the sleeping bag. The distant mountain range to the east was a narrow sawblade of black, outlined against a greenish blue illumination that tapered off into darkness. It was as yet too early to distinguish colors, but the sleeping camp showed objects in gray outlines.

Mason struggled to a sitting position and, as his back and shoulders emerged from the sleeping bag, the body warmth which the down covers had wrapped around him was whisked away in the cold still air, and Mason promptly shot back down into the warm covers.

The burros had seen him move, and, walking with dainty, careful feet, moved over to his sleeping bag. Mason felt a silky soft nose nuzzling around his ear. Then, after a moment, lips nibbled at his hair.

The lawyer laughed and struggled out of the sleeping bag and into his clothes. Apparently the braying of the burros had not aroused any of the other sleepers. The bags were motionless mounds in the increasing light of early dawn.

Mason kept feeling colder as he dressed. There was no breath of air stirring, but the crisp mountain air was definitely cold. He looked around for feed for the burros and could find none, nor did the animals seem to expect any. Apparently they had only wanted human companionship, desired only to see the camp stirred into life. Once Mason started moving around, the burros sagged into a posture of contentment, ears drooping forward, heads lowered.

Mason broke up dry sagebrush, kindled it with a match, soon had a fire going. He was looking around for supplies when Salty Bowers, a businesslike six-shooter strapped to his hip, came swinging out from behind the rock outcropping and into the open.

Salty nodded to Mason, apparently avoiding conversation that would waken the other sleepers. He moved over to the burros, rubbed his hand along their necks and ears, poured ice-cold water from a canteen into a basin, washed, then put coffee on the fire. As Mason washed, the bracing water stung glowing circulation into his face and hands.

"Cold up here," he said.

"Nights are cold," Salty agreed. "You're way up, up here. Wait until the sun rises and you won't be bothered none with cold."

Mason helped with the cooking, noticing that Della Street's sleeping bag became convulsed with motion as she did most of her dressing under cover of the bag. A few moments later she joined him at the fire.

"Sleep?" Mason asked.

"Sleep!" she exclaimed. "The most marvelous sleep I've ever had in my life. Usually when I sleep so heavily, I wake up feeling drugged. Now my lungs feel all washed out and—When do we eat?"

"Pretty soon," Salty said.

The east became a dazzling sheet of vivid orange. The edges of the silhouetted mountains seemed coated with liquid gold. The first small segment of sun put in a dazzling appearance. The desert began taking on pastel shades of color. Mason, seeing the need for more firewood, broke up brittle, dry sage and brought it in to where Salty was slicing bacon with a razor-keen knife.

The sun swung clear of the mountains, hung poised for a few moments as though gathering strength, and then sent rays of golden warmth flooding the camp. For the next quarter hour, Mason was too busy assisting in the preparations to pay too much attention to his surroundings. Then suddenly he realized that not only had he ceased being cold, but that it was getting hot.

The aroma of coffee mingled with the smoky tang of bacon. Velma Starler and Dr. Kenward joined the group around the fire. Soon they were eating golden brown hot cakes swimming with melted butter, rich with sirup, with strips of meaty bacon to add just the right tang of smoky salt. The coffee was a clear deep brown with plenty of full-bodied flavor.

"What's the secret?" Velma Starler asked, laughing. "Doesn't rationing bother you?"

Salty grinned. "Banning Clarke laid in a cache of canned goods up here a while back."

"Didn't he declare them?" Mason asked.

"Sure he declared them. They'll be tearing half the coupons out of his book from now until the middle of nineteen-seventy-six. He liked his grub, and he hated to carry too much stuff in by burro-back, so he trucked stuff out part way and got packers to bring it in. You'd be surprised how long canned butter keeps when it's buried in a cool place. Same with vacuum-packed coffee. —Rationing's all right for people in the city," Salty went on with some feeling, "but you take a prospector that has to go in and load up with enough provisions to last him for months, and he just can't get by on ration stuff. He has to use all canned goods and dried foods.—Oh well, *we're* all right, thanks to the stuff we got cached around here. You can eat all you want an' stay as long as you like and it won't hurt a bit."

"Thanks for your hospitality, Salty, but we're heading toward Mojave right after breakfast."

Della glanced quickly at the lawyer, fighting surprise back from her eyes.

"Better look up Nell Sims when you get there," Salty said.

"We intend to."

"Maybe she'll have her pies going by today. She said she would."

"Suppose Pete went with her?"

Salty's lips clamped into a tight line. "I wouldn't know."

"You don't care much about Pete?"

"He's all right."

Mason grinned. "Well, I'll go take a look at Mojave."

"You don't know when—That is—the funeral?"

"No. They won't release the body for a while, Salty. Not until tomorrow anyway."

Salty suddenly thrust out his hand. "Thanks," he said.

They said good-by to the others, loaded their car and started down the dusty, winding road, Della Street at the wheel.

"Thought you planned to stay for a day or two," Della said.

"I did," Mason admitted. "I wasn't exactly running away, but I didn't want to be available for questioning until the situation had clarified itself somewhat. If I don't produce that stock certificate, I'm in bad. If I do, it becomes apparent that the endorsement is, as matters now stand, a forgery. Then there's one other thing that bothers me. The minute Mrs. Bradisson finds that other will has disappeared she'll know who has it. You see she *knows* I couldn't have gone in that room and fallen asleep, because she left it only a relatively short time before I was discovered in there at the desk."

"What will she do when she finds out, Chief?"

"I don't know. Her position will then be untenable,

so she may decide to beat me to the punch. All in all, I thought it would be better to keep out of circulation for a while. But that information about the ipecac—well, if they start anything, we can fight back."

"At that you're in hot water again," she observed after a few minutes during which she silently concentrated on driving the car.

"It's hot all right," Mason admitted, "and it keeps getting hotter. It won't be long until it starts boiling."

"Then what?"

"Then I'll become even more hard-boiled."

"For one like that, you deserve to be conversationally ostracized," she proclaimed. "I'm going to put you in verbal quarantine."

"It's really justified," he admitted, letting his head drop back to the cushions, closing his eyes. "I really *should* be shot."

Mason dozed while the dusty miles slipped behind. Then the dirt road joined a ribbon of paved highway and the car purred smoothly toward Mojave, topped a little rise, and the town of Mojave sprawled out across the face of the desert as listless, when seen from this distance, and as sun-bleached as a dried bone.

"Well," Della Street said, easing the pressure on the foot throttle, "here we are. Where do we go?"

Mason, still with his eyes closed, said, "Nell Sims' restaurant."

"Think we can find it all right?"

Mason chuckled. "Her return should be quite an event in the history of Mojave. Doubtless there will be some manifestation. Her individuality is too strong to be swallowed without a trace in a town of this size."

The road swung along for a short distance parallel to the railroad track. Della Street said, "Looks as though it had been snowing."

Mason opened his eyes. Pieces of paper were plastered

up against every clump of greasewood that dotted the face of the desert.

"Railroad track over here," Mason said with a gesture, "and the winds come from that direction, and you've never really seen the wind blow until you've been in Mojave. Trains always spew out pieces of paper, and along here the winds blow them against the little greasewood bushes so hard that they stick. The accumulation of years along here. Down here a way, a man had a hat farm."

"A hat farm?" Della asked.

"That's right. It gets hot in the desert and people stick their heads out of the train windows. A certain percentage of hats blow off, and the wind rolls them along the ground like tumbleweeds until they fetch up against the greasewood on this fellow's little homestead. His neighbors plowed up the ground on their homesteads and tried to grow things. The country starved them out. This man left all the natural brush in place and picked up enough hats in the course of a year to keep him in grub."

Della Street laughed.

"No kidding," Mason told her; "it's a fact. Ask some of the people around here about the hat farm."

"Honest injun?"

"Honest injun. You ask them."

The road went down a little dip, made a slight curve and entered Mojave. At closer range the little desert metropolis presented more signs of external activity.

"There was a time," Mason said, "when the only people who lived here were those who didn't have carfare enough or gumption enough to get out of town. This was too civilized to have the real advantages of the desert, and too much of the desert to have the advantages of civilization. Now, with air-conditioning and electric refrigeration, the place is quite livable, and you can see the difference in the whole appearance of the city.—I guess

171

this is the place we want, Della, dead ahead. See the sign?"

A sign made of bunting had been rigged up and hung out across the sidewalk. It proclaimed in vivid red letters at least three feet high, *"NELL'S BACK!"*

Della Street eased the car to a stop. Mason held the car door open while she slid out from under the steering wheel, across the seat, and, with a flash of trim legs, stood on the sidewalk beside him.

"Any particular line we use?" Della asked.

"No. We just barge in and start talking."

Mason held the restaurant door open for her. As they entered the room, after the glare of the desert, their sun-tortured eyes took a second or two to adjust themselves so they could see into the shadows. One thing, however, which was clearly visible as soon as they entered the room was a long thin piece of bunting stretched over the mirror behind the lunch counter. On it was painted in big letters: "BECAUSE I RUN A BETTER RESTAURANT, THE WORLD HAS BEAT A MOUSE TRAP TO MY DOORS."

"This," Mason announced, "is *undoubtedly* the place."

From the dark coolness near the back of the room, Nell Sims exclaimed, "Well, for the land sakes! Now, what on earth are *you* two doing here?"

"Just looking for a cup of coffee and a piece of pie," Mason said, grinning and walking across to shake hands. "How are you?"

"I'm fine. Well, you folks certainly *do* get around."

"Don't we?" Della said laughing.

"It's just a little early for me to get my shelves stocked with pastry," Nell Sims apologized, "but I've got some pies coming out of the oven in just a minute now. How'd you like a piece of hot apple pie with a couple of scoops of ice cream on top of it and a nice big slab of cheese on the side of the plate?"

"Can you do that?"

172

"Do what?"

"Serve pie, cheese, and ice cream at one time?"

"I ain't supposed to, but I can. Out in these parts Hospitality can't read—at least, any of these new-fangled government regulations. Sit right down and I'll have those pies out of the oven in just a minute or two. You'll like 'em. I put in plenty of sugar. Never did care for desserts that were just half sweet. I put in lots of butter and sugar and cinnamon. May not be able to bake so many pies, but those I do bake certainly taste like something."

"Anything new around here?" Mason asked casually, as he slid up to the counter.

"Lots of excitement in town over the new strike. If you ask me, there's something awfully fishy about it."

"What?" Mason asked.

"That prospector," she said, and stopped.

"The man who located the mine?"

"The man who *says* he located the mine."

"What's wrong with him?" Mason asked.

"He's a tenderfoot. If he's a prospector, I'm a diplomat. He's certainly got the gold, though. Showing it around everywhere."

"What's he doing?" Mason asked.

"Drinking mostly."

"Where?"

"Just any place around town where he can find a parking place and a bottle. That cattleman is with him, and they're doing the craziest things."

"Where," Mason asked, "is your husband?"

"Haven't see him since I landed. When they going to have the funeral, do you folks know?"

"I don't think anyone does. There's a lot of red tape in connection with post-mortems and things of that sort."

"A mighty good man," Nell Sims said. "It's a crying shame men like him have to go. He was just like a brother to me. Leaves me all broken up. Don't s'pose they've

173

found out who did it yet. . . . Land sakes! I'm almost forgetting about my pies."

She dashed back into the kitchen. They heard an oven door open and, a moment later, the delicious aroma of freshly baked pie warmed their nostrils.

The door opened. Two men entered the restaurant. Della Street, looking back at the door, closed her fingers on Mason's forearm. "It's Paul Drake and Harvey Brady," she said in a whisper.

"Hi!" Paul Drake exclaimed in the loud voice of a man who has been drinking and feels that his thoughts become increasingly important as they are expressed in a louder voice.

Mason's back was rigid.

"Madam," Paul Drake said, a slightly thickened tongue interfering a little with his grandiloquent manner, "I have been advised that the civic life of this c'-munity has turned over a new page, with the aushpicious advent of your return to the scenes of your earlier triumphants. In other words, Madam, to express myself more directly, they say you make damn good pie."

Harvey Brady said, "Unless my nose is mistaken, the pies are just about ready to come out of the oven."

Mason slowly turned.

Brady regarded him with the casual interest a man bestows upon a total stranger.

Paul Drake lurched forward, peered up at Mason with the intense scrutiny of someone who is having some difficulty focusing his eyes. "Hello, stranger," he said. "Let me introduce myself. My name's Drake. I'm half owner in the richest bonanza ever discovered in the whole mining history of the West. I'm happy. You, my boy, look hungry. You look thirsty. You look dissatisfied. You look unhappy. In short, my lad, you look like a Republican on an appropriations committee. There's nothing I can do here in the form of liquid refreshment to alleviate

174

your deplorable condition, but I *can* show you the true hospitality of the West by buying you a piece of pie."

"His pie is already spoken for," Nell Sims said.

Drake nodded owlishly. "How many pieces of pie?" he asked.

"One," Mrs. Sims said.

"That's fine. I'll buy him the second piece. The first piece he has on himself. The second piece he has on me."

Drake turned to Harvey Brady. "Come on, partner. Sit up to the counter. Let's have pie. What do we care for the various vicis—s—s. . . . Whoa! Guess I'd better back up and take another try at that one." He took in a deep breath. "What do we care for the various vicis—viciss—ssitudes of life when we have pie? Madam, we shall have pie, or as you would doubtless express it, eat —drink—and be merry, for tomorrow we pie."

Nell Sims said, "That isn't the right quotation."

"What *is?*" Drake asked belligerently.

"Eat, drink, and be merry, for tomorrow and tomorrow and tomorrow roll on their dreary course."

Drake put his head in his hands and thought that over. "You're right," he agreed at length.

Mrs. Sims said, "I've just taken the pies out of the oven. Just a minute and I'll bring them in."

She retired to the kitchen.

Paul Drake leaned forward and said in a confidential voice that was almost a whisper, "Look, Perry, let's make some dough on the side. I've met a *real* prospector who's working some property he thinks doesn't amount to much. There are some black pebbles that constantly get in his sluices. Perry, those pebbles are gold nuggets once you scrape off the black. The poor chap doesn't realize this. I wouldn't outsmart him on the whole claim, but I can get a half interest in it."

Mason drew back from the detective's breath. "Paul, you've been drinking."

"Of course I've been drinking," Drake said truculently. "Why the hell shouldn't I be drinking? How can I act the part of a drunk without drinking—at least in this town where people watch every move you make. Hell's bells! I'm *famous!*"

Nell Sims appeared with the pie, served Della Street and Mason, then cut off smaller pieces for Brady and Drake.

The cattleman gave Mason's arm a surreptitious re-assuring squeeze, then settled down at the table next to Drake.

Drake turned once more to Mason, regarded him with the alcoholic persistence of a drunk who has been re-buffed and has made up his mind he isn't going to take it. "Another thing," Drake said, "is that. . . . Say, how's it happen *he* gets ice cream on *his* pie, and *we* don't get ice cream on *our* pie?"

"That's government regulations," Nell Sims said; "least-wise I think it is. That's what they told me when I took over the restaurant."

"How about him?" Drake demanded, pointing his finger at Perry Mason.

Nell Sims never batted an eyelash. "He has an A-1-A priority rating from the local war board."

Drake regarded Mason with widened eyes. "I'll be a son-of-a-gun!" he exclaimed.

Mason, watching his opportunity, said in a low voice, "Want to see you alone as soon as we can get out of here, Paul."

Brady, keeping his voice equally low, said, "So does all the rest of Mojave, Perry. Stick your head out of the door and you'll see ten or fifteen people sort of casually hanging around the sidewalk. The point is that wherever we go those same ten or fifteen people—"

He broke off as the screen door banged open. A fright-ened little whisper of a man scuttled through the doorway and made for the kitchen.

"Hey, Pete!" Paul Drake yelled, jumping to his feet,

his manner enthusiastically cordial. "Come on over here. Right over here, Pete old boy!"

Pete Sims either didn't hear him or paid no attention. "Nell!" he half screamed. "Nell, you've got to see me through this! You—!"

Once more the door banged open. Sheriff Greggory's form bulked large against the eye-dazzling glare which beat down on the town's single main street.

"Hey, you!" he yelled. "Come back here. What the hell did you run for? You're under arrest."

Drake gave Mason a woebegone look. "Oh, my gosh," he said dolefully. *That's* the guy who was going to sell me a half interest in the mining claim."

■ 19 ■

Sheriff Greggory pushed his way toward the counter, his face hard lines of determination.

Pete skidded around the counter to stand beside his wife. His frightened little eyes regarded the sheriff apprehensively.

Nell Sims said, "Pete, *what* have you been up to now?"

Behind the officer, venturing somewhat tentatively through the doorway, appeared Mrs. Bradisson and her son.

Pete Sims caught sight of Mason and, his voice chattering with fright, said, "There's my lawyer. I demand an opportunity to talk with my lawyer. You can't do anything to me until I've seen a lawyer."

"Pete," Nell Sims said sternly, "you tell me what you've been up to. Come on now, make a clean breast of it."

Greggory said, "Ask him to tell you what he was doing with twelve ounces of arsenic."

"*Arsenic!*" Nell exclaimed.

"That's right. What were you doing with it, Pete?"

"I didn't have it, I tell you."

"Don't be silly. We've found where you bought it. The druggist identifies your photograph."

"It's all a mistake, I tell you."

"It's a mistake as far as you're concerned all right."

"I'm going to talk with a lawyer."

"Pete Sims, did you put poison in that sugar? Why, if I thought you'd done that, I'd—I'd—I'd kill you with my bare hands."

"I didn't, Nell. Honest I didn't. I got this poison for something else."

178

"What did you want with it?"

"I can't tell you."

"Where is that poison?" Nell demanded.

"You've got it."

"*I* have?"

"Yes."

"You're crazy!"

"Don't you remember that paper bag I gave to you and told you to save?"

"You mean that stuff that— Good Heavens! I thought it was some stuff for mining. That's what you said it was. You didn't *tell* me it was poison."

"I told you to keep it where no one could possibly touch it," Sims said.

"Why you. . . you. . . ."

"Come on," Sheriff Greggory said; "what did you buy it for?"

"I—I don't know."

Mason turned to Nell Sims. "Where did you put it?" he asked.

Her face told its own story of agonized dismay.

"Near the sugar?" Mason asked.

She nodded, too overcome for words.

"And," Mason went on gently, "could you, by mistake, have reached into this bag instead of the sugar bag, and—"

"I couldn't," she said, "but Dorina could have. You see, with the rationing of sugar, the way things are nowadays—well, I told Dorina to use her stamps and get a bag of sugar. She handed it to me. After she'd gone, I opened the bag and dumped it into the big sack with the other sugar; but this bag Pete had given me was in there on the shelf, and she might have seen it and thought it was the bag of sugar she'd bought. And then, if she thought the sugar bowl needed filling. . . . Pete, why didn't you tell me that was poison?"

"I told you not to touch it," Pete said.

179

"Don't you see what you've done? If Dorina got into that bag by mistake and filled up the sugar bowl, you've been the one that poisoned Banning Clarke."

"I didn't poison him. I tell you I didn't have anything to do with it. I just handed you this bag."

"Why did you buy that arsenic in the first place?" Sheriff Greggory asked.

"I wanted to do some experiments in mining, and I had to have some arsenic to do them with."

"Then why didn't you use it?"

"Well, I just never got around to doing those experiments."

There was a moment's silence.

Mrs. Bradisson said, "But while that might account for the fact that arsenic was mixed in the sugar, Sheriff, it would hardly account for the fact that arsenic had been mixed in with the salt the night my son and I were poisoned."

"That's right," the sheriff agreed. "I hadn't thought of that. That shows it was deliberate, not an accident."

"Just a moment," Mason interposed smoothly. "I hadn't intended to spring this at this time, but under the circumstances and since you seem to be narrowing the circle down, Sheriff, I'm going to tell you that Mrs. Bradisson wasn't suffering from arsenic poisoning."

"Nonsense," Mrs. Bradisson said. "I guess I know what the symptoms were, and Dr. Kenward said that's what it was, also the nurse."

"Nevertheless," Mason said, "you didn't have arsenic poisoning. You had certain symptoms and you perhaps simulated others, but your nausea was induced by ipecac—probably deliberately induced."

"Why, I never heard of any such thing. What do you mean by that?"

"I mean," Mason said, "that Dr. Kenward told me he placed a portion of the stomach contents in a sealed glass bottle and delivered it to a laboratory for an examina-

180

tion and anlysis. The report came back a few hours ago. There was no sign of arsenic, but there *were* traces of ipecac. The same situation is true of both yourself and your son."

"Why, I never heard of such a thing," she stormed.

"Now then," Mason went on smoothly, "arsenic *might* have been administered accidentally, or with homicidal intent; but the strong probabilities are that the ipecac was taken deliberately. Now suppose you and your son tell us why you took ipecac, and then simulated the symptoms of arsenic poisoning. Why did you do it?"

"I never did any such thing," Mrs. Bradisson said.

James Bradisson moved forward. "I think it's about time for me to take a hand in this, Mason."

"Go ahead," Mason said. "Walk right in."

Bradisson said in a low voice to Greggory, "I think you should find out why Mason is so deliberately pulling a red herring across the trail."

"It's no red herring," Mason said. "I'm simply showing that the theory that the arsenic got into the sugar accidentally is quite tenable. The only thing that stands in the way of such a theory is that arsenic is supposed to have been in the saltcellar the night before."

Mrs. Bradisson tilted her chin. She said with dignity, "*I* can tell you why Perry Mason has suddenly brought up all of this stuff about the ipecac."

Sheriff Greggory looked at her expectantly.

"Because," Mrs. Bradisson went on, "Perry Mason *stole* something from Banning Clarke's study."

"What's that?" Greggory demanded. "Say that again."

Mrs. Bradisson spoke, the words coming out in a rush. "I said that Perry Mason stole a document out of Banning Clarke's desk, and I know what I'm talking about."

"How do you know?" Greggory asked.

"I'll tell you how. When I heard Banning Clarke was killed, I knew that there was something very dark and sinister behind it, and that someone would be almost certain to try to go through his things, and—if he had left a will—to tamper with it. So I went into his room, went through his roll-top desk, found a document that I considered very important evidence. I fastened it to the bottom of the drawer on the lower left-hand side of the desk with thumbtacks and then put the drawer back."

"Why did you do that?" Greggory asked ominously.

"So that anyone that came in and tried to tamper with his things wouldn't be able to find that document and destroy it."

"Why would anyone want to destroy it."

"Because it purported to be a will in Banning Clarke's handwriting. It wasn't in his writing at all. It was a forgery. It left property to Perry Mason. And if you'll use your head a little you'll see some very sinister things have been happening. Perry Mason meets Banning Clarke only a few days ago. In that short time, Mason gets all of Banning Clarke's stock, then Clarke leaves a will leaving property to Mason, and then Clarke dies. Rather a nice series of happenings—for Perry Mason—who is also named in the will as executor."

Greggory turned toward Perry Mason, started to say something, changed his mind and whirled back to Mrs. Bradisson.

"And why do you think Perry Mason took the will?"

"Put two and two together. When I went down to Banning Clarke's room I didn't close the door. I simply went into the desk and found this forged will and hid it. Remember that Banning was my son-in-law. I felt toward him just as though he had been my own child."

"And," Mason asked, "you substituted a will in place of the one you took out of the desk?"

She smiled at him with exaggerated sweetness. "Yes, Mr. Mason, I did. And thank you very much for calling my attention to that fact, because it shows that you *were* watching me."

"I was," Mason admitted.

She turned triumphantly to the officer. "You see," she said, "he was watching me. As soon as I left, he entered the room, found where I had left that forged will, and probably destroyed it. He knew by that time that I suspected the truth. I went back the next morning and the will had been removed. There were only the thumbtacks left in the bottom of the drawer—no will. And you'll remember you found Mr. Mason sitting at the desk when you went in there to search. I believe he *said* he'd been asleep. Well, that was only about ten or fifteen minutes after I had left the room. Banning had left his *real* will in my custody. I put it in the desk."

Greggory said ominously, "Mason, this is serious—damn serious. You yourself admit you took that will?"

"I admit nothing," Mason said suavely. "I only asked Mrs. Bradisson a question. She took it as an admission."

"So did I."

Mason bowed. "That's your privilege. I only said I watched."

"Where's that will?"

"What will?"

"The one Mrs. Bradisson has described."

"You'll have to ask her. She's the one who described it."

"You deny having it?"

"I haven't any such document as *she* described."

"It said something about a clue in a drawer in the desk," Mrs. Bradisson went on, "and there was nothing in there but a mosquito in a bottle."

Mason smiled at her. "I believe I was accused of dragging red herrings across the trail, Mrs. Bradisson, so I feel free to make the same accusation. Now, since you have tossed the hand grenade which was to have stampeded the investigation in an entirely different direction, perhaps you'll be so good as to explain to the sheriff how it happens that you took ipecac in order to simulate the symptoms of arsenic poisoning twenty-four hours before Banning Clarke was given a fatal dose."

Sheriff Greggory seemed somewhat dazed as he turned his frown from Mason to Mrs. Bradisson.

James Bradisson interposed, "Look here, this is all news to me, but I don't like the way this is being handled. My mother is nervous and unstrung. If she has any statement to make, she'll make it to the sheriff privately. I don't like the idea of Perry Mason standing here bulldozing her."

Mason bowed. "I wasn't aware I was doing it, but if you feel I am upsetting your mother, I'll withdraw."

"No, no!" Bradisson exclaimed. "That isn't what I meant. I meant she would make her statement later, after the sheriff had finished with you."

"It may not have been what *you* meant," Mason said, "but it's what *I* meant. Come, Della."

"Wait a minute," Greggory said. "I'm not finished with you, Mason."

"You're quite right," Mason said, "but your most important angle at the moment is to find out about that ipecac before mother and son have a chance to confer, and *I* refuse to be questioned in the presence of the Bradissons." He started for the door.

"Wait a minute," Greggory interposed. "You're not going to walk out of here until I've searched you for that document."

"Really, Sheriff!" Mason said. "Has it ever occurred to you what county you're in? Such high-handed procedure will hardly go over now that you've left your jurisdiction. And you really should question the Bradissons before they get a chance to patch up a story. Come, Della."

It was the reference to the fact that Greggory was outside his own county that brought sudden dismay to his face. Mason calmly pushed past him to the door.

Paul Drake, who had been a fascinated spectator, suddenly burst into applause.

184

The sheriff whirled on him angrily. "Who the hell are *you?*" he demanded.

Drake, with alcoholic dignity, said loftily, "If you want to put it that way, who the hell are *you?*"

Mason didn't wait to hear Greggory's answer.

As the door banged shut behind them, Della Street let out her breath. "Whew! That was close. How's the water now, Chief? Hot enough?"

"Coming to a boil," Mason said.

"You have to hand it to Mrs. Bradisson for having the courage to stage a counter-offensive," Della said.

Mason frowned as he slid in behind the steering wheel. "Unless she set a trap, and I walked into it."

"What do you mean?"

"Suppose she left that door open on purpose so I could see her juggling wills. Naturally I'd promptly jump to the conclusion that the will she was hiding was genuine. If it should turn out to be forged, that, coupled with the phony endorsement on that stock certificate, and the fact that Banning Clarke was poisoned at a meal we shared with him—"

"Chief!" Della Street interrupted in an exclamation of frightened dismay.

"Exactly," Mason said, and stepped on the foot throttle.

"But, Chief, there's no way out."

"Only one possible avenue left open," Mason said.

"What's that?"

"We don't know too much about the drowsy mosquito," Mason told her. "Velma Starler heard it. She turned on the light. The mosquito ceased flying. She turned out the light, went to the window carrying a flashlight. Someone was standing near the wall—almost directly below her window. He fired two shots. Those shots perforated the upper windowpane above Velma Starler's head. They were less than three inches apart. Is there anything about that which strikes you as being particularly unusual?"

"You mean about the shots?"

185

"Yes. That's partly it. Quite evidently the man didn't want to hit her. He wanted to frighten her away from the window. If he had enough skill to put those bullets within three inches of each other, he must have been a darn good shot."

"But why try to frighten her away from the window?"

Mason smiled. "The drowsy mosquito."

"What do you mean, Chief?"

"Did you notice," Mason asked, "that when Salty Bowers made his demonstration of black light last night there was some sort of an induction coil in the mechanism by which the current of a dry battery was stepped up to sufficient voltage to work the bulb?"

She nodded.

"And," Mason went on, "if you had been somewhere in the dark and heard that rather faint buzzing, it would have sounded very much like a mosquito that was in the room."

Della Street was excited now. "It would, at that," she said.

"A peculiar, somewhat lazy mosquito—perhaps a drowsy mosquito."

"Then you think the sound Velma heard was caused by one of those black-light devices?"

"Why not? When she looked out the window, someone was standing near the wall. Put yourself in the position of Banning Clarke. He had a bad heart. He had very valuable information. He didn't dare trust that information to anyone. Yet the possibility that he might die and take the secret to the grave with him must have occurred to him. Therefore, he must have tried to leave some message. His reference to the drowsy mosquito becomes very significant in view of the demonstration we saw last night of fluorescent lighting."

"You mean that he worked out a code message somewhere?"

"Exactly."

"Then it must be in that rock wall!"

"Exactly. Remember he had all of those different rocks brought in from the desert."

Della Street's eyes sparkled. "And I suppose that means we're going to be the first ones to throw a beam of invisible light on that wall and see what the message is?"

"We're going to *try* to be first," Mason said.

"But the prowler must have been using one of these machines."

Mason was thoughtful. "The machine *may* have been one that Salty Bowers or Banning Clarke was using at a place on the wall a short distance from where Velma saw the prowler. The prowler *may* have been trying to find out what was going on. In any event, I think we've found an explanation for the drowsy mosquito."

■ 20 ■

It was too early for the distorted moon to lift itself over the horizon. For the moment, the night was dark save for the stars which, in this ocean-misted atmosphere, seemed distant, impersonal pin points.

Della Street held the flashlight. Mason carried the long, box-like apparatus for generating black light. The house at the north end of the big grounds was silhouetted against the night as a dark rectangle. There was no sign of human occupancy anywhere in the building.

Mason took up a position some ten feet from the wall. "All right, Della," he said, "let's have it dark."

She snapped out the flashlight.

Mason turned a switch. From the interior of the box came a low, distinctive hum, and a moment later, the darkness of the night seemed to turn slightly luminous and a deep violet.

Mason directed the rays of ultraviolet light against the wall. Almost instantly a series of colored lights winked back at him. In silence the lawyer and Della Street studied them.

"Do you make anything out of it, Chief?" she asked anxiously.

Mason didn't answer immediately. When he did, there was discouragement in his tone. "Not a darn thing. Of course, it may be in some sort of code. . . . It's just a succession of isolated dots. There doesn't seem to be any particular pattern."

Mason moved on down the wall. "Looks pretty hopeless," he remarked, and Della's keen ears could detect the disappointment in his voice, showing to what extent he had banked on his theory.

"Perhaps it's something *else* that has to do with this ultraviolet light," she said, knowing how much it meant to them, and realizing that Mason was in a predicament from which he could extricate himself only by quick, clear thinking and that solving the mystery of the drowsy mosquito was but the first step. Failing in that, they were beaten on everything else.

"I can't imagine what it could be. The deuce of it is, Della, we're working against time. . . . Hello, what's this!"

Mason had been moving down the wall, coming to the lower portion where the wall tapered down until it was hardly four feet high.

"It's a straight line," Della exclaimed. "Those fluorescent stones have been arranged so they make a straight line, and over here— Oh, look!"

Mason had swung the portable light over to the left so that an entirely new section of wall was brought into their field of vision. A whole series of luminous lines appeared, as though someone had etched a roughly rectangular diagram with a phosphorescent pencil.

Della said, "There's some kind of flower with pointed petals. It's hanging upside down."

Mason frowned as he looked at the object: apparently a five-petaled flower, hanging downward from a slightly curved stem. Abruptly he exclaimed, "By George!"

"What?" Della asked.

"The Shooting Star," Mason said in low tones. "That's not a flower hanging upside down—it's a shooting star, and those lines must be the boundaries of the claims, and this cross must mark the point where Banning Clarke discovered the evidence showing it's the original Goler discovery."

"That's it," Della exclaimed, excitedly. "Gosh, Chief, I feel as though we'd just located a valley full of gold. My knees are all trembly."

Mason, apparently thinking out loud, said, "That's

why he wanted to put up a fight on the fraud case. You can see his position, Della. If he tried to get any property *back* from the mining company, that would be the pay-off—the clue that would enable Bradisson to go and locate the lost Goler claim. But, by pretending he was trying to beat a hopeless case, and trying to keep Mrs. Sims from getting her claims back, Clarke managed to pull the wool over everyone's eyes—including my own."

"Then Mrs. Sims will get her claims back?" Della asked.

"Hang it," Mason muttered with exasperation, "I fixed it so she won't. I trapped Bradisson on his deposition into making statements that changed that fraud case from a hopeless case to an ironclad cinch—and by doing it, deprived my client of a fortune. Now I've got to find some way of executing a legal flip-flop before they get wise to the real value. . . . And there's always the possibility someone else knows about this."

"About the Shooting Star and the secret of the drowsy mosquito?"

"Yes."

"You mean the prowler?"

"Yes."

"But don't you think the prowler was simply spying on Banning Clarke who was using the light to help arrange the rocks in the wall? And the prowler may have been frightened away before he learned the secret? After all, Banning Clarke *could* have stripped off his outer garments after he heard the shots the prowler fired."

"That's right," Mason said. "But remember that this prowler could always come back. He shot *after* Velma had seen him, but to keep her from turning the flashlight on him. Therefore, he shot, not to prevent discovery but recognition, and—"

"Someone's coming!" Della exclaimed.

"Quick, Della. We can't afford to be caught here. Lucky

190

we left our car away from the house." Mason started around behind the cacti looking for a place of concealment as two dazzling headlights came crawling through the gate and turned into the driveway.

Della Street came to stand at his side, and Mason could feel her fingers digging into his arm as they stood waiting breathlessly.

The car rattled to a stop.

The motor quit its tin-pan rhythm. The headlights snapped off. After a moment, they heard the car doors open and then bang shut.

"Probably Salty coming back," Della whispered. "Sounds like his car."

"Wait a minute," Mason cautioned in a low voice.

They heard Nell Sims saying, "Now then, Pete Sims, you march right in to that pantry. If you've made my daughter poison Banning Clarke, I'm going to lift the scalp right off your head."

Pete's voice had that pleading, apologetic whine which was so characteristic of him in his moments of explanation. "I tell you, honey, you don't know anything about a man's business. Now this mining business. . . ."

"I know enough to know that when a man gives his wife arsenic to put in the pantry alongside the sugar bowl, he's just crazy."

"But listen, honey, I. . . ."

The sound of the side door of the house opening and shutting swallowed the rest of the conversation.

Mason bent down, shoved the long box back under the heavy growth of a thick clump of spineless cactus. "We've got to see him, Della."

"How do we arrange it?" Della asked.

"Bust right in the side door as big as Life. We've got to make a hit-and-run play. I want to see Sims and get out before the District Attorney arrives on the scene."

They started up the walk which led to the back of the house, and reached the side door. Mason tried it, found it unlocked, and walked in; then, using Della Street's flashlight, went back toward the kitchen.

Lights were on here, and they could hear the sound of voices. They heard Nell Sims says angrily, "Now you look at that bag, Pete Sims. That's been opened and a whole lot of the stuff taken out."

Sims said, "It isn't my fault, Nell. I tell you—"

Mason opened the door, said, "Perhaps you wouldn't mind if *I* asked a few questions."

They turned to face him in surprise, Nell Sims holding a paper bag in her hand.

"Is that the arsenic?" Mason asked.

She nodded.

"Sitting in there next to the sugar container?"

"Well, not right next to it, but pretty close."

"What's that written on it?"

Sims said hastily, "That's something I wrote on there so nobody would make a mistake. You can see for yourself. I printed on here: 'GUARD CAREFULLY. PETE SIMS. PRIVATE.' "

Mason stretched out his hand. "Pete," he said, "I want to ask you a few questions. I—" Abruptly he stopped and frowned down at the printing on the bag.

"I want you to be my lawyer," Pete said. "I'm in awful bad, Mr. Mason and. . . ."

The swinging door abruptly slammed open.

Mason whirled as he heard Della Street's gasp.

Sheriff Greggory was standing in the doorway. For a moment, there was anger on his face. Then he smiled triumphantly.

"And *now*, Mr. Mason," he said, "I am in my own bailiwick, vested with the full authority of the law. The District Attorney is waiting in his office. Either you can come along and make a statement, or I'll hold you in jail, at least until you can get a writ of *habeas corpus*."

Mason hesitated just long enough to make an accurate

appraisal of the determination in Sheriff Greggory's face. Then he turned to Della Street and said quietly, "You can drive the car up to the courthouse, Della. I think the sheriff prefers that I ride with him."

21

District Attorney Topham was a cadaverous man with hollow cheeks, a haunted expression of nervous futility, and restless mannerisms. He fidgeted slightly in the big leather-backed swivel chair behind his office desk, regarded Perry Mason with large lackluster eyes, said in the voice one uses in reciting a memorized speech, "Mr. Mason, there is evidence indicating that you have committed a crime within the limits of this county. Because you are a brother attorney who has achieved a certain prominence within the limits of your profession, I am giving you an opportunity to explain the circumstances before any formal action is taken against you."

"What do you want to know?" Mason asked.

"What have you to say to the charge that you committed larceny of a paper?"

"I took it."

"From the desk of Banning Clarke in his residence in this county?"

"That's right."

"Mr. Mason, surely you must understand the damaging effect of such an admission?"

"*I* don't see anything wrong with it," Mason said. "What's all the commotion about?"

"Surely, Mr. Mason, you understand that, entirely apart from the statute making it a crime to alter or deface an instrument of such a nature, the law provides that an instrument is property; that the taking of such an instrument constitutes larceny; that because the degree of the larceny is determined by the value of the property to be distributed by the instrument—"

"Now listen," Mason interrupted. "I didn't spring this

before because I didn't want to have to produce the will at this time and explain the terms of it; but I'll tell you this: It is my position that this is a genuine will made by Banning Clarke in his handwriting, and dated the day prior to his death. I am named executor of that last will and testament. As such, it was my duty to take that will into my custody. In fact, if any other person had discovered that will—even you yourself—I could have demanded that you turn it over to me as the person named as the executor, or that you turn it over to the clerk of the probate court. Now then, try and find some flaw in the legality of that reasoning."

Topham ran long bony fingers over his high forehead, glanced at the sheriff, twisted his position in the chair which had apparently learned to squeak a protest against the constant fidgeting of its occupant. "You are named as executor?"

"The sheriff's own witness admits that."

"May I see that will?"

"No."

"Why not?"

"I will produce it at the proper time. I believe that under the law, although I haven't looked it up, I have thirty days."

The swivel chair squeaked again, this time a high-pitched drawn out sque-e-e-e-ak. The district attorney faced the sheriff. "If that's the truth, there's nothing we can do about it."

"No matter if he entered the house and surreptitiously removed this from the desk?" the sheriff insisted.

Mason smiled as the chair gave forth a whole series of short, sharp squeaks.

"You see," Topham explained, "if he is executor, then he is entitled to take charge of all the property of the deceased. It was not only his right, but his duty, to go through the effects of the decedent, and I believe that he is absolutely correct in regard to the provision of the

195

law that the will must be surrendered either to the executor or to the county clerk."

"Why didn't you tell me this before?" Greggory demanded of Mason.

"You didn't ask me."

"Well, you weren't dumb, were you?"

Mason said apologetically, "Sometimes when I'm embarrassed, Sheriff, I find myself a little tongue-tied. You'll remember, Sheriff, you have threatened me with drastic action on several occasions. That embarrassed me. I became a little diffident."

The sheriff flushed. "You're not a damn bit diffident now," he said angrily.

Mason smiled at the district attorney. "Because I am not a damned bit embarrassed, Sheriff."

22

Mason found Della Street parked in his automobile in front of the courthouse.

"How did you come out?" she asked anxiously.

"I squeezed out," Mason said, "through the front door, and it was a close squeak."

"The legal wolf is chained?" she asked.

"Not chained—roped. Because the sheriff thought he had a cinch case against me on taking that will, he went after me on that. I made him so mad he forgot all about the stock certificate. But it won't take long for him to start off on that as a new angle of approach. Hang it, at the time endorsing that stock certificate so that Moffgat couldn't trap my client seemed the only logical thing to do. Now it seems a terrible blunder to have made."

"How long a period of grace do you suppose we have, Chief?"

"Half an hour perhaps."

"Then let's start for Salty's camp."

"Not right away," Mason said. "You see, Della, in that half hour we've got to find out who killed Banning Clarke, all about the poison and who was prowling around in the grounds the night Velma heard the drowsy mosquito. When the sheriff finally starts looking for us, we'll be in the one place he'll least expect to find us."

"Banning Clarke's house?" she asked.

Mason nodded.

"Hop in," she said, "and hang on."

Mrs. Sims answered the bell. "Oh, hello," she chirped. "You're back just in time. Long Distance is trying to get you from Castaic. I didn't *think* they'd hold you long."

Mason flashed Della Street a significant glance, entered the house and went at once to the telephone. A few moments later, he heard Paul Drake's voice on the wire. "Hello, Perry. Are you sober?"

"Yes," Mason said shortly.

"All right," Drake said. "Remember, I asked you first. Now listen, Perry, I'm a little foggy, but I think a fish is nibbling at your bait."

"Go ahead."

"Man by the name of Hayward Small, a spindly chap with a gift of gab. Has a way of trying to look right through you. Know him?"

"Yes."

"Is he the fish you want?"

"If he's taking the bait, he is."

"Someone," Drake said, "has leaned on him."

"What do you mean?"

"Against his left eye. It's a beauty."

"A shiner?"

"A mouse, a shanty."

"What's his proposition?"

"Says he knows that the mine I've discovered is on the property of the Come-Back Mining Syndicate, that he has a pull with the company; if I'll take him into partnership on a fifty-fifty basis he'll guarantee to get us a thirty-three percent interest as our share, and I'll cut with him."

"If you accept the proposition, what does he want to do?"

"I don't know, but he's taking me to San Roberto with him if it's a deal. I'm on my road to Los Angeles with Harvey Brady. What do I do?"

"Does he know you're telephoning?"

"Thinks I'm telephoning a girl in Los Angeles. It's a booth in a restaurant. I've ridden this far with him."

"Okay," Mason said. "Accept the proposition and come on down."

"What do I do when he wants the information?"

Mason said, "Tell him you'll draw him a map and give him the exact location when you get to San Roberto."

"And not before?" Drake asked.

"Not unless you want to get poisoned," Mason said and hung up.

Mrs. Sims said, "Mr. Moffgat telephoned. Seems like the company wants to settle that case. He says he can't make a proposition directly to me because it wouldn't be ethical, but he says we can settle."

"Yes," Mason announced, smiling, "I feel quite certain he wants to settle it. Where's your husband?"

"He's in the kitchen."

Mason went out to where Pete Sims was sitting slumped dejectedly in a kitchen chair.

"Oh, it's you," Pete said.

Mason nodded. "I want to talk with you, Pete."

"What about?"

"About Bob."

Pete squirmed. "Bob don't ever cause me nothing but trouble."

Mason said, "Come with me. You haven't seen anything yet. Bring your typewriter and brief case, Della."

And Mason led the worried, sheepish man up the back stairs and into the room Banning Clarke had used in his lifetime.

"Sit down, Pete."

Pete sat down. "What do you want?"

"I want to know something about claim salting."

"What about it? I ain't ever done any, but I know how it's done."

"You load a shotgun shell with little nuggets of gold?" Mason asked. "And then fire it into a ledge of quartz, and . . ."

Pete Sims shuddered.

"What's the matter?" Mason asked.

199

"That's crude, Mr. Mason. You don't do it that way at all."

"How do you do it, Pete?"

"Well, it's what Hayward Small would call a psychological proposition. You've got to make the sucker try to slip something over on *you*."

"I'm afraid I don't understand," Mason said, glancing out of the corner of his eye to make certain Della Street was taking down the questions and answers.

"Well, it's like this, Mr. Mason. People are pretty well educated nowadays. They're getting smart. You try to sell them a gold brick, or try to shoot gold into a ledge of quartz, and chances are like as not they'll have read about it or seen it in a movie somewhere and just give you the horselaugh. In fact, you try to *sell* anybody a mining claim and he gets suspicious right away. If he knows mines, what you tell him don't make any difference, and if he don't know mines, he's suspicious of everything."

Quite obviously, Pete Sims was vastly relieved that Mason was asking for information rather than making direct accusations or demanding explanations. That relief made him talkative.

"I'm afraid I don't understand," Mason said.

"Well, Mr. Mason, you work it this way. You get the sucker all lined up, then you fix it so the sucker is the one that's trying to sell you."

Mason said, "You didn't work it that way with Jim Bradisson, Pete."

Pete shifted his position in the chair. "You don't know that whole story, Mr. Mason."

"What is the story, Pete?"

Pete shook his head doggedly.

"Aren't you going to tell me?"

"I've told you all I know," Pete said, his manner changing from glib friendliness to surly reticence.

"All right, Pete. No offense. Let's go back to discussing

200

generalities. How can you make the sucker try to slip something over on you?"

"There's lots of ways."

"Can you tell me one?"

"I'll give you the basic idea back of the whole thing," Pete said. "You pretend to be the innocent guy and let the sucker be the smart guy. You're just an innocent, ignorant son of the desert, and the city slicker decides you're so dumb it would be a shame to cut you in on any profits."

"I don't see how you could work that, Pete."

Sims once more warmed to his subject. "You've got to be ingenious, Mr. Mason. You've got to do a lot of thinking, and you've got to have imagination. That's why lots of people think I'm lazy. When I'm sitting around doing nothing is when I'm thinking, when I'm ... I guess I'm doin' a lot of talking, Mr. Mason."

"That's all right, Pete. You're among friends," Mason said. "I'm interested in how you can get the city slicker to try to take advantage of you."

"They'll do it every time. You be simple and take them out and show them some property that you want them to buy. You get enthusiastic about that property and show them all the good points. They keep drawing back into their shell. Then about lunch time you take 'em around to some property that you tell 'em belongs to you, or belongs to a friend of yours, and sit down there to eat lunch. Then you make an excuse to wander away and you've planted something that the sucker can find for himself, something that makes it look like the claim is lousy with gold. You get me, Mr. Mason? He finds it while you're gone. When you come back, he never says to you, 'Look, Pete, we've struck it rich right on your own claim.'—I'll tell you the truth, Mr. Mason. I've been salting claims for twenty years and I've never had one of these birds pull that line on me yet."

"How do you get the customer looking around?" Mason asked.

"Shucks, they'll all do it. Tell 'em a claim's rich and they'd ought to buy it, and they take only a halfway interest in it. But take 'em down to some place that looks sort of promising with nice colored rock on it and tell 'em it's no good—and then walk away and leave 'em, and they start prowling. They'll do it every time. That's one thing about a sucker in the desert—he always thinks he knows more than the old-time mining men."

Mason nodded.

"Well," Pete went on, "that's the way it's put across. He begins looking around. You've got some rocks that's so rich the gold is just stuck in them in chunks. You've blasted away a section of rock outcropping and grafted these little pieces of rock into place. If you're good with dynamite and mixing up a little rock cement, there's nothing to it. You can put those pieces in place so they look as though they'd been there since the Year One.

"The sucker sticks the sample of rock in his pocket and when you come back he starts asking you a lot of casual questions about the title to the property, when your option expires, and all that. Then, next thing you know, he's sneaking around behind your back, trying to double-cross you and get the property. Or if you've told him you own it outright, he starts telling you about how this is such a swell place for a desert cabin; he's never been in a place that seemed more restful to him, and all that sort of stuff. Since the thing doesn't amount to so much as a mine, he'd like to buy it for a cabin site—or he says he has a friend who has bad sinus trouble, and he would like to get this place for his friend.

"If *you'd* been the one who discovered the chunk of ore the sucker would have been suspicious. He'd have wanted to call in a couple of mining engineers and had you give him bank references before he'd even listen to you. But when *he* discovers it, and thinks he's slipping one over on you, *he* becomes the salesman and *you're* the customer. That's all there is to it. It's his own baby and he's putting it across."

"A most interesting example of practical and applied psychology," Mason said. "I think, Sims, I can use that in my business."

"Well, Mr. Mason, if that's all you want, I'll be getting back. But that's the secret of the whole business. You've got to get the sucker trying to sell you."

"Just a minute," Mason said. "Before you go, Pete, there's just one more question I want to ask."

Pete sat on the extreme edge of the chair. "Go right ahead, Mr. Mason."

Mason said, "You planted that six-gun on Banning Clarke, didn't you, Pete?"

"Why, *what* do you mean?"

Mason said, "You salted that group of your wife's claims. You sold them to Jim Bradisson. Then, after the corporation commenced its action for fraud, you realized you were in hot water, so you thought you might as well have a second string to your bow. You fixed things so Banning Clarke would think the famous Lost Goler Mine was situated on properties controlled by the Shooting Star Group, didn't you?"

"*Why, Mr. Mason!*" Sims exclaimed reproachfully.

"And in order to do that," Mason went on, "you found this old six-gun somewhere and etched the name Goler on the handle. But what you overlooked, Pete, was the fact that you have a very distinctive method of printing a capital G. And the printing you put on that bag of arsenic —'*GUARD CAREFULLY*'—had the same capital G as was on the handle of the gun."

For a moment, Pete looked Mason squarely in the eyes, then his eyes slithered away. "I don't know what you're talking about," he mumbled.

Mason turned to Della Street, "All right, Della, go

get the sheriff. Tell him to bring up that bag of arsenic. We'll get that gun and compare the printing. . . ."

"No, no, no!" Sims exclaimed. "Don't do that. Now don't go off half-cocked like this, Mr. Mason. Don't bring that sheriff into it again."

Mason grinned. "Make up your mind, Pete."

Sims heaved a long sigh. "Give me a cigarette."

Mason gave him one, and Sims lighted it. All the resistance seemed to have oozed out of him. "All right," he said. "I did it. That's what happened."

"Now tell us about the arsenic," Mason said.

"It's just like I told the sheriff. I got that for. . . ."

"For what?" Mason asked as Sims hesitated.

"Just for experimenting." Sims twisted his position in the chair.

"Perhaps you'd better get the sheriff after all, Della."

Pete might not have heard. He went on as though he had never balked at the question in the first place. "This lost mines business could be quite a racket, Mr. Mason. I realized that when I saw the way Banning Clarke fell for that six-gun business. I'd been a fool—going around salting claims and juggling samples and all of that kind of business. All you've got to do is see that people know about some of these famous lost mines, and then leave just a little clue that will make 'em think they've got hold of a lost mine. You pretend that you don't know a thing in the world about the significance of it or what it is. You get me?"

Mason nodded.

"Now on that Shooting Star claim," Pete went on, "the time I sold it to Jim Bradisson I certainly went at it crude. I'll tell you the truth. I was pretty well plastered at the time, and Jim kept shooting off his mouth about what a big mining executive he was—and he was so damned easy I just didn't take any pains to cover my tracks.

"But when I realized I needed to fix it up so he

204

wouldn't yell he'd been stuck, I tumbled onto this idea of planting a six-shooter and letting Banning Clarke find it and tell Jim. I'd found this old six-shooter out in the desert quite a while back. I simply etched the name Goler on the handle and rubbed wet tea leaves over it until the printing looked good and old. Then I planted it down by a little spring that's on the property, leaving just a few inches of the muzzle sticking up, the rest of it buried in the sand. I got Banning Clarke out there with me. That was before his heart got so bad he couldn't travel at all, but it was bad enough so he had to keep quiet. I told him I wanted to do just a little prospecting around, and I knew he'd go over to the spring and sit down. I'd planted a whole bunch of nuggets in the spring right near the gun. Well, there was nothing to it. As soon as I came back, I saw the gun wasn't there, and Clarke was so excited he could hardly talk. I pretended I didn't notice nothing.

"I thought Clarke, being a stockholder in the company, would see that they didn't make any squawk about the deal I'd handed them, but Clarke got so sold on the idea he'd uncovered the lost Goler Diggings that he actually wanted my wife to get the claims back. He thought she was entitled to them more than the corporation, I guess. Well, there I was, in a devil of a fix, Mr. Mason.

"Later on, I managed to see that Jim Bradisson got tipped off that Clarke had discovered the Lost Goler Diggings. Clarke hadn't been out in the desert for six months before that time he'd been with me. I thought Bradisson would be smart enough to put two and two together and figure the mine must be located on the Shooting Star Group. But Jim wasn't smart at all. He went ahead with the fraud action, and darned if Banning didn't get *you* to fight the lawsuit. By that time, it was all mixed up. I didn't know just what he was doing. I see it now. He was trying to have Nell put up enough

205

fight in the case so that Jim wouldn't get suspicious and decide to hang onto that property.—Now, that's the absolute truth."

"And this arsenic?" Mason asked.

"Well, if you want to know the real low-down, Mr. Mason, I decided to go into this lost mines as a racket. I guess I'm just a miserable, no-good skunk. But don't get me wrong. I ain't reformin' none. I'm scared stiff now, but I know myself well enough to know I'll keep right on being a claim-salter.

"If you was someone else I'd pull an act about being sorry, and make such a swell job of it I'd even convince myself. . . . I used to be a damn good liar, Mr. Mason. That was before I met Hayward Small and he tried to hypnotize me, and told me a lot about these here secondary personalities. I pretended he'd hypnotized me. I don't know but what maybe he did, at that. And then I rung in this secondary personality.

"Well, it just ruined me as a liar, Mr. Mason. It was so easy blaming things on Bob, I got all out of practice on real good lying. It came to me with a shock when that lawyer tied me all up in knots the way he did.

"Believe you me, I ain't going to let anybody do my lying for me from now on. I'm getting rid of Bob, *pronto!* I've got to brush up. You understand?"

"I understand, Pete. But specifically, what did you intend to do with the arsenic?"

"Well, now, this Lost Peg-Leg Mine," Sims said "and a couple of other mines that have been lost out in the desert—the reason they get lost is because the gold is black. It's covered on the outside with some sort of a deposit that turns it black. When you scratch down inside, it's good yellow gold, but the nuggets look like little black rocks. I heard that it was some kind of arsenic compound, and I decided to get this arsenic and experiment with some gold and see if I could get that black coating on it. If I could, I thought I'd trim the next sucker by letting him think he'd discovered the Lost Peg-Leg Mine. That cattleman and his partner who think *they've* discovered the Lost Goler Mine—that cattleman's all swelled up with the idea he can go out and locate lost mines by scientific methods. Well, I was going to let him get the Lost Peg-Leg."

"Did you use this arsenic?" Mason asked.

"No, Mr. Mason, I didn't have to. To tell you the truth, I'd forgotten all about that arsenic. Shortly after I got it I found where there was some of this black gold —not much of it, but enough so I could salt a claim."

Mason said, "You've had some arrangement with Hayward Small."

Sims shifted his position. "Now, Mr. Mason, you're all wet on that. That's one thing you shouldn't say. Hayward Small is just as square a shooter as there is in the world. My wife don't like him because he's kind of shining up to Dorina, but Dorina's got to get married some day and she'll go a long, long ways before she gets a better boy than Hayward Small."

Mason smiled and shook his head. "Remember the sheriff, Pete."

Sims sighed wearily. "Oh, all right. What's the use? Sure, I stood in with Hayward Small, and Small's got some kind of a club he's holding over Jim Bradisson."

"What?"

"I don't know, but I know it's a club. I've been salting claims for Small, and Small's been selling them to the corporation."

"And he was in on this Shooting Star deal?"

"Nope. That was on my own. Understand, I ain't been partners with Small. He's just been paying me so much a job to salt mines for him. He's fooled on that Goler mine, himself."

"Hayward Small knew that you had this arsenic?" Mason asked.

"He knew about it, yes. He was the one who told me

207

not to use it. He said he knew where we could get some of this black gold."

"And did you poison Banning Clarke?" Mason asked.

"Who, me!"

Mason nodded.

"Gosh, no. Get that idea out of your head."

"Or shoot him?"

"Listen, Mr. Mason, Banning Clarke was a square guy. I wouldn't have touched a hair of his head."

"And you haven't any idea who put the poison in that sugar bowl?"

"No, sir, I haven't."

Mason said, "You don't know what hold it is that Small has over Jim Bradisson, do you?"

"No, sir, I don't, but it's a hold all right. You can take it from me, Jim Bradisson is afraid of Hayward Small. It's some sort of blackmail."

"You don't really think Small is a proper person to be Dorina's husband, do you?"

"I'll say he ain't. If I'd been here, he'd never have had the nerve to go to Nevada with her."

"But they didn't get married?"

"The way I get the story," Sims said with a grin, "that soldier boy that's been sort of sweet on Dorina got himself a twenty-four-hour leave and was sort of hanging around Las Vegas—and I guess when the soldier got done with him, Hayward Small decided he wasn't going to marry anybody. He didn't feel like a bridegroom. He's still got quite an eye on him."

Mason said, "Well, I guess that covers it, Pete. Thanks a lot."

Pete got eagerly to his feet. "Mr. Mason, I can't begin to tell you how much it means to me to talk right frank with someone that can really understand. If you've ever got any desert property you want to get rid of at a fancy price—No, you wouldn't have; but if there's ever anything I can do, you just call on me."

When he had gone, Mason grinned over at Della Street.

"We're going to use some of Pete's psychology," he said. "Feed some stationery in your portable typewriter. Put it up on that desk—right under the light."

"How many copies?" Della asked.

"One," Mason said.

"What is it," she asked, "a document for someone to sign, a letter, or. . . ."

"It's a piece of claim salting," Mason announced, "and we're going to let the sucker discover it. Our interview with Pete Sims is going to be highly productive."

Della Street ratcheted the paper into the machine, held her fingers poised over the keyboard.

Mason said, "We'll start this in the middle of a sentence up near the top of the page. Put a page number on it—make it page twenty-two, and then put just below that, *'Transcript of statements made to Sheriff Greggory.'* "

Della Street's fingers rippled the keyboard into a swift staccato of noise. When she paused, Mason said, "Just down below that, write *Continuation of statement of James Bradisson.*—All right, now let's start the top of the page in the middle of a sentence, say, *'that is, to the best of my knowledge and belief.'*—Now then, make a paragraph and put *Question by sheriff: 'Then you are prepared to swear, Mr. Bradisson, that you saw Hayward Small tampering with the sugar bowl?' Answer: 'I did. Yes, sir.'* Paragraph. *Question: 'You not only saw him put the note under the sugar bowl, but you are willing to swear you saw him raise the lid of the sugar bowl?'* Paragraph. *Answer: 'I did. Yes, sir. But I want you to remember that there are certain reasons why I must not be called as a witness until the time of trial. Once you get him before a jury, I'll be the surprise witness that will get a conviction. I can afford to go on the stand when you've already made a case against him, but you'll have to make up a case against him based on other testimony than mine.'* Paragraph. *Statement by Sheriff Greggory: 'I understand that, Mr. Bradisson. I've told you that we would try to respect your confidence. However, I can't promise definitely. Now, about the arsenic. You say that Pete Sims had told him about having a supply of arsenic on hand?' Answer: 'That's right. Sims wanted to use it in connection with some gold treatment, but Small told him not to use it, that he could get some of the black gold Sims wanted elsewhere.' Paragraph. Question: 'Who told you that?' Paragraph. Answer: 'Sims.' Paragraph. Question: 'Hayward Small never confirmed that?' Paragraph. Answer: 'Not in so many words, no.'*

"Getting down to the end of the page?" Mason asked Della Street.

"Right at the end," she said.

"All right," Mason said. "Leave that in the typewriter. Leave the light on. Take your brief case with you. Now, wait a minute. We'll want to plant some cigarette stubs around here as though the room had been used for a conference. Tear some cigarettes in two. We'll light them and leave stubs around.

"It's touch-and-go, Della. If the sheriff ever thinks to question Dorina about whether she knows anything about the signing of the endorsement on that stock certificate, the fat's in the fire."

Della Street looked at him curiously. *"Did* Hayward Small poison the sugar?" she asked.

Mason smiled. "Ask Mrs. Sims what the proverb is about the goose that lays the golden eggs coming home to roost."

"Then why are you putting that in the written statement?"

Mason's face was suddenly serious. "To the best of my ability," he said, "I am carrying out the wishes of a dead client."

210

23

Sheriff Greggory plunged ahead with his midnight investigation with the bulldog tenacity of a man who has both rugged health and stubborn determination. District Attorney Topham, on the other hand, plainly felt that the matter could well have waited until Monday morning. He hadn't the physical stamina to waste energy arguing the matter, however, and showed his disapproval only by the passive resignation of his countenance and the manner in which he kept himself in the psychological background.

Sheriff Greggory looked at his watch. "It shouldn't be long, now," he said. "I'm going to get at the bottom of certain phases of this matter before leaving here."

Mason stretched his hands high above his head. He yawned, smiled at the District Attorney, and said, "Personally, I see no reason for such nocturnal haste."

The District Attorney lowered and raised his eyelids with slow deliberation. "I think we should place a limit on it."

"The limit," Greggory said, "will be when we find out what's been going on around here. There's evidence that the signature on those stock certificates is *not* the signature of Banning Clarke." He glowered at Mason.

Once more Mason yawned. "If you ask me," he said, "the place fairly reeks with mysteries. If Banning Clarke was dying with poison and had only a few gasps left in his system, why did someone have to hurry it along with a .38 caliber automatic? What could Clarke have done with those last few breaths that would have been so devastating to the one who fired the shot?

"And what are you going to do if you *do* find the

211

poisoner? He'll claim the murderer was the man who fired the gun. And how about that person? He'll claim the victim was suffering from a fatal dose of poison. On the whole, gentlemen, you have a tough nut to crack."

The chimes at the front door tinkled into noise.

"I'll open it," Mason said.

Greggory pushed past him, jerked the door back.

An inebriated Paul Drake elevated a long forefinger, then brought it down on a level with the surprised sheriff's coat lapel.

"Never jerk a door open like that," Paul reproached. "If your guests should fall in, flat on their faces, they could bring suit."

"Who are you?" the sheriff demanded. "Oh yes—I know now. You're the man who found the mine."

" 'Discovered' is a better word, Sheriff. Finding implies an element of luck. Discovery denotes planning and—"

"Oh, there's Small. Come on in, Small. I want to question you."

Small extended his hand. "How are you, Sheriff? I hardly expected to find you here. How are you?" he greeted. "And Mr. Mason. Good evening, Mr. Mason. I brought a friend with me."

Sheriff Greggory said, "Small, I want you to answer this question fairly and frankly. Do you know anything about the endorsement on the shares of stock that—"

"Just a moment," Mason interrupted. "I am going to suggest that any statements from any of these witnesses be made where the answers can be taken down in shorthand. You've asked other witnesses various questions in a manner that I don't think was fair."

"You don't have anything to say about *my* questions," Greggory interrupted angrily. "I am conducting this investigation."

"Go right ahead, if you feel that way about it," Mason retorted.

Paul Drake said, "But not in a drafty hallway, please."

"What are *you* doing here?" Greggory asked.

"Waiting for a drink," Paul told him. "The hospitality with which you greeted me, all but jerking the door off its hinges, seems a most favorable omen. But I find your attitude, my dear sir, sadly at variance with the initial cordiality with which you answered the bell."

"Get this drunk out of here," Greggory ordered.

"On the contrary," Mason announced. "This man has come to talk with me on a business proposition—a matter which relates to the estate of Banning Clarke, deceased. And as the executor of Banning Clarke, I have the right. . . ."

"You come with me," Greggory said to the reluctant Hayward Small.

Mason handed Hayward Small a key. "Go on up to Banning Clarke's room," he said. "You and the District Attorney can conduct your investigation up there."

"Very good," Greggory grunted.

They were halfway up the stairs when Mason called, "Oh, Sheriff."

"What?"

"There's one thing I think you should know before you proceed with that questioning."

"What is it?"

"Something that—May I speak with you and the District Attorney for a moment, please?"

Greggory hesitated. Mason started up the stairs, said, "Go right on up to Banning Clarke's room, Small. I just want a word with the sheriff."

Small went on up the stairs. Mason climbed to Sheriff Greggory's side. "Look here, Sheriff," he said in a low voice, "there's no need for us to get at loggerheads over this. If you'll calm down a bit, you'll see that I'm working toward the same end that you are. I want to solve this murder case."

The District Attorney said, "Gentlemen, can't we get

it over with without so much friction? After all, it seems to me that all we can hope to do now is to get preliminary statements and then adjourn."

"I want to warn you," Mason said, "that you'd better have your interview with Hayward Small reduced to writing; otherwise, you'll regret it."

"I haven't a court reporter here," Greggory said. "This is merely a preliminary."

"My secretary can take it."

The sheriff's smile was skeptical.

"That's better than nothing," Mason said.

The sheriff turned angrily away. "I think not," he said. "I am beginning now to sympathize with my brother-in-law."

"Well," Mason announced, "anything that *I* say will be taken down by my secretary."

"I don't give a damn what *you* say," Greggory told him.

"Can't we keep the questioning on a more dignified plane?" Topham protested wearily.

"Come on," Greggory said, and started up the stairs.

Mason, descending the stairs, grinned at Della Street. "Now," he announced, "we'll find out whether Pete's psychology actually works in practice."

Drake said, "Perry, I'm comparatively sober. The long ride in the cool of the night has brushed cobwebs from my brain, but it has also given me something of a chill. Wouldn't it be possible for you to scare me up a drink?"

"No drink," Mason told him. "You're going to need to have your wits about you."

Drake sighed. "Well, there was no harm in trying."

"Come on," Mason said in a low voice. "Give me the low-down. What have you found out?"

"I assume," Drake said with alcoholic verbosity, "that you wished me to pump the gentleman who accompanied me from Mojave—to turn him inside out, as it were."

"I did."

214

"Your wishes have been followed to the letter."

"What did you find out?"

"Small has some hold over Bradisson."

"How long has he had this hold?"

"That," Drake admitted, "is something that also occurred to me. I realized that one could hardly expect the man to tell me the nature of his strangle hold on Bradisson, but that there might be other and more devious ways of getting the information. I therefore endeavored to ascertain the exact date when Small first became acquainted with Bradisson. Now, Small only met Bradisson in January of nineteen forty-two, and almost immediately moved right into the charmed circle."

"January of nineteen forty-two, eh?" Mason said musingly.

"That's right. He—"

A door opened explosively in the upper corridor. Pounding feet came toward the head of the stairs.

"Sounds like our impulsive sheriff," Drake observed.

Greggory shouted, "Mason, come up here!"

"The summons is a bit peremptory," Drake observed. "I'm afraid, Perry, you've been doing it again."

Mason nodded to Della Street, then halfway up the stairs said, "You'd better come along, Paul. I may want a witness."

"Your assignments," Drake said, "range from the sublime to the ridiculous. How in hell can I climb stairs?"

As Mason entered the room, Greggory indignantly pointed at the typewriter. "What the devil is this?" he demanded.

"Why," Mason said, "the notes of the investigation you made. . . ."

"But I made no such investigation."

Mason looked nonplused. "I'm afraid I don't understand, Sheriff. Della Street certainly took down. . . ."

Greggory's face purpled. "Damn it, don't try to pull that innocent stuff with me. You've interfered in this case too damn much. I'm conducting this investigation, and I'll conduct it in my own way."

"Yes, Sheriff. Certainly."

"The idea of leaving that sheet of paper there in the typewriter. What are you trying to do?"

Mason turned to Della Street reproachfully. "Della, I thought the sheriff told you to get all of those papers cleaned out of this room and then lock it."

Della's eyelashes lowered demurely on her cheeks. "I'm sorry."

Topham glanced from Mason to the sheriff. There was quiet reproach in his eyes.

Mason said, "I'm sorry, Sheriff," as one apologizing for a justifiable oversight.

The sheriff's anger made him all but inarticulate. "I tell you I didn't conduct any investigation here. I merely had an informal inquiry before you got here, Topham."

"Yes, of course," Mason agreed hastily—too hastily, in fact. "You wouldn't want to investigate without Mr. Topham."

Hayward Small's restless eyes moved from face to face, missing no flicker of expression, taking in every word that was said.

Mason nudged Della Street quite obviously.

Della said hastily, "That's right, Mr. Topham. There wasn't any investigation. I'm sorry."

Mason ripped the page out of the typewriter, said to Small, "It's a mistake. We're sorry, Sheriff."

Greggory glared at Mason. "You'll pay for this. You'll . . . ."

"But I told you I was sorry. My secretary shouldn't have left it here. We've apologized. We've told Small that there wasn't any investigation. We've told Topham that. We've all agreed on it. *You* say there wasn't any, and *we* say there wasn't any. Now, what more do you want? The more you say now, the more suspicious you make your witness."

216

For the moment, Greggory was at a loss for words.

Mason went on smoothly enough, "And, frankly, I don't see any reason why you should adopt this attitude. Ever since January of nineteen forty-two, Hayward Small has been blackmailing Bradisson. Of course, that gives Bradisson a motive to pin the murder on Small; but if you ask *me,* Sheriff, I think Bradisson is—"

"No one's asking you," the sheriff interrupted.

Mason bowed after the manner of one who is rebuked by a person in authority. Thereafter, he became conspicuously silent.

Greggory turned to Hayward Small. "What I'm trying to find out," he said, "is about that stock."

Small moistened his lips with his tongue, merely nodded.

"What about it?" Greggory asked.

"All I know is what Dorina told me."

"Well, what was that?"

Mason said reproachfully, "Hearsay testimony. I wouldn't repeat it, Small. You can't vouch for it, you know."

"You keep out of this," Greggory shouted.

"After he gets that out of you, he'll start giving you a third-degree on the murder charge, you know," Mason observed. "How about a cigarette—anyone want a cigarette?"

He calmly took his cigarette case from his pocket.

"Thank you, I'll take one," Della Street said sweetly.

Greggory said angrily, "Get out of here. Clear out!"

"But I thought you wanted me," Mason said.

"I wanted an explanation of this. . . ."

"Oh, yes. Do you want to go into that again?"

"No, I don't."

Hayward Small, who had been doing more thinking, said suddenly, "Look here, I'm going to come clean on this thing. I had absolutely nothing to do with that poisoning. I did—well, I did bring a little pressure to bear on Jim Bradisson about eighteen months ago."

"January, nineteen forty-two, wasn't it?" Mason asked.

"That's right."

"Very shortly after Mrs. Banning Clarke passed away, I believe."

Small said nothing.

"And Moffgat began exerting a little pressure at about the same time," Mason said.

"I'm not interested in any of this," Greggory announced.

"I am," Topham said, his voice packing quiet authority. "Just let Mr. Mason continue, please, Sheriff."

Greggory said angrily, "He's stage-managed this whole damn business. He's trying to cover up the forgery of a stock certificate and save his own neck by—"

"Nevertheless," Topham interrupted in a quiet tone which cut through the sheriff's anger with the force of a cold rebuke, "I want Mr. Mason left entirely alone. Go right ahead, Mr. Mason."

Mason bowed. "Thank you." He turned to Small. "About the time Mrs. Banning Clarke died, wasn't it?"

Small's eyes met Mason's for a moment, then shifted. "Well . . . yes."

"Now," Mason went on, "we have a very interesting situation. We have Mrs. Bradisson tiptoeing into Banning Clarke's room and substituting an old will in place of the new one. A very adroit method of validating a spurious document. A will, of course, is revoked by a later will where the testator's intention to revoke is plainly evidenced by the later will; but unless the earlier will is destroyed, there is nothing on its face to show that it has been superseded—a point which, ordinarily, a layman wouldn't figure out. Such an ingenious bomb-proof little scheme would be far more apt to have been hatched in the mind of some clever attorney. I can't help wondering whether Mrs. Bradisson's idea of exchanging wills didn't date back to an earlier episode. You wouldn't know anything about that, would you, Small?"

218

Hayward Small raised his hand to the collar of his shirt, twitched it as though the neckband were exerting unusual pressure. "No."

Sheriff Greggory started to say something. Topham motioned him to silence.

Mason said, almost musingly, "You see, gentlemen, we are confronted with a poisoning and with a shooting—two entirely different crimes. Yet we must not overlook the fact that they may have been actuated by the same motive. Two different murderers, each pursuing his way independent of the other because he didn't dare to take the other into his confidence—one using poison, the other using lead.

"Because of the peculiar circumstances, we are forced to think back over everything that happened, interpreting each clue, and making pure deduction give us the answer we want.

"Now, I submit, gentlemen, here was Hayward Small, a friend and acquaintance of Moffgat, the lawyer, a virtual stranger to James Bradisson, and to his mother, Mrs. Bradisson. In the early part of January, nineteen hundred and forty-two, Mrs. Banning Clarke dies. A will is offered for probate leaving all of her property to her mother and her brother, and intimating that it is no great amount of property. Almost immediately afterwards, Moffgat and Hayward become very favored personages. The lawyer becomes a stockholder in the company. Hayward Small becomes a mining broker, though he has never sold any mines before. Now, however, he sells mines right and left—and sells them all at fancy prices to the corporation which now consists largely of Mrs. Bradisson and her son James. What's the answer?"

"You're crazy," Hayward Small said. "I don't know what you're getting at, but you're all wet."

"Could it possibly be," Mason said, "that Small was one of the witnesses to a will made at a later date, and

219

that—with the connivance of all parties concerned—this will was suppressed?"

"You're making a grave charge," Greggory blurted.

"Certainly I am," Mason said, eyeing him coldly. "Perhaps, Sheriff, you have some other logical explanation of what happened."

"That's a lie," Small said. "Nothing like that happened."

"And," Mason went on, turning to the District Attorney, "that, Mr. District Attorney, would account for Bradisson's anxiety to see that the crime was pinned on Hayward Small. It would account for the testimony given by Bradisson and his mother that is so damaging to this witness. *If* he had been blackmailing them, and *if* they could get him convicted of murder, without appearing to do so, it would—"

"But," the sheriff all but shouted at the District Attorney, "there wasn't any such investigation. Bradisson never made any such statement."

Topham turned reproachful eyes on the sheriff. It was quite apparent that he didn't believe him either.

"Call Bradisson in. Ask him," the sheriff interpolated angrily.

Mason's patronizing, superior smile disposed of that suggestion without words.

Small blurted abruptly, "Listen, I'm not going to be framed with any murder rap. If Jim Bradisson is trying to push off anything on me, I'll . . ."

"You'll what?" Mason asked as Small became abruptly silent.

"I won't stand for it, that's all."

Mason said, "Don't worry, Small. You don't stand a chance. The sheriff in this county is one of the old-fashioned type who believes in acting on secret tips, on keeping his witnesses in the background. You've seen the extent to which he's gone to convince you that Bradisson didn't do anything of the sort. You won't ever see

220

Bradisson's hand in the matter until after you're stand-ing up in front of the judge to hear the death sen-tence."

Greggory said, "I'm not going to stand for—"

"Please!" Topham interrupted.

Greggory checked himself under the domination of the District Attorney's tired eyes.

"Now," Mason went on, "personally I'd be very much inclined to doubt Bradisson's statement. It doesn't sound logical to me. I see no reason why Hayward Small should have put arsenic in the sugar bowl. On the other hand, there are plenty of reasons why Bradisson should have put the poison in the sugar. Look at the evidence impar-tially, gentlemen. Bradisson and his mother apparently developed symptoms of arsenic poisoning. It turns out that this poisoning was self-induced, caused by taking ipecac. Need we look far for a reason? They intended that on the next night Hayward Small should die of arsenic poisoning. Then you'd have a baffling mystery in which the real poi-soners would never be suspected because they themselves had apparently been first on the list of victims. A person who is blackmailing doesn't want to kill the goose that lays the golden eggs, but the person who is being black-mailed always wants to kill the blackmailer."

Topham glanced speculatively at Small, almost imper-ceptibly nodded his head.

Small said, "You're making all this up. You're just talking."

"But," Mason went on, "the scheme went astray be-cause that night Hayward Small didn't go over and help himself to his usual evening cup of tea. The reason he didn't was that he was planning to run away with Mrs. Sims' daughter, and he knew that Mrs. Sims didn't ap-prove of him. He was somewhat afraid of her uncanny intuitive powers, her sharp tongue, and her shrewd eyes. So he kept on the outskirts, leaving Dorina to put the note under the sugar bowl. That upset Bradisson's plans.

"Now, we can almost determine the exact time when that arsenic was placed in the sugar. It was placed in there *after* Della Street, Banning Clarke, Mrs. Sims and I had had our first cups of tea, because Mrs. Sims poured herself a *fourth* cup of tea, was the *fourth* to take sugar from the bowl—And she felt no ill effects. Then the persons who had been at that stockholders' meeting entered the room. There was, of course, a certain amount of confusion with people passing back and forth around the table. *Then* Banning Clarke had a second cup of tea and put sugar in it. At that time he got the largest dose of poison, showing that the arsenic was at that time on top of the sugar, so that he got nearly all of it. . . . Then, Della Street and I had a second cup, had sugar, and received a relatively small amount of arsenic. Now then, gentlemen, I submit that Bradisson was trying to poison Hayward Small, counting on Small's habit of usually having a cup of tea when he entered the kitchen. Failing in his attempt at poison, Bradisson now tries to accomplish his end by making a highly confidential statement to the sheriff that he knows Hayward Small is guilty, and if the sheriff will get Small to trial on other evidence, Bradisson will be the surprise witness who sends him to the death cell."

Mason stopped talking, apparently centering his attention entirely on the District Attorney, paying no more attention to Hayward Small than if Small had been a mere casual spectator.

"How does that sound, Mr. District Attorney?"

"It sounds very, *very* logical," the District Attorney said.

Small blurted out, "The lawyer's right. Damn Jim Bradisson for a double-crossing back-stabber. I should have known he'd try something like that. All right, damn him. Now *I'll* do a little talking, and *I'll* tell the truth."

"That," Mason said, "is very much better."

Small said, "I knew Moffgat, used to hang around his office a bit. I dug up a little business for him. Nothing

222

like an ambulance chaser, you understand, but just a friend of his who brought in business, and he did favors for me. I happened to be in his office one Friday morning. I'll never forget the date—the fifth of December, nineteen hundred and forty-one. The reason I'll never forget is that we all know what happened on December seventh. Well, I was waiting in the outer office to see Moffgat. Mrs. Banning Clarke was in the office with him. I'd never met her. Moffgat opened the door of the private office and looked out to see who was in the outer office. He saw me sitting there and asked if I'd mind stepping in and acting as witness to a will."

"And you did so?"

"Yes."

"And what happened subsequently?"

"You know."

"You don't know what was in that will?"

"No. I only know that along in January I read about Mrs. Clarke's dying and about a will's being offered for probate. I asked Moffgat if I didn't have to testify as a witness to that will, and he acted so strangely about it I began to do a little thinking. I went and looked up the records. Well, it didn't take me long to figure out what had happened when I saw that they were probating a will dated a year or so earlier and signed before two other witnesses.—I just climbed aboard the gravy train, that's all. Nothing crude, you understand, but I made myself a broker of mining properties. Then I called on Bradisson, mentioned casually that I had known his sister, that I'd been a witness to a will she'd made very shortly before she died. That was all I needed to say. After that, when I suggested that the mining company should buy one of my properties at the price I put on it, the money was forthcoming. I didn't run a willing horse to death, you understand, but I saw to it that my business was reasonably profitable."

"Now," Mason said to the District Attorney, "if we

223

could locate the *other* witness to that will, we might find out something about Banning Clarke's murder."

Small said, "The other witness was named Craiglaw. He was waiting in the office at the same time I was. We happened to strike up an acquaintance. That's all I know about him—that his name was Craiglaw, and that he was a man about fifty-four or fifty-five years old."

Mason said to the District Attorney, "There is one phase of this matter that has never been explained. When Banning Clarke left the room immediately after drinking the poisoned cup of tea, Moffgat was trying to get me to stipulate to taking his deposition. Moffgat had a subpoena all ready to serve on him, and Moffgat said that he was going to serve that subpoena. It would have been logical for Moffgat to try to do so; yet apparently he made no such attempt. That would seem to indicate that he had other plans.

"At the time, I was just a little stupid. I underestimated Moffgat's intelligence. I thought that he was dumb enough to let a witness he wanted slip through his fingers. But Moffgat wasn't dumb—he was shrewd enough to know that if he flashed this subpoena on me, I would signal Banning Clarke to get out of the way. Then, Moffgat would have had an excellent excuse to go out in the cactus gardens to try and serve his subpoena. If he had been caught there, he could simply have said, 'Why, I'm here trying to serve this subpoena.' But if he *wasn't* caught there, if no one saw him enter, if he found Banning Clarke lying asleep on the sand, then he needed only to squeeze the trigger on an automatic and get off the premises. I notice that the sheriff checked on where everyone was at the time. Dr. Kenward was wounded, but he didn't check on Moffgat. Moffgat had announced he was driving back to Los Angeles, and for some reason, Sheriff Greggory took that entirely at its face value.

"A short time ago Moffgat was trying very hard indeed to have the sale of the Shooting Star Group rescinded on the ground of fraud. More lately, he's been talking about settling the case and keeping the claims. There's just a chance that Moffgat spied on Banning Clarke when he was working on his wall. Or Moffgat may possibly have manipulated a beam of invisible light from a machine of his own. And if you turn a beam of invisible light on the lower part of that rock wall you'll see what I mean—the low portion where even a man with heart trouble could manipulate the little rocks around.

"Evidently Banning Clarke was beginning to suspect something about what Moffgat had done, something of the true nature of Small's hold over Bradisson. I wouldn't doubt that Banning Clarke had some rather damaging bit of evidence which he was keeping in his desk. I do know that evidence had been tampered with. *I* found only a small phial and a dying mosquito. If Clarke had put that mosquito in the little bottle at the time he made the will, the insect would have been dead before I ever saw it.

"You know, Sheriff, if I were you, and if *I* had a brother-in-law in Los Angeles who is as clever and adroit as Lieutenant Tragg, I think I'd ring him up and suggest it would be a feather in both of your caps to apprehend Moffgat on a charge of first-degree murder, and whisk him out of Los Angeles County and up to San Roberto before he had a chance to start using any *habeas corpus* or taking steps to bring pressure to bear on the witnesses."

■ 24 ■

Afternoon shadows were collecting in purple pools on the desert floor far below when Mason and Della Street drove around the last turn in the grade, to roll out on the plateau where Salty had his camp.

Salty Bowers came ambling over toward the car as Mason brought it to a stop. There was hostility and suspicion in his manner until he recognized the car. Then he slouched into friendliness.

Mason and Della Street clambered out and stretched travel-stiffened limbs.

"Brought you some news," Mason said. "And then we're going to stay up here for a day or two and get some of the so-called civilization purified out of our minds. Your murder is all solved."

"Who did it?"

"Sheriff Greggory and Lieutenant Tragg working in Los Angeles."

"No. I mean who did the murder?"

"Oh— Moffgat killed Banning Clarke. He took a shot at Dr. Kenward first, thinking he was shooting at the sleeping figure of Banning Clarke. After he found out his mistake, he learned about your departure in the house trailer and started looking for you. He probably would never have found you if it hadn't been that, just by chance, you drove under a street light a couple of blocks in front of him. Banning Clarke had been poisoned and you were looking for medical attention. When you went in to telephone the hospital, Moffgat simply opened the door of the house trailer, walked in, pulled the trigger, and walked out. It was that simple and that fast."

"*Why* did he do it?" Salty asked.

226

"That," Mason said, "is the part of it that has a direct bearing on you."

Salty raised his eyebrows.

"Mrs. Banning Clarke made a will in December of nineteen forty-one. She died in January of nineteen forty-two. Hayward Small was a witness to the new will. The other witness was a man by the name of Craiglaw. The Bradissons bribed Moffgat to say nothing about the latter will and to offer the earlier one for probate. That earlier will had been made before Banning Clarke gave his wife the stock in the mine. At that time, she didn't have a great deal of property in her own name, so she left it all to her mother and brother, share and share alike."

"But why kill Banning Clarke?" Salty asked.

"Because Banning Clarke had uncovered a clue. In going through some of his wife's papers he found a diary, and under date of December fifth there was an entry in the diary: *'Went to Los Angeles—witnesses, Rupert Craiglaw and Hayward Small.'* That clue in the diary was all that Banning Clarke had to work on. You remember that he told me he was going to want me in connection with another matter. His pooling agreement and getting me to represent Mrs. Sims in that fraud suit were just excuses to give him an opportunity to size me up. He'd been double-crossed by one lawyer. He didn't want to repeat the experience.

"After the shooting, and the poisoning of the Bradissons, Clarke thought his life might be in danger. He wasn't quite ready to confide in me as yet, but, in the event something happened to him, he wanted me to go ahead and see that justice was done. You must remember that he knew the seriousness of his heart condition, and had to plan every move with the constant thought in mind that he might die at any minute."

Salty fished a plug of tobacco from his pocket, bit off a corner and rolled it over into his cheek.

"Moffgat came out to the house after he had killed Clarke. The Bradissons weren't there. Della and I were lying asleep, under the influence of drugs. Velma Starler was engaged in waiting on Dr. Kenward, who had, of course, been wounded by Moffgat when he shot him.

"Moffgat looked through Clarke's desk. He would have destroyed Clarke's will if it hadn't been that he was afraid Clarke might have told me about it, and—if so—that when the will couldn't be found I'd become suspicious of what had really happened. But Clarke had mentioned in his will that the clue he was leaving me was contained in a certain drawer of his desk; it was where he had left his wife's diary. But Moffgat, with diabolical ingenuity—knowing that I would be looking for some clue, and remembering what Velma had said about the drowsy mosquito, and because Clarke had also mentioned that in his will—emptied some gold out of a little phial, caught a mosquito, put it in the phial, and left it there for me.—The noise of the drowsy mosquito, of course, was the noise made by one of those black-light machines as Moffgat either surreptitiously deciphered the message Banning Clarke had left in the stone wall, or spied on Clarke when Clarke was putting the finishing touches to the fluorescent diagram he left there.

"Clarke's will left everything to you, Salty. The mining stock that was placed in my name, I am of course holding as trustee for you, although I didn't dare admit it earlier. The estate not only includes that, but also all of the other property which was fraudulently distributed to the Bradissons."

Salty said nothing for several seconds. His tongue rolled the moist bit of tobacco from one cheek over to the other. "How did *you* find out all of this?" he asked.

"Lieutenant Tragg arrested Moffgat in Los Angeles, found Mrs. Clarke's diary in his pocket. I instantly decided that this was the real clue Banning Clarke had left in his desk drawer. We managed to locate Rupert

Craiglaw, got him on long-distance telephone, learned that he remembered the occasion of having witnessed the will. We also tricked Hayward Small and Bradisson into making recriminations. That cracked the case, and Moffgat finally made a complete confession.

"Bradisson got tired of being blackmailed, and he also wanted Clarke out of the way. He planted arsenic in the saltcellar used by himself and his mother, then got some ipecac. He and his mother took it, pretended to have exactly the symptoms they would have had if they'd taken the arsenic. That was just window-dressing to divert suspicion from themselves over what was due to happen twenty-four hours later, when they opened Pete's bag of arsenic, took out some and waited for an opportunity to plant it where Small would get it. Right after the directors' meeting, they saw their chance. They saw Dorina put a note under the sugar bowl, and knew that Hayward Small usually had a cup of tea in the evening, taking sugar in it. When Jim saw Small looking at the teapot, he introduced the arsenic into the sugar. His mother was standing so as to partially shield what he was doing. But Small, for reasons of his own, didn't take tea that night, and Jim couldn't say anything without giving himself away."

"The dirty rats," Salty said. "If Banning had only told me about that evidence. . . . Oh, well, we can't change things now."

"That's right. It's finished now. There are a few more incidental angles," Mason told him, "but those are the main points."

"Never mind the incidental angles," Salty said. "I reckon you're pretty well fed up with murder stuff, and so am I. Suppose you and Miss Street come over to the camp and we'll fix up a little chow. Lucille's coming up tonight and we're going in to town on a marrying party tomorrow. I thought for a while we'd put it off on account of Banning's death; but I know how Banning would

229

feel about it—he'd want us to go ahead. So we decided we'd make it a foursome."

"A foursome?" Mason asked.

Salty twisted the small piece of tobacco back to the other side of his mouth, nodded. "Dr. Kenward and the nurse decided they were going to Las Vegas and get spliced, and I thought Lucille and I would go along. Well, I'll be getting the food together. We'll have a little banquet tonight. Expect Lucille up almost any time."

Salty turned abruptly away, walked over to the blackened stone fireplace, and got a fire going.

Mason turned to Della Street. "Know something?"

"What?"

"I bet the preacher would make a reduced rate on marrying three couples instead of two."

She looked up at him with wistful tenderness. "Forget it, Chief."

"Why?"

Her eyes looked out over the long reaches of desert that stretched out far below. "We're happy now," she said. "You can't tell what marriage would do to us. We'd have a home. I'd be a housekeeper. You'd need a new secretary. . . . You don't want a home. I don't want you to have a new secretary. Right now you're tired. You've been matching wits with a murderer. You feel as though you'd like to marry and settle down. Day after tomorrow you'll be looking for a new case where you can go like mad, skin through by a thousandth of an inch. That's the way you want to be, and that's the way I want you. You'd never settle down and I don't want you to. And besides, Salty couldn't leave the camp all alone tomorrow."

Mason moved to her side, slipped his arm around her shoulders, held her close to him. "I could argue with you about all that," he said softly.

She laughed up at him. "You could argue all right,

but even if you could convince *me,* you couldn't convince *you.* You *know* I'm right."

Mason started to say something, then checked himself, tightened the pressure of his arm. They stood in silence, looking out at the desert where varicolored peaks thrust up into the red sunlight.

"And," Della said, laughing, "we're hardened campaigners who can't waste time with romance when there's work to be done. Salty needs help with that fire, and perhaps he'll let me do some of the cooking."

"Ten to one he won't," Mason said.

"What?"

"Let you help with the cooking."

"No takers. Come on. You don't see Salty wasting time with desert scenery when there's work to be done."

They walked over to where Salty was bending over the fireplace, saw him straighten up, saw him turn toward the boxes of provisions, then pause to stand looking out over the desert.

As they joined him, Salty said almost reverently, "No matter what I'm doing, I always knock off for a few minutes along about this time of day just to look out over the desert—makes you realize man may be pretty active, but he ain't so darn big. You know, folks, the desert is the kindest mother a man ever had, because she's so cruel. Cruelty makes you careful and self-reliant, and that's what the desert wants. She don't want any softies hanging around. Sometimes, when she's blistering hot and the light burns your eyes out, you see only the cruelty. But then, along about this time of day, she smiles back at you and tells you her cruelty is really kindness, and you can see it from her viewpoint—and it's the right viewpoint."

The Case of
the Empty Tin

CAST OF CHARACTERS

■ 1 ■

Mrs. Arthur Gentrie managed her household with that meticulous attention to detail which marks any good executive. Her mind was an encyclopedic storehouse of various household data. Seemingly without any mental effort, she knew when the holes which showed up in Junior's socks were sufficiently premature to indicate a poor quality in the yarn. When her husband had to travel on business, she knew just which of his shirts had already been sent to the laundry, and could, therefore, be packed in his grip. His other shirts were scrupulously hand-laundered at home.

In her forties, Mrs. Gentrie prided herself on the fact that she "didn't have a nerve in her body." She neither ate so much that she bulged with fat, nor had she ever starved herself so as to become neurotic. Her hips weren't what they had been twenty years ago, but she accepted that with the calm philosophy of a realist. After all, a person couldn't keep house for a husband, three children, an old-maid sister-in-law, rent out a room, keep household expenses down, and still retain the slim silhouette of a bride. As Mrs. Gentrie herself expressed it, she was "strong as an ox."

Her husband's sister wasn't much help. Rebecca obviously was not a bachelor woman, nor could she be described as an "unmarried relative." She was very definitely and decidedly an old-fashioned maiden lady, a thin, tea-drinking, cat-loving, gossip-spreading, talkative, critical, yet withal a good-looking old maid.

Mrs. Gentrie didn't rely on Rebecca for much help around the house. She was too slight physically to be of assistance with the work, and too scatterbrained to help

1

with responsibilities. She had, moreover, frequent spells of "ailing," during which there seemed to be nothing particularly wrong save a psychic maladjustment seeking a physical manifestation.

Rebecca did, however, keep the room which Mrs. Gentrie rented in order. At present this room was occupied by a Mr. Delman Steele, an architect. Rebecca had two hobbies to which she gave herself with that enthusiasm which characterizes one whose emotions are otherwise repressed. She was an ardent crossword-puzzle fan and an amateur photographer. A darkroom in the basement was equipped with printers, enlargers, and developing tanks, most of which had been built by Arthur Gentrie, who had a distinct flair for tinkering and loved to indulge the whims of his sister.

There were times when Mrs. Gentrie bitterly resented Rebecca, although she tried to fight against that resentment and always managed to keep from showing it. For one thing, Rebecca didn't get along well with the children. In place of sympathizing with their youthful indiscretions, Rebecca sought to hold them to the standards by which one would judge a grown-up. This, coupled with the fact that she had an uncanny ability to mimic voices and enjoyed nothing better than watching the children squirm while she re-enacted some bit of their conversation over the telephone, introduced a certain element of friction into the household which Mrs. Gentrie found highly annoying.

Nor would Rebecca, who did excellent photographic work, ever take the trouble to get good pictures of the children.

On Junior's nineteenth birthday, she had condescended to take a picture at Mrs. Gentrie's urgent request. The ordeal had been as distasteful to Junior as it had been to Rebecca, and Junior's picture showed it, which would have been bad enough, had it not happened that Rebecca, who was experimenting with some of the new photo-

2

graphic wrinkles, had made an enlargement on a sheet of paper which had been held on an angle. The result had been a picture which was similar to the distorted reflections shown in the curved mirrors of penny arcades.

There was nothing slow about Rebecca's mental processes when dealing with anything that interested her. Nothing ever went on around the house which she didn't ferret out. Her curiosity was insatiable, and the manner in which she ferreted out secrets from an inadvertent remark or some casual clue would have done credit to a really good detective. Mrs. Gentrie knew that Rebecca had consented to take care of Delman Steele's room largely because she enjoyed snooping around through his things, but there was nothing Mrs. Gentrie could do about this, and, inasmuch as the cleaning was always done while Steele was away at the office, there wasn't much chance he would ever discover Rebecca's surreptitious activities.

Hester, the maid, who came in by the day, was a strong, stalwart, taciturn, childless woman who lived in the neighborhood. Her husband was an intermittent sufferer from asthma, but was able to get around, and had a job as night watchman in one of the laboratories where new-model planes were given wind-tunnel tests.

Mrs. Gentrie paused to make a mental survey of the house. The breakfast things had been cleared away. Arthur and Junior had gone to the store. The children were off at school. Hester was running small table napkins through the electric mangle, and Rebecca, at her perennial crossword puzzle, was struggling with the daily offering from the newspaper, a pencil in her hand, her dark, deep-set eyes staring in frowning concentration. Mephisto, the black cat to which she was so attached, was curled up in the chair, where a shaft of windowed sunlight furnished a spot of welcome warmth.

The morning fire was still going in the wood stove. The big tea kettle was singing away reassuringly. There was a

3

pile of mending to be done in the basket and . . . Mrs. Gentrie thought of the preserved fruit in the cellar. It simply had to be gone over. Hester was always inclined to reach for the most accessible tin, and Mrs. Gentrie strongly suspected that over in the dark corner of the cellar there were some cans which went back to 1939.

She paused for a moment, trying to remember the location of a flashlight. The children were always picking them up. There was a candle in the pantry, but . . . She remembered there was a flashlight in Junior's bedroom that had a clip which enabled it to be fastened to the belt. She'd borrow it for a few moments.

The flashlight in her hand, she descended the cellar stairs. The big gas furnace with its automatic controls had been on earlier in the morning, heating the house. Mrs. Gentrie had cut it off as soon as the family had got out of the way, but the cellar was still slightly warm from the heat which had been given off. She noticed cobwebs on the pipes in the back. Hester would have to get down here for a little cleaning. There was a neat array of canned goods and glass jars on the long shelves which stretched across the full length of the cellar. Mrs. Gentrie gave only a casual glance to the section near the window which marked this year's canning. She passed up the first part of last year's canning, and back in the dark corner used Junior's flashlight to inspect the remnants.

She knew at once Hester had been neglecting this corner. There were cobwebs which showed as much, and the beam of Junior's flashlight picked up two cans of 1939 pears almost at once. There were some jars of strawberry jam, cans of homemade apple butter—1939. . . .

Mrs. Gentrie stood perfectly still in puzzled perplexity. The white circle of illumination thrown by the flashlight was centered upon the glistening sides of an unlabeled tin which certainly looked as though it was fresh from the store.

4

Mrs. Gentrie couldn't understand how an unlabeled tin could possibly have intruded itself upon her systematic classification of preserves. She used adhesive tape for labels so there would be no trouble with them dropping off. There was, moreover, something about the appearance of the tin itself which made it seem an intruder. The sides were so new and shiny. Not even a cobweb or a smudge on it.

Mrs. Gentrie reached out with her left hand. Unconsciously she measured the muscular effort in terms of a full quart, and, as a result, the light tin seemed to fairly jump off the shelf before she realized that it weighed no more than an empty can.

She looked at it with the frowning displeasure of a systematic individual finding something definitely at variance with an established system.

Holding the tin in her hand, she turned it around, looking at it from all angles. The top was crimped on, sealed carefully in place as though it had been filled with fruit and syrup. But the smooth glistening, somewhat oily surface of the tin indicated that it was just as it had come from the store—except that it had been so carefully sealed.

Mrs. Gentrie frowned at the offending object as she would have regarded evidences that a mouse had been in the shelf which held the spare bedding. She walked back to the cellar stairs, raised her voice, and called, "Hester! Oh, Hester!"

After a few moments she heard the heavy thud of Hester's steps across the kitchen floor, then the stolid, "Yes, ma'am."

"How did this tin get here?"

Hester advanced a tentative step or two down the cellar stairs, looked at the can in Mrs. Gentrie's hand. The vacancy of her expression was sufficient answer to the question.

Mrs. Gentrie said, "It was right over in that corner.

5

And I notice, Hester, you haven't been cleaning up the 1939 preserves. We had 1940 pears last night, but there are still several cans of '39 pears."

"I didn't know that," Hester said.

"And this tin," Mrs. Gentrie observed, "was in with the '39 preserves."

Hester shook her head. Long experience as a domestic had taught her that nothing was ever gained by argument. When the lady of the house took a notion to blame you for some slip, you stood there, let her speak her piece, and then went back to work. As it was, Hester was losing just this much time from the mangle, and her mind was half occupied with the unfinished ironing which remained in the kitchen.

There was a big wooden box over by the furnace where Arthur threw odds and ends of scraps, bits of old tin, pieces of wood, and an occasional can. Mrs. Gentrie tossed the offending can into this box.

"It doesn't seem," she said as she started upstairs, "that it would have been possible for anyone to have put an empty can on that shelf. I can't imagine you doing anything like that, Hester."

Hester walked back up the three or four stairs she had descended, and returned to the mangle without a word.

Rebecca looked up from her crossword puzzle. "What is it?" she asked. ". . . No, don't tell me. I don't want to know. I'm timing myself on this puzzle. The newspaper gives the time it should take a person of average intelligence. What in the world, Florence, *could* be the name of a young salmon with only four letters and the last three *a-r-r*?"

Mrs. Gentrie shook her head. "Too deep for me," she said, her manner indicating that she was interested only in dismissing the question. She went over to the basket of mending.

The shaft of sunlight which had been falling on Mephisto had moved over to the edge of the chair. The cat stretched, yawned, moved over a few inches, and squirmed over half on its back.

Rebecca frowningly studied the crossword puzzle.

Mrs. Gentrie said to Hester, "I can't understand why anyone would seal up an empty can in the first place."

"No, ma'am."

Rebecca said, "If I could get the five-letter word meaning the side of a ditch next the parapet, I'd have the first letter of that word for the young salmon."

"Why not look up parapet?"

"I have. It says, 'a wall, rampart, or elevation to protect soldiers; a breastwork.'"

"Perhaps that dictionary isn't complete enough to give it."

"Oh, but it is. It's the Fifth Edition of Webster's Collegiate Dictionary. It's got everything in it you need for these newspaper puzzles."

Rebecca once more regarded the crossword puzzle, then looked at her watch. The exclamation which left her lips was one of definite annoyance.

She put down the pencil. "It's no use. I just can't keep my mind on it, and I'm running behind. *What* is all this talk about a can?"

"Nothing," Mrs. Gentrie said, "except that I found a new empty can had been put in with the preserves over in the 1939 corner. I notice that when Junior put the new preserves up on the shelf, he shoved the old ones back over into that dark corner. Next year I'm going to have him do it just the opposite so that we naturally have to use up the old stuff first."

"But why would anyone put an empty tin in with the full ones?" Rebecca asked.

"I don't know. That's what bothers me."

"Wasn't there *any* label on it?"

"No."

"Where is it?"

"I threw it in the scrap box down in the cellar."

7

Rebecca frowned and said, "I wish you hadn't told me about it."

Mrs. Gentrie laughed. "*You* asked *me*. Haven't you *any* of the letters in your parapet word?"

Rebecca said, "The second two are *c-a*."

Mrs. Gentrie held up her fingers. "Five letters?"

"Five letters."

She checked off letters on her fingers, suddenly said, "I have it, Rebecca. It's . . ."

"No, no, don't help me! I want to get it by myself. I want to see if I can't beat this 'average intelligence' time. Don't interrupt me, Florence."

Mrs. Gentrie smiled, picked up the box of mending, carried it over to the breakfast nook, picked out one of Junior's socks, thrust the darning egg in it, and picked up her needle.

Rebecca said sharply, "Well, I don't know how you could have found any five-letter word so soon."

Mrs. Gentrie said soothingly, "Isn't there a clue in the fact that the second two letters are *c-a,* Rebecca? Not many letters would go with *c-a.* You have some of the vowels which would hardly fit. Then in the consonants, I would say that *s* is about the only one that would go with *c.* That gives you *s-c-a.*"

"Oh, I have it," Rebecca said. "*S-c-a-r-p* . . . but whoever heard of a young salmon being called a *parr?*"

"You might look it up."

Rebecca turned the pages of the dictionary. "Yes. Here it is. *P-a-r-r.*"

She worked quickly with her pencil, then looked at the watch again. For a moment there was silence, then she threw down the pencil. "I don't know what good it does a body to try and concentrate when you keep thinking about empty tins being found on the shelves. Why would an empty tin be put on a shelf, anyway?"

Mrs. Gentrie smiled indulgently. "I'm sure I can't tell you. Go back to your puzzle, Rebecca. I'm certain you'll

8

have much better than average intelligence. What else are you having trouble with?"

"A four-letter word meaning 'an East Indian tree used for masts.' "

"Do you have any of the letters?"

"Yes. I've got the first two letters. —*P-o*."

"What other words would give you a clue?"

"A four-letter word meaning 'of domestic animals, vehicles, etc., on the left.' Now what in the world would that mean?"

Mrs. Gentrie puckered her forehead. "Don't they talk about the *'near'* side and the *'off'* side of an animal? Wait a minute. It's *'nigh.'* Would that fit in?"

Rebecca moved her pencil tentatively, then faster. Abruptly, she reversed the ends of the pencil to make an erasure and said, "That's right. It's *nigh*. That makes that tree *p-o*-something-*n*."

"Why don't you take the dictionary and look under *p-o?* There certainly wouldn't be so terribly many words."

Rebecca's fingers moved with a fluttering rapidity. "Oh, I've got it—*poon*. Now I've got the whole thing. *Saber-toothed* and *poon* were the two words that were sticking me, and I've got a high intelligence rating. I'm way ahead of the average. Isn't that splendid?"

Mrs. Gentrie said, "That's really fine. Don't you think you'd better straighten up Mr. Steele's room?"

"Oh, it isn't time for that."

"It's ten-thirty."

"Good heavens, how time flies. Yes, I suppose I should. Sometimes he comes home at noon. Do you know, Florence, I wonder if he's *really* an architect. He left some sketches in his room yesterday, and they looked very crude and amateurish to me."

"I don't think we should bother about his sketches, Rebecca."

"Well, good heavens, they were right where a body

would notice them. They were right in his upper bureau drawer, right where I couldn't help seeing them."

"Did he leave the bureau drawer open?"

"Well, no; but you know how the dust collects on those handles, and when I was dusting, it pulled the drawer open just a little, so I peeked."

"An architect doesn't necessarily have to be an artist."

"Well, perhaps not, but he certainly should be able to draw the floor plans of this house so it would look—well, professional."

"The floor plans of *this* house!"

"That's what I'm telling you. There was a complete sketch of the basement floor plan with the garages, my darkroom, the shelves, window, stairs, and everything."

Mrs. Gentrie said, "Well, I should think that would prove he was an architect and was interested in this old architecture."

Rebecca sniffed. "Like as not he'll turn out to be snooping for some of these agencies, and a building inspector will show up to tell us that our foundations are defective and that we're going to have to do a lot of expensive repair work."

"We'll cross that bridge when we come to it. In the meantime, run along in and clean up the room, Rebecca."

Mrs. Gentrie had utilized an outside entrance two years ago to create a room and bath which could be rented. Delman Steele was a very recent tenant. He had moved in within the last ten days. Yet in that short time he had made himself quite one of the family. In the evening he frequently sat with Rebecca, helping her solve crossword puzzles or assisting her in the darkroom.

The huge, rambling, old-fashioned house had its defects. It was hard enough to heat and to keep clean, but there was lots of space, and the rental from the room more than made up for a lot of the inconveniences due to the size of the house.

Moreover, because the house was on a slope, two garages had been cut out of the basement. One of these garages was rented to R. E Hocksley, who lived in one of the flats next door. Mrs. Gentrie had never seen Hocksley himself, but his secretary, who came in by the day, Opal Sunley, was always on hand to pay the garage rent promptly in advance. That started Mrs. Gentrie thinking about Junior. Junior had been evidencing quite an interest in Opal Sunley lately. Junior was only nineteen. In a way, he was old enough to take care of himself; but lately there had been a smug expression about Opal's eyes that Mrs. Gentrie didn't like. Opal was four or five years older than Junior, and Mrs. Gentrie felt certain she'd been married and was separated from her husband. It would be a lot better if Junior would spend more time with some of the girls in his own set. Suppose Opal was twenty-three or twenty-four. Those few years made a big difference.

Mrs. Gentrie sighed with the realization that the years, of late, had begun to flit by with smooth, streamlined speed.

■ **2** ■

Mrs. Gentrie awakened sometime during the night with the vague feeling that she had heard a door open and close, and steps on the stairs—the cautious steps of someone trying to be quiet and succeeding only in being furtive.

It was that time of the night when weary muscles and tired nerves wrap themselves in the mantle of slumber as in a protective cloak, drugging the senses into an oblivion so deep that sounds, penetrating through to the consciousness, are robbed of significance.

11

Mrs. Gentrie felt no apprehension, only a mild irritation. Her sleep-numbed senses struggled with her uneasiness and won the argument. As soon as the sounds themselves ceased to register, she slipped tranquilly back into a deeper slumber, from which she was aroused abruptly by some sound so sinister that she found herself sitting bolt upright in bed, trying to call back a noise which had already become an echo in her ears.

At her side, Arthur Gentrie said sleepily, "Whatsmatter?"

"I thought I heard something, Arthur."

"Goschleep."

"Arthur it sounded like—like a door banging or—or—or a shot."

Arthur Gentrie rolled over, said, " 'Sall right," and almost immediately settled down into a rhythm of breathing which soon deepened into a gentle snore.

Mrs. Gentrie could hear sounds on the stairs again, the steps of someone trying to be quiet, yet someone who was in a hurry. A board creaked.

Mrs. Gentrie switched on the light over her bed. She looked at the sleeping form of her husband; then realized that before she could waken him to a realization of the emergency, it would be too late to do anything about it. She slid out of bed, flung her robe around her, kicked her feet into slippers, and opened the door which led to the hallway.

Down at the far end of the corridor, by the bathroom door, a dim night light furnished a vague sort of illumination which was hardly brilliant enough to penetrate the shadows near the doorways.

Mrs. Gentrie rubbed sleep from her eyes, walked over toward the head of the stairs. She paused to listen, and could hear nothing. The insidious chill of the night air stole the warmth from her body, and Mrs. Gentrie wrapped the robe more tightly around her. She shivered nervously. She knew that an ominous noise had wakened her yet her mind could conjure up only an uncertain memory of that sound. It might have been a slamming door. It might have been that someone had fallen over a chair, or . . . well, it might have been the sound of a backfire from a truck somewhere. Mrs. Gentrie, sufficiently wide awake now to be more matter-of-fact, refused to consider the possibility of a shot.

Then from the dark bowels of the house there came another sound, a dull, muffled, thudding noise as though someone had struck against something in the dark, or knocked something down. This noise came very definitely from the lower floor. That called for activity on the part of her husband.

Mrs. Gentrie hurried back to the bedroom. She was shivering now, and abruptly conscious of the fact that a night wind was blowing the lace curtains, billowing them into miniature balloons that remained distended for a while, then collapsed, letting the curtains fall against the screen with an audible slapping noise.

Mrs. Gentrie had been the first to bed. Her husband had been puttering around with painting in the cellar. That was what came of trusting Arthur to open the windows. He'd neglected to pull back the curtains. There might be an intruder on the lower floor, but Mrs. Gentrie considered the curtains to be the matter of paramount importance just then. Slapping against that dusty screen, they'd get themselves filled with dirt. . . . "Arthur," she called as she crossed the room and looped back the curtains.

Her husband failed to respond. She had to shake him awake, impressing upon him the fact that there'd been a series of noises.

"Junior coming in," he said.

Mrs. Gentrie looked at the clock. It was thirty-five minutes past midnight. "He'll have been in long before this," she said.

"Look in his room?"

"No. I tell you it was someone running, stumbling over something."

"It was Junior coming in and the wind blowing a door shut."

"But I heard some other noises from down on the lower floor."

"Wind," he said, then as her very silence became sufficiently pronounced to constitute a contradiction, "Well, I'll go take a look."

She knew that Arthur's look would be perfunctory. She could hear him moving around on the lower floor, switching on lights. She wondered about Junior. Once more she walked down the corridor toward the head of the stairs. Junior's room was the first on the right as you came up the stairs. His door was closed. She opened it gently, looked inside.

"Junior."

There was no answer.

Somehow, the dark interior of the room indicated that it was empty. She clicked on a light switch. Junior wasn't in his room. The unwrinkled, smooth, white counterpane seemed to Mrs. Gentrie a fresh cause for alarm. But the plodding steps of her husband, climbing wearily back up the staircase, seemed, somehow, reassuring in a matter-of-fact sort of way. And suddenly, she wanted to shield Junior—didn't want her husband to know he wasn't in.

"Was anyone down there?" she asked, moving away from the door of Junior's room.

"Of course not," he said. "You heard the cellar door bang shut. The wind blew it shut, and Mephisto jumped . . ."

"The *cellar* door!"

"Yes, going down from the kitchen."

"Why, it's always kept closed. It . . ."

"No. I left it open tonight. I did some painting down there, and wanted to let the air circulate. The wind blew it shut, that's all."

14

Mrs. Gentrie felt sheepish. The very weariness in her husband's voice, the dejected slump of his shoulders as he walked down the corridor, carried conviction to her mind. She had become nervous, permitted herself to magnify and distort noises of the night. Arthur, plodding down the corridor, had the attitude of a man who has learned from twenty-one years of married life that women *will* get those ideas and send men prowling around on nocturnal investigations. Nothing can be done about it, so there's no need to remonstrate after it's all over; just get back into bed, try to get warm again, and back to sleep.

Mrs. Gentrie, feeling apologetic, followed her husband to bed. She snuggled close to him, heard once more the gentle rhythm of his breathing, felt the delicious warmth of drowsiness stealing over her like some powerful drug dragging her into the welcome oblivion of sleep.

The alarm wakened her in the morning. She shut it off and pulled down the window. Putting on her robe, she moved around the upper floor, pressing the controls which turned on the gas furnace in the cellar. In the dim light of early morning, her fears of the night before seemed rather ludicrous. But she couldn't resist looking into Junior's room.

His clothes were piled in a careless heap on a chair by the window. He lay wrapped in the blankets, deep in slumber.

It was only after she had seen him that Mrs. Gentrie realized how much she had feared that when she opened the door the unwrinkled counterpane and smooth white of the pillowcases would greet her once more, just as they had done at thirty-five minutes past midnight.

Mrs. Gentrie closed the door quietly. Junior didn't need to get up for an hour yet.

So the big house took up once more the burden of its daily routine—a routine which differed no whit from that of any other day until the sound of screaming sirens

15

tore the silence of the neighborhood into shreds, and completely disrupted the smooth functioning of Mrs. Gentrie's domestic machinery.

■ **3** ■

Perry Mason was standing at the cigar counter buying a package of cigarettes when Della Street came through the doorway, carried along by the stream of people pouring in from the street. Several masculine eyes looked at her with approval as she swung to the outer edge of the file of in-pouring office workers. From the straight seams of her stockings to the tilt of her chin, she represented a feminine bundle of neat efficiency which was remarkably easy on the eyes.

Perry Mason, tossing a quarter on the glass counter and turning back toward the elevators, encountered Della Street's smiling eyes looking up at him. "What is the rush?" she asked.

Mason gripped her elbows with his hand. "Surprise!" he said.

"I'll say it's a surprise. What's bringing you down this early? Is there a murder in the air that I haven't sniffed? I didn't expect to see you before eleven, not after the way you were working last night when I went home. I suppose the office is a litter."

"Your supposition is entirely correct," he said, "and don't try putting away the books in the law library. I've worked out a new theory in that Consolidated case. The books are all lying face open, piled one on top of the other in the exact order that I want to follow in dictating an office brief."

They walked together into one of the crowded elevators, stood back from the door, being pushed into the intimacy of a close proximity by the packed humanity. Mason's hand, still on Della Street's arm, tightened into that little gesture of friendship and understanding which was the keynote of their relationship.

"Going to win that case?" she asked.

He nodded, smiled at her, but said nothing until the elevator stopped to let them out, then as they walked down the long corridor, he said, "It's a cinch now. I always thought it should have been presented on the doctrine of 'last clear chance,' but I couldn't find the authorities to support that contention. Last night about eleven o'clock I uncovered just the line of decisions I wanted."

"Nice going," she said.

Della Street unlocked the door of Mason's private office, said, "I'll take a peek at the outer office and see what's doing. I suppose you'll want the mail?"

Mason grinned. "Not all the mail. High-grade it for checks. Throw the bills away, and put the other correspondence in the deferred file."

"Where it will duly repose for a week or two, and then get transferred to the dead file," she said.

"Oh, well, if there's anything important, you'll know what to do about it."

Mason, who hated all letters with the aversion a man of action feels for routine work, hung up his hat in the cloak closet, walked over to the window, looked down for a moment at the confusion of tangled traffic, then turned back to his desk. Picking up a law book which lay open on his blotter, he started studying the decision. As he followed an obscure legal principle through an intricate maze of legal reasoning, the corners of his eyes puckered with the enjoyment of concentration. Slowly, as though hardly aware of what he was doing, he pulled out the swivel chair and settled down at his desk without interrupting his reading.

Several minutes later the door opened and his confidential secretary, easing her way into the room, waited for him to look up. It was almost five minutes before, turning a page, he saw her standing there. "What is it?" he asked.

"An aviator who wants to see you on behalf of his stepfather," Della Street said. "He's in the outer office."

"Not interested," Mason said. "I have this Consolidated case on my mind and don't want to be disturbed."

"He's a tall, handsome devil," she said, "and knows it. He says that his stepfather is a cripple and can't come himself, that he has a most important legal matter to take up with you, that because there was a shooting affair last night in the flat below, he's afraid the situation may be complicated."

Mason put down the law book somewhat wistfully. "The gunshot does it," he announced with a grin. "I never can concentrate on a brief when there's shooting going on. What's his name, Della?"

"Rodney Wenston. He's one of these playboy aviation enthusiasts; living, I gather, largely on funds inherited from his mother. I doubt if his stepfather entirely approves of him, and I also doubt if he entirely approves of his stepfather—refers to him as the guv'nor."

"How old?" Mason asked.

"Somewhere around thirty-five. Tall, straight, and has that slow-moving assurance of a man who's accustomed to the best in life. He has a lisp when he's embarrassed or self-conscious and you can see it annoys him."

"He's not flying for a living, just as a sport?"

"A hobby, he calls it."

"You seem to have found out a good deal about him."

"What it takes to get information I have," she told him coolly. "But this time I didn't even have to work. The man *really* loosened up. Perhaps that's why I'm prejudiced in his favor. He doesn't regard a secretary as a wall to be jumped over or detoured but as a necessary part of a business organization. As soon as I told him I

18

was your secretary and asked him about his business, he opened right up."

Mason said, "With that in his favor and the gunshot as a lure, we'll certainly give him an audience. What about the lisp, Della?"

"Oh, it isn't bad. He's really very distinguished looking, tall, straight, blue eyes, blond hair and lots of it, a nice profile, probably more than a little spoiled, but quite definitely a personality. The lisp embarrasses him a lot but he gets over it somewhat after he's warmed up to his conversation."

"All right, let's talk with him," Mason said.

Della Street picked up the telephone, said, "Send Mr. Wenston in, Gertie." She dropped the telephone receiver, said to Mason, "Now, don't start reading that law book again."

"I won't," Mason promised.

"Your mind is just about half focused on that book right now."

Reluctantly, Mason turned the book face down on his desk. The door of his private office opened, and Rodney Wenston bowed deferentially. "Good morning, Mr. Mason. I hope you'll pardon this early intrusion but the fact ith the guv'nor is all worked up. Apparently, there's been a shooting in the lower flat, and he's afraid officers will be thwarming all over the place to interfere with what he wants to see you about. He says it's dreadfully important and I'm commissioned to get a *habeas corpus, mandamus,* or whatever you lawyers call it, to see that you get there at once. My stepfather promises to pay you anything you want if you'll come immediately."

"Can you tell me the nature of the business?" Mason asked.

Wenston smiled. "Frankly, I can't. My stepfather ith one of those rugged individualists. I was to act as intermediary. He's . . ."

The telephone rang. Della Street picked it up, said,

19

"Hello," then, shielding the mouthpiece with her hand, said to Mason, "This is he on the phone now. Elston A. Karr. Says he sent his stepson to explain matters, and he'd like to talk with you personally."

Mason nodded acquiescence to Della Street, took the telephone from her, and said, "Hello." He heard a thin, high-pitched voice saying in a crisp, meticulous accuracy of enunciation, "Mr. Mason, this is Elston A. Karr. I have given my address to your secretary. I presume she has made a note of it. Apparently a murder was committed in the flat below mine sometime last night. The place is crawling with police. For certain reasons which I cannot explain at the present time or over the telephone, I want to talk with an attorney. It's about a matter about which I've been thinking for several days. I want to get it disposed of before police start messing into my private affairs. Can you come out here immediately? I am confined to a wheelchair and am unable to get to your office."

"Who was murdered?" Mason asked.

"I don't know. That matter is highly immaterial except as it will interfere with what I want to do."

Mason, conducting a psychological experiment, asked, "Do you think you'll be suspected of complicity in this murder?"

The man's close-lipped accents said scornfully, "Certainly not."

"Then why all this hurry about seeing me?"

"It's a matter I'll explain when you get here. It's highly important. I am willing to pay any fee within reason. I want you personally, Mr. Mason. I would not be satisfied with any other attorney. But you'll have to make up your mind quickly."

Mason turned to Della Street. "Tell Gertie not to touch those books on the library table. Okay, Mr. Karr, I'll be right out. Just a minute. Della, you have the address?"

"Yes."

Mason dropped the receiver into place. "Come on, Della. We're going places."

Wenston smiled. "Glad you talked with him, Mr. Mason. He'th a card. I'll not be going out with you. Sometimes we don't get along too well. I fly him around and do errands for him, but we're not too thick. Just a tip —don't let him dominate you. He'll try fast enough— and lose all respect for you as soon as he does it.

"And, if you want another tip, remember he's a deep one. He may seem simple enough, but he has an oriental angle of approach. You know, when he wants to go north, he starts to the east and circles back. He's rented the flat in my name. You'll see Wenston on the door.

"Well, I'll be on my way. Thank you for your courtesy in seeing me. Good morning."

Mason was putting on his hat as Wenston went out. He and Della caught the next elevator down, and crossed to the garage where Mason's car was parked. The lawyer drove swiftly through the congestion of morning traffic, parking the car half a block from the address his client had given Della Street. Four or five cars were already parked in front of the two-flat stucco house, its cream-colored sides and red-tiled roof contrasting in architecture with the old-fashioned rambling frame house on the corner where the Gentries lived.

As they walked rapidly along toward the flat, Della said, "That corner house certainly goes back."

Mason looked at it curiously. "A lot of those houses were put up around 1900. They were then the last word in luxurious mansions. Of course they seem hopelessly antiquated now. That's because this section of the country is so young and styles have changed with such bewildering rapidity. Take some of the older parts of the country and old houses don't look so much out of place. You'll find lots of houses seventy-five to a hundred years

21

old which don't seem nearly as old as this place. This flat is the one we want, isn't it?"

"Yes. We ring the bell on the left. This one on the right says Robindale E. Hocksley."

Mason said, "Hope he doesn't keep us standing here. It would be just our luck to have Lieutenant Tragg pop his head out of the door and . . ."

Abruptly the door of the left-hand flat opened. A tall Chinese, clad in somber, dark clothes, said, "How-do? Mistah Mason? You please come in, velly quick please."

Mason and Della walked through the door the Chinese was holding open and climbed the stairs. The door was swung quietly shut behind them by the swift-moving Chinese.

Nearing the head of the stairs Mason heard the sound of rubber-tired wheels rolling rapidly along the hardwood floor. The same high-pitched, reedy voice he had heard over the telephone said, "It's all right, Johns. Don't bother. I'll make it." Then a wheelchair shot through a curtained doorway. An emaciated hand applied a brake, and Mason found himself scrutinized by a pair of piercing gray eyes, deep-set beneath shaggy brows, in a face which seemed all skin and bones.

The man in the wheelchair gave the impression of boundless nervous energy. It was as though the strength which had been denied the body had gone into nervous vitality. So intense was the concentration in those gray eyes that the man seemed to entirely forget the amenities of the situation. Della Street he ignored, utterly and completely, devoting all of his attention to a study of the lawyer.

It was a man who came hurrying from the room behind the curtained doorway who broke the tension. "Mr. Mason?"

The lawyer nodded.

The man came forward, smiling. Powerful shoulders pushed out a short, muscular arm. Thick, strong fingers grasped Mason's hand. "I'm Blaine," he said. "Johns Blaine."

Karr lowered the lids of his eyes. In that moment, so transparent and waxlike was his skin that he seemed almost as a corpse. Then his eyes slowly opened. The look of intense concentration had departed. There was a smile on his lips, and a kindly twinkle in his eyes. "Forgive me, Mr. Mason," he said. "I need a good lawyer. I've heard a lot about you. I wanted to see if you measured up."

He raised his hand from the arm of the wheelchair and extended it. Mason folded gentle fingers about the hand, noticing that the skin was cold, that the bones seemed delicately fragile.

"My secretary, Miss Street," Mason introduced.

The others acknowledged the introduction, then Karr said, "And my number one boy, Gow Loong."

Mason regarded the Chinese with undisguised interest. He had, somehow, more the air of a companion or partner than of a servant. His high forehead, the calm placidity of his countenance, the steady inscrutability of his dark eyes gave him a distinguished appearance.

"Don't get interested in him," Karr warned, in his quick, nervous voice. "He's too much like the Orient. You want to understand him, but can't. A perpetual mystery. Arouses your curiosity and then slams the door in your face. We've got too confounded much to think about—too much to talk about. Glad you brought your secretary. She can take notes, and I won't have to go over the thing twice. Makes me terribly impatient when I have to repeat things. What are you standing there for? Come on, let's go in where we can sit down and be comfortable, and get this over with."

He grasped the big rubber tires of the wheelchair, spun it in a quick turn, lunged forward with his thin shoulders, and, mustering surprising strength, sent the chair shooting back through the curtained doorway at such speed that the others, following along behind, were hopelessly in the rear.

The room beyond the curtained doorway was a well-furnished drawing room with hardwood floors, sumptuous Chinese rugs and furniture which had quite evidently been brought from the Orient. The dark wood of this furniture had been cunningly carved with a design in which the dragon motif predominated.

Karr spun the wheelchair into a quick turn and stopped it instantly. He handled his chair with the deft, expert skill born of long practice. "Sit down. Sit down," he said in his high-pitched, piping voice. "Don't stand on formality, please. There isn't any time. Mason, sit over here. Miss Street, if you'll use that table for your writing. No! Wait a minute. There's some nested tables over there. You can get one just the right height. Gow Loong, put that table over by her elbow. All set? Sit down, Johns. Damn it, you make me nervous, hovering around over me. I'm not going to break in two."

"What has happened?" Mason asked.

Karr said, "Listen attentively, please. You got your notebook there, Miss Street? That's fine. I'm right in the middle of a delicate matter. I won't go into details right now, but I had a partner in China. A rough partnership it was, too. We were running guns up the Yangtze. Slice you up in fine pieces if they caught you. Death of a thousand cuts, they called it.

"Well, anyway, my partner and I kept 'em supplied with guns. There was excitement in it, and money. I won't go into that, though, not now. I'll only say I'm doing something in connection with that old partnership—and I've got to keep under cover until it's done. I can't stand any notoriety—don't want anyone to know of me. Far as anyone knows, Elston A. Karr was killed up the river.

"I rented this apartment in the name of my stepson,

24

Rodney Wenston. He signs all the checks, pays the rent, and all that. I don't enter into the picture at all.

"However, there are some of the boys who aren't fooled easily. Don't ever underestimate the Oriental. They're slow but sure. Sometimes they aren't so slow, either. Well, as I said, I've got to avoid any publicity. No one must see me here. I can't be questioned.

"Well, this matter I want to talk to you about has to do with the old partnership. I didn't start the ball rolling until I was certain any interest which might have been aroused by my having moved in here had quieted down. So I picked this particular time to go ahead, and then that murder happened downstairs. Puts me in the devil of a predicament. I suppose the newspapermen will describe the house and the tenants. Worst possible time it could have happened."

Mason asked, "Why not let this other matter wait?"

"Because I've already started it," Karr exclaimed irritably. "Dammit, Mason, I told you that already. I've started the ball rolling. I can't stop it now. And the more of a mystery they make of that murder downstairs, the longer the thing drags out, the more notoriety I'll get, and the more dangerous it is for me."

"Have the police been here yet?" Mason asked.

"No. That's why I was in such a hurry to get you. I want you to help me handle them."

Mason frowned. "How does it happen they haven't been here before this?"

Karr said, "Talked them out of it. Sent Johns and Gow Loong down to find out what it was all about. The police questioned them. Some lieutenant from the Homicide Squad down there. What's his name, Johns?"

"Tragg."

"That's right, Tragg. Lieutenant Tragg. Know him, Mason?"

"Yes."

Karr said, "They told Tragg I was sick, that he'd have

25

to come up to interview me, that I didn't know anything, anyway. That's not true. I heard the shot, but that's all I know about it."

Mason said, "Perhaps if you'd tell me why you felt it necessary to call me, we'd have a more satisfactory starting point."

Karr jerked his head into a sharp turn. His eyes were blazing now with the fire of that devastating, nervous energy which seemed to be too much for his frail body to hold. "How about this secretary of yours? All right?"

"All right."

"You can vouch for her?"

"Yes."

"This is important—important as the devil."

"She's all right."

Karr said, "I don't know what happened downstairs. I don't give a damn. I'm confined to my wheelchair. I can't get around. Have to be lifted in and out. Don't have any opportunity to be neighborly. Don't *want* to be neighborly. All I ask is to be left alone. Now this confounded murder comes along, and I suppose the newspaper reporters will start snooping around. One thing I can't stand, Mason, is publicity. Don't want any of it. Can't have it."

"Why did you send for me?" Mason asked.

"I'm coming to it. Don't interrupt me. When I get started, let me go. And don't make me repeat. It makes me nervous to have to repeat. Where was I? Oh, yes, publicity. I'll tell you why I can't stand any publicity. I'm hiding. They're trying to murder me. Wouldn't be surprised if this murder downstairs was because some hired assassin got his numbers mixed. I used the greatest care getting this flat. It's an ideal location for what I want. But I made one mistake. I should have rented the lower flat as well, and put Gow Loong in there. But when I moved in, the lower flat was untenanted and had been for over a year. Neighborhood's gone to hell, but the still want too much money for their rentals. I rented this place, moved in at night. . . ."

"Why didn't you take the lower apartment for yourself?" Mason asked. "The stairs must make a difference."

"Don't make any difference at all," Karr said. "Can't go any place except in a wheelchair. Have no desire to go out of doors except to get a little sunlight. There's a fine balcony here on the south and west side. I can get out there and get the sunlight. That's why I like the place. No buildings over on the south side to shut off the sunlight. That big old-fashioned mansion over on the north literally blankets the north side, shuts off any cold north winds. I want it warm. My blood's thin. Too long in the tropics. Too much dysentery. Too much malaria. Too much other stuff. Never mind. Don't need to go into that now. How'd I get talking about stairs? Oh, yes, you asked me."

He raised his hand and pointed a long, bony finger at Mason. "I told you not to interrupt me. Let me talk."

Mason smiled. "There are certain things I have to know."

"All right, I'll come to them. Wait until I've finished, and then ask me for anything I haven't covered. What was I talking about?"

"Publicity," Johns Blaine said in the half second of silence which followed Karr's request.

"Murder," corrected Gow Loong.

Mason's eyes shifted to the face of the Chinese, regarding him with keen interest. The one word which he had spoken had been without emphasis, without accent, and without hesitation. It was the one word of prompting which Karr needed.

"That's right," Karr said. "It's murder. I'm a wanted man, Mr. Mason. There are people who want to know where I am. If they find out, I'm finished. In my condition, I can't move around rapidly. I took a lot of trouble getting into this place unobserved. Johns Blaine

27

rented it, and moved in. He and Gow Loong smuggled me in under cover of darkness. No one has ever seen me. That's the beauty of the place. That balcony out there gets the sunlight, but it can't be seen from any direction. There isn't any other house which can command a view. That's the advantage of that deep gully along there —'barranca' they call it in this country. That's one of the reasons I didn't think they'd ever rent the lower part of the house. Too many people are afraid there's going to be an earthquake, and the whole thing will slide down into the gully—barranca.

"There may be better places out here in Hollywood, but we didn't have time to look around too much. They were after me. They were pretty hot on my trail, if you want to know the truth. A man who has to move around in a wheelchair isn't exactly what you'd call inconspicuous. Johns did a good job in the limited time he had. It's a satisfactory place. But I can't stand any investigation. I don't want to talk with the police. I don't want them to talk with me. I can't see any newspaper reporters."

"What do you know," Mason asked, "and what happened?"

"A man moved in down in the lower flat about a week after I'd rented this place," Karr said. "I haven't ever seen him. He's never seen me. His name's Hocksley. Guess you saw it on the mailbox—didn't you?"

Mason nodded.

"I don't know what he does. I think he's connected with the studios, some sort of a writer. Damned irregular habits. I can hear him dictating sometimes at night. Always seems to dictate at night. Don't know what he does during the daytime. Guess he sleeps."

"Does he dictate to a stenographer?" Mason asked.

"No. To a dictating machine. That's the way it sounds, and I think that's right. Has a girl who comes in every day and pounds the typewriter. He seems to keep her busy. She's the one who discovered the murder."

"She comes in each day?" Mason asked.

"Yes."

"He lives down there alone?"

"No, he doesn't. He has a housekeeper. What's her name, Gow Loong?"

"Salah Pahlin."

"That's right, Sarah Perlin. Never can remember names. That's an odd name, anyway. I've never seen her. Johns has seen her. Tell him what she looks like, Johns."

Blaine said very tersely, "Fifty-five, tall, angular, dark eyes, thin gray hair, keeps it combed tightly back, flat-footed, doesn't try to make herself look attractive. She lives in the place, has the back bedroom, I think. About five-foot-four or five, weighs a hundred ten or a hundred and fifteen. Is there to work, and that's all, closemouthed, does the cooking, takes care of the place, doesn't do washing, evidently a good cook. There's lots of baking. You can smell it up here. Doesn't seem to do much frying."

Karr held up his hand. "That's enough," he said. "Gives Mason the picture. He doesn't have to know too much about her. Just wants a description—doesn't want to know what brand of toothpaste she uses. She's disappeared."

Abruptly, the sound of the buzzer on the door interrupted Karr's speech.

Mason said, "That'll be the police."

Karr said, "Keep me out of it, Mason. You've got to keep me out of it."

Mason said impatiently, "You've spouted out a lot of rapid conversation, but you haven't got anywhere. That's because you wouldn't let me interrupt you and ask questions. Gow Loong, go to the door. If that's Tragg, keep him down there for a minute or two. Karr, tell me exactly what happened."

Karr frowned irritably. "Don't interrupt me. I . . ."

"Shut up," Mason said. "Answer my question. What happened?"

Johns Blaine stared at Mason in sudden consternation, said, "Mr. Karr gets nervous when he's interrupted, Mr. Mason. He . . ."

"Shut up," Karr said to Blaine, and to Mason, "Last night about half past twelve, a shot. After that, some moving around downstairs. I didn't do anything about it. I couldn't. I could have yelled, that's all. I didn't try yelling. Wouldn't have done any good, anyway."

"How about these other people?" Mason asked. "Where were they?"

"I was here alone," Karr said. "I don't ordinarily stay alone. I . . ."

Mason said to Gow Loong, "If that's Tragg, stall him along as much as you can, but let him in. Go ahead and open the door. All right, Karr, let's hear the rest of it."

"Heard someone running, heard a door slam," Karr said. "Then I didn't hear anything more for ten or fifteen minutes. Then I heard someone moving around cautiously. I heard a man's voice talking. Might have been telephoning."

"Then what?" Mason asked.

"Nothing more for an hour. Then things moving again, a sound of something being dragged across the floor, and out the side door. It sounded like a body being dragged by someone who couldn't lift it. There were two people, I think. I was in bed. I couldn't even get to the window or the telephone. Never have a telephone by my bed. Makes me too nervous if it rings at night."

"The *side* door?" Mason asked.

"That's right. The side door is right opposite the garage over at the other house—that one on the north. Hocksley rents that garage, keeps his car there. His stenographer uses it sometimes."

"Hear anything else?" Mason asked.

"Voices. I think one of them was a woman. I heard a car start and drive out. It was gone about an hour, came back to that garage. Gow Loong was back by that time."

"And Mr. Blaine?" Mason asked as he heard steps on the stairs.

Blaine said, "I got in about two o'clock."

The steps on the stairs were louder. Gow Loong said, "You come topside upstairs, please. Solly no come sooner. No savvy policee man. Massah in here, please."

Lieutenant Tragg, standing in the doorway, surveyed the group for a minute before his eyes segregated Perry Mason from the others. As he recognized the lawyer, a slight flush deepened his color, but there was no other indication of surprise or annoyance. "Well, well," he said, "fancy seeing you here! May I ask what's the occasion of the visit?"

Mason said, "My client, Mr. Karr, is nervous. You understand how it is when a man of law-abiding habits is suddenly brought into contact with lawlessness. He naturally becomes apprehensive. Mr. Karr has been intending to make a will for some time, and the unfortunate occurrence downstairs tended to emphasize the uncertainties of life. He sent for me to . . . to come on a legal matter."

"So you're drawing a will?" Tragg asked skeptically.

Mason started to say something, then apparently caught himself, and said, "Well, I don't think there's anything to be gained by discussing Mr. Karr's private business. You may draw your own conclusions, Lieutenant."

"I'm drawing them," Tragg said significantly.

Mason performed the introductions. "Mr. Karr," he said, "Mr. Johns Blaine, and Gow Loong, the number one boy."

Lieutenant Tragg said, "I've met the others. Mr. Karr's the one I want to talk with."

Mason said, "I'm afraid Mr. Karr can't help you very much. I've been asking him generally about the murder. Just the natural questions that one would ask out of curiosity, you know."

31

"Yes," Tragg said, and added, after a duly significant pause, "just out of curiosity."

Mason grinned. "Certainly, Tragg. I hope you don't think that if I were interested in what had gone on downstairs, I'd be approaching it in this roundabout method."

Tragg said, "Experience has taught me that your methods of approach are sometimes oblique, but always deadly."

Mason laughed. "Come on over and sit down. I'm afraid Mr. Karr can't help you very much. You see, he heard two shots in the wee small hours of the morning, but thought they were from the exhaust of a truck, and . . ."

"*Two* shots!" Tragg interrupted.

Mason regarded him with wide-open, innocent eyes. "Why, yes. Weren't there two?"

Tragg said, "What time was this?"

"Oh, perhaps one or two in the morning. He didn't look at his clock. But he thinks it was right around in there."

"Why does he place the time as being around in there if he didn't look at the clock?"

"Well, he'd awakened about twelve-thirty, and he was just getting back to sleep again," Mason said.

Tragg frowned. "That doesn't agree with statements made by some of the other witnesses."

"The deuce it doesn't," Mason said in apparent surprise. "Well, Mr. Karr can't be very certain about any of it, Tragg. There is, of course, a chance he actually *did* hear a truck backfiring, and didn't hear the actual shots, which may have been fired earlier in the night."

"Shot," Tragg said. "There was only one."

Mason gave a low whistle.

Tragg looked at Karr. "You're certain there were two?"

Karr said, "I don't think I can add anything to what Mr. Mason has said."

"I've been talking it over with him," Mason observed

easily, "and he isn't certain of a thing, Tragg. That's why I told you I didn't think he could help you much."

Tragg said to Karr, "What do you know about this man, Hocksley, who lived in the flat below you?"

"Not a thing," Karr said. "I've never so much as set eyes on the man. You see, I'm confined to my wheel-chair and bed. I'm not interested in the neighbors, and I don't particularly care about having them interested in me. Even if Hocksley had lived a completely normal, ordinary life, I probably would never have seen him; but he didn't."

"In what way didn't he?"

"I think," Karr said, "the man must have slept most of the day, because I'd heard him up at all hours of the night. He did a lot of talking down there. It sounded as though it was dictation he was pouring into a dictating machine . . ."

"Why not to a stenographer?" Tragg asked.

"It may have been," Karr said, "but it sounded more like a dictating machine, a steady, even monotone of fast dictation with virtually no pauses. I've noticed that when people dictate to stenographers, they pause every little while—that is, most of them do. Then they'll have inter-vals of real long pauses while they're waiting for ideas. Something about a dictating machine which speeds up a man's concentration. He feeds the stuff right into it. Anyway, that's the way I've always thought about it."

Tragg frowned and looked down at the toes of his shoes. After a while he said, "Humph," then turned to regard Mason thoughtfully.

"Oh, well," Mason said cheerfully, "it'll probably work out all right. It's been my experience there are always these little discrepancies in a case. What happened, Tragg?"

Tragg said, "Hocksley had that flat downstairs. He had a housekeeper, a Mrs. Sarah Perlin. A stenographer, Opal Sunley, came in and transcribed records. You're right,

Mr. Karr. The man dictated to a machine. In any event, that's what Opal Sunley says, and I was glad to get your corroboration on that."

"What was his line of business?" Mason asked.

Tragg said, "I don't know."

"You don't know!" Mason exclaimed. "Haven't you talked with his stenographer?"

"That's just it," Tragg said. "His stenographer tells an absolutely impossible story."

"What do you mean?"

"Apparently, Hocksley was engaged in some sort of exporting business. He wrote a great many letters giving detailed specifications about bills of lading, shipments, shipping directions, and all that sort of stuff. He wrote to a manufacturer's agent about buying merchandise. He wrote to steamship companies about deliveries. And every damn letter in the outfit was a phoney."

"What do you mean?" Mason asked.

Tragg said, "The letters were some sort of code stuff. Because from what the Sunley woman tells me, I know darn well that, with shipments in the condition they are today, the letters weren't what they seemed to be on their face."

"Did she know it?" Mason asked.

"No. She's one of the slow, plugging kind that sticks a head clamp over her head, turns on the dictating machine, transcribes the letters, and forgets about them."

"How about carbon copies?" Mason asked.

"That's just it. Hocksley would have her make carbon copies, but she didn't do any filing. She doesn't know where the carbon copies are, or what became of them, and we can't find any."

"Hocksley was killed?"

"Hocksley or his housekeeper or both. They're both missing, and there's evidences of a shooting. We'd been acting on the theory that either Hocksley killed his housekeeper, or the housekeeper killed Hocksley, because we'd

34

only been able to account for one shot. But if there were *two* shots, that might make the situation entirely different."

Mason said, "If there's anything we can do, don't hesitate to call, Tragg. But Mr. Karr is intensely nervous. He's had a nervous breakdown, and his doctors have told him to live in seclusion where he wouldn't meet strangers, not to cultivate acquaintances, or form any new friendships. It would be a lot better if you'd limit his contacts as much as possible."

Tragg pushed back his chair, got to his feet, shoved his hands down deep in his trousers pockets, and looked down at Karr. "You won't think I'm getting too nosey if I ask you why the wheelchair?" he inquired.

Karr said tersely, "Arthritis. In my knees and ankles. Can't stand any weight on them at all. Have to be lifted. Get in one position and I'm fairly comfortable. Make any moves with my legs, and there's intense pain. Doctors recommended diathermy. I tried it for a while and came to the conclusion I could do the same thing by keeping a blanket over my legs and keeping them warm all the time. I drink lots of water and fruit juices. I'm getting better."

"You haven't a doctor now?"

"No, sir. Got tired of paying them so much money, and having them do me so little good. Man gets something acute wrong with him, and a doctor can help cure him. When it's something chronic, doctors can't help. They know it. They try to kid the patient along so he keeps cheerful. To hell with that stuff. I don't want it. I never have been kidded along, and I don't want to start in now. Put it up cold turkey to the last doctor. He got mad and told me I never would get any better, that in the course of time, I'd probably get worse. They've looked me all over for bad teeth and focal infections. I'm getting along all right. Last few months I've been better than ever before. Keep my legs warm all the time."

Tragg regarded him with an air of detached interest, as though he were looking at some specimen in a glass case. Then he turned to regard Mason thoughtfully. Abruptly, he said, "Well, I'm sorry I disturbed you, Mr. Karr. I just had to complete my checkup. Just a matter of routine, you know. It probably won't be necessary to bother you again. Sorry you've been having your troubles and hope I didn't aggravate them too much."

"Oh, that's all right," Karr said. "Like to talk with a man who has intelligence. Afraid some square-toed, brow-beating cop was going to come messing around here, asking a lot of damnfool questions. You're all right. Come in any time."

"Thanks," Tragg said. "I'll try and handle this end of it myself, so you won't be meeting new people."

"I'll certainly appreciate that," Karr said. "I will for a fact."

"Now then," Tragg went on in a deliberately casual manner, "how about Rodney Wenston? Does he . . ."

"Just a blind," Karr interrupted. "He's my stepson. Lives down toward the beach somewhere. I have the telephone in his name, and his name on the door. In fact, he rents the flat. I've done that deliberately so as to let myself stay in the background. When peddlers come here and ask for Mr. Wenston, we can tell them quite truthfully he's out and we don't know when he'll be back. I don't want to be annoyed with people. I use Wenston as a sort of buffer."

Tragg appeared quite favorably impressed with the explanation. He nodded his head sympathetically and said, "I understand perfectly. Is there any particular reason why you are avoiding people, Mr. Karr?"

"There certainly is," Karr snapped. "I'm a nervous man—irritable—highly irritable. The doctors tell me to conserve my nervous energy. I can't do it when I meet people, particularly strangers. Strangers ask too damn many questions. Strangers get sympathetic. Strangers talk too damn much. Strangers come to visit and stay too long. I don't like them."

Tragg laughed good-naturedly, and said, "And, I take it, the fewer questions I ask and the shorter I make my stay, the more popular I'll be?"

"Poppycock," Karr exploded. "I didn't mean you, didn't mean you at all. You're here on business."

"In any event, I'll be going," Tragg said. "I trust it won't be necessary to bother you again, Mr. Karr."

Mason watched him out of the room, then frowned and lit a cigarette. He was still frowning at the cigarette smoke when the sound of the lower door closing seemed to ease the tension.

Karr said, "What was the idea telling him about *two* shots, and making the time later, Mason?"

Mason said, "It would have been a good gag if it had worked."

"Don't you think it did?"

"I don't know."

"Why was it a good gag?"

"Because when an officer's working up a case, he talks with a lot of witnesses. From them he gets a pretty good idea of what happened and when it happened. Naturally, an officer likes to get newspaper publicity, so he stands in pretty well with the newspaper reporters. Otherwise he doesn't stay on the force. The newspapers see to that. So when you tell a man like Lieutenant Tragg to keep your name out of the newspapers, it doesn't mean a damn thing. But if you give him testimony which is at variance with the facts in the case he's working up, then he's certain to see your name is kept out of the newspapers."

"Why?"

"Because if the newspapers state you don't recollect things just as the other witnesses do, or that your testimony is at sharp variance with theirs, it means that the person who actually committed the murder, and whom the police are after, is encouraged. It means that when that person is arrested, the lawyer he retains will know immediately where to go to find a witness who will contradict the testimony of the prosecution's witnesses."

Karr's face lit up into a smile. "Clever," he said. "Damned clever. That's what I wanted you for, Mason. Fast thinking . . ."

"Well, don't be too happy about it," Mason warned, "because I don't think it worked."

"Why not?"

Mason said, "Tragg's too damned intelligent. That man's just nobody's damn fool."

"You think he saw through what you were doing?"

"I'm practically certain of it," Mason said, "but that isn't what's worrying me."

"What is?"

Mason said, "The way he suddenly started getting sympathetic, and telling you that he'd keep the reporters from annoying you."

"Well, isn't that just what we want?"

"It is except for one thing," Mason said.

"What's that?"

Mason looked down at the blanket thrown over Karr's knees. "If any of this invalid business is part of the build-up you're using to give yourself an alibi, and if your legs are in such shape you *can* walk, you're going to find yourself Lieutenant Tragg's very favorite suspect—leading the rest of the field by about a dozen lengths."

Karr's face, which had twisted with some emotional reflex as Mason expounded his theory of Tragg's reactions, suddenly broke into a relieved smile. "Well, as far as that's concerned," he said, "I can give you absolutely definite assurance, Mr. Mason. I can't walk. I can't put any weight on my legs. I can't even move from a chair to a bed or a bed to a chair. I have to be lifted. I can't even get to a telephone without help."

"If that's the case," Mason said, "it might simplify

38

matters to have me suggest to Lieutenant Tragg that he call in his own doctor and make an examination."

"Wouldn't that indicate that I had something on my mind? Wouldn't it be going out of my way to make it appear that I thought he was considering me as a suspect?"

"Sure it would," Mason said. "After all, you're a man of average intelligence. You were in the house. You were alone when the shot was fired. You've surrounded yourself with a good deal of mystery. Your Chinese servant isn't going to help any. Blaine here could very well be considered a bodyguard. The way he described that housekeeper, you know at once he's been a cop. Lieutenant Tragg comes up here to find what you know about what happened. Your story is at variance with that of everyone else. He finds you talking to me. In fact, by this time, it's doubtless occurred to him that *I* was the one who furnished just about all the information. In other words, I did most of the talking."

"Well?"

"Unless Lieutenant Tragg has uncovered some clues pointing to the person who actually did commit the murder, he's getting ready to pin the blue ribbon right on your chest."

Karr said, "That would be unfortunate."

"I gathered as much," Mason said, "and may I remind you that Tragg's inopportune arrival prevented you from telling me just why it was you wished to consult me?"

Karr sighed. "It's about that old partnership," he said, "but I don't feel up to going into it now. Tell me, Mr. Mason, what's the legal position of a surviving partner with reference to partnership business?"

Mason said, "The death of a partner dissolves the partnership. It's the duty of the surviving partner to wind up the affairs of the partnership and make an accounting to the executor or administrator of the dead partner."

"What do you mean by winding up the affairs of the partnership?"

"Reduce them to cash."

"Suppose there isn't any executor or administrator? What happens to the property?"

"It goes to the heirs."

"I'm not *positive* there are any heirs."

"You should have an administrator appointed, anyway, to protect yourself."

Karr shook his head emphatically.

"Why not?" Mason asked.

"That would have to go through court, wouldn't it?"

"Yes."

"Suppose the business was something you couldn't take to court?"

"Why not?"

"Too dangerous."

"For whom?"

"Me."

Mason said, "Then you could absolve yourself from responsibility by paying the dead partner's share of the funds to his heirs. But under those circumstances, you would have to take all the responsibility of seeing that you got all of the heirs and met the . . ."

"You mean," Karr interrupted, "that if I paid money to someone who wasn't the nearest relative, I might have to pay it all over again?"

"That's right. Moreover, the nearest relative isn't always the heir. Suppose a partner left a son, for instance, and sometime later on it appeared that he had been secretly married or he might have left a will which might not have been offered for probate."

Karr fastened Mason with his alert, intense eyes, and said, "I understand. It's better to take that risk than to have the court asking a lot of questions."

"Was that the matter that you wanted me to handle?" Mason asked.

40

Karr leaned back in the chair and closed his eyes. After a few moments he said, "That was it—at first. I wanted you to investigate the possibility of my late partner having left an heir. Now this other matter has come up."

"You mean the murder?"

"Yes."

"And you want me to do something in connection with the murder?"

"Yes, I think I do. I think I'd like to have you see that it's cleared up just as quickly as possible. I can't afford to have that develop into one of those mysteries that they spread all over the front pages of the newspapers. How soon do you think Tragg will solve it?"

"It shouldn't take him long. He's a good man."

"Tell you what you do. *You're* a good man. Give him a hand. See that the thing gets cleaned up and cleaned up fast."

"You want me to find out who committed the murder?" Mason asked.

"That's right."

Mason said, "Make a note of that, Della."

Her pen still poised over the notebook, Della said, "I did."

"Why do you want a note of that?" Karr asked.

Mason said, "Because if you're guilty, and I uncover the evidence that sticks your neck in the noose, I want to be in a position to send your estate a bill for doing it."

Karr laughed. "You're a great one! You really are. You measure up to expectations. Salty character. Individuality. All right, Mason, go ahead. Start working. Get that detective agency of yours on the job. Uncover everything you can. Help Tragg find out what actually happened. Turn over any evidence you find to him. Gow Loong, go massah's bedroom. Drawer, on right-hand topside. Ketchum money. You savvy? You bring'm money. This lawyer man wants cash money now."

"Can do," Gow Loong said, and started for the bedroom.

Johns Blaine said easily, "Don't let that idea of having Karr as a suspect cramp your style any, Mason. Just go right ahead. Karr's absolutely in the clear, and I'd say the best way to get Lieutenant Tragg off his neck was to help him get some evidence."

Mason said, "It's all right, but I just wanted to have all the cards on the table. In this business, we find that a person who has anything to conceal wants to cover it up. You take a witness who's lying on the witness stand, and he almost invariably starts stroking his cheeks with the tips of his fingers, then slides his hand around so that he's concealing his mouth as much as possible while he talks. We know those signs and get to look for them. Mr. Karr's idea about keeping his legs warm may be all to the good, but as far as Lieutenant Tragg is concerned, that heavy robe over his legs gave him the idea Mr. Karr was covering them up because he had something to conceal."

Karr threw back his head and laughed. "And gave you the same idea, Mason?" he asked. "Come on, now, be frank. Didn't it?"

Mason looked down at the heavy blanket.

"Yes."

Gow Loong returned from the bedroom, carrying a tin cash box. He placed it gently on Karr's lap. Karr threw back the lid of the box, reached in, picked up a sheaf of currency, and said to Mason, "How much do you charge in these cases, Counselor?"

Mason regarded the bundle of currency. "Usually all the traffic will bear," he said.

Once more Karr threw back his head and laughed. "I like you, Mason. I mean I *really* do! You don't beat around the bush."

"No," Mason said. "I don't beat around the bush.

"And may I ask whether you want to retain me to

solve that murder or to advise you in connection with your old partnership?"

"Both," Karr said, "but we'll do one thing at a time, Mason. I want that murder case off my neck. That's a nightmare. Couldn't possibly have happened at a more inopportune time. As I see it, the only way to keep it from becoming a mystery is to clean it up—only way to clean it up is to solve the damn case. Perhaps you can solve it by this afternoon. That'll give me a chance to do what I have to do. Personally, I don't see why the devil this man What's-his-name couldn't have picked a more opportune time to get himself killed. Damned inconsiderate, I call it."

■ 4 ■

Mrs. Gentrie seemed somewhat overawed by the importance of her visitor. Aunt Rebecca and Delman Steele, sitting together at the dining-room table working a crossword puzzle, looked up as Mason introduced himself to Mrs. Gentrie. They stood up as Mrs. Gentrie escorted Mason toward them.

Mrs. Gentrie performed the introductions. "Mr. Mason, the lawyer you've read about," she announced. "This is my husband's sister, *Miss* Gentrie." It was always necessary to emphasize the "Miss" in introducing Aunt Rebecca. So many people were inclined to call her Mrs. if they hadn't been paying attention when the introduction was performed, and that led to a correction later which, somehow, always seemed like an embarrassing explanation. "And Mr. Steele, a roomer, who is also a crossword addict," Mrs. Gentrie added.

Aunt Rebecca was by no means overawed. She looked Mason over critically, said, "Humph! You don't look so formidable. Reading about you, I'd always imagined you bristled with hostility like a battleship."

Mason laughed, sized up Delman Steele, a young man in the twenties, who met his eye steadily enough, yet who seemed, somehow, on the defensive. He was good looking, and there was plenty of character in his face, but something about the tight line of his lips indicated that he might, perhaps, have something to conceal.

Mrs. Gentrie said, "Mr. Steele is usually at his work by this time, but after what happened next door, the police insisted on holding everyone here—except they *did* let the two younger children go to school. Junior, that's the oldest, is around somewhere. Here he is coming up from the basement now. Junior, come and meet Mr. Mason, the lawyer. He's here because he—well, what *are* you doing here, Mr. Mason?" she asked as Junior shook hands with the lawyer.

"Just investigating the case," Mason said.

"You have a client who's interested in it?"

"Well, only indirectly. Not the person who's charged with murder."

"Have they charged anyone yet?"

"No," Mason said and laughed. "That's why I can speak with assurance when I say I'm not representing the person who's charged with the murder."

He turned to study Junior, a lad of about nineteen, who had a high, sensitive forehead which seemed at odd variance with the thickness of his lips. However, his nose was straight and well proportioned, and Mason realized that while the young man would never be considered as a matinée idol, he was, nevertheless, sufficiently good looking to get by nicely with the opposite sex.

Junior looked at the dictionary on the table in front of Aunt Rebecca. "No wonder that's never in my room," he said. "Every time I have to use it, I put in half an hour looking for it."

Aunt Rebecca rattled into quick reproach. "Now,

44

Junior, don't be selfish with your things. After all, it doesn't wear your dictionary out to look up a word once in a while. You should learn . . ."

"*And* my flashlight," Junior interrupted. "Somebody's always taking that and running the batteries down."

"Why, Junior," Mrs. Gentrie said, "I don't know what you're talking about. I only borrowed it for a few minutes yesterday when I was looking at the preserves on the shelf in the cellar. I didn't have it on for as much as a minute or a minute and a half altogether."

"Well, somebody must have left the switch on for a while," Junior said. "The batteries were all run down this morning."

"Perhaps you used it last night."

He said, "That's the point. I couldn't find it last night."

"Why, I put it back in your room. I . . ." Her voice suddenly lost its assurance, and Junior, wise in the ways of family life, said, "You mean you *intended* to put it back in my room, but I suppose you left it hanging around some place."

"I . . . well, perhaps I did leave it down here. I had that basket of mending, and I put it . . . Where did you find it, Junior?"

"In my bedroom this morning."

"Wasn't it there last night?"

He shook his head.

Mrs. Gentrie laughed and said, "Well, Mr. Mason isn't interested in all of our domestic troubles. That's the way it is with a large family, Mr. Mason. Someone's always feeling that his rights are being infringed upon."

Aunt Rebecca said, "Well, I suppose Mr. Mason wants to ask us a lot of questions, but before he does, I'm certainly going to take advantage of his being here to find out about that thing that was bothering us in the crossword puzzle."

45

Mrs. Gentrie said, "Oh, Rebecca, don't intrude your silly . . ."

"If I can help, I'll be only too glad to," Mason said. "Fire away."

"It's a five-letter word, and the second two letters are *u-a*. It's a legal term, meaning—what is it, Delman? How did they express it?"

Steele ran his finger down a list of numbers and then said, reading, "A legal term meaning *'as if; as though; as it were.'*"

"Five letters?" Mason asked.

"That's right."

The lawyer frowned a moment, then said, "Why not try *quasi?*"

Rebecca grabbed up the pencil, lettered in the word, moved her head back, and perked it on one side as though she had been a bird critically examining a dubious bug. "Yes," she said abruptly, "that's right! That's absolutely right! That's exactly what it is. *Quasi.* I never heard of it before."

"It's a term used extensively by lawyers," Mason said.

"Well," Rebecca announced, "that is going to get us over the hump, Delman. I suppose Mr. Mason wants to know everything—just as the police did. . . ."

"Please be seated, Mr. Mason," Mrs. Gentrie invited.

As Mason sat down, Rebecca said, "I certainly hope you don't start asking a lot of questions, Mr. Mason. I'm all on edge. I started this crossword puzzle to try and quiet my nerves. Mr. Steele's been kind enough to help me on quite a few of them. Do *you* do crossword puzzles, Mr. Mason?"

"I'm afraid I don't have much time for them."

"Well, perhaps I should be doing something else— and yet I don't know what else to do. I think it's a lot better to do crossword puzzles than just fritter away your time. After all, Mr. Mason, it does do wonders for your vocabulary."

"I assume it does," Mason said.

Mrs. Gentrie said, "Come, Rebecca. Mr. Mason's time is valuable. He didn't come here just to talk about crossword puzzles."

"Well, I don't want to start talking about that murder again. It all happened yesterday when you upset me with that story about the empty can. I haven't been able to concentrate since."

"Empty can?" Mason asked.

Mrs. Gentrie said indulgently, "That's just a household mystery. You mustn't mind Rebecca. She's always digging up little household mysteries."

"*I'm* interested in mysteries," Mason said, his eyes twinkling. "I collect mysteries the way your sister-in-law collects crossword puzzles."

"Well," Rebecca said, "I wish you'd solve this one, Mr. Mason. I just can't get it off my mind."

"Rebecca!" Mrs. Gentrie rebuked.

"No, go ahead. I'd like to hear it," Mason said. "I really would."

Mrs. Gentrie, evidently quite embarrassed, said, "It was nothing, Mr. Mason. I went down in the cellar yesterday to check over the tins and jars of preserved fruit. I found an empty tin on the shelf."

"Just an empty tin?" Mason asked.

"Yes."

"No. That isn't all of it," Rebecca interpolated. "It was an absolutely brand new tin, Mr. Mason. It had been put up on that shelf with the preserves. There wasn't any label on that tin, and it had been sealed up—you know, crimped over, the way you seal preserves in a can."

"You have one of those sealing machines here?" Mason asked.

"Yes. We put up a good deal of fruit and vegetables. Some we put up in jars, and some we put up in tins. We have a sealing machine which crimps the top on."

"And this can was empty?"

47

"Just exactly as it came from the store," Mrs. Gentrie said.

Rebecca said, "It wasn't any such thing, Florence. The more I think of it, the more I realize there was *something* strange about that can. A can isn't hermetically sealed when it comes from a store."

"What did you do with the tin?" Mason asked.

"Tossed it in the box of old tins," Mrs. Gentrie said, laughing.

"You didn't open it to look inside?"

"Gracious, no. It was too light to have had anything in it. It was just an empty can."

"But you didn't look inside to make *certain* it was empty?"

Rebecca said, "Arthur did that. That's Florence's husband, Mr. Gentrie, you know."

"Was he here when you found it?"

"No. He was looking around for a tin to mix some paint in last night. He found this tin down in the box."

"It was empty?" Mason asked.

"That's what *he* said."

Delman Steele said, "*I* saw the can, Mr. Mason. I went down in the basement last night to ask Mr. Gentrie a question. He was painting around the woodwork of the windows, and the door which leads to the garage. I asked him if he'd seen the tin . . ."

Rebecca interrupted, "*I'm* the one that asked Mr. Steele to go down and dig that tin up. I just couldn't get it off my mind."

Steele laughed and said, "And thereby almost got me in bad with this lieutenant who's investigating the shooting next door."

"How did that happen?" Mason inquired.

"He was checking up on all of the persons who had been down in the basement last night," Steele said. "I sometimes go down to chat with Arthur Gentrie or look in on Miss Gentrie when she's in her darkroom. But I don't think I'd have gone down last night if it hadn't been for Miss Gentrie asking me about the can."

"What's being in the basement got to do with the murder?" Mason asked.

Steele said, "It's beyond me. Tragg was down there prowling here and there, then came back and asked a lot of questions."

Rebecca said, "I'm going to put a lock on my darkroom door. They pulled the door open and flung the dark curtain to one side, let daylight stream in, and fogged half a dozen films for me. Personally, I think the police should be more considerate."

Mason said, "I find myself getting interested in that can. You say that Mr. Gentrie had used it to mix paint in, Mr. Steele?"

"That's right. I guess it's still down there."

"How did he open it?"

"Oh, there's a can-opening machine down there in the cellar."

Rebecca said, "I'm certain you'll agree with me, Mr. Mason, that it's something that should be looked into. That tin didn't *grow* on the shelf. It was a brand new tin. It hadn't been there long—and why should anyone hermetically seal up an empty can?"

"I'm certain I don't know," Mason said.

"Well, neither do I, but someone did."

"You mentioned a garage door," Mason said to Steele. "That's a door which communicates with the garage where Mr. Hocksley keeps his car?"

"That's right," Mrs. Gentrie said. "There's a double garage with one door leading to the cellar. You see, the house is built on a sloping lot, and the ground is so steep they made the cellar in two levels. I presume the house was built before the days of automobiles—or at least before people appreciated the importance of having a garage in connection with the house. Then, later on, someone remodeled that end of the basement so as to include

49

a two-car garage. We keep our machine in one of them, so we have the other one for rent. The side that has the door to the cellar is a little the more desirable, so we rent that, and, of course, use that door to the cellar to come in and out of our house, particularly when it's rainy."

Mason said, "If you don't mind, I'd like to take a look at the garage."

"You can come right down the cellar stairs, Mr. Mason, and open the door—or you can walk around the sidewalk and come in through the garage door."

"I think I'd prefer to go in through the cellar."

Mrs. Gentrie said, "If you'll just come this way, Mr. Mason."

Rebecca firmly pushed the dictionary and the crossword puzzle to one side, got to her feet, and smoothed down her skirts. "If you think you're going down in that cellar with Mr. Mason and talk about that empty can, and have me sitting up here where I can't hear what you're saying, Florence Gentrie, you're very much mistaken. The more I think of it, the more I think that empty tin may just as well as not be a clue to what happened."

"How could it be a clue?" Mrs. Gentrie asked, her eyes twinkling.

"I don't know," Rebecca said firmly, "but it might just as well be. Don't you think so, Delman?"

Steele's laugh was magnetic. "Don't involve me in a family argument," he said. "I just room here. They take me in as one of the family—but I'm not a charter member. I am not entitled to take part in the discussions."

Mrs. Gentrie laughed. "I've never drawn the line there, Delman. When you rented that room and asked if you could move in as one of the family, I told you there was only one thing that was absolutely forbidden—and that was the privilege of the telephone."

She turned to Mr. Mason, smiling, and said, "We should have three lines in here. What with three children all making dates and scrambling for the phone every time it rings, I sometimes think I'll smash it—and I can never get to it in the morning or evening to place my orders at the grocer's or call up my own friends."

Rebecca said, "We were talking about the tin, Florence."

Junior said, "Your clutch is slipping, Aunt Rebecca. How the heck could an empty tin have anything to do . . ."

"Junior!" Mrs. Gentrie broke in. "No one asked you for your opinion. Come on, Mr. Mason, down this way."

They all trooped after the lawyer down to the cellar. Mason looked the place over. Mrs. Gentrie pointed out where she had found the tin. Junior showed him the door leading to the garage. Mason tested the paint with his finger. "This what Mr. Gentrie painted last night?" he asked.

"A quick-drying enamel of some sort," Steele said by way of explanation. "Mr. Gentrie runs a hardware store, you know. This was a sample of a new brand of paint one of the salesmen for a paint company had given him. He wanted him to try it out. He was telling me about it last night."

"It's necessary to mix it?"

"Half and half with some thinner," Steele explained. "Gentrie seemed to think it was a distinct improvement over any other of the brands he'd been handling. It comes in two cans. One of them has the color; and the other is some sort of a quick-drying thinner. You mix the two together, half and half, and apply. It's supposed to dry within six hours."

Mason indicated a spot near the garage door. "Someone evidently didn't know it had been freshly painted. It looks very much as if someone, groping for the doorknob in the dark, got his hands on the paint."

"It does for a fact," Steele said.

"Let *me* see," Junior insisted, pushing forward with an eager curiosity.

Steele said, "That's odd. I hadn't noticed that before. I was down here with the police, too. It's just a little smear."

Mason said, "The paint's dry now. You say it dries in six hours?"

"Yes, four to six hours. That's what Mr. Gentrie told me. Of course, that's the only way I have of knowing."

"Let's look for that tin," Rebecca said, moving along the workbench, sniffing and peering at the assortment of tools. "Here's a can with paint brushes in it. Could this be it, Delman?"

"That's it," Delman said. "You can always tell the way Mr. Gentrie opens a can. He never runs the opener all the way around. He stops just before he cuts the lid entirely free. He always leaves a strip of tin of about a sixteenth of an inch, then twists the lid off."

"That's right," Mrs. Gentrie confirmed. "He says that if you go farther than that, the top of the can falls down on the inside. I always hold up the lid and then finish cutting. Arthur twists. You can see where the top of this can was twisted off."

Mason thoughtfully regarded the tin. "Let's take a look at the *top* of the can just to make our investigation complete," he said.

"At the *top* of the can!" Mrs. Gentrie asked.

Mason nodded.

"Well, probably we can find it if we look through this box of scraps, but, for the life of me, I can't see what . . ."

Steele said, "I noticed it lying here on the bench last night. There it is, over there near the corner. He used it to set a paint can on."

Mason picked up the circular tin top and examined the distinctive place where it had been twisted off.

"This the one?" he asked.

"That's it," Steele said. "I remember that little distinctive twist on the tin. You can see where it was turned . . ."

Mason's eyes showed keen interest. "Wait a minute," he said. "This isn't right."

"What's wrong with it?"

Mason said, "The lid that was on the tin was twisted off to the left. This one is twisted off to the right."

Steele bent forward and regarded the circular piece of tin, then went over to look at the can. "Well, I'll be darned," he said. *"I* saw that piece of tin lying here on the counter last night and naturally supposed it had come off this can. Why in the world would Mr. Gentrie have opened the can, thrown the top away, then taken the top from another tin out of that box of scraps? But Gentrie is left-handed. You're right about that top—but, why . . .?"

"I don't know why," Mason said, "but that's very evidently what he did. Let's take a look over here in this box of scraps."

Rebecca said tartly to Mrs. Gentrie, "I *told* you it had something to do with what happened over there. You can see what happens when a trained mind starts working on the problem."

Mrs. Gentrie sighed. "I'm afraid I'd make a poor detective," she said. "It certainly seemed trivial enough."

Mason smiled. "I'm afraid I'm like your sister-in-law Mrs. Gentrie. Whenever there's anything the least bit out of the ordinary, I start making a mystery out of it. After all, you know, it *is* rather a peculiar place for an empty tin, and I can't imagine why anyone would seal up an entirely empty tin. There must have been *something* in it."

"Well, I shook it and didn't hear anything. And goodness knows the can was light enough to be empty. It *couldn't* have had anything in it. Of course, now that I see everyone making so much of a point of it, it . . ."

"And unless I'm mistaken," Mason, who had been leaning over the scrap box, interposed, "this is the top which came off the can." He reached down into the tangled mass of tin.

"Watch out you don't cut your hand in there," Mrs. Gentrie warned sharply.

Junior laughed and said, "Mr. Mason doesn't need to be a detective to tell you're the mother of three children, Ma. 'Don't do this, and don't do that.' "

Mason straightened up with a piece of tin in his hand, walked over to the can in which the paint brushes were deposited, and held the circular piece of tin over the top so that the little twisted nipple of tin which had been left on the can was placed against the corresponding point on the circular piece.

"That's it all right," Steele said.

Junior reached out eagerly. "Gee, Mr. Mason, let me take a . . ."

"Junior," Mrs. Gentrie rebuked, "don't interfere with what Mr. Mason is doing."

Mason said, "The underside seems to be all scratched up. It feels rough to the touch. Let's just examine those scratches. We'll tilt it over here near the window so that the light comes across it from the side, and . . ."

"It's a code," Rebecca shrilled excitedly. "Something written on there . . . scratched on the tin! I knew it! I just *knew* it! I told you so, Florence. You wouldn't listen to me, but . . ."

Mason whipped a pencil from his pocket and tore a sheet of paper from his notebook. "Will someone write these letters as I read them off?" he asked.

Rebecca said eagerly, "I will."

Mason handed her the paper and pencil, tilting the lid, so that he could get a side lighting on the letters as he read.

"CKDACK CJIAJ DLACC HEDBCE CEIADD GIKADC CLDGBD KFBCH CLGGBJ."

Mason took the piece of paper from Rebecca and carefully checked the letters she had written with the original.

"I don't see how this could have had anything to do with what happened across the street," Mrs. Gentrie said, frankly puzzled.

Mason slipped the sharp-edged circle of tin into the side pocket of his coat. "It may be just a coincidence," he agreed. "Rather peculiar, that's all. How many of you heard the shot?"

"I did," Mrs. Gentrie said.

Steele said, "I was sleeping soundly, and was wakened by the noise. I suppose it was all over when I woke up, but I tried to reconstruct what had wakened me, and somehow had the impression there were *two* shots."

"Did you mention that to Lieutenant Tragg—the head of the Homicide Squad?" Mason asked.

"I don't think I did," Steele said. "He seemed quite positive there was only one shot, and I didn't contradict him. Of course, my impressions were very vague, just trying to recall a noise which has wakened you from a sound sleep. It's just a vague feeling, anyhow—an echo in the back of the consciousness, if you know what I mean."

Mason said, "I know exactly what you mean, and you express it very well indeed. It might be a good plan for you to get in touch with Lieutenant Tragg and tell him that, after thinking it over, you believe it's very possible there were two shots."

"There weren't," Rebecca said positively. "Only one. I was wide awake at the time. I thought it might have been a backfire from an automobile or truck. I know there was only one shot."

Mason turned to Junior, raised his eyebrows.

Junior shook his head. "I can't help you at all. I slept right through the whole commotion. I couldn't have been in bed very long when it happened either, probably not more than fifteen or twenty minutes."

55

"What time was the shot?"

"Around twelve-thirty, I believe."

"What time did you get to bed?"

"Ten or fifteen minutes after midnight. I just shed my clothes all over the room and dove into bed. I'd been out with a young lady, and had taken her home. I thought I was going to have to work today, and—well, I just can't seem to get enough sleep."

Mrs. Gentrie said solicitously, "Junior, don't you think you should tell Mr. Mason with whom you spent the evening?"

Junior colored. "No," he said shortly.

"I noticed that you avoided mentioning her name to that Lieutenant— What's his name?"

"Tragg," Mason prompted.

"No need of dragging a woman into this," Junior said hotly.

"Junior, was it . . ." Mrs. Gentrie started to ask.

"Don't you mention any names," he interrupted with intense feeling. "I don't want you snooping around in my affairs. It's bad enough to have Rebecca always camping on my trail. My gosh, I'm grown up and big enough to take care of myself. I don't go around snooping into your . . ."

"Junior!"

"All right, I'm sorry, but don't you mention any names. I mean that. This is stuff that gets in the papers, and I don't see that it makes a particle of difference who I was with."

Rebecca said, "Well, what are we going to do about that code message on the can? Here we are, standing talking and letting the murderer slip through the fingers of the police."

Mason said, "Let's be certain about that can before we do anything. You feel quite positive you didn't put it up on that shelf with the preserves, Mrs. Gentrie?"

"I *know* I didn't, and I don't think Hester did either.

She's stupid at times, but certainly not that stupid. Further-more, I don't think that can had been there for more than a day or two at the most. I don't see how it could have . . . well . . ."

Mason said, "Well, let's notify Lieutenant Tragg of ex-actly what happened, and he can draw his own conclu-sions. After all, that's his business."

■ 5 ■

Seated in his private office, tilted back in the big swivel chair, Mason propped his heels on the corner of his desk, held his interlocked fingers behind his head, and regarded Della Street with a lazy smile.

"Well," he said, "this is one case where I have a free hand. Carr says I'm to do everything I can to uncover the truth. It makes no difference who gets hurt."

"Even if it's Karr himself?" she asked, studying him searchingly.

Mason nodded. His eyes, preoccupied now, were gaz-ing through Della Street out past the walls of the office.

"You certainly did make *that* plain enough to him," she said. "What were you trying to do, frighten him, or make him mad?"

"Neither. I just didn't want any misunderstanding—and I wanted to know where I stood. Lieutenant Tragg is no one's fool. One of the big things which keeps Karr from being rated as a likely suspect is the condition of his legs. Tragg isn't going to take anyone's word for that. He's going to check up on it."

"Ask permission to make an examination?"

"Oh, he won't be that crude, not unless he gets some-thing else to work on. After all, he's not in a position to go around offending prominent taxpayers. He'll go about

57

it in a roundabout way, but he'll be very thorough. Don't worry about that."

"You think he'll be suspicious of Karr's legs?"

"I would if I were in his place."

She laughed. "Well, in a way, you are."

Mason took his hands from behind his head, stretched out his left wrist, and consulted his strap watch. "Paul Drake's late. He said he'd be in here ten minutes ago, and make a preliminary report. He . . . here he is now."

Della Street was up out of her chair as soon as Paul Drake's distinctive knock sounded on the door of the private office. She crossed over and opened it.

Paul Drake, head of the Drake Detective Agency, tall, thin, and with a look of perpetual, puzzled perplexity on his face, said, "Hello, gang."

"Come in and sit," Mason invited.

Della Street picked up her notebook, settled herself at a small secretarial table, and held her pen poised. Paul Drake slid into the big leather chair, squirmed around so that he was seated crosswise, took a notebook from his pocket, and said, "Well, it looks like one of those things."

"How so?"

"The reason Lieutenant Tragg wasn't particularly communicative," Drake said, "is that he's running around in circles. He doesn't want to talk with anyone until he knows more what he has to talk about."

"Let's have it," Mason said.

"I'm somewhat the same way myself, Perry. I've picked up as much as I can of what the police know and done a little snooping on my own."

"What did you find out?"

"This man Hocksley is a mystery. I think Opal Sunley, that stenographer who comes in to transcribe the cylinders he dictates, knows more than she's admitting. I think Mrs. Perlin, the housekeeper, knew a whole lot more than was good for her."

"Just what did Hocksley do?"

"No one knows. Apparently he slept most of the day and spent the nights dictating. He'd use a dictating machine. The girl would come in and find anywhere from two to fifteen records waiting to be transcribed. Sometimes she'd have an easy day. Sometimes she'd have a hard day. Occasionally she wouldn't be able to even finish the work that was laid out for her. She says it was virtually all correspondence, and that she didn't pay much attention to the contents of the letters, simply typed them out, made sure there were no typographical errors, and left them for Hocksley to sign. She also made one carbon copy. She left that for Hocksley. She doesn't know what he did with them. The point is there aren't any files in the house, just a dictating machine, a cylinder-shaving machine, a transcribing machine, cylinders, a big stock of stationery, envelopes, postage stamps, a pair of scales, and that's about all in the line of office equipment—except the safe."

"What about the safe?"

"The safe is apparently the key to the whole situation," Drake said.

"Tragg seemed very evasive about that safe when I talked with him," Mason said.

"He would be. It's a safe that cost money. It stands in the corner of Hocksley's bedroom. It isn't the sort of safe you'd pick up second hand somewhere and use to keep the ordinary bunch of office junk. It's a safe that has individuality and distinction."

"What was in the safe?" Mason asked.

"That's another thing," Drake said. "When the police got there, there were fifty dollars in cash, about a hundred dollars in postage stamps, and not another damned thing in the safe."

"Was it locked?"

"It was locked. Opal Sunley gave Tragg the combination."

"Then if a burglar had been working on it, he hadn't done himself any good."

59

"Perhaps not. . . . He could have closed and locked it again."

"Well, a hundred and fifty dollars is a hundred and fifty dollars," Mason said.

"Uh huh. But the point is, the man who bought that safe didn't buy it just for postage stamps and chicken-feed currency."

"Okay, what about the shooting?"

"The shooting took place in that room where the safe is," Drake said. "There's some chance Hocksley surprised someone trying to get in the safe. It may have been the housekeeper."

"How do they know the safe figured in it?" Mason asked.

"There's blood on the floor in front of it, quite a little pool. That might indicate that it was a burglar who was shot. But Hocksley is missing, and the housekeeper is missing. There's a trail of blood drops around through several rooms in the house, and more to the point, there's blood in Hocksley's automobile. So you pay your money and take your choice. Either a burglar killed Hocksley and the housekeeper and carted away the bodies, or Hocksley shot a burglar, then put him in the automobile and took him away. The blood in the automobile indicates that the person who had been shot was stretched out on the back seat of the car. That brings us to what seems to be the most logical explanation."

"What's that?"

"The housekeeper was the one who was trying to get in the safe. Hocksley shot her, wounded her, put her in the automobile, and took her away. Hocksley was a big, strong man who could have picked up the housekeeper and carried her out to the automobile. She was a slender woman in the fifties. She couldn't have carried him. There were some burnt matches lying on the floor in the corridor of Hocksley's flat—about half a dozen of them."

"How much have you found out about Hocksley?" Mason asked.

"Not much. Hocksley's a big, powerful man who walks with a decided limp. He's very eccentric, and apparently interested primarily in being left absolutely alone."

"That makes two of them," Mason said.

"What?"

"Tenants in the same building who didn't want to have anything to do with neighbors."

"I gather it was a different situation with Hocksley, from what it was with Karr. Karr is a neurotic old crab. Hocksley was engaged in doing something he wanted kept an absolute secret. Hocksley worked at night, and slept during the daytime. The people who sold him the safe, the agent who rented him the house, the company that sold him his automobile all remember him more or less vaguely. But by putting the descriptions together, we have a pretty good picture of the man, about forty-eight or fifty with very broad shoulders and flaming red hair. His limp was quite noticeable—not the sort of limp you'd get from a stiffness in a leg, but the kind where one leg is shorter than the other."

Mason asked, "Any connection between Hocksley or his housekeeper and anyone over in the Gentrie house?"

"No. The connection there is between Opal Sunley and Arthur Gentrie, Jr. That's also something."

"What?"

"Arthur Gentrie, the boy's father, had been painting that night down in the cellar. I believe you're the one who first noticed that someone who evidently didn't know about that fresh paint had been groping for the garage door and had smeared paint on his fingertips. After you pointed this out to Tragg, he had the police look the automobiles over pretty carefully to see if they couldn't find some trace of paint on the handles of the doors or on the steering wheels. They couldn't find a thing, but over in Hocksley's flat they found two fingerprints outlined in paint of exactly the same color as that used on the garage door."

"Where were those paint fingerprints?" Mason asked.

Drake said, "On the desk telephone, and the desk telephone was on Hocksley's desk, and Hocksley's desk was in the room where the safe was located, and the telephone was right near the door of that room. Moreover, there's a side door on the garage that Hocksley used to get in and out. That door opens into a little yard between the flat and the Gentrie house. It's right near a side door leading to the Hocksley flat."

"Were the fingerprints clear enough so the police could do anything with them?"

"Very clear. I think Tragg's getting ready to do something there. He's just waiting for the right time to strike."

"Meaning he . . ." Mason broke off as the door from the outer office opened, and the girl who had charge of the switchboard timidly entered.

"I didn't know whether to disturb you, Mr. Mason," she said. "I told this woman you were in conference on an important matter, but she says that she wants to see you about the matter you're talking over."

"Who is she?" Mason asked.

"Her name is Gentrie, and there's a young man with her, her son."

Mason glanced at Drake.

Drake, consulting his notebook again, quoted: "He was in bed and asleep when the shot was fired. He came in, however, just about fifteen or twenty minutes before the shooting. He'd been out with Opal Sunley, the stenographer who handled Hocksley's work."

"You're certain?" Mason asked.

"Uh huh."

"I understood he was refusing to divulge the name of the woman . . ."

"Oh, sure," Drake interrupted. "Some of that kid gallantry stuff, but Opal Sunley didn't make any secret of it.

She told the police right at the start. Young Gentrie didn't rate the use of the family automobile, not for her, anyway. They were using streetcars. He took her to a movie, bought her a chocolate sundae afterwards, did a little mild necking in the park, and took her home about eleven-thirty. They said good night on the stairs for half an hour, and young Gentrie left about midnight. Evidently, he went right home and upstairs to bed."

"He must have moved pretty fast if he left her home at midnight and was in bed at quarter past," Mason said. "How far from Hocksley's place does she live?"

"About twelve blocks. You *can* walk it in fifteen minutes if you're young—and have just spent half an hour saying good night to your best girl."

Mason said to the girl in the doorway, "Show them in. I have an idea something is weighing on that young man's mind."

■ 6 ■

Mrs. Gentrie entered Mason's private office with Junior trailing along behind her, very much as though he were being led.

Mrs. Gentrie's attitude was one of parental indignation.

"Mr. Mason," she said, "you'll have to help us. It's about Junior."

Mason looked at the young man's sullen features, and said, "Don't tell me anything in confidence, Mrs. Gentrie, because, in a way, I'm not a free agent. It's quite possible I won't be able to help you."

"Well, I've got to talk with someone, and I don't know anyone else to whom I can turn. This thing has been preying on my mind ever since I heard what Junior said to the police. I thought at first my duty was to back up my son in a chivalrous attempt to protect some young woman's good name. Then, when I began to think of how serious it might be because—well, because perhaps that murder is linked with—well, I can't keep quiet any longer."

"What's eating you?" Junior demanded. "What's got into you, Ma?"

She kept looking anxiously at the lawyer. "Don't you think I'm doing the right thing, Mr. Mason?"

"Go ahead," Mason said. "I've warned you."

Young Gentrie spoke up to say, "You folks go ahead and talk about me all you please, but nothing anyone can do is going to change my position, or make me change my story. I want that definitely and finally understood."

Mrs. Gentrie said, "I wish you'd try to impress on my son the importance of telling the truth, Mr. Mason."

"Have you," Mason asked the young man, "been taking liberties with the truth, Junior? Perhaps just fudging the least little bit?"

"No, I haven't," Gentrie said sullenly.

"Arthur, I know that you have. I tell you I heard that shot and got up. I looked in your room. *You weren't in your bed*. You hadn't been in your room."

"Then you looked in before midnight. I got into my room at midnight, or just ten or fifteen minutes after."

"I looked at the clock. It was thirty-five minutes past twelve."

"You read it wrong. It was thirty-five minutes past eleven, and you thought it was thirty-five minutes past twelve. You didn't have your glasses on, did you?"

Mrs. Gentrie said, "I didn't have my glasses on, but I didn't make a mistake in the time. I'm certain I didn't. And everybody else says that was when the shot was fired."

"What do you mean, everybody else?"

"Well, the other people in the house, all of them."

Junior said, "Well, if you ask me, that fellow Steele

is a phoney. I wouldn't trust him as far as I could throw a loaded truck. Look at the way he's always hanging around Rebecca, helping her with her crossword puzzles, stringing her along. What's he really want, anyway? He isn't supposed to be one of the family. He's supposed to have a room rented, and that's all. You know as well as I do Aunt Rebecca's full of prunes, and she keeps her tongue rattling against the roof of her mouth all the time. It's impossible to have any secrets around her. She spills everything she knows."

"Junior, that's not a nice way to talk about your Aunt Rebecca."

Junior went on hotly, "The other night I was looking for my dictionary and couldn't find it, and came downstairs to see if she had it, and she was telling him a whole lot of stuff about me. She hasn't any right to do that."

"You're altogether too sensitive," Mrs. Gentrie said. "She probably wasn't talking about you at all."

"The heck she wasn't. I heard the whole business, all about how you were worried about me having an infatuation for an older woman. She said . . ." Junior's voice suddenly choked up. His face changed color. "She said altogether too darn much," he finished.

Mrs. Gentrie said, "Mr. Mason isn't interested in our family squabbles, Junior. I came here because . . ."

"I'm old enough now to get out and get a job. I don't need to work in Dad's store. I'm worth the wages I'm getting from him and more. I can support myself. I'm a man now."

Mrs. Gentrie turned to the lawyer, "I'm so worried," she said. "Junior *wasn't* in his room when that shot was fired. He keeps insisting that he was, but I know he wasn't. Now, I understand that the police have found some fingerprints over in Hocksley's flat, and I . . . well, I just wish Junior would tell the truth. That's all. So I'd know what to expect."

"You mean the fingerprints which were outlined in the paint?" Mason asked.

She nodded.

Junior said, "I tell you I was in bed."

Mrs. Gentrie said, by way of explanation, "He'd been out with that stenographer, Opal Sunley, and he swears he took her home about midnight. I'm afraid, Mr. Mason, that he's just doing it to—well, to give her sort of an alibi. Now you look here, Junior. You were just coming up the stairs to your room when that shot was fired, weren't you? You took your flashlight and went sneaking down the stairs."

Junior said, "I thought you said I wasn't in my room."

"You weren't when I looked in there. The bed wasn't even so much as wrinkled. But I'd heard someone sneaking along the corridor and on the stairs."

"I tell you, you didn't have your glasses on, and you made a mistake in the time."

"But everybody says the shot was at twelve-thirty-five."

"Phooey," Junior said. "Because you didn't have your glasses on and . . ."

"Then you think the shot was fired at *eleven*-thirty-five?" Mrs. Gentrie interrupted.

"Why, sure, if I wasn't in my room . . . no, wait a minute. . . . Yes, sure, that's right. The shot was fired at *eleven*-thirty-five."

She said, "Arthur, you're stalling for time. You're trying to think whether you can give her a good alibi for eleven-thirty-five."

Arthur jumped to his feet. "Oh, let me alone," he cried. "You make me tired! You're always twisting everything I do so as to make it seem I'm trying to think of Opal. Can't you leave her out of it ever?"

Mrs. Gentrie glanced at Mason.

Mason, without raising his voice, but putting the tim-

66

bre of authority into his command, said, "Sit down, Arthur. I want to talk with you."

Arthur's eyes met the lawyer's. The young man hesitated for a moment, then seated himself somewhat tentatively on the edge of a chair.

Mason said, "This is your first murder case. I've seen dozens of them. I don't know very much about Miss Sunley. I've seen enough to know that you're trying to protect her. Perhaps it hasn't occurred to you that the most certain way to turn the limelight of pitiless, hostile publicity on her would be to twist the truth to try to keep her out of it."

Arthur Gentrie was interested despite himself. "I don't get you," he said.

"You start suppressing or distorting facts to keep Opal Sunley out of that case," Mason said, "and you'll find that you've not only dragged her in, but have painted her with a crimson brush doing it."

"What's that crimson-brush crack?" Arthur Gentrie asked, suddenly belligerent.

Mason said, "Nice young men don't tell lies in murder cases for nice young women. Do you get me?"

"I'm not certain that I do."

"You make a good impression. The public would look on you as a nice young man. They would consider that the motivation which would cause you to lie to protect a woman would have to be more powerful and more compelling and, frankly, a little more sinister than the ordinary attraction which a nice young woman would or should have for you.

"Now, I'm not going to argue with you. I'm not going to plead with you. I've told you facts. If you want to drag Opal Sunley into this thing, if you want to smear her reputation, if you want the newspapers to treat her as an older woman who was leading a young boy around by the nose . . ."

Gentrie came up out of the chair as though he had

been a fighter springing for an antagonist at the sound of the gong. "No, you don't," he shouted. "You can't . . ."

Mason held up his hand, palm outward. Aside from that, he made no move. "Hurts, doesn't it?" he said. "It hurts because you know it's the truth. Now, what have you to tell me?"

"Nothing."

Mason said, "All right, go on home. Get out. I told you I wasn't going to argue with you, and I wasn't going to plead with you. I've told you. There's truth in what I've told you, and truth is an acid which burns through every falsehood. The only thing it won't touch is the pure gold of unvarnished truth. My words are going to eat into your consciousness until they've cut through the falsehood and got down to the real truth. Then you're going to make a clean breast of things, either to your mother or to me. And after that you're going to feel better. Now, I'm busy. I haven't time to discuss things further. Good-by."

Gentrie, who had quite evidently braced himself when he was taken to the lawyer's office for resistance against cajoleries and blandishments, appeared somewhat dazed by this abrupt dismissal. He said, "Why, I haven't told any . . ."

Mason said, "I'm sorry, Gentrie. I haven't the time to waste. Don't bother to say anything more until you've had a chance to think over what I've said. Good afternoon, Mrs. Gentrie. Let me know if you want to see me again."

Her eyes were troubled but grateful. "Thank you, Mr. Mason. Come, Arthur."

Arthur hung back at the door, then suddenly squared his shoulders, pushed up his chin, and marched out, jerking the door behind him. He would have slammed it violently had it not been for the automatic door check.

Mason grinned across at Della Street. "Hot-headed youth on the rampage."

Della Street said, "I thought he was going to hit you when you said what you did about Opal Sunley."

"He was trying to make himself think so, too. At his age, it was what he considered the manly thing. Sometimes, Della, I don't know but what hot-blooded, impetuous youth which has no time for weighing disadvantages against advantages, or consequences against acts, is a darn sight better than what we are pleased to call the mature outlook."

Her eyes smiled at him. "Obey that impulse, eh?"

"Exactly," he said.

She was laughing now. "Well, it's a good idea. More the philosophy one would expect to hear in a taxicab driving home than in a law office. How about that code message?"

Mason said, "You would bring my nose back to the grindstone. Well, I'll bite. *What* about the code?"

"Given it any thought?"

"Lots of thought, probably too much."

"Look, Chief, if it's a cipher, couldn't you read it? There are nine words in the message, and I've always understood any cipher can be solved if there's a long enough message."

Mason said, "I guess that's right, but I don't think it's an ordinary cipher in which letters are transposed."

"Why not?"

"Let's analyze this. There are nine words. Five of them begin with the letter *c*. The letter *c* is in every single word at least once."

"Wouldn't that indicate it was either *e* or *a?*"

"I'm afraid you're missing the most significant thing about the whole message, Della."

She studied the typewritten copy of the message which Mason pushed across to her. After an interval of silence, she said, "I'm afraid I don't get it."

"Look again. It's relatively simple."

"You mean that there are no short words in it?"

"That's one thing," Mason said. "The shortest word in there has five letters. The longest has six. That's an interesting peculiarity of the message. Nine words. Three of them have five letters, and the other six have six letters. But there's something that's far more significant than that."

"What?"

"Give up?" he asked banteringly.

She nodded.

"The last fourteen letters of the alphabet aren't represented there at all," he said. "The entire message is composed of words made up from the first twelve letters of the alphabet."

Della Street frowned, stared down at the typewriting, then said thoughtfully, "That's right. What does it mean?"

Mason said, "I'll tell you one other significant thing. Every word contains either the letter *a* or the letter *b*."

"I don't see that that's as important as the frequency with which the letter *c* occurs."

"Perhaps not, unless we also consider positions. Every word has either *a* or *b* in it, but neither *a* nor *b* appears at the first of the word or at the ending. They're always either the second or third letter from the end of the word."

There followed an interval while she checked his conclusions, then nodded again.

Mason said, "That empty can is significant in a good many ways. I'm wondering whether Tragg has overlooked some of those things, or is just sitting tight and awaiting developments."

"What, for instance?" Della asked.

"That can conveyed a message to some person," Mason said. "That means two persons were concerned in the crime. That, in turn, means that the someone who put the can there must have had easy access to the basement. It also means that the person for whom the message was intended must have had easy access to the basement. Yet it also means that *those two persons didn't have access to each other."*

"I don't get you," Della Street said.

"It's simple," Mason pointed out. "If the two persons could have met and talked with each other, there would have been no necessity for going to all that elaborate trouble of scratching a message in the top of the can, sealing the can, and placing it in the cellar."

"Yes. That's true."

"The fact that the cellar was chosen as the place where the message was to be left means that both parties must have had access to the cellar."

She nodded.

"Therefore," Mason said, "we have a peculiar situation. Two persons have access to the same place, yet those persons don't have contact with each other, and that place is highly unusual—the cellar of a big, rambling, frame residence."

Della Street said excitedly, "Now that you analyze it, it's plain as day. One of the persons had to have access to the cellar through the garage that Hocksley rented, and the other one because he lived in Gentrie's house."

Mason said, "That's one of the possibilities."

"But, Chief," Della Street said, "that brings up all sorts of complications."

"That's just the point."

"Then you think Junior is mixed up with it—and Opal?"

Mason said, "The evidence *seems* to point the other way."

He said, "Then the message in the can becomes perfectly meaningless . . . so far as the murder is concerned."

"Why? Oh, I get it. Because he and she were together. Is that right?"

"That's right."

Della Street said with a smile, "Once that message is deciphered, it may turn out to be 'I love you, darling, no

71

matter what happens.' Persons in love are inclined to do things like that, you know—or do you?"

Mason nodded, said, "Frankly, Della, if it had been a simple cipher where letters had been transposed in order to make a message, I would have been very much surprised if it had had anything to do with the murder. But as it is, I'm inclined to attach more importance to it. But the perfectly obvious and logical point seems to have escaped everyone."

"What's that?"

"The one real clue as to the identity of the person for whom the message was intended."

"What's the clue?"

Mason said, "The fact that only one person got it, of course."

"You mean . . . ?"

"Arthur Gentrie."

"Junior? I thought you said he . . ."

"No, the father. He's the one who went down in the cellar. He says he found the can lying in the box and opened it in order to mix up paint in it. Then he threw the top away, but you notice that when Steele became interested in the top, Gentrie saw that the tops were substituted. The one with the code message on it remained in the box, and one that had no message was put on the workbench."

Della Street said, "My gosh, Chief, it's perfectly obvious, now that you mention it. The way you sum it up, it sounds rather damning."

Mason pulled the sheet of typewritten paper over to him, started studying it. Abruptly, he laughed.

"What is it?" she asked.

"That code," he said. "It's absolutely simple."

"You mean you can read the message?" Della Street asked.

Mason nodded. "It's absurdly simple when you approach the problem from the right angle."

"What's the right angle?"

"Notice," Mason said, "that only the first twelve letters in the alphabet are employed. Notice that every word contains *either* a or b, and that a or b, whenever it appears, is either the second or the third letter from the end of the word. That, coupled with the fact that the words have either five or six letters, is absolutely determinative of the whole business. I wonder if Tragg has got it by this time."

Della Street said, "I don't get it."

"Twelve letters," Mason said. "Good Lord, Della, it fairly hits you in the face."

"It doesn't hit me in the face," Della Street laughed. "It doesn't hit me anywhere. I miss it altogether."

Mason pushed back his chair. "I'm going out for fifteen or twenty minutes, Della. Think it over while I'm gone."

She said, "Ordinarily, I'm a peaceful woman. I'm not given to homicidal mania, but if you arouse my curiosity this way and then try to go out of that door without telling me what the message says, I'm very apt to assault you with a deadly weapon before you get as far as the elevator."

Mason said, "I don't know what the message says."

"I thought you said you did."

"No. I said the solution was simple. Good Lord, Della, I can't give you any more clues than that. I've virtually told you the whole thing now."

"You'll be back in twenty minutes?"

"Yes."

"And you'll tell me what the message says then?"

"Shortly afterwards, yes."

"But I'm supposed to get the secret of this while you're gone?"

"You should."

"What does twelve letters have to do with it?"

"How much is twelve?" Mason asked.

She frowned. "You mean six and six?"

"That's not it."

"You don't mean that since two and two make four, six and six make twelve?"

"No, not that way."

"You mean it's eleven and one?"

Mason smiled. "Try ten and two," he said, "and you'll be on the right track. And if you can't get it from that, you're going to have to buy me the drinks."

Mason took his hat out of the coat closet, grinned at her, and started for the elevator.

■ 7 ■

Della Street was sitting at her desk frantically scribbling with a pencil when Mason returned, an oblong package under his arm.

"Get it?" he asked.

"Uh huh. That ten plus two crack did it."

"Got it deciphered?"

She said, "I've got it figured both ways. Either the figures start with *a* and end with *j*, or they start with *c* and end with *l*."

"They start with *c* and end with *l*," Mason said. "The *a* and *b* are true letters."

"How do you know?"

"Because the *a* and *b* are always either the second or third letter from the end of the word."

"Well, I've got it worked out that way," she said.

"How does it check out?"

She said, "Well, if *c* represents one; *d* represents two; *e*, three; *f*, four; *g*, five; *h*, six; *i*, seven; *j*, eight; *k*, nine; and *l* a cipher, the message breaks down into 192A19

187A8 20A11 632B13 137A22 579A21 1025B2 94B16 1055B8."

"I think we can safely rely on that," Mason said.

"But that's a code within a code," she said. "It still doesn't give us the message."

"No," Mason said, untying the string around the oblong package, "but I think this will."

"What is it?"

"There are two books that might have been used as keys, two books that would naturally have large vocabularies, and in which the pages would be divided into an A column and a B column. They're the Bible and the dictionary."

"And because Junior mentioned his dictionary, you think . . ."

"There's been a lot of talk about a dictionary," Mason agreed, taking the wrappings off the package. "No one's said very much about a Bible. Junior has his dictionary, and he isn't able to keep his hands on it because his Aunt Rebecca is constantly borrowing it. She says that her interest in it is due to crossword puzzles, but that *might* not be true. In any event, the dictionary looks like a good lead."

"How do you know which dictionary?"

"I happened to notice the dictionary on the table when I was out at Gentries'. It's a Webster's Collegiate Dictionary, Fifth Edition."

"Then the numbers refer to pages?"

"That's right. For instance, the first word in the code message would be the nineteenth word from the top in the A column on page 192."

"And the A column would be the first one?"

"That's right. The one on the left."

Della Street said, "Gosh, Chief, I'm so excited. I'm trembling. Let's see what it is."

Mason turned the pages in the dictionary, then counted down the column.

"What is it?" she asked.

"Coast," Mason said.

"Coast." She frowned. "That doesn't sound right."

"Well, let's try the next one. What is it?"

"The eighth word in the left-hand column on page 187."

Mason turned back a few pages in the dictionary, then announced, "That word's 'clear.' What's the next one?"

Della Street's voice showed her excitement. "Gosh, Chief, that makes it 'Coast clear.' Let's see. The next one's the eleventh word in the A column on page 20."

Mason made a brief search, then announced, "That's 'after.' What comes next?"

"The thirteenth word in the B column on page 632."

When Mason found that word, he whistled.

"What is it?" she demanded impatiently.

"Midnight," Mason said. "Get it? 'Coast clear after midnight.'"

"We've got it. We've got it," she said. "And the crime was committed after midnight. It ties up. This is the solution of the whole business."

"Don't be *too* certain," Mason warned. "What's our next word?"

"The twenty-second word in the A column on page 137."

"But," Mason announced after a moment. "What's next?"

"The twenty-first word in the A column on page 579."

Mason turned pages. "Lift," he said. "What's next?"

"The second word in the B column on page 1025. Gosh, Chief, hurry."

Mason turned the pages. Once more he gave a low whistle.

"What is it?"

"Telephone receiver," Mason said.

Della Street regarded him with startled eyes. " 'Coast

clear after midnight but lift telephone receiver.' And the police found fingerprints on the telephone receiver!"

"That's right. What's next?"

"The sixteenth word in the B column on page 94."

"Before," Mason announced. "What's the last word?"

"The eighth word in the B column on page 1055."

Mason turned the pages and said, "That's 'touching.' That gives us the message, Della. *'Coast clear after midnight, but lift telephone receiver before touching.'* "

"Before touching what?" she asked.

He shrugged his shoulders. "Obviously not the telephone receiver. You can't lift a telephone receiver without touching it."

"What are you going to do about this, Chief?"

"Darned if I know."

"Going to tell Tragg?"

"I think not—not yet."

"And you think this implicates Rebecca?"

He said, "I don't know. After all, Arthur Gentrie was the one who *got* the message, and apparently the only one. That tin was left there for a purpose. It contained a message. The person who left it knew it contained a message, and the person who was to have received the message knew that it contained a message. Apparently, the only one who made any attempt to *open* the can was Arthur Gentrie."

"But he was in bed at the time the shot was fired."

"Exactly."

The telephone, which was connected with Mason's private unlisted line—a number which less than half a dozen people had—buzzed into activity. Mason picked up the receiver, said, "Let's have it."

Paul Drake's voice said. "Giving you a hot tip right off the bat, Perry."

"What is it?"

"Remember I told you there were fingerprints on the telephone receiver?"

"Yes."

"Tragg isn't saying anything just yet, but he's found out whose prints they are."

"Whose?"

"Arthur Gentrie's."

"The old man," Mason said triumphantly. "I was just telling Della that . . ."

"No," Drake interrupted. "The young chap—the one they call Junior."

Mason frowned. "Darn it, Paul. You kick the props out from under me just when I'm showing off to my secretary. Why the hell couldn't you have waited a half hour with that information?"

"Well," Drake said cheerfully, "that's the way with theories. You form them, and they get upset."

"But everything in this pointed absolutely to one logical conclusion," Mason said. "It just doesn't fit in to have those fingerprints belong to young Gentrie."

"Well, they're his prints all right. Keep it under your hat. I got a straight tip from one of the newspaper boys. Tragg isn't saying anything. The newspaper guys got it straight from the fingerprint man in the D.A.'s office, but had to promise not to use it until he got a release. Apparently, Tragg's going to give the boy a little rope and see if he'll get himself tangled up."

"Okay," Mason said, "keep me posted, Paul." He dropped the receiver into place, looked at Della Street, and shook his head. "The darn thing just doesn't fit."

"They're Junior's fingerprints?" she asked.
He nodded.

"Then the message *must* have been for him."

Mason pushed his hands down deep in his pockets. "That is what comes of sticking my neck out," he announced.

■ 8 ■

The strident bell summoned Perry Mason from the depths of slumber. While his drugged senses were still trying to adjust themselves, his hand automatically reached for the telephone. He said thickly, "Hello."

Only Della Street and Paul Drake had the number of that telephone which was by Mason's bedside, a telephone which rang only in cases of grave emergency.

Paul Drake was on the line. "Hello, Perry," he said. "Sorry to bust in on your slumbers, but snap awake, because this is important."

"All right," Mason said, "I can take it. What is it?"

"Remember," Drake said, "the evening paper mentioned that you were working on the case and that you had employed the Drake Detective Agency to make an investigation?"

"Yes," Mason said, switching on a light.

"Well, she read the paper and called me up."

"Who did?"

"I'm coming to that in a minute. I want to make certain you're awake before I give you this."

Mason said impatiently, "I'm awake all right. I've got the light on. What is it?"

"Mrs. Sarah Perlin, Hocksley's housekeeper, telephoned the office and said that if she could talk with Mr. Mason personally, she'd make a complete confession. She wanted to know where she could reach you. What do I do?"

"A complete confession?" Mason asked.

"Yes."

"Where is she?"

"Waiting on one of the other trunk lines."

"Trace the call?" Mason asked.

"Yes. It's from a public pay station. I didn't know what to do. I thought I'd get in touch with you and let you be the goat. If we don't relay the information on to the police and try to hold her there until a radio car can get on the job, we're sticking our necks out. But, on the other hand . . ."

"Tell her to call this number," Mason said. "Tell her she can talk with me here."

"And how about the police?"

"Forget 'em."

"Okay," Drake said, "I'm stalling her along on the other line. Hold the phone, Perry, until I see if she's still on the line."

Mason held the telephone, hearing only the slight buzzing sound of the wire. Then he heard Drake's voice once more. "Okay, Perry, she says she'll call you in twenty minutes. She thinks I was having the call traced and notifying the police. She says she'll go to another pay station. She says if I've notified the police, it won't do a bit of good, that you're the only one she'll talk with."

"Said she'd call in about twenty minutes?" Mason asked.

"That's right."

"Okay, Paul. What are *you* doing up at the office this time of night?"

"No rest for the wicked," Drake said wearily. "A lot of stuff has been coming in. I'm up here sifting the reports, and juggling the men around on new assignments. I was just ready to quit."

"What time is it?"

"About one o'clock."

"How did that woman sound on the telephone, Paul?"

"She didn't seem particularly excited. She has a good speaking voice."

"But she said she was going to make a confession?"

"That's right. I guess that'll crack the whole case. The way the police figured it out, there was only one shot. Two people had disappeared. That meant Hocksley had killed his housekeeper, removed the body, and was in hiding, or that she had killed him."

Mason said, "In that latter event, I think there was an accomplice. She didn't give you any inkling of who it was, did she?"

"No, not a thing. Just said that if she could talk with Mr. Mason personally, she'd make a complete confession. Otherwise, there was no dice."

"Better stick around," Mason said, "in case I need you."

"For how long?"

"Oh, until I tell you to quit."

Drake said, "Okay, there's a couch here in the office. I'll bed down on that, and the night operator will call me in case you phone in."

"Hate to bust up your sleep," Mason apologized.

"Oh, it's all right. I'm used to that."

"Okay," Mason said, "I'll give you a ring."

He hung up the telephone, stretched, yawned, got out of bed, closed the windows in the room, dressed, and was smoking a cigarette when his telephone rang.

Mason picked up the receiver, said, "This is Perry Mason talking," and heard a low voice saying in a tone of calm finality, "This is Mrs. Perlin. It's all over. I've decided to confess."

"Yes, Mrs. Perlin."

"Don't try to have this call traced."

"I won't."

"It won't do you any good if you do try."

"I tell you I won't try."

"I want to talk with you. I *must* talk with you."

"Go ahead. You're talking with me now," Mason said.

"Not this way. I want to be where our conversation can be absolutely confidential."

Mason said, "Do you want to come here?"

"No. You'll have to come to me."

"Where are you?"

"You promise you won't notify the police?"

"Yes."

"You'll come alone?"

"Yes."

"How soon?"

"As soon as I can make it. That's on the understanding that you're going to play absolutely fair with me and will make a frank statement."

She said, "Come to six-o-four East Hillgrade Avenue. Don't park your car directly in front of the house. Leave it half a block down the hill. Don't go to the front door. It will be locked, and I won't answer the bell. Go around to the garage in the back of the house. Wait there until you see a light turned on in the house. When you see that light turned on, go in through the *back* door. It will be open and unlocked. Be certain you come alone and don't try to tip the police off."

Mason said, "It will take me fifteen or twenty minutes to get there."

"That's all right, only remember to do just as I told you."

Mason said, "That's all very well, Mrs. Perlin, but I certainly can't go chasing around at night simply on the strength of a telephone conversation with a woman who says she has something confidential to tell me."

"You understand who this is talking, don't you?"

"Mr. Hocksley's housekeeper?"

"Yes. I'm going to tell you the truth. I want someone in whom I can confide."

Mason, trying to draw her out, said, "That's all rather vague, Mrs. Perlin."

She hesitated, then said slowly, "I shot him. I had a right to shoot him. I destroyed the body so it can never be found. And then I wondered if that was the wise thing to do. That made it look as though I were a criminal. That's what I have to ask you about, whether I shouldn't tell the whole truth. I was absolutely justified in what I

82

did. No jury would ever convict me—not ever. Now, do you want to see me, or do I have to call some other lawyer?"

"I want to see you," Mason said. "You're at that address on Hillgrade Avenue?"

"I'll meet you there—if you play fair. Otherwise you'll never see me. Be sure you do just as I told you. Don't come in as soon as you get there—and when you do come, come in through the *back* door. I have to do it that way so I can be certain you're playing fair with me. You probably think I'm hard to get along with, but you'll understand after I tell you the circumstances."

Mason said, "All right, I'll be out," and hung up the telephone.

He looked at his watch to verify the time, then wrote the address 604 East Hillgrade Avenue on a sheet of paper, folded the paper, put it in an envelope, addressed the envelope to Lieutenant Tragg, sealed it, and placed it on the little table by the side of the bed, then he called the Drake Detective Agency. When he had Paul Drake on the line, he said, "Paul, I'm going places. It doesn't sound any too good. There's just a chance we're dealing with a woman who is a homicidal paranoiac. In case you don't hear from me within an hour, bust out to six-o-four East Hillgrade Avenue—and be damn sure you get in. Also be sure you have a gun in your hand when you go in, and you'd better have a couple of hard-boiled men with you."

"Why not let me pick up a couple of tough operatives and go out there with you, Perry?"

"I don't think it would do any good. She's given me certain specific instructions. She's evidently where she can check up on me to see if I'm following those instructions. I wouldn't doubt if she's planted right across the street waiting to see what I do."

"Okay, Perry, I'll crash the joint in exactly one hour if I don't hear from you."

Mason slid the receiver back into place, put on a light topcoat, pulled his hat down low over his eyes, and left his apartment. Walking to the garage where he kept his car, Mason was careful to avoid looking around, as though afraid someone might be shadowing him. He slid in behind the wheel of his car, warmed up the motor, nodded to the night attendant in the garage, and rolled out into the dark, all-but-deserted street.

Following instructions to the letter, he left his car in the five-hundred block on Hillgrade Avenue and walked up the steep incline toward the intersection.

Six hundred and four was the first house on the right, after he had passed the intersection. It was a typical Southern California bungalow, neat, cool, efficiently arranged, and without anything to differentiate it from thousands of other bungalows. The house seemed dark and deserted. Mason, however, had expected this. If Mrs. Perlin had decided to follow him, to make certain he wasn't leading police to the place, it would normally take her some little time, after she had satisfied herself, to enter the house and turn on the lights. It was quite possible she'd deliberately keep him waiting. The fact that she had instructed him to wait until he saw the light and then go in through the back door convinced him that the woman herself would slip in through the front door, divest herself of hat and coat, and subsequently claim she had been in the house all the time.

Mason, keeping to the shadows, moved around toward the garage at the back of the house. A moon in the last quarter furnished a faint yellowish light which enabled him to find his way down the side street and into the driveway which led to the garage. Beneath the deep shadows of a spreading pepper tree, the lawyer found an empty box which he improvised as a chair, and waited.

He watched for a light to come on in the house. The luminous hands of Mason's watch ticked through an interval of minutes without anything happening—fifteen minutes—twenty minutes.

Mason moved restlessly. He'd have to reach Paul Drake soon or there would be complications.

Mason eased himself off the box, tiptoed toward the house. A vague, disquieting thought intruded itself upon his mind. If this should be some elaborate hoax, some runaround by which Mason was to be placed on a spot, what could put him in a more embarrassing position than to be caught prowling around the back yard of a house at nearly two o'clock in the morning. After all, he'd been unusually credulous, too credulous in fact. It had been because of some quality in that voice, as well as because he'd been aroused out of sound slumber. Her voice had held a note of well-modulated poise which had, somehow, impressed Mason with its sincerity.

He looked at his watch again and reluctantly determined he'd have to go telephone Paul Drake, and call off his vigil. Quite evidently, she had anticipated he might do something like that, and had determined to keep him waiting until . . .

A light was switched on in the house.

Mason could see the beam pouring through an unshaded window. It splashed across a strip of lawn, and against an ornamental hedge. At the same time, Mason became acutely conscious that this all might be some clever trap. A voice on the telephone—Mason sent to the back yard of a strange house. Then they had only to put through a telephone call to the occupant of that house. When he switched on the light to answer the phone, Mason would come up to try the back door. Anyone would be legally justified in shooting him as a burglar.

There was a vast difference between making a rendezvous over the phone with a reassuringly calm voice and actually waiting in the midnight chill of a strange back yard.

Mason decided to let the back door determine the is-

85

sue. If it turned out to be unlocked, he would go in, come what may. Otherwise, he'd return home and say nothing.

He tiptoed up the walk, paused for a moment as he encountered the back steps, then felt his way up, opened a screen door, winced inwardly at the creak of a rusty spring, stepped across a linoleum-covered surface, and tentatively tried the knob of the back door.

It opened readily enough.

Mason gently pushed the door. He could see the faint gleam of a reflected light trickling through from some room down a corridor. He took a cautious step forward —and the light was suddenly switched off, leaving the entire interior of the house in darkness. His eyes accustomed by now to this darkness, Mason could find no clue to indicate in which room the light had been turned on and then off again.

Standing in the midst of a darkness which had suddenly become a baffling barrier to further progress, smelling those peculiar homey smells which invariably attach themselves to a kitchen, Mason waited for some development that would give him a cue on which to proceed.

Abruptly the break he had been waiting for came. He heard the gasping intake of a sobbing breath, then the sound of light feet coming groping down a corridor. The steps were coming toward him. From the kitchen there might be a swinging door. . . .

He heard hinges creak cautiously. A door was pushed back. For a fleeting instant, he had the feeling that someone was standing on the threshold of a swinging door, listening. Then the door swung back, and Mason realized someone was groping toward him, looking either for him or for the back door.

Mason moved back a cautious step, his left hand groping for the light switch which he realized must be on the wall in the vicinity of the back door. The person in the room was groping blindly. Mason heard this person stumble against a table, and took advantage of the noise

86

to turn toward the back door so he could see more clearly the location of his objective. His foot kicked a chair. He heard a quick startled intake of breath, then a woman's voice saying quickly, "Who's there? Who is it? Speak up or I'll shoot."

Mason said, "I've come to keep my appointment."

He realized then that she was no longer coming toward him, but was backing away under cover of the darkness, moving quickly, trying not to make any noise, yet he could distinctly hear the sound of groping motion. His fingers, sliding along the wall, found the buttom of the light switch. He pushed it.

It was a light on the screened porch, but the illumination from it, seeping through the open door and into the kitchen, gave sufficient light so that they could see each other.

She was evidently young. Her body held the lithe lines of resilient youth. It was impossible to see the expression on her face, but he could see the arm which was stretched out in front, and the ominous glint of metal in the hand, which was extended toward him.

Mason said, "Don't be foolish. Put down the gun."

The hand didn't so much as waver. "Who are you, and what do you want?"

"I'm here to keep an appointment."

"With whom?"

"With the woman who made it. Are you she?"

"I most certainly am not. Stand to one side and let me out."

"You don't live here?"

She hesitated a moment, then said, "No."

Mason stood to one side. "Go ahead," he said.

She came toward him cautiously. Light coming through the doorway struck her face. He could see deep brown eyes, a rather short, pert nose, light golden hair which fluffed out from under the rolled-up brim of a small hat perched jauntily on one side of her head. She was rather tall, and her short skirt disclosed legs which had a long graceful sweep from knee to ankle.

"Just keep back out of the way," she warned, holding the gun on him as she came forward.

"Why the artillery?" Mason asked, trying to trap her into conversation.

She did not deign to answer his question, simply kept moving forward with that slow, wary approach as though she were stalking him.

"Don't get nervous and pull the trigger on that gun," Mason said apprehensively.

"I know what I'm doing."

"Then look out for that chair in front of you," he warned. "You'll hit that, the gun will go off, and . . ."

She turned her head slightly in the direction indicated, and Mason's long arms shot out. His left hand clamped down over her right wrist. He felt her muscles bunch into tension. His fingers squeezed the strength out of her wrist. When he felt her fingers grow limp, he took the revolver from her hand, and slipped it into the side pocket of his coat.

The realization that she was disarmed gave her the strength of panic. She jerked her arm, trying to free her hand. When Mason held tight, she raised her right leg high, and kicked out at him hard, driving the heel of her shoe toward the pit of his stomach.

Mason swung to one side, jerking on her wrist as he moved. He threw her off balance and toward him. Then as she lowered her leg to keep from falling, Mason grabbed her around the waist with his left hand, circled her shoulders with his right, pinning her arms to her sides. "Now let's be sensible," he said.

He could feel the resistance drain out of her. The slender body crushed up against his grew limp.

"No kicking now," Mason warned, and relaxed his grip.

"Who are you?" she asked.

"My name's Mason. I'm a lawyer. You didn't telephone me?"

"You're—you're Perry Mason?"

"Yes."

She clung to his arm. There was something of desperation in that grip. He could feel the tremor of tortured nerves in the tips of her fingers. "Why didn't you say so?"

"You're the one who telephoned for me?" Mason asked.

"No."

"What are you doing here?"

"I . . . I came here—to meet someone."

"Whom?"

"It doesn't make any difference. I think now it was a trap. I want to get out. Can't we leave here?"

Mason said, "*I* was to meet someone here. Suppose you tell me who you are?"

"I'm Opal Sunley—the one who called the police yesterday morning."

"Whom were you going to meet here?"

"Mrs. Perlin."

"So was I," Mason said. "Suppose we wait together? I think perhaps she wanted to see us both together. She told me she was going to make a confession."

"She won't make it now," the girl said.

"Why not?"

Mason could feel her trembling. It was more than mere nervousness. It was trembling of one who's in the grip of a fear which threatens momentarily to become blind panic.

"Go on," Mason said. "Where is she?"

The girl's fingers were digging into his arm. "She's—she's in the bedroom. She's dead."

Mason said, "Let's look."

"No, no! You go alone!"

"I'm not leaving you at the moment. You'll have to come along."

"I can't. I can't face it. I can't go back there!"

Mason slid his arm around her waist. "Come on," he said. "Buck up. It's something you've got to do. The quicker you start, the easier it will be."

He accompanied his words with a gentle pressure, urging her toward the door at the other end of the kitchen. He opened this door, and struck a match. The flickering flame showed him a light switch. He pushed it. The room blazed with a light which seemed dazzling. The furniture was of that nondescript variety which robbed the room of personality. He knew then that this was merely a house, cheaply furnished, and rented furnished.

"Where is she?" Mason asked.

"Down . . . the corridor."

The dining room had two doors. One of them opened into a corridor, the other into a living room. The corridor then ran the length of the house to broaden into a reception room by the front door. Mason switched on a light in the hallway. On the right were two doors which apparently led to bedrooms with a bath in between. Mason moved cautiously along this hallway.

"Which bedroom?" he asked.

"The front."

Mason kept gently urging her forward. He opened the door of the bedroom, pushed a light switch, and paused, surveying the interior. Opal Sunley jerked back away from the door.

"I can't," she said. "I can't! I won't! Don't try to make me!"

"Okay," Mason said, "take it easy."

The woman who lay sprawled on the floor in front of the dressing table had quite evidently fallen from the padded bench. She was dressed for the street, even to her hat, which had been pushed to one side of her head when she fell. She was lying on her left side, her left arm stretching out, her left hand clutching at the carpet. The fingers were short, stubby, and competent. The nails were close-cut, uncolored. The right arm lay across the body. The fingers of the right hand still clutched the handle of a grim snub-nosed revolver. She had evidently been shot once, just slightly to one side of the left breast.

Mason walked across the room, bent over, and placed his forefinger on the woman's left wrist.

The young woman in the doorway stood staring as though torn between a desire to run screaming from the house, and an urge to see every move that was made.

Mason straightened from his examination. "All right," he said, "we'll have to notify the police."

"No, no, no!" she cried. "You mustn't! You can't!"

"Why not?"

"It . . . They wouldn't understand. It . . ."

"Wouldn't understand what?"

"How I happened to be here."

"How *did* you happen to be here?"

"She telephoned me, and told me to come."

"She telephoned me, and told me to come," Mason said.

"She—she said she had something she wanted to confess."

"When did she telephone you?" Mason asked.

"About an hour ago. Perhaps not quite that long."

"What did she say?"

"Told me to come to the front door, walk in, switch on the lights, and wait for her in case she wasn't here."

"Did she say where she was, or what she was doing?"

"She was keeping an eye on someone. I didn't get all there was to it. She didn't talk with me herself."

"She didn't?"

"No. . . . Let's get out of here. I can't talk here. I can't . . ."

"Wait a minute," Mason said. "Do you know this person?"

"Why, yes, of course."

91

"Who is it?"

"Mrs. Perlin, Hocksley's housekeeper."

"Did she live here?"

"No. She lived in the flat with Mr. Hocksley. I don't know how she happened to come here."

"Had you seen her at all today?"

"I'm not going to be questioned about this."

Mason said. "That's what *you* think. You're going to be questioned about this until your eardrums get calloused. *Who* telephoned you?"

"I don't know. It was a woman with a nice voice, who said Sarah had given her a message to pass on to me, that I was to leave my car about half a block beyond the house up the hill. I was to walk back to this house and come right in. In case Sarah wasn't here, I was to switch on the lights and make myself at home. She said Sarah would be here within a very few minutes of the time I arrived. She said Sarah was keeping a watch on someone who might be trying to double-cross her, and she couldn't break away long enough to talk with me herself."

"Did you think it might be some sort of a trap?"

"Not then."

"Did the one who spoke to you say anything about not telephoning the police?"

"Yes."

"And you didn't think of this as being a trap of some sort to get you? In other words, didn't you feel somewhat diffident about coming out into a residential neighborhood and simply walking into a strange house at two o'clock in the morning, switching on the lights, and making yourself at home?"

"I tell you, I didn't at the time. I did later."

"How much later?"

"When I got near the house and began to think over the things I was supposed to do. This woman told me the front door would be unlocked. I decided that I'd see if the front door actually was open. If it was, I'd go in. Otherwise, I wasn't even going to try to ring the bell or do anything about it."

"So you tried the front door and it was open."

"Yes. I came in. No one seemed to be home. I thought I'd find the bathroom . . ."

"What did Mrs. Perlin want to confess?"

"She didn't say. That is, the one who was talking with me didn't have anything to say about that. She simply said that Sarah had told her to tell me she wanted to make a confession, and ask my forgiveness."

"Ask *your* forgiveness!"

"Yes."

"And you don't know who this person was?"

"No. She said she was simply passing on the message, that Sarah was busy, and . . ."

"Yes. You've gone over all that, but did this person give you any idea of who *she* was?"

"No. Somehow, I got the impression she was a waitress in some restaurant where Sarah had established headquarters. You know, where Sarah could stand by the door to wait and watch. She said Sarah was over at the window, watching to see if a man to whom she'd telephoned was double-crossing her."

"You have your own car?"

"Yes. That is, it isn't mine. It's a car I can borrow when I need one."

"And you parked it a half a block beyond the house up the hill?"

"Yes."

"She distinctly told you a half block beyond the house, and *up* the hill, did she?"

"That's right."

Mason said, "That shot was instantly fatal. She's dead. There isn't the faintest trace of pulse. You can tell from the location of the wound and the direction of the bullet that death was virtually instantaneous. Now then, why should she have committed suicide?"

"I tell you I don't know."

"And why can't you tell your story to the police?"

"Because—because I'm afraid I'm in an awful jam, Mr. Mason. Sarah was the only one who could have vouched for me in case—well, in case the police turn up certain things."

"And you want me to suppress all of this," and Mason included the room and the body with a sweeping gesture of his hands, "simply in order to save you from being questioned by the police?"

"It isn't going to hurt anything if you do this for me," she said. "There's nothing you can do to help solve this."

Mason studied her thoughtfully. Abruptly, he asked, "This Mrs. Perlin, was she a woman who had had much experience as a housekeeper, or had she perhaps had money at one time, run into hard luck, and had to get work as a housekeeper . . . ?"

"No. She'd been a housekeeper for years. I remember checking on her agency card when Mr. Hocksley hired her."

Mason strolled down the corridor toward the dining room. His hands were pushed down in his pockets, his head thrust forward. She followed him, apprehensive, silently pleading. Abruptly, Mason whirled to face her. "You know what you're asking?" he demanded.

She said nothing as he paused, her eyes pleading eloquently, her lips motionless.

"You're asking me to square a murder," Mason said, "to get my neck in a noose, and you're doing it as casually as though you were wanting to know if I wouldn't buy you an ice cream, or sign my name in your autograph album."

She kept looking at him, pleading with her eyes. Her hand came out to touch his arm.

Mason said, "Once I walk out of this house without calling the police, I've put myself in the middle of a great big spot. I've given you a stranglehold on me. How deeply are you mixed in this business?"

She shook her head.

"Come on. Speak up."

"I'm not in it at all."

Mason said, "That's what you think. You called the police yesterday morning, didn't you?"

"Do we have to talk here?"

"We have to do *some* talking here."

"It's dangerous just being here."

"It's dangerous just walking away."

"I came to work yesterday. No one was in the house. Usually Mrs. Perlin is there, and nearly always there are some records for me."

"Records?" Mason asked.

"You know, the wax records that have been dictated on a dictating machine."

"Oh."

"This morning there weren't any records. Mrs. Perlin wasn't there."

"How about Hocksley?"

"I very seldom see him. He sleeps most of the day. He works rather late at night."

"But you have seen him?"

"Oh, yes."

"Go ahead."

"I couldn't understand there not being any work laid out for me or any message. Then I started looking around, and I saw the door to Mr. Hocksley's room was open. Then I saw spots of blood. I went in and saw the safe with a great pool of blood in front of it, and then I went out to the garage where we keep the car."

"That's in the house next door?"

"Yes. The Gentries rent Mr. Hocksley a garage."

"And the car was there?"

"Yes; but there were bloodstains in it, all over the

back seat. Really, Mr. Mason, that's all I know. Then I called the police."

"Why not call them now?"

"I can't explain my being here. I can't explain—lots of things."

"What, for instance?"

"Things—complications that would be brought about by what's happened here. Don't you see. They'd think that Mrs. Perlin and I had worked together to get Mr. Hocksley out of the way."

"Why should you want him out of the way?"

"I don't know. I only know that's what they'd say. It looks as though I must have had some connection with Mrs. Perlin, as though she'd communicated with me some-time today, and I hadn't told the police."

"She did communicate with you, didn't she?"

"Well, in a way, yes."

"And you didn't tell the police?"

"She told me not to."

Mason looked at his watch, hesitated a moment, then said, "If I do this for you, what'll you do for me?"

She met his eyes without flinching. "What do you want?" she asked.

Mason said, "I don't want you to run out on me if the going gets tough."

"All right."

"You'll stick?"

"Yes—only—only don't kid me."

"What do you mean?"

"Don't tell me that you're going to give me a break, and then as soon as I've left, call the police."

Mason said, "As far as that's concerned, I'll go you one better. I know a roadhouse that's still open. I'll buy you a drink, and a sandwich, and you can watch me to make certain I don't even go near a telephone."

She hugged his arm. "You don't know what this means to me! It—it means everything!"

Mason said, "Okay, let's go."

"Shouldn't we—turn the lights off?"

"No," Mason said. "Leave things just as they are."

"But I'm the one who turned the lights *on.*"

"All right, leave them that way."

"How about locking the doors?"

"No. Leave them just the way they are."

"Why?"

"Suppose something happens. Suppose we're picked up within a block by a prowl car. Suppose someone sees us leaving. We tell our story, and police find the doors locked."

"I see. Look here, we have two cars. We can't . . ."

Mason said, "You get in my car. I drive you up to your car. You get in, turn it around, and follow me for four or five blocks, park your car, get out, and go to the nightclub with me. I bring you back to where your car is parked. In that way, you'll know I'm not doing any telephoning."

Looking up, she said, "I think you're wonderful. I can't imagine why you're doing this for me."

Mason said, "Neither can I."

■ **9** ■

Paul Drake, his face gray with fatigue and worry, looked across the desk at Perry Mason, and said, "Some day when you play me for a sucker, I'm going to wriggle off the hook."

The lawyer raised his eyebrows. "Why, Paul, what's the idea?"

"You know darn well what the idea is," Drake said.

"You mean piling so much work on you I kept you up all night?" Mason asked. "Shucks, think of me. I was pulled out of bed around one o'clock in the morning to go out on a wild-goose chase."

Drake said, "And I suppose you haven't heard anything at all about the wild goose?"

Mason said, "Spill it. What's on your mind, Paul?"

Drake said sarcastically, "Oh, no, *you* don't know what it's all about. *You* haven't the faintest idea. *You* wouldn't have got me in a jam for worlds."

"What the devil are you talking about, Paul?"

"Why didn't you telephone me?"

"When?"

"When! When you said you were going to."

"Why, did I say . . ."

"How about that date to go out and save your bacon at Hillgrade Avenue if you didn't call inside of an hour?"

Mason said, "I had some trouble, Paul. I was talking with a witness. I couldn't break away to get to a telephone without jeopardizing the whole thing. And after all, it only meant a trip out to Hillgrade Avenue for you. That was only a matter of twenty minutes, and it was better to send you on a wild-goose chase than to jeopardize what I was working on."

"Oh, yes, a wild-goose chase," Drake said. "I see."

"Well," Mason said, "that was the way it looked to me. House standing there, gloomy and sedate, with a light or two in it, but no one to answer the doorbell."

"And the doors all unlocked and waiting for you to go right on in?" Drake asked.

Mason shook his head. "Not me."

"Why not?"

"Be your age, Paul. Somebody rings you up at one o'clock, tells you to go to a certain address, and walk right into a house you've never seen before. You go blundering on in. Someone comes out with a double-barreled shotgun, says, 'Burglars, eh,' and lets you have both loads of buckshot right in the middle of your stomach. No, thank you. None of that in mine. They answer bells or I don't open doors."

"You mean to say you didn't go in?"

"I mean to say I don't make a practice of having strangers tell me to go out to some residence and walk right in. But what are *you* crabbing about? You had a wild-goose chase out there, and that was all. You got back in twenty or thirty minutes. You found out that I wasn't there. You knew I'd either been kidnaped, or was working on some new angle of the case."

Drake said sarcastically, "Oh, yes. It's nothing to me, just the few minutes necessary to run out there and back."

"Well, what *are* you beefing about?" Mason asked, letting a note of impatience creep into his voice.

Drake said, "I don't suppose *you* went inside. I don't suppose *you* found the body and didn't want to take the responsibility of telephoning the police and trying to explain to them how it happened you were out there. I don't suppose *you* decided you'd discovered enough bodies and that it would be a smart idea to let Paul Drake take the rap on this one. You knew damn well I'd have some hard-boiled detectives on my staff who would bust right on into that house. You knew damn well I'd find the corpse, and when I found it, I'd *have* to telephone the police."

Mason said, "What body?"

"Oh, I don't suppose *you* knew there was a body in the house?"

"What about the body? Who was it?"

"Apparently," Drake said, "it's the body of Mrs. Sarah Perlin, the housekeeper for Hocksley. She *may* have committed suicide, and she may have been shot."

Mason said excitedly, "You mean she was actually *in* that house?"

"Of course, she was in that house, in a bedroom in front

99

of her dressing table. After the shot had been fired, she'd slumped down on the floor. Her own gun did the job."

Mason's face held an expression of puzzled surprise. "Paul, you're not kidding me about this? You mean she *was* there?"

"Of course, she was there."

"And that's who it was? What I mean is, the body's been identified?"

Drake nodded.

"Then she must have been killed *after* she telephoned me and . . . Gosh, Paul, she said she wanted to confess. She must have telephoned me then started getting ready to meet me. The thought of what she'd done began preying on her mind, and she decided on suicide. What is there that indicates it wasn't a suicide?"

"The course of the bullet, and position of the body," Drake said.

"Tell me what happened, Paul."

"I waited for you to telephone. At first I didn't think very much of it. Just a matter of routine. Then when about forty-five minutes had gone by and you hadn't phoned, I began to worry. After all, it could pretty easily have been a trap. You work on a case in an unorthodox manner. You keep two or three jumps ahead of the police. You're usually pretty close to the murderer. A man who was being crowded could bump you off, and, by shutting your lips, might save himself a one-way trip to the gas chamber at San Quentin. One o'clock in the morning was a hell of a time to be calling a lawyer out of bed. The more I thought of it, the less I liked it. I rounded up a couple of tough operatives and sat here with my eye glued on the clock. Somehow, I had a feeling in my bones you weren't going to call. I wanted to get started. I felt that seconds were precious, but you'd said an hour, so I decided to give you the full hour.

"Believe me, boy, when the second hand on that electric clock swung around to the sixtieth minute, I was on my way. And maybe you don't think we burnt up the roads getting out to Hillgrade."

"Good boy," Mason said. "I knew I could count on you. Then what happened?"

Drake said, "I didn't even bother to waste any time sizing up the lay of the land. I got to six-o-four East Hillgrade and saw lights in the house. I slammed the car to a stop right in front of the house, jumped out, and the three of us ran up the steps to the front porch and started jabbing the bell button. I could hear the doorbell jangling on the inside of the house, but nothing happened. So I pushed the door open. It was unlocked. We went in. You know what I found."

Mason shook his head. "What did you find, Paul?"

Drake said, "There was a reception corridor with an arched entrance into a living room, and back of that a dining room and kitchen. Over on the other side was a door which led to a hallway. A light was on in the hallway, and the bedroom door was open. I was the one who walked down the hallway while the other boys took the living room and dining room. Believe me, I had my gun where I could reach it right quick. Okay, I get down to the second bedroom door. It's open. I take a look inside. I see the top of a woman's head, gray hair sprawled out over the floor. I see a left arm stretched out, and a right hand holding a gun. I let out a yell for the other boys, then I go over and make sure she's dead. Then we go through the house looking for you. By that time, my gun's out, and I'm having the jitters.

"We can't find any trace of you anywhere, so I find a telephone and call the police and tell them to rush me out some radio officers and also to notify Homicide."

"Mention my name?"

"No. I didn't see where that would do any good. I knew they'd look things over pretty thoroughly. At the time, I thought it was suicide."

"You don't think so now?"

"I'm darned if I know what to think now. I'm beginning to swing over toward the murder theory."

"What did the police say?"

"They wanted to know how I happened to go walking into the house at that time in the morning, and how I happened to find the body."

"What did you tell them?"

Drake said apologetically, "I only had four or five minutes after I telephoned headquarters before the radio officers showed up. I didn't have time to think up an absolutely iron-clad story. I could have improved it if I'd had a little more time. I . . ."

"What was it?" Mason asked.

"I couldn't be absolutely certain who she was. Looking at things fast, it looked like an open-and-shut case of suicide. So I told the cops that I'd got a telephone message from a woman who said she wanted to tell me something before it was too late, that if I'd jump in my car and get out to that address fast, I'd find out something in connection with the Hocksley murder that would interest me."

Mason grinned. "You couldn't have done any better than that if you'd tried all night, Paul."

Drake shook his head. "You overlook the weak point in it."

"What?"

"I didn't see how I could tell them I'd stalled around very long after getting that telephone call. I didn't know just when she'd pulled the trigger, but I surmised it had to be after she'd talked with you on the telephone. That would mean a medical examination would show she'd been dead for perhaps as much as an hour before I'd notified the cops. That wouldn't look so well. So I told the cops I was working on something at the time which kept me from leaving the office, that I'd told her I'd be right out, but had put my car in the garage and there'd be a little delay. I felt that that way I could stall her along. That's what I told the cops."

"Go ahead," Mason said.

"They wanted to know how long it was after the telephone conversation before I got there. I told them it might have been an hour, and I could see they didn't believe that. They said that if I'd been on the track of something as important as that sounded, I'd have got out there sooner."

"So then what?" Mason asked.

"So I told them that I hadn't paid too much attention to time, that it had seemed quite a long while to me because I had so much to do, but that it might have been less than an hour; perhaps forty-five minutes, or perhaps even half an hour. And then I got myself in a jack pot. The times were all wet."

Mason frowned. "You mean," he said, "that she had been dead for more than . . ."

"She'd been dead ever since midnight," Drake said, "and probably before."

"How do they know?"

"Taking the temperature of the room and the temperature of the body and estimating how long it takes a body to lose a degree of heat, and all that stuff," Drake said.

Mason frowned. "It *couldn't* have been midnight. She talked with me over the telephone."

"That's what I thought," Drake said, "but I wasn't in a position to do any arguing."

Mason said, "I guess that's it, Paul."

"What?"

"She was killed around midnight. That makes it murder."

"But she talked with you and . . ."

"No," Mason said. "A woman talked with me, a woman who had a rather well-bred voice. That is, the tones were smoothly harmonious, but there was something

103

wrong with the way she spoke, as though she had a marble in her mouth. That explains it."

"Explains what?" Drake asked.

Mason said, "It was a woman who talked with me. This woman said she was Mrs. Perlin. It was a cinch to pull that on me because I'd never heard Mrs. Perlin speak and didn't know her voice. But the one who called the other person was one who said she was speaking for Mrs. Perlin because she was unable to come to the phone."

"What other person?" Drake asked.

Mason said, "Right at the moment, Paul, that's neither here nor there."

The detective looked at him, sighed, and said, "It's probably there, but it sure as hell ain't here."

Mason said, "When I looked down at the body, it didn't seem to me that she'd been a woman who would have had a voice such as the one I'd heard on the telephone. So I asked—this other party—if the housekeeper had been up in the world at one time, and then had some bad luck. Had to go to housekeeping. That would have accounted for the well-bred voice, you know."

"What was the answer?"

"Negative."

Drake lit a cigarette. "That means," he said, "that the party who was with you was someone who knew the housekeeper pretty well, someone who knew the housekeeper's past, someone who was interested in the Hocksley case because a message brought that person out there. Probably a girl. Give me one guess, Perry."

"Don't take it," Mason warned.

Drake removed the cigarette from his mouth, blew smoke at the smoldering end. "I don't suppose it's occurred to you, Perry, but there's just a chance you and some feminine accomplice could be nominated for a murder rap. You might even be elected."

"If the woman died before midnight?" Mason asked.

"That's what you say."

"I ought to know."

Drake said, "If you're going to keep messing around in murder cases, you'd better get married—so you'll have some corroboration when it comes to bedtime alibis."

"What the deuce are you talking about?" Mason said irritably. "Why the devil should I need an alibi?"

"Darned if I know," Drake said, "but I have a hunch Lieutenant Tragg is going to become *very* inquisitive about what you were doing last night."

"Tragg doesn't even know I was anywhere within a mile of Hillgrade Avenue."

Drake said, "Tragg gets around."

Mason pushed back his chair. "You've been up all night, Paul. It gives you a pessimistic outlook."

Drake regarded him moodily. He said, "You're always pulling fast ones, and then expecting me to back your plays without telling me what it's all about. I'm warning you that if Lieutenant Tragg finds out you were out at Hillgrade Avenue last night, or if he finds out the real reason why you didn't call me back inside of an hour, you're going to have trouble."

"What is the real reason I didn't call you back inside of an hour?" Mason asked.

Drake regarded the lawyer thoughtfully. "If it's what I think it is, I hope I'm not right."

Mason laughed. "Come on. Out with it."

Drake held up his left hand with the fingers extended. With the forefinger of his right hand, he checked off the points as he made them. "First," he said, "you aren't kidding *me* a bit. The reason you didn't call me was because something very important did turn up. Two, that something important was of a nature which would interfere with a telephone call. Three, you didn't discover anything from that contact which was particularly new. Otherwise, you'd have passed along the information, so I'd have something to work on. Four, it was a contact which knew a lot about the housekeeper, but one you

105

had to keep absolutely dark. Five, it put you in such a spot that you don't dare to confide even in me. You're trying to kid me out of it. Now then, what's the answer to those five points?"

Mason said, "I'll bite, Mr. Bones. What is the answer to those five points?"

"Opal Sunley," Drake said.

Mason got up. "I warned you not to make that guess, Paul. I try to keep you out in the clear and you jump right into the middle of the fire."

Drake grinned. "I was in the frying pan, anyway," he said.

■ **10** ■

Della Street, humming a little tune as she opened the door to Mason's private office, carrying the morning mail under her arm, stopped short with surprise, said, "Well, well, is this getting to be a habit?"

Mason grinned at her. "Come on over and sit down."

She went back to close the door to the outer office. "What's the idea?" she asked. "Been up all night?"

"No," Mason said. "I got a few hours' sleep. I guess that's more than Drake did."

"What happened?"

"A woman telephoned me about one o'clock in the morning, said she was Sarah Perlin, and she wanted to confess to the murder of R. E. Hocksley, wanted me to come at once to six-o-four East Hillgrade Avenue, said if she wasn't there to wait until I saw a light, then open the back door and walk in. I took the precaution of telling Paul Drake to follow up in an hour if I didn't telephone him everything was okay."

106

"How did she get in touch with you?" Della Street asked.

"She called Paul Drake, and Paul held her on the line while he got in touch with me. I told Paul to give her my private number."

"This was Mrs. Perlin, Hocksley's housekeeper?"

"The voice said it was Mrs. Perlin. I don't think it was."

"Why not?"

"I think Mrs. Perlin was dead at the time. When I got out to the house on Hillgrade, I found her lying on the floor with a gun in her right hand and a bullet through her heart. It could have been suicide."

"Did you report to the police?"

"Not directly," Mason said. "I had other fish to fry. Opal Sunley came wandering in with a story that was just about as wild as mine. I didn't realize how utterly incredible my story would sound to Lieutenant Tragg until I heard Opal Sunley telling me her version of about the same thing."

"What did you do?"

Mason grinned. "I let Paul Drake hold the sack," he said. "The hour was about up. Opal Sunley offered to play square if I wouldn't notify the police, but give her a chance for a getaway."

"Isn't that compounding a felony?"

"It most certainly is—if she was guilty of a felony."

"And how about not reporting the finding of the body?"

"I can get by with that in a pinch because I knew that Drake was on his way up. It only made a difference of a few minutes. The thing that bothers me is this Sunley woman."

"What did you do with her?"

"Took her to a night spot and tried to get her tight."

"Do any good?"

Mason shook his head. "She is a very bright young

107

woman, or else I telegraphed my punch pretty badly. She started taking defensive measures even before I'd ordered the first drink."

"What were the defensive measures?" Della Street asked. "I might have occasion to use them sometime."

"Crackers and butter," Mason said, "and *lots* of butter. She'd eaten about five squares before I got the first cocktail into her. After that, I knew it wouldn't be much use."

"Evidently the young woman knows her way around," Della Street said.

Mason nodded. "I got her telephone number—Acton one-one-one-one-o."

"What did she tell you about young Gentrie?"

"Not a great deal. Young Arthur Gentrie is madly in love with her. She's older than he is and considers it a case of puppy love, but doesn't want to destroy his illusions. She says that it's very, very serious when a young man starts putting an older woman on a pedestal and becomes really infatuated for the first time in his life."

"Is it the first time with Junior Gentrie?" Della Street asked.

Mason said, "He told her it was."

"I don't believe it."

"He said there'd been puppy loves in his life before, but nothing that could approach the devastating effect of this feeling that he has for her."

"And so she keeps on going out with him and encouraging him?"

"She says she isn't encouraging him. She's trying to be an older sister to him, but Junior won't, as she expresses it, cool off. She said she had been trying to find some younger woman who would be sufficiently attractive to Junior to get his mind into what she calls a more normal state. The hell of it is, Della, she's got a boy friend—some chap she's crazy over—and she's keeping all this about young Gentrie away from her regular boy friend because he's insanely jealous. Of course, she's also keeping all news of the boy friend from Gentrie because she doesn't want to destroy his illusions."

Della Street said, "It's nice business if you can get it. How old is she?"

"Around twenty-two or twenty-three according to her looks, but something she said made me place her at about twenty-five."

"What did Opal Sunley tell you about what happened in Hocksley's flat?"

"According to her story, she arrived for work at the usual time in the morning, saw bloodstains, went out to look at the automobiles, saw that someone had been riding in the back of Hocksley's automobile, and spilling blood. She couldn't find either Hocksley or Mrs. Perlin. So she notified the police."

"That's all she told you?"

"Just about. I had to worm it out of her about her boy friend. I think that was the main reason she didn't want the police to report her as having been in that bungalow at one-forty-five in the morning. Yet she was driving a borrowed car. I got the license number, of course."

"The boy friend's car?"

"No. Strangely enough it's not. It belongs to a girl by the name of Ethel Prentice who is evidently a close friend of Opal's—lets her take a jalopy in times of need."

"Anything else?"

"Oh, she told a few things about her job over there. This man Hocksley was very much of a man of mystery, and so is Karr who lives in the flat above him. Somehow, that's taxing credulity just a little bit too much. Two men of mystery drifting into an apartment house. They arrive within a week of each other, and, before that, the flats have been vacant for five months."

"You think Karr and Hocksley have some connection?"

Mason shrugged his shoulders and said, "It's rather a coincidence. Have you seen Karr's ad in the paper?"

"No. What is it?"

"Opal Sunley told me about it—and said she noticed it because she'd seen Wenston's name on the door of the other flat. It's been running two days."

Mason took the morning paper from the desk, opened it to the classified ad section, turned to the personals, and said, "Listen to this. 'Personal. Wanted information concerning the daughter of the man who was a partner in a gun-running expedition up the Yangtze River in nineteen-twenty-one. Detailed information is purposely withheld from this advertisement, but the right party will know who I am, who her father was, and will be able to give proof of our association in the expedition in the fall of 1920, and the first part of 1921. I do not wish to be pestered, and, therefore, give warning that any imposter will be prosecuted to the limit of the law. On the other hand, the young woman who is the genuine daughter will be given a considerable sum of partnership assets which I have held for her in trust because I did not know until recently, and by accident, that my partner left any heirs at law. Do not seek to obtain an interview until after first writing Rodney Wenston, 787 East Dorchester Boulevard or telephoning Graybar 8–9351.' "

Mason finished reading the ad, pushed the newspaper to one side. Della Street pursed her lips. "Whew! And Opal Sunley told you about the ad?"

Mason nodded.

"I'd say that was rather significant, wouldn't you?"

"Uh huh. Karr mentioned he started the ball rolling to clean up his partnership, but he didn't mention this ad."

"How did Opal happen to tell you about it?"

"Just talking."

"What did she tell you about Hocksley?"

"Nothing much I didn't know already. She got all of her work from wax cylinders. Hocksley dictated at night, and spent most of the day in bed."

"Sleeping all day?"

110

"No. He'd be in his room. He'd get up along in the afternoon and read the papers, have coffee and toast, and sometimes do a little dictation."

"To the machine?"

"Yes. Mrs. Perlin, the housekeeper, was the only one to go in and out of Hocksley's room. She'd wait on him as soon as he wakened, bringing him the work Opal Sunley had typed, bringing out cylinders for Opal to transcribe, taking him his meals—the newspapers—sometimes sitting in there and talking with him. Opal could hear the hum of low-pitched conversation."

"Any heart throbs between Hocksley and the housekeeper?" Della Street asked.

"Opal says she doesn't know."

"She considers it's a possibility then?" Della Street asked.

"Apparently a very definite possibility."

Della Street thought that over for a few seconds, then shook her head and said, "That isn't right, Chief."

"What isn't?"

"That story of hers. No girl on earth would go on working for a man under those conditions without making it a point to learn more about him. In the first place, there'd be legitimate questions she'd have to ask about the work. In the second place, all that attempt to be secretive would simply arouse her curiosity."

"Then you think she was lying to me?" Mason asked.

"I know darn well she was lying."

Mason smiled reminiscently. "She did it *most* convincingly," he said.

Della's eyes were twinkling. "The hussy!"

Mason said, "Well, there's no percentage in sitting around waiting for something to break. Why wouldn't this be a fine time to communicate with the murderer?"

"Fine—but how are you going about it?"

"You could go down to a hardware store, Della, and buy a sealing machine for cans. Also get a new tin. We'll

111

scratch a message on the lid, seal it up, make certain there are no fingerprints on it, and plant it on the shelf at the Gentrie residence."

"Think the murderer would get it?"

"It would be interesting to find out."

"What sort of a message?"

"Oh, something that would tend to keep things moving," Mason said. "We don't want the case to get static. It would give the police too much of a chance to catch up on us."

Della Street picked up the dictionary from Mason's desk. "Think up a nice message, and I'll put it in code for you."

Mason said, "Well now, let's see, Della. We want something that will get some action. Suppose we left the murderer a message. Let's see. It will have to be dictionary words. We can't use participles or plurals. We want something that will get swift action. Suppose we did this: *'Lawyer Mason has fingerprint photograph his wallet fatal unless recovered.'* No, let's see. We couldn't use *recovered*. That's past tense. The word in the dictionary would be *recover*."

Della Street, frowning down at her shorthand notebook, said, "We could use *recovery,* Chief. That would be a noun, and would be listed. We could use the words *recovery made* instead of *recovered*."

"Okay, let's try putting it in code."

"I don't like the idea."

"Why not?"

"It's too much risk."

"It'll bring me into contact with the murderer."

"That's just it. The murderer will choose the time and the place of making the contact. He may even shoot first, and look in your wallet afterwards."

"There's always the chance," Mason admitted, "but he'd be more apt to make a stick-up of it. And I'll be careful."

She said, "Yes, I've got a picture of you being careful —and when the murderer finds your wallet without a fingerprint in it, what . . ."

Mason walked across the office to a bookcase. On the top of this bookcase was a choice example of Japanese pigeon-blood cloisonne. He took a handkerchief from his pocket, polished the vase, ran his right hand through his hair several times, then pressed three of his fingertips against the surface. He said to Della, "Take that down to Paul Drake's office. Have him develop the latent fingerprints on it, and photograph them. Don't tell him why we want them. I'll carry a copy of that photograph in my wallet. Then in case anything slips, the murderer won't get suspicious."

"Chief, I wish you wouldn't do it. There's no need for you to take the risk personally. Why not say that you have them in your office safe?"

"No. We can't guard the office without letting someone else in on it. I want to handle this myself."

"Why?"

"Because it won't look like a trap then. But if I try to decoy the murderer into some office and have that office guarded, it's going to look very much like a trap. The person with whom we're dealing is far too intelligent to walk into so obvious a trap."

Della Street reached for the dictionary. "Well," she said, "I'll put it in code. Only I do wish you wouldn't do it, Chief."

Mason said, "Here. Give me the dictionary. I'll help you . . . 'Lawyer.' That's in column *a* on page 569, the seventh word."

Della Street spelled out the code word. "GHKAI."

Mason turned through the pages again, said, "Isn't it nice I have a name that's listed in the dictionary?"

"You might wish it on Paul Drake," she said. "We could use 'Detective Drake' just as well as 'Lawyer Mason.'"

"No," Mason said with a grin. "Paul isn't feeling too friendly right now. He might object to being selected as the victim of a hold-up. At that, it's a tempting thought. Detective Drake has an alliteration which is lacking in Lawyer Mason."

"Shall we use it?" Della Street asked eagerly.

"No, absolutely not. Get thee behind me, Satan. Let's get back to our knitting. Here's Mason on the *a* part of page 615, the sixth word from the top."

Della Street said, "Six-fifteen-A-six. That'll be HCGAH. What's next?"

Mason said, "I'll look up 'has.' Let's see. That's the second word in column *b* on page 455."

"That's FGGBD."

"Fine," Mason said. "Now, 'fingerprint.' That's page 377, the seventh word on the page."

Della Street said, "Three-seven-seven-A-seven. That'll be EIIAI." Abruptly, she looked down at what she had written and began to laugh.

"What?" Mason asked.

"I was just wondering what would happen if Lieutenant Tragg got hold of this message," she said. "Has it occurred to you, Chief, that out of four words, two of them have ended in AI?"

Mason frowned, scratched his head. "That isn't so good," he said. "It'll give Tragg too much of a clue. He'll know darn well then it isn't just an ordinary cipher, but some sort of a code."

"You don't think he'll get hold of this, do you?"

"He may."

"I don't see just what you're planning to do. Won't the man who gets the message know it's a trap?"

"Not if my idea is correct. The persons who are using this means of communication both have access to that place in the cellar; but for some reason, they don't dare to be seen talking together. Now if that's the case, they won't have any opportunity to clarify an ambiguity

114

in the case. In other words, the person who gets the message can't pick up a telephone and say, 'Hello, Bill. I got your message. What do you mean, a fingerprint? Your fingerprint or my fingerprint. Or . . .' " Mason broke off suddenly to stare at Della Street. "Do you realize," he demanded, "what I have just said?"

"About the telephone?"

"Yes."

"What about it?"

"Why the devil should anyone resort to the complicated means of putting a code in the top of a can if he could get to a telephone? After all, you know, Della, my idea has been that the code idea was necessary because we had two persons who needed to communicate with each other, couldn't see each other, and so had to leave messages in a can at a certain place."

"Well, what's wrong with that?"

"But why the devil couldn't they *telephone* to each other? There wouldn't be any danger in that. A person can go into a telephone booth anywhere, drop a nickel, dial a number, and talk with any person he wants. In that way, a man could give another complete instructions without the possibility of having them garbled, or, as happened in this case, having the woman of the house find the can and toss it into the discard."

She frowned. "Well, why not?"

"That's just it. There's only one explanation. The person *can't use a telephone.*"

"Why?"

Mason said, "Either because they can't get to a telephone, or because they couldn't use it if they did."

"How do you mean?"

"Well, a deaf person couldn't use a telephone."

"Oh, I see."

"And," Mason said slowly, "a crippled person might not be able to get to a telephone."

Della Street said, "Wouldn't a crippled person have a

115

telephone by the side of his bed? After all, a person who could put a can on a shelf, could certainly get to a telephone."

Mason said, "There's one person who doesn't have a phone by his bed, yet is crippled. Remember Karr said he got so nervous at the sound of a bell he wouldn't have a phone by his bed?"

Della said, "You've put your finger on something there."

Mason stroked the angle of his jaw. "This begins to look like something," he admitted. "But why should Karr communicate in code with anyone in the Gentrie house?"

"He's the only one in the case who really couldn't get to a telephone when he wanted one," Della said.

Mason pursed his lips. "He is, for a fact. We'll have to keep our eye on Mr. Elston A. Karr. It's beginning to look very much as though he engineered the burglary of Hocksley's flat. Of course, that doesn't mean he suggested the murder of Hocksley."

"Wouldn't it make him legally responsible for it though —if he engineered the burglary?" Della Street asked.

"It would," Mason agreed, a slight twinkle in his eyes, "on one condition."

"What's the condition?"

"That they can prove it on him."

Della said, "You've just about done that by cold, remorseless logic."

"I have, but that doesn't mean Tragg's going to. He *may* overlook that angle entirely."

"Bosh! He pretends to be just dawdling along, and then—Wham!"

Mason abruptly walked over to the hat closet. "Be sure to get that can and the sealing machine, Della. Take that vase down to Paul Drake's office. I'm going out to get a shave, a face massage, a manicure, and a quart of coffee."

"I will," Della Street said, then added, "and don't you

116

let that Sunley girl mix any more sex, simpers, and sweetness to kid you along."

"You could have added pseudo-sincerity," Mason grinned. "That also is alliterative."

Della said, "Damn! I knew we shouldn't have bought that dictionary."

■ 11 ■

Lieutenant Tragg rang the front doorbell, then raised his hat as Mrs. Gentrie opened the door.

"I'm sorry to keep on disturbing you," he said, "but there are one or two minor matters on which I have to get more information."

She seemed apprehensive for a moment, then smiled and said, "Come right on in, Lieutenant."

"I'm not inconveniencing you?"

"Not at all, but now those other officers just came bursting in here without so much as a by-your-leave or without taking their hats off. You're always a perfect gentleman."

"Thank you," he said, and then added after a moment, "but let me put in a good word for the hardboiled officers. They're overworked and have so many things to do, they simply don't have time to think of people as human beings. They regard them as witnesses, suspects, possible victims, and accomplices—if you know what I mean."

"Yes, I see," Mrs. Gentrie said, ushering Tragg into the living room.

Rebecca looked up with a quick smile, a smile that was almost a simper. "Good afternoon, Lieutenant."

Tragg came across to stand before her. "And how are you today?" he asked.

117

"I'm fine, thank you."

"Well, you're certainly looking well."

"Isn't she," Mrs. Gentrie said. "I believe murder cases agree with her. She's perked up no end."

"Now, Florence," Rebecca said, "you're talking as though I had been an invalid."

"Don't be silly. But you must know you're looking a lot better, and I think you're feeling a lot better. Now that you have something to interest you." She turned to Lieutenant Tragg, and said, "Rebecca spends too much time in her darkroom, and she stays in the house too much of the time. I keep trying to persuade her to get out, and take more exercise, but I don't have much luck."

"Well, sakes alive, what's a body going to do?" Rebecca demanded. "I never stand a chance at getting the family car—even if I knew how to drive, which I don't. And as far as walking is concerned, it isn't any pleasure to get up and pound your feet to pieces on the cement sidewalk while automobiles go whizzing by and spewing a lot of poison gas into the atmosphere. I don't see why they allow automobiles on residential streets, Lieutenant. I think it's an outrage and a menace to health."

"It may be at that," Tragg agreed. "Are there any new developments?"

Mrs. Gentrie shook her head.

Rebecca, having started to talk, rambled on. She said, "Mr. Mason was out here just about an hour ago. He was making what he called a final check-up."

Tragg's finely chiseled features lost some of their boyish look. "Oh, yes," he said. "Mr. *Mason.* He's been out here several times, hasn't he?"

"Well, off and on," Rebecca said.

Lieutenant Tragg was looking at Mrs. Gentrie. "I wonder just what Mason's interest is in the case," he said.

"Why, what do you mean?"

Tragg said, "Mason is a lawyer. He doesn't go around

solving mysteries. He isn't particularly interested in apprehending murderers. He's interested in making fees, and he makes fees because he represents some one client. I haven't been able to find out whom he's representing in this case. He hasn't said anything, has he?"

Mrs. Gentrie said, "Well . . . no. I can't say that he has."

He frowned. "Rather strange. Mrs. Gentrie, I am going to have to talk frankly with you about rather a disagreeable matter."

"What is it?" she asked.

"It's about your oldest son."

"Yes."

"I'm wondering if you've found him always truthful?"

Mrs. Gentrie said somewhat defiantly, "Junior is a *good* boy."

"Of course he is," Tragg said. "But I am asking you if you have found him entirely truthful."

Rebecca, who had been squirming uneasily on her chair, anxious for an excuse to enter the conversation, said, "Of course, Florence, you must admit that since he's started going . . ."

Florence turned to her. "Please, Rebecca," she said.

Tragg was apologetic, but insistent. "This is rather embarrassing to me," he said, "but I think your sister-in-law was commenting on the exact phase that I wanted to bring up, Mrs. Gentrie." He turned to Rebecca. "You were going to say that since he became interested in that stenographer next door, he's been a little secretive, weren't you?"

Rebecca sniffed. "Secretive's no name for it. There's no good going to come of it, if you ask me. A young boy like him running around with a woman that's so much older. They certainly didn't do anything like that when *I* was a girl."

Mrs. Gentrie said doggedly, "Rebecca, I think it would be better if you left Junior out of it."

119

Rebecca said, "It isn't anything against Junior as much as it is against that little minx. She has that butter-won't-melt-in-my-mouth manner of looking at you. And she says"—and here Rebecca's voice changed entirely to assume a startling likeness to that of Opal Sunley—" 'Good *moa*hning, Miss Gentrie—ahnd how's all the fahmily to-day?' I feel like up and giving her a piece of my mind, just coming right out and saying, 'They'd be very well, thank you, if you'd just leave your painted finger hooks out of Junior and let him grow up as a normal boy should.' "

Mrs. Gentrie said sternly, "Rebecca! Stop it!"

Tragg flashed Mrs. Gentrie his best smile. "I'm sorry. I'm quite certain it was my fault. I led her into it, and, as you probably realize, I did it with a purpose. Mrs. Gentrie, are you absolutely certain that your son was in bed when that shot was heard next door?"

Mrs. Gentrie said slowly, "No. I'm not certain he was in bed."

"Are you perhaps certain that he wasn't?" Tragg asked, his voice quietly insistent.

"I don't know. What makes you say that?" she asked.

"I'm not certain that I know myself," Tragg observed, still smiling, "only it impresses me that you're a very efficient mother, that you keep an eye on your children, that in the event you heard something you thought might be a shot, your first idea would be to look for the safety of your children. And, as I understand it, Junior's bedroom is between your room and the head of the stairs."

Mrs. Gentrie met his eyes steadily, and asked, "Is there some particular reason why you're trying to drag Junior into this?"

"I'm not trying to drag him into it, Mrs. Gentrie, but I think it's only fair to tell you that the two fingerprints on the telephone in Mr. Hocksley's house are those of your son."

Mrs. Gentrie started to say something, then changed her mind and was silent.

"The paint-smear fingerprints on the telephone were made by someone who had touched the paint your husband had placed on the garage door. He didn't finish that painting until around nine-thirty at night as I understand it. Obviously then, your son, who was out at the time, returned home sometime after that, entered this house, probably in the dark, went down to the cellar for some purpose. Without realizing that the garage door had been painted, he came groping his way toward it. I think you follow me, Mrs. Gentrie. If he'd been using a light, or if a light had been on in the cellar, he'd have seen the fresh paint on the door, and, moreover, wouldn't have been groping along with his hands outstretched."

Rebecca said, "I think you're quite right, Lieutenant. Personally, I *thought* I heard someone moving around here in the corridor just about the time the noise of the shot wakened me."

"Someone moving around in the house?" Tragg asked her.

"Yes."

"And you said *you* thought you heard someone moving, Mrs. Gentrie?"

"No. I heard Mephisto, the cat."

"Yet you got up and got your husband to go downstairs?"

"Well, yes."

"Why?"

"Because I was worried."

"About what?"

"I thought that noise might have been a shot."

"You didn't think it came from this house?"

"Well, no—that is, I didn't think very much about it."

"You got your husband to get up and investigate things here in this house?"

"Yes."

121

Tragg remained silent for several seconds, letting the significance of those questions and replies soak into Mrs. Gentrie's mind; then he went on smoothly, "Your son went downstairs in the dark. He groped for the garage door, opened it, and went into the garage. Then he opened the other door and went across to Hocksley's flat. In groping for the garage door in the dark, he got paint on the fingers of his left hand. After he got over to Hocksley's flat, he struck matches to light his way. Your husband is left-handed. Your son, however, is right-handed. He was taking matches from his pocket with his right hand and striking them with his right hand. So he didn't touch anything with the fingers of his left hand until he picked up the telephone over in Hocksley's flat. The paint on his fingers was still wet. It's obvious that must have been within a very few minutes of the time he got his fingers in the paint on the garage door. When he came back, he . . ."

Rebecca suddenly sucked in her breath as though she had been about to make some exclamatory statement.

Tragg turned to her. "Well?" he asked after a moment as she failed to speak.

Rebecca said, "I was just wondering if . . ."

"I don't think Lieutenant Tragg is interested in any of your wild theories, Rebecca," Mrs. Gentrie cautioned.

Tragg kept smiling affably. "What were you thinking, Miss Gentrie?"

"Well," Rebecca said, "I suppose it's nothing, but my darkroom door opens into the basement, and there's a curtain hanging just inside that door, so that when you open the door to come into the darkroom, you don't let light in."

"You mean the curtain is far enough behind the door so you can open and close the door before you go through the curtain?" Tragg asked.

"That's right."

Tragg said, "It's a very nice darkroom you have."

Rebecca beamed with pride. "It has the finest equipment! And we've made it ourselves. I have a daylight enlarger, so I can use diffused daylight in enlarging my pictures and . . ."

"But there was something about the darkroom itself you were going to tell me?" Tragg asked.

"That's right, there was."

"What was it?"

"Well," she said, "I had some cut film lying in a box on the darkroom shelf. I hadn't developed some exposed film in the other plate holders, and I was going to put this new film in . . ."

Mrs. Gentrie interposed to say to Lieutenant Tragg, "She thinks that the officers were careless. They opened the door of her darkroom, and then pulled the curtain all the way back. That let light into the darkroom, and fogged . . ."

"No, that isn't what I was going to say," Rebecca said. "I'm quite capable of doing my own talking, thank you, Florence."

"What were you going to say, Miss Gentrie?"

"Simply that those films *might* not have been fogged during the daytime by the police, but might have been fogged the night before by someone who struck a match. I found a burnt match stub on the floor of my darkroom. I thought at the time one of the officers had lit a cigarette, but I'm just wondering now if it mightn't have been someone who was looking for something in my darkroom and struck a match. Lots and lots of people don't realize that striking a match in a darkroom is just the same as turning on a light. It can cause just as much damage as though you'd switched on an electric light."

Tragg said, "That's very interesting. You keep a pretty fair stock of materials in your darkroom, Miss Gentrie?"

"Well, no, I don't. I don't have the money to buy them."

"It's rather an expensive pastime," Mrs. Gentrie said.

"Well, you don't need to talk. It pays its own way."

"You do work for others?"

Rebecca said, "Occasionally."

"A few of the neighbors," Mrs. Gentrie supplemented.

"Not much developing and printing," Rebecca said. "There's no money in that, but I do do enlargements occasionally. I do wish I had enough money so I wasn't always worrying about expense. I could really turn out marvelous work if I had enough money to get myself a little car so I could get out and . . ."

"She does very fine work," Mrs. Gentrie explained to Tragg. "I've often told her that if she'd specialize in taking pictures of children and . . ."

"Children!" Rebecca flared. "That's the mother complex of yours. You want pictures of the little darlings taken on their birthdays, pictures when they first put on long pants, pictures in their new suits. Those sort of pictures clutter up the house and don't mean a blessed thing."

"They mean a lot to Arthur and me," Mrs. Gentrie said.

"Well, they mean nothing to me. They simply are a waste of good photographic material. You find family albums filled up with that sort of junk." She turned to Lieutenant Tragg and said, "What I want are pictures of unusual cloud effects, of trees against the sky, of flowers. I could win prizes if I just had enough money to get myself a car and didn't always have to use photographic material which had expired."

"What do you mean by material that has expired?" Tragg asked.

"Oh, you know, films are only good while they're fresh. They'll keep for a certain length of time. You must have noticed that whenever you buy film, there's an emulsion date on it."

"You mean the little rubber-stamped date which says develop before a certain date?"

"That's right," Rebecca said.

"But you can use it after that date?"

"Oh, yes. It depends on the sort of care the film has had, the place where it's been stored. You can use it very nicely for as much as six months after the expiration date, and if it's been in a cool, dry place, you can use it for years afterwards."

"And you buy this film and paper which has expired?" Tragg asked.

"That's right. You can get it at certain places at a very great discount."

Tragg thought that over for several moments, then said, "What happens, however, when it finally gets too old?"

"Well, then, of course, it does different things. Usually it fogs."

Tragg said, "Then these films which were in the box were old films—that is, the expiration date had passed?"

"Yes."

"And couldn't the fact that the films had fogged been due to the age of the emulsion?"

"Well, I guess it *could,*" Rebecca said hesitatingly, "but I've never had any trouble before with films I've got from this particular source. This person handles only the best."

"But they were fogged?"

"Oh, yes, very definitely."

Tragg said, "That's very interesting. But it's rather a definite change of subject from the thing I was trying to impress upon Mrs. Gentrie. That is the fact that her son is in a very dangerous position. He's seen fit to try and confuse the issues in a murder case. It's quite possible that he's protecting the guilty party."

"I don't know what makes you say things like that,"

Mrs. Gentrie said indignantly. "Junior's a good boy. He . . ."

"The reason I'm saying that," Tragg interrupted firmly, "is that I'm satisfied your son *is* a good boy. I'm satisfied, however, that he's very young, very romantic, and inclined to carry gallantry altogether too far. He's trying to protect someone in a murder case, and that's a particularly dangerous thing to do. Now I think your boy's a mighty good kid, Mrs. Gentrie, but I think Opal Sunley is a woman who is older, more experienced, and knows her way around. I'm not satisfied the companionship would have been a good thing under any circumstances. And now that a murder has been perpetrated, I'm absolutely satisfied something about that companionship is causing your son to withhold information from us, and put himself in a very questionable position with the law."

Mrs. Gentrie averted her eyes, said almost under her breath, her voice choking in a sob, "He wouldn't do anything wrong."

Tragg said, "That's not it. If he doesn't tell the truth, we're going to take steps to get the truth. I felt I should come to you and talk frankly, since you're so deeply concerned and so fond of him."

Rebecca said, "You see how it is, Florence. You wouldn't listen to me. I hope you'll listen to the lieutenant. When a boy starts trying to conceal things from his own mother . . ."

"What did Junior ever try to conceal?" Mrs. Gentrie demanded angrily.

"Plenty," Rebecca said with a disdainful sniff. "He and that girl started making all kinds of surreptitious dates. You know as well as I do they didn't make them over the telephone. He never called her—at least not from here, and yet they were having their dates, dates he never told you about. I tried to warn you about it and . . ."

"I think," Mrs. Gentrie said, "it's going to be better if you wait until we're alone to go into this, Rebecca. You always make it a point to listen when the children are making dates on the telephone, and then you ask them questions. Junior's getting to the age where he resents that. He isn't a boy any more. He's growing into real manhood."

"Well, this creature has got him mixed up in a murder case," Rebecca said with self-righteous approval, "and I'm trying to help Lieutenant Tragg, that's all. It's just as distasteful to me as it can be. I consider Junior just as much a part of me as though he were my own boy, but after all, when a young man starts gallivanting around—and now, the evidence of those fingerprints makes it just as plain as the nose on your face. He's been sneaking over there at night. . . ."

"Stop it!" Mrs. Gentrie commanded indignantly. "You don't know that he's been sneaking over there, and as far as that's concerned, Opal Sunley doesn't stay over there nights."

"How do you know she doesn't?"

"Well, she comes in and works by the day."

"But she's over there quite frequently at night."

"Only when she has to work."

Rebecca sniffed.

Lieutenant Tragg, who had been keenly observing the trend of the conversation and the facial expressions of the two women, interposed soothingly, "I'm sorry I gave the wrong impression, Mrs. Gentrie. All I'm interested in is finding out just how it happened your son left those fingerprints on the telephone."

"You're absolutely certain they're his?"

"Absolutely."

"Couldn't he have been using that paint—well, later?"

Tragg raised his eyebrows. "You mean after the shot was fired?" he asked.

Mrs. Gentrie thought that over. "Well, no. I mean before—before his father started to paint."

127

"I believe his father mixed up the paint from some he'd brought home from the hardware store."

"I guess so," Mrs. Gentrie said.

Hester came through from the kitchen, stood silently in the doorway.

"What is it, Hester?" Mrs. Gentrie asked.

"You want me to get some more preserves from the pantry shelves?"

"Yes. . . ." Mrs. Gentrie looked at Lieutenant Tragg and said, "I wonder if you could pardon me for just a moment, Lieutenant. It seems as though I haven't been able to keep abreast of my work all day, and . . ."

"Certainly," Tragg interposed. "I can understand just how it is, Mrs. Gentrie. Go right ahead."

Mrs. Gentrie said to Hester, "Clean out all of those '39 and '40 tins and jars over on the left side of the shelf, Hester. Bring them up and put them on the pantry shelves. We'll start serving them until we've used them all up."

Lieutenant Tragg said, "If you're going down in the cellar, I'll take a look around after you are finished."

"Certainly," Mrs. Gentrie said.

Hester opened the cellar door. The heavy, flat-footed pound of her springless steps sounded on the stairs.

Rebecca said, "Well, if you ask me, I think that can had a lot to do with what happened over there across the street. Don't you think that message was intended for someone who . . ."

Mrs. Gentrie interrupted firmly, "Now, Rebecca, Lieutenant Tragg isn't interested in your theories, and I certainly am not going to have you make any veiled insinuation that it was a code communication between Opal Sunley and Junior. Thought your crossword-puzzle club was having a meeting today."

Rebecca sniffed. "I'm quite capable of arranging my own affairs, Florence. I don't have to leave for an hour yet, and the way you're trying to get rid of me only makes Lieutenant Tragg all the more suspicious of Junior. You know just as well as I do that these messages in the can may as well as not be the way they made their dates. They never dared to do it over the telephone. Land sakes, you'd have thought she was a married woman from the way Junior was acting! She might have . . ."

From the cellar came Hester's voice, calling out without emotion, "Mrs. Gentrie, here's another one."

Mrs. Gentrie walked toward the cellar door, looking back over her shoulder, conscious of the fact she was leaving Rebecca and Lieutenant Tragg alone, conscious also that this might well be what Lieutenant Tragg wanted. It was certainly what Rebecca wanted.

"What is it, Hester?" she called.

"Another one."

"Another what?"

"Another empty tin on the shelf," she said.

Mrs. Gentrie turned to where Lieutenant Tragg was drawing up a chair close to Rebecca, preparatory to the intimacy of a low-voiced conversation.

Tragg looked up.

Mrs. Gentrie said, "Hester says there's another empty tin on the shelf in the basement, Lieutenant."

Tragg came up out of the chair and reached the cellar door with long, quick strides. He pushed past Mrs. Gentrie and took the cellar stairs two at a time.

"Where is it?" Tragg asked Hester.

"Here. I . . ."

"Good Lord, don't touch it!" Tragg shouted.

There was the sound of an empty tin clattering to the cement floor.

"I didn't mean for you to drop it."

"You said not to touch it," Hester said stolidly.

Tragg carefully picked up the tin, holding it in such a way that his fingers touched it only in one place. He placed it on the workbench and took from his pocket a

129

small leather case across the top of which was a zipper, a case not much larger than a flexible spectacle case.

The two women who had dashed down the cellar stairs after him, watched him in silent fascination as he slid open the catch on the zipper, took out a camel's-hair brush, and three small containers. Selecting one of the containers, he removed the top to disclose a fine powder. With the camel's-hair brush he dusted the powder evenly over the surface of the can.

Carefully, Tragg examined the fingerprints which the powder brought to light.

"Let me see your hands," he said to Hester, and when she had extended her hands for his inspection, he opened one of the other small tins to disclose a sticky black ink which he placed upon the tips of her fingers. He recorded her inked impressions on paper in his notebook.

"What's the matter?" Hester asked sullenly. "I didn't do nothing."

Lieutenant Tragg had nothing of the bulldozing, arrogant manner of the detective who has graduated from pavement-pounding to the Homicide Squad. He was, instead, suavely courteous and never more so than when he was hot on the trail of a significant clue. "I'm sorry," he said with a reassuring smile. "I thought you'd understand. I am trying to find the fingerprints of the person who placed the tin on the shelf. In order to do that, I have to eliminate your fingerprints."

Mrs. Gentrie knew that Hester didn't quite know what Tragg meant by eliminate, so she added by way of explanation, "He just wants to find out which fingerprints are yours, so he can rub them off, and get them out of the way, Hester."

But Tragg didn't rub off any of the fingerprints. He did, however, check them off one at a time, after comparing them, with the aid of a magnifying glass, with the prints Hester's fingers had left on the paper. During the time he was doing this, he was exceedingly careful not to get any of his own fingerprints on the surface of the can.

"Where *was* that tin?" Rebecca asked.

Lieutenant Tragg seemed to feel it was unnecessary to answer the question. Rebecca turned to Hester. "Where did you find it, Hester?" she demanded.

Hester mutely pointed toward the shelf.

"Humph," Rebecca said. "The exact place where that other can was!"

Mrs. Gentrie nodded.

Rebecca said, "There was something written on the top of that other tin on the inside. Mr. Mason discovered that."

"I overlooked a bet there," Tragg said, laughing. "Don't ever underestimate the ability of Mr. Perry Mason. He's a very shrewd, very adroit attorney. And is there a can opener here I can use, Mrs. Gentrie?"

"Yes. How about fingerprints?"

He shook his head. "Everyone of them that we can use seems to have been made by Hester. Apparently, whoever placed the tin there had first taken the precaution of wiping it free of fingerprints."

"Well, a person couldn't have put it up there without leaving *some* prints," Rebecca said.

"Not unless he'd deliberately tried to avoid doing so," Tragg said.

Mrs. Gentrie showed him the location of the can opener. Lieutenant Tragg fed the can into the holder, rolled the rotating blade around the edges, and then shook out the detached circle of tin which was the top of the can.

Hester remained sullenly aloof, but Mrs. Gentrie and Rebecca crowded close to look over his shoulder as Tragg tilted the circle of tin so that the light would enable him to examine the surface closely.

"Well," he said, "we've got something here. Looks like another code message."

"You *don't* say!" Rebecca said, her voice quivering with excitement. "Now, don't tell me there's going to be another murder, Lieutenant."

Tragg turned to Mrs. Gentrie. "Can you read these letters off for me while I copy them into my notebook?"

Mrs. Gentrie squinted at the top of the can. "I haven't
my reading glasses and this print is pretty fine. . . ."

"I can," Rebecca volunteered.

"Her eyes are sharp as needles," Mrs. Gentrie said.

Tragg said, "Hold it by the edges so you don't get your
fingerprints on it. After I've seen what the words are, I'm
going to try dusting it for fingerprints."

Slowly Rebecca spelled off the code words while Tragg
made a note of them in his notebook. Then Tragg stood
behind Rebecca so that he could look over her shoulder
and compare what he had written with the message which
appeared on the tin.

"Right," he said at length. "Now let's just try dusting
it. I don't think we'll find any fingerprints, but we'll go
through the motions just the same."

When he had found no fingerprints, Tragg said, "Well,
that's that."

Rebecca sniffed. "If you ask me," she said pointedly
to Mrs. Gentrie, "it's a lovers' post office, and that stenographer is getting Junior to pull some more chestnuts out
of the fire."

"Where *is* Junior?" Tragg asked Mrs. Gentrie.

"At the hardware store with his father."

"I think it might be a good idea to call him on the telephone and ask if he can come home at once," Tragg said.

Mrs. Gentrie obediently moved toward the stairs, but
halfway up she paused to inquire, "Am I to tell him why
you want him?"

"No. Just that I'm here and want him to come at once."

Mrs. Gentrie said, "As far as that tin is concerned,
Junior wouldn't . . ."

"I understand," Tragg interrupted, "but wouldn't it
be better to let Junior speak for himself?"

Mrs. Gentrie resumed her climbing up the stairs, closed

the kitchen door behind her. Tragg turned to Rebecca, said, "We'll try . . ."

"Look," Rebecca exclaimed, her eyes bright with excitement, "I've just thought of a way to find out if it's Junior."

"Yes?" Tragg's tone was only politely courteous.

Rebecca said, "We can seal this tin again and put it back on the shelf." She was plainly trying to make an impression on Tragg, smiling coquettishly.

Tragg's eyes narrowed. "You might have something there," he said. "Provided, of course, we could get that top back into the can without it appearing the tin had been opened."

Rebecca countered that objection with the rapid-fire retort of an enthusiast upholding a pet idea. "We could copy the message on to the top of *another* can and seal that one up and put it up there on the shelf. After all, the person who's going to get that message couldn't tell one tin from the other."

Tragg regarded Rebecca with a certain respect appearing in his eyes. "That might be an excellent thing to do," he admitted.

Rebecca, conscious of the impression she had made, modestly lowered her eyes. Her skirt swung slightly as she moved her bony hips from side to side. "Somehow, you really inspire a person to get ideas, Lieutenant."

Tragg hesitated for only a moment, then he was running up the cellar stairs two at a time, calling Mrs. Gentrie away from the telephone.

"Now look," he said when he had the three women gathered around him in the basement, "I'm going to take this tin for evidence. But I'm going to copy this message in another new tin, seal it, and place it on the shelf. I don't want anyone to know anything about what I've done. That means *anyone*. None of you women are to communicate to a soul what has happened. Do you understand, Hester?"

133

She looked at Mrs. Gentrie. "If Mrs. Gentrie says so . . ."

"I do, Hester," Mrs. Gentrie said. "You mustn't tell a soul."

"And you?" Tragg asked Rebecca.

The spinster clamped her lips together tightly and nodded with vehemence.

Tragg shifted his glance to Mrs. Gentrie. She said, "I can't understand the fact that my cellar is being used for . . ."

"But you do appreciate the necessity of keeping this matter absolutely to ourselves?" Tragg asked.

Slowly, Mrs. Gentrie nodded.

"That means that you mustn't tell even your husband about it," Tragg said.

"I don't keep secrets from Arthur. I . . ."

"But this is a secret you *must* keep. Everyone must maintain absolute and complete silence about this. Do you understand?"

"Well, if you say so."

"I do say so, and that means particularly that Junior isn't to know anything about it."

Mrs. Gentrie glanced resentfully at Rebecca. "I suppose I have you to thank . . ."

"Do I have your promise?" Tragg interrupted.

"Yes," Mrs. Gentrie said. "I guess so—yes, if you say so. But you'll see Junior isn't the one who will walk into your trap."

Tragg said, "Now let's go some place where we can get a can. I'll etch these letters in the top of the can with the point of my jackknife."

Rebecca beamed at Tragg with the smile an unattached woman in the forties bestows upon an attractive male. "I'll get the can for you and show you how to seal it."

"Thanks," Tragg said. "First, however, I want to use the telephone. Is it where I can have absolute privacy?"

"Well," Mrs. Gentrie said apologetically, "it isn't in a

phone booth, if that's what you mean. It's in the living room, but . . ."

"I guess that will do," Tragg said.

"We won't listen," Rebecca assured him.

"And to make certain we don't," Mrs. Gentrie said with the ghost of a smile twitching the corners of her lips, "we'll *all* go out in the kitchen."

Rebecca said indignantly, "Well, I don't see any reason for us being herded around like . . ."

"We'll *all* go out in the kitchen," Mrs. Gentrie interrupted firmly.

Rebecca, her lips compressed into a thin line of indignation, marched up the cellar stairs and followed Mrs. Gentrie into the kitchen while Hester tagged along behind her. Tragg turned toward the living room. Carefully closing the doors behind him, he surreptitiously twisted the key. To his discomfiture, the lock clicked noisily. But there was nothing to do about it now. Tragg picked up the telephone, took out his notebook, called for Detective Texman, and when he had him on the line, said in a low voice, "This is Tragg, Tex. Get that dictionary and look up these words. Got a pencil? . . . Okay. The seventh word in the first column on page 569. The sixth word in the first column on page 615. The second word in the second column on page 455. Seventh word in the first column, page 377. Twelfth word in the first column, page 748. Seventeenth word in the second column, 472. Eleventh word in the second column, page 1131. Sixth word, second column, page 364. Twenty-second word, second column, page 1094. Fourth word, first column, page 832, and the twenty-sixth word in the second column on page 600. When you have that list of words, call me back at the residence of Arthur Gentrie. I'll be sticking around here, stalling along until I get your call. It shouldn't take long. Read me those words in that order. And keep absolutely mum about this message. I don't want a word of it to get out to the newspapers—not even to anyone else on the force. Keep this as the most closely guarded secret in the office. Got it? All right, good-by."

Tragg hung up, and went back to the kitchen where Hester was matter-of-factly engaged in peeling potatoes, where Mrs. Gentrie was rubbing a tin can with a rag and watching her sister-in-law with tolerant good humor.

Rebecca, sitting in the straight-backed kitchen chair, was tapping the floor with her toe. Her thin, rigid form fairly quivered with indignation. She got to her feet to face the officer.

"Was it necessary to lock that door?" she snapped.

Tragg regarded her with candid surprise in his blue eyes. "Good heavens," he exclaimed. "Did I do that? That's what the force of habit does for a man who's detecting murders for a living. Miss Gentrie, I apologize. No hard feelings, I hope."

He extended his hand, and as Rebecca hesitantly placed her thin, bony hand in his, Tragg put his left hand over hers, and stood for a moment smiling down at her.

The indignation vanished from her face. Her smile became coy and arch. "No one could withhold forgiveness from so attractive a penitent," she said.

Mrs. Gentrie said matter-of-factly, "Forget it, Rebecca. The lieutenant's a busy man. He doesn't have time to think of all the little things. After all, he isn't a suitor."

Rebecca turned to her sister-in-law, started to say something, then changed her mind. The anger in her face gave way once more to a smile as she turned back to Lieutenant Tragg. "Do be seated, Lieutenant."

He bowed, holding her chair gallantly. "After you, Miss Gentrie," he said.

Rebecca sighed with satisfaction. She settled down into the straight-backed kitchen chair as though she had been the star in a movie receiving a penitent but ardent swain. "Do you ever do crossword puzzles—on your days off, Lieutenant?" she asked invitingly.

12

Mason left the elevator and came walking down the long corridor of his office building. His hat was tilted back on his head at a jaunty angle, and his hands were thrust deep in his pockets. He was whistling the catchy chorus of one of the popular tunes and his manner was that of a man who was very well pleased with himself and the world.

The door of Paul Drake's office opened, and Della Street, thrusting out her head, came running after him down the corridor.

Mason turned and looked down at her with smiling eyes. "Hi, Della," he said. "What's the rush?"

"I was waiting for you," she said. "I've been trying to get you."

"What's the excitement?"

She looked up and down the corridor, slipped her hand through his arm, said, "Come on into Paul Drake's office."

Slowly the smile faded from Mason's eyes. He walked back the half dozen steps which took him to Drake's office, and Della Street piloted him past the girl at the switchboard, down the glassed-in partition to Paul Drake's private office.

Drake looked up as Mason entered, said to Della Street, "See you got him."

She nodded.

Mason perched a casual hip on the edge of Paul Drake's desk. "What is the excitement?" he asked.

Drake said, "They found out something about that telephone, Perry."

"Which one?"

"The one in Hocksley's flat."

"You mean the fingerprints on it?"

"No. Something else."

"What?"

"The thing had been rigged up into an ingenious burglar alarm. There was a small hole in the base which looked as though it might have been a place for a wire. In reality, it was a little lens. A beam of invisible light ran through it, and when anyone stepped across that beam, it worked the alarm. Lifting the telephone receiver disconnected the whole thing. Then you had only to walk over to a switch by the safe, throw that, turn back, and put the telephone receiver back in place. Because it was a dial phone, the thing didn't interfere with the operation of the telephone."

Mason said, "Oh-oh."

Della Street and Paul Drake were watching him anxiously.

"See where that leaves young Gentrie?" Drake asked after a while.

Mason nodded.

"And," Della Street said, "it all ties in with the message in the tin. Tragg can really go to town on that."

Mason lit a cigarette. "Yes," he said thoughtfully, "that would account for it. The tin itself was a signal. Whenever the can was placed on the shelf, it meant the time had come to rob the safe. If any unforeseen developments necessitated a minor change in plans, that would be noted in code on the inside of the tin top."

"It *was* noted," Drake said, "and the person for whom the message was intended got it all right."

"And acted on it," Della Street supplemented with a meaning glance at Mason.

"And," Drake added, "they're Junior's fingerprints on the telephone. Now just suppose, for the sake of the argument, Perry, that message has something to do with the telephone. You could see where that would leave young Gentrie.

138

"Of course," Drake went on, "they may never decipher that code. But they have some pretty clever cipher men knocking around these days. Whatever that message is, it's an even money bet Tragg will have it all worked out within a week or two, perhaps a lot sooner than that."

Mason lit a cigarette, blew out twin streams of smoke through his nostrils. "Just as a gambling proposition, Paul, what would you say the percentage of chances was?"

"Percentage on what?"

"That the message has anything to do with the telephone."

"I'd say it was even money," Drake said.

"Well," Mason told him, avoiding Della Street's eyes, "we'll cross that bridge when we come to it. Anything else new?"

"Yes," Della said. "Rodney Wenston's waiting in the office. There's a woman with him who claims to be the daughter of Karr's partner. Wenston thinks she's an impostor, and wants you to trap her."

"Has she seen Karr?"

"No. Karr arranged with Wenston to answer the phone and handle all calls that came in on that ad. Wenston says that unless she can really produce some evidence, he's not even going to let her talk with Karr. He said he was against Karr's putting that ad in the paper. He says it's certain to attract swindlers. He thought that if Karr wanted to do anything, he should quietly engage a firm of private detectives to find out what had happened to the daughter. Karr got impatient and said he couldn't wait."

"Where is this woman now?" Mason asked.

"Waiting in the office with Wenston. He hasn't let her tell her story. He wants you to be with him the first time she tells it."

Drake said, "There's one other thing, Perry."

"What?"

"Wenston acts the part of the wealthy playboy. He has quite a place down between Culver City and Santa Monica. There's a hangar and a swell little private landing field. He flies back and forth to San Francisco quite a lot. Guess who he has for a passenger on nearly all of the trips?"

"Karr?" Mason asked.

Drake nodded.

"Anything else?"

"Yes. When Karr's taking the plane, a big limousine comes to Wenston's place. The driver opens a locked gate in the fence around the estate, follows the driveway around back of the house to the hangar, then past the hangar out to the far end of the flying field. Wenston has his plane all warmed up. He taxies out there, and turns around; then a door opens, a couple of men get out— that Chinese servant and Johns Blaine, who apparently is a bodyguard. Then Karr gets out and . . ."

"Wait a minute," Mason interrupted. "You say *gets* out?"

"That's what I said."

"You mean he walks?"

"Uh huh. Not very well, but he walks."

Mason said excitedly, "How did you get that, Paul?"

Drake said, "Talking with a queer old hobo who lives in a scrap house down on the edge of the railroad right of way near where Wenston has his landing field. You know the sort. They squat down on waste land that no one cares anything about and build houses out of flattened-out coal-oil tins, old pieces of corrugated iron, and a few boards here and there."

Mason nodded.

"This chap's seen Wenston take off and come back from trips. Occasionally a passenger gets aboard or gets out down at the far end of the landing field. A heavy-set man who's probably Johns Blaine is always on hand.

140

Also there's a Chinese. The passenger usually walks the few steps from the plane to the automobile, and gets in. He walks rather slowly, but he walks. From the description, it has to be Karr."

"Is that hobo on the level?" Mason asked.

"I can't guarantee him," Drake said. "I think he's okay, but he's a queer cuss. I spotted his shack and thought it might be worth while trying to pump him for information. You told me to get a line on Wenston. I don't think any amount of money would have bribed the old codger, but I got some old clothes and a roll of blankets and came walking along the railroad. I stopped to pass the time of day with him, and had a bottle of cheap liquor in my blanket roll. We got pretty well plastered. I've still got a headache from it. But he loosened up and told me a lot of stuff."

Mason grinned. "Perhaps I'd better go out and talk with him."

Drake said, *"You!* Hell's bells, Perry, if you'd had to go through what I did, you'd have died. That booze was awful. My head feels like a toy balloon just before it busts."

Mason slid off of Drake's desk, said, "Why don't you get better booze when you want to get plastered, Paul? It's on the expense account. First time I ever knew you to economize on it."

Drake said grimly, "Yeah. A nice time I'd have hitting the rails as a hobo, and then pulling a bottle of bonded hooch out of my blanket roll. Here I sit up most of the night finding bodies for you, grab a couple of hours' sleep, go out and get drunk on cheap rotgut, and this is all the thanks I get."

Mason started for the door. "It's lack of imagination, Paul. You should have told him you were a hijacker, or poured some bonded stuff in a bottle with a cheap label."

141

Drake snorted. "Let's see you try *that* stunt on *this* coot. Go right ahead, my lad. Hop to it."

Out in the hallway, Mason asked, "These people waiting, Della?"

"Yes. I told them you were in conference in another lawyer's office, and I couldn't reach you on the telephone, as you'd left word you weren't to be disturbed, but I thought I could go over, explain the situation, and get you to come back with me. How about it? Did you plant that tin?"

"Nothing to it," Mason said. "I walked in with a bulging brief case and wearing gloves, said I wanted to look the premises over again, and particularly wanted to see the smudges of paint on the garage door. They sent Hester, the stolid servant who certainly seems none too intelligent, down to show me around. I waited until her back was turned and slipped the tin up on the shelf."

"You don't think she spotted it?"

"She didn't even so much as look back when I started upstairs. She's either just an ox, or she's trying to keep out of the mess by seeming to be one. So now we've baited the trap, and we'll wait to see what walks in."

"I don't like the bait," Della said. "Be careful someone doesn't steal it."

"I'll do that little thing," Mason promised.

He unlocked the door of his private office, and pushed it open. Della Street said, "I'll go and bring them in. Mr. Wenston wants to talk with you before you see this girl."

"All right, get him in. Let's see what's on *his* mind."

Wenston, looking very trim and military, entered Mason's private office. He had a courteous bow for Della Street, a handclasp for Mason. "This ith a complication," he said. "This girl ith an imposter. I have refused even to listen to her. I want you to hear her story the first time she tells it. I don't want to take her to the guv'nor until after you've talked with her. After that, I won't have to. You can trap her, and expose her as an impothtor."

"What makes you think she's an impostor if you haven't talked with her?" Mason asked.

"I don't know," Wenston said, "unless it's some sort of a telepathic intuition. She doesn't theem genuine. There's something phoney about her whole approach."

"And you want me to talk with her?" Mason asked.

"I want you to cross-examine her—give her the works."

"Wouldn't it be better to do that in front of Mr. Karr?"

"No. I know most of the facts. I want to see if she's telling the truth. If she isn't, I'm not going to let her even get near Karr."

"And you want me to cross-examine?" Mason asked.

Wenston nodded.

Mason said, "Well, let's have her in here and see what she looks like."

Doris Wickford followed Della Street into the office. She was between twenty-seven and thirty, Mason judged, with very dark hair, dark, thin eyebrows, long lashes, slate-colored eyes, and a pale skin which, coupled with a poker-faced immobility of countenance, gave her a peculiarly detached manner. She said, "Good afternoon. You're Mr. Mason, aren't you?" and came over to give him her hand. The slate-gray eyes gave him a long, steady scrutiny. She said, "I presume Mr. Wenston has told you I'm an imposter."

Mason laughed.

Wenston said with dignity, "I told him to give you a croth-examination."

"I expected that," she said. "The reason I didn't tell Mr. Wenston all the details is that I don't want to keep going over them again and again. I don't mind telling you, Mr. Mason, that I know Mr. Wenston isn't the one who put that ad in the paper. For one thing, it's very apparent that Mr. Wenston is rather young to have been in partnership with my father in 1920. I also know it because I know something about the persons with whom my father had that partnership. One of them was a man by the name of Karr, and I presume that he's the one who's really back of this ad in the paper. I've asked Mr. Wenston if that wasn't a fact, and he refused to answer. I've asked him if he isn't related to a Mr. Karr or employed by him, and he told me we'd go over that when we got to your office. Well, the way I look at it, if Mr. Karr is the one who's really interested, why can't we go to see him and then have it settled one way or the other?"

Wenston shook his head firmly. "I won't subject the guv'nor to the strain of such an interview unleth I know it's justified. You've got to convince me before you can ever see him."

"How much convincing are you going to require?" Miss Wickford asked, her eyes surveying Wenston in a head-to-toe glance, which was something less than cordial.

"*I'm* going to need lots of convincing."

"All right, here goes," Miss Wickford said cheerfully, drawing up a chair and unfastening the snap on a large purse which she had carried under her arm.

"Tell me the name of your father," Wenston said, glancing at Mason meaningly. "It might save time."

Her glance was scornful. "His name was Wickford. He had trouble with creditors, so he went to the Orient. While he was in Shanghai, he took the name of Tucker."

Wenston frowningly studied her. "He had rather an unusual firtht name. Perhaps you can tell us what *that* was."

"I can tell you what it was," she said, "and I can tell you how he happened to take it. The name was D-O-W, and it consists of the initials of my name. Doris Octavia Wickford. Octavia was my mother's name, and when my father wanted some distinctive first name, he coined the word *Dow* from those initials."

144

This time Wenston managed to keep his face more of a mask. "What else?" he asked. "Have you any proof?"

She took a somewhat dog-eared envelope from her purse. The envelope had a Chinese stamp and postmark. She said, "This letter was sent from Shanghai, January 8, 1921."

Wenston and Mason both moved over to take a look at the envelope. Wenston reached for it. She pushed his hand back with a quick gesture and said, "Naughty, naughty! You can look, and that's all."

"Your father wrote that?" Wenston asked.

"That's right, and you'll notice the name, Doris O. Wickford, written on the envelope."

"The return address in the upper left-hand corner," Mason said, "is that of George A. Wickford at Shanghai."

"That's right. That was his real name. Here's a photostatic copy of his marriage license to my mother. September, 1912, and here's a copy of my birth certificate, November, 1913. You'll notice my mother's name was Octavia, and you'll note that I was christened Doris Octavia Wickford."

Mason examined the photostatic copies of the documents, then raised his eyes to meet Wenston's perplexed gaze.

She said, "Now I'll read you some of the excerpts from this letter. After all, remember I was a child of eight at the time, and he's written to me the way a father would write to a girl of that age."

She took some folded sheets of paper from the envelope. They were written in pencil. The paper was a thin, limp rice paper characteristic of Chinese manufacture. She read, " 'My dear daughter: It seems like a very long time since your daddy has seen you. I miss you very much and hope you are being a good girl. I don't know just when daddy is coming back to you, but I hope it won't be long. Over here, I am doing some good business and expect to return and clean up all of the debts I owe.

145

You must remember not to mention to anyone where daddy is because some of those people who made so much trouble for me would try to keep me from getting enough together to pay off what I owe. If they will only leave me alone for a little while longer, I can not only pay off everything, but have money left. Then I will come back to you, and we will be together for a long time. You can have nice dresses and a pony if you still want one.' "

She looked up and said, "I had written him saying that I wanted a pony for Christmas."

"Your mother?" Mason asked.

"She died when I was six, just before Dad went to China."

"Go ahead."

She turned back to the letter and read, " 'I have a very fine business here now, but I can't tell you what it is. I have a partner. His name is Karr. Don't you think that is a funny way for a man to spell his name? But he is a good partner, and he has lots of courage. Three weeks ago we were on a trip up the Yangtze River, and the boat he was in tipped over. Some of the Chinese boatmen clung to the overturned boat, but one of them was swept away. The current was very swift. This man couldn't swim. He was only a Chinese, and over here the life of a laborer is not very valuable. I doubt if any one of the Chinese would have tried to rescue him, even if they had been strong swimmers. But my partner, Karr, swam out to the aid of this Chinaboy and brought him back to the boat. By that time my boat had come alongside, and the coolies managed to get it turned right side up. But we lost a lot of things in the river which we never recovered.

" 'The water of this river is very yellow. It is filled with a kind of mud. Even after it flows out into the ocean, it stains the whole region around the mouth of the river. It

146

is a very big river, and Shanghai is on a branch of it called the Whangpoo.

" 'Shanghai is a very big city. You would never dream of the noise and bustle of one of these Chinese cities. It seems as though everyone is always screaming something at the top of his voice. You wouldn't believe people could make that much noise.

" 'Now daddy wants Doris to be a good little girl, and study hard in school. Your daddy is sorry he couldn't send you that pony for Christmas, because there is no way of sending a pony from China to the United States, but some day soon when your daddy comes back, you shall have your pony. Lots of love from a lonely father to his little girl. Your loving *DAD*. P.S. When you write me over here, you can write the letter addressed to me, but be sure you put it care of Dow Tucker and send it care of the American Express Company. I will get it all right.' "

She folded the letter, held it for a moment in her fingers as though contemplating whether she should pass it over to Mason for his inspection. Then abruptly she pushed it back into the envelope, and said simply, "I saved that one because it was the last letter I ever received. There were other letters, and I lost them. This one I kept. I never heard any more from him. I didn't know what had happened to him."

Wenston tried to keep from seeming impressed. "You have someting else? Some better proof, perhaps?"

She looked at him with the impersonal appraisal one would give an insect impaled on a pin and said, "I've got lots of proof. Here's a picture—a family group taken the year my mother died. I was six at the time, almost seven."

She extracted a somewhat faded photograph from her purse. It was of the peculiar muddy tone which characterized the matte-surface prints of that period. It was a square picture three and a half inches by three and a

147

half inches, and showed a man and a woman seated on what was apparently the upper step of a front porch. The man was holding a girl on his knee. Despite the pigtails and extreme youth of the girl in the picture, the resemblance to Doris Wickford was very pronounced.

Wenston pursed his lips, caught Mason's eye, and almost imperceptibly nodded.

"You remember your father?" Mason asked.

"Naturally. Of course, it's the memory of a girl of seven years of age. I was seven the last time I saw him. I suppose there are some things on which my memory is distorted, and you'll have to make allowances for youth, but aside from that, I remember him quite distinctly, numerous little things about him, his tolerance, his unfailing consideration of the rights of others, and, what didn't impress me as being particularly remarkable at the time but what does now that I've seen more of the world, is that I never knew him to lose his temper over anything, or say a sharp word to anyone. And yet the man must have been beset by worries."

"Where did you live?"

"The address is on this letter," she said. "It was in Denver, Colorado."

"You lived there all the time until your father disappeared?"

"He didn't disappear. He simply went away. There weren't any jobs in Denver, and . . ."

"All right, have it your own way," Mason interposed. "Had you lived there long? I notice that your birth certificate says that you were born in California."

"That's right. We lived in California for a while, then went to Nevada, and then to Denver. My father had work in the mines. Conditions got so bad Dad made complaints and eventually started organizing the men. Unions had never gotten a hold in that locality, and the company fired him. Dad opened up a little store, and the miners all started buying their things from him. Then the company simply ruined him. They forced him into disastrous competition. They wanted to get him out of the country. They said his cracker-box socialism was going to ruin the country. That's when he incurred all those debts. He . . ."

Wenston said, "I guess, Mr. Mason, we're going to have to see the guv'nor, after all."

Mason said, "We can check the incident of that upset boat in the Yangtze River before going any farther."

"We don't have to," Wenston said. "I've heard the guv'nor speak of it half a dozen times."

Mason sat at his desk for a moment drumming thoughtfully with his fingers on the edge of the desk. Abruptly, he asked Miss Wickford, "And you saw this ad in the paper this morning?"

"No. The one that appeared yesterday morning."

"Why didn't you answer it at once?"

"I was working, and I—well," she said with a little smile, "I arranged with my relief to have today off. I went to a hairdresser and then called the number mentioned in the ad. I asked for Mr. Karr. Mr. Wenston answered, said he was handling the preliminary interviews, and made an appointment. I never did have a chance to tell him any of my story. He rushed me right up here. Now, if that ad is on the level, I want to see Mr. Karr. It's a matter of money with me. I'm not going to kid you, Mr. Mason, and I'm not going to kid myself. If there's any money coming to me from my father, I need it."

"You're employed?" Mason asked.

"Yes. I'm an actress, and I can't get a part. I had some bits in New York. A man promised he could get me a part in pictures if I came to Hollywood. He lied. Right at present I'm working as cashier in a cafeteria. And I don't like it. It would be worth a good deal to be able to slap the boss's face and walk out."

"With whom were you living while you were going to school?"

"An aunt. She died about three years ago. Really, Mr. Mason, *all* of this can be verified. If there's really anything back of this ad in the paper, we're wasting a lot of time."

"I think the guv'nor would want to see her," Wenston said to Mason and then added, "Right away."

Mason reached for his hat. "Okay," he said, "let's go."

■ 13 ■

The people in the room were grouped in a tense-faced circle around the wheelchair occupied by Elston A. Karr. The day had been warm, yet the blanket covered his legs. His skin was no longer wax-like but was flushed. As his hand touched Mason's, the lawyer noticed that the skin was dry and hot. Karr turned over the photograph and the letter, looked first at Johns Blaine, then at Gow Loong, the number one boy.

"Well?" he asked.

Blaine said nothing.

Rodney Wenston said, "When I brought her to Mason, I thought she wath a damned imposter, but this proof is pretty convincing."

Doris Wickford said indignantly, "I'm *not* an impostor, and I'm tired of being treated like one. After all, this was *your* idea. *I* didn't advertise to try and get in touch with you. *You* advertised to try and get in touch with *me*. If my father left any money, it isn't yours, and there's no reason why you should act as though giving it to me would be an act of generosity or charity on your part. After all, we have courts to protect the rights of people in cases like this."

Karr didn't so much as glance at her. He kept his eyes on Gow Loong.

Gow Loong extended his forefinger. The nail protruded a good half inch from the end of the finger. He placed this long nail on the face in the photograph. "Alla same Dow Tucker," he said.

Karr nodded.

Gow Loong turned to Karr. "Maybe-so you tired. Too much work. Too much tlouble. Maybe-so you go sleep. Maybe one two hours. Wake up, feel more better. Too many people. Too much talk. Velly much no good."

Karr turned to Johns Blaine. "I see no reason for prolonging the matter. This girl seems to be it. We'll have to make an additional check, but that's Dow Tucker's picture all right. What she says about how he came to adopt the name of Dow sounds logical. Get me that album of pictures out of the desk in my bedroom."

Gow Loong became merely a part of the scenery. He effaced himself beyond a point of silence. It seemed that even his personality had retired behind the expressionless composure of a calmly indifferent face. Johns Blaine hurried toward the bedroom.

Mason asked casually, "Keep those pictures in your bedroom all the time?"

"Prints," Karr said. "The negatives are in a safe place. Wouldn't take a million dollars for those negatives. Adventures in China that would curl your hair. I've seen things that white men aren't permitted to see, things that no person should ever see. The Temple of the Passionate Buddha under the walls of the Forbidden City—the living dead man called up out of the grave to make obeisance to a Lama god. You might think it's hypnotism, might think it's superstition, might think it's imagination, but I've seen things you can't explain, things you can't understand, things you don't even dare to talk about. Take a look through that album, Johns. Get some of those

151

pictures taken at Shanghai in the fall of '20 and the spring of '21."

Blaine turned the pages of the photograph album. "Here's a picture taken on a junk on the Whangpoo," he said. "That shows him pretty well."

"Show it to Mason," Karr said. "Want him to see it."

Mason looked at the picture of three men seated on the high stern deck of a big junk. The camera had been focused upon the faces. Back of them was a hazy sheet of water, the dim line of a bank, and the fuzzy outlines of an out-of-focus pagoda rising against the sky. The men were smiling affably at the camera with that peculiarly inane expression with which one obeys the command to "look pleasant." On a table before them was a huge teapot. Three Chinese cups were nestled into the distinctive hole-in-the-center saucers which furnish a sturdy resting place for Chinese soup-bowl cups. Behind the group, standing a little to one side, looking solicitously down at the man in the center, was a Chinese who was undoubtedly Gow Loong. The man in the center was Elston A. Karr, more robust, twenty years younger, but still with that same cold-eyed concentration glittering from his eyes, that ruthless, indomitable purpose stamped upon his face. There had been change in the twenty years. He had lost weight. His skin had stretched taut across his cheekbones, and there were puffs under his eyes; but there could be no mistaking Elston Karr.

The man on his right was the man shown in the photograph produced by Doris Wickford. There could be no doubt of that, and the two photographs must have been taken at about the same time. The partially bald head, the snub nose, the long lower lip with the deep calipers stretching down from the nostrils, the cleft chin, the bushy eyebrows, the protruding batlike ears were unmistakable.

The third man in the photograph caught Mason's eye. He was a thick-chested, heavy-necked individual with

152

thick lips that were twisted into a smile, but even in the photograph it was apparent that the eyes were not smiling. They were the sort of eyes that wouldn't smile. They were staring in sullen contemplation at the lens of the camera. It was as though the man had been brooding so long upon some sinister scheme that his thoughts had stamped themselves indelibly upon his face.

"Who's this man?" Mason asked.

Karr said, "A Judas—a dirty traitor—sold us out for his pieces of silver—almost brought about my death." He looked up at Doris Wickford and said, "He was responsible for the death of your father. I shan't forget him—ever."

There was something in the way he said that last that was as whisperingly ominous as the sound of a carving knife being sharpened on a steel.

Mason compared the photograph in the book with that produced by Doris Wickford. Slowly he nodded his head, then asked, "Got any more pictures of Tucker?"

Karr jerked his head to Johns Blaine, and Blaine, turning the leaves of the photograph album, paused four times more to show Mason photographs. Always there were the photographs of the same four men: Karr; his partner, Tucker; Gow Loong; and this heavy-set, sullen-faced man who had apparently betrayed them.

Abruptly Karr said to Miss Wickford, "I want to check up on you. Where you lived, what you did, whom you knew."

"Of course. You realize I was rather a child when Dad left, but I have rather distinct memories. I can tell you the houses we lived in—some of them, at any rate. Would you mind telling me whether my father left any considerable amount of property?"

"We had a partnership venture," Karr said. "I didn't know your father had any heirs. There was a partnership. We made some profit. He was killed. I didn't make any formal accounting of his share. It wasn't the sort of

153

business you could offer for probate. We'd have been be-headed or hung if we'd been caught at it. Most danger-ous, most risky business in the world, and the most fas-cinating. Betrayed by a damned Judas. But I got out of there with the money. I invested that money. The invest-ments turned out well. Recently, Gow Loong mentioned that one night when Dow Tucker had been standing by the rail of the junk looking down at some little girls danc-ing on the landing in a Chinese village, he'd pointed out one little Chinese girl about seven or eight years old, and said that he had a daughter at home just about her age. He never spoke to me about it—very reticent about his private and family affairs. Gow Loong never realized the significance of it until later, when I was talking with him about the night Tucker was captured and killed. I'm tired. I'll think it over. I'll follow Gow Loong's ad-vice and rest. Give Mr. Blaine all the data you can think of, where you live, for whom you've worked, where you went to school, all the rest of it. Answer all questions Mr. Mason may ask."

She nodded.

"One more thing," Karr said abruptly. "You lived with an aunt?"

"Yes."

"Perhaps there are more letters from your father in your aunt's things."

"I never thought of that."

"Know where they are?"

"No."

"Try and find them. He might have written to her. See me again. No, don't see me again. Keep in touch with Mr. Mason. He's my lawyer. Don't let Rodney Wenston's hostility impress you much. He has nothing whatever to say about it. I told him to be skeptical in dealing with claimants. If you're my partner's daughter, I want to be friendly with you. If you're an impostor, I want to send

154

you to jail. I don't want to waste too much time finding out which it's going to be."

Mason heard a quick intake of breath as though Gow Loong had been about to say something. Then the number one boy changed his mind. By the time Mason had raised his eyes, Gow Loong was standing absolutely motionless. Apparently he hadn't even been listening to the conversation.

"Something you wanted to say, Gow Loong?" Karr asked.

"Maskee," the Chinese number one boy said.

The girl looked questioningly at Karr. "Is that Chinese?" she asked innocently enough.

Karr's frosty eyes twinkled into a half smile. "Near enough to Chinese," he said. "The pigeon English of the treaty port. The greatest word of all, 'maskee.' It means never mind, no matter. And now run along, my dear. I think I'll have some very important news for you soon, but let Mr. Mason check up on you and . . ."

The harsh sound of the door buzzer interrupted him. He looked quickly at Gow Loong. "See who it is," he said. "I don't want to see anyone."

But as it turned out, Gow Loong had nothing to say on that score. They heard him descend the stairs, heard the door open, and then the crisp tones of an authoritative voice, and the feet of the two men on the stairs.

Lieutenant Tragg preceded the Chinese houseboy up the stairs. "Good afternoon, everyone," he said. "Good afternoon. Ah, Mason again. *And* a young woman. Hope I'm not intruding. Your houseboy said you were busy, Karr, but just as I put my duties ahead of my own personal convenience, I have to adopt that attitude elsewhere. I trust you'll understand." Tragg ceased speaking and looked inquiringly at Doris Wickford.

"Miss Wickford," Mason introduced. "Lieutenant Tragg of the Homicide Squad."

"Homicide!" Miss Wickford said with a little startled exclamation.

"That's right," Tragg explained. "You probably aren't interested in murder cases, Miss Wickford, but if you'd been reading the papers, you'd know that a man and his housekeeper were . . ."

"But are you working on *that?*" she asked.

Tragg eyed her narrowly. "Yes, ma'am," he said, his voice suddenly noncommittal. "They lived in the flat below here."

"Lived below *here?*" she asked, her eyes widening, and seeming suddenly to take on a darker hue.

"In the flat right below here," Tragg repeated. "Didn't you know it?"

There was no flicker in her glance, no waver in her eyes. "No," she said.

"Sorry," Tragg said, "but I've got to ask a few questions. Let's go back to the night of the murder, gentlemen. Now, Gow Loong where were you?"

"Down China city. I visit my cousin."

"How many cousins?" Tragg asked.

There was just the bare suggestion of a flicker of triumph in Gow Loong's eyes. "Twenty-one."

It was Miss Wickford who broke the silence with a little laugh. *"Twenty-one cousins!"* she exclaimed.

Karr said to Lieutenant Tragg, "Chinese cousins are different from ours. In China they properly have only one hundred names. Everyone who has the same surname is supposed to be related. It's a vague relationship. There's nothing to compare with it in this country. That's why a Chinaboy will say of another Chinese, 'He allee same my cousin.' "

"I see," Tragg said. "Most interesting. And your name is Loong?"

"That's not really his family name," Karr interposed again. "Gow Loong he calls himself. Literally translated, it means 'nine dragons'—Cantonese. So don't try looking

156

it up in the official Mandarin dictionaries. Cantonese is a different language. Sort of a Chinese nickname. Means he has the strength, wisdom, daring, and courage of nine dragons. Each one of them furnishes some attribute: Loyalty, courage, perspicacity, endurance, shrewdness in money matters, ability to study—let's see. How many's that? Seven. I've forgotten the other two. Virtue and filial respect, probably. No matter. It illustrates the point. Anyway, he's got twenty-one witnesses. He wasn't here. *I* know he wasn't here. If you want to check up on him, that's easy. Who else do you want?"

Tragg turned to Blaine.

Blaine said, "I believe I've explained that at the same time the murder was committed I was flying down from San Francisco with Mr. Wenston here. We left San Francisco at eleven o'clock. I had some friends come down to the plane to see me off."

"Good thing you did too," Wenston interposed. "Otherwise I couldn't have prethented any alibi myself."

Tragg suddenly whirled to Karr. *"You,"* he said.

Karr met his eyes with cold defiance. "I was here—alone."

"That's rather unusual, isn't it?"

"Yes."

"In your wheelchair?"

"No. In bed. I believe I've gone over all that with you before, Lieutenant."

"You haven't," Tragg said meaningly. "Mason has."

"What do you mean?" Karr asked.

Karr kept staring at the detective with the cold concentration of one who is completely the master of his own soul, and resents uninvited familiarities. "Do you have any fault to find with what Mr. Mason answered?" he asked.

"I may have," Tragg said.

"Under those circumstances," Karr announced with cold dignity, "I am afraid it will be necessary for me to ask Mr. Mason to speak for me again. I am not feeling well, Lieutenant, and this interview has wearied me."

Tragg said affably, "Let's not get off to a bad start, Mr. Karr. I'm trying to save you future trouble."

"Thank you for your consideration. You don't need to try to save me anything. I'm quite capable of looking after myself."

"Despite the fact that you are unable to walk?" Tragg asked.

"Despite the fact that I am unable to walk."

"I don't want to have any misunderstanding about that," Tragg observed.

Karr said, "You don't need to have any. I can't walk."

"You were here alone in this flat," Tragg said. "So far as is known, you, the housekeeper, and Hocksley were the only three persons under this roof."

"Hocksley!" Miss Wickford exclaimed.

Tragg turned to look at her. "Hocksley," he said.

"Why . . . !"

"The name mean anything to you?" Tragg asked.

She smiled and shook her head somewhat dubiously.

Tragg kept his eyes boring into hers. "But," he asked affably in the manner of one making small talk, "you've known a Hocksley somewhere, I take it, Miss Wickford?"

She said, "No."

"The name has some association for you? Come now, let's not beat around the bush."

She said, "My father mentioned a Hocksley in one of his letters."

"How long ago?"

"Oh, perhaps twenty years."

Karr laughed mirthlessly. "Hardly the same Hocksley," he said.

Tragg didn't shift his eyes. "You were a child at the time?"

"Yes."

158

"How old?"

"Seven."

"Where was your father?"

"China."

"What did he say about Hocksley?"

She shifted her eyes to Karr as though looking for some signal. Tragg said insistently, "This is just between you and me, Miss Wickford. What did your father say about Hocksley?"

"My father was in a partnership in China. I believe Hocksley was one of the partners."

Tragg thought that over for a few seconds, then asked abruptly, "When did you meet Mr. Mason?"

"About an hour and a half ago."

"Karr?"

"About forty minutes."

"Known anyone here longer than that?"

"I met Mr. Wenston before I met Mr. Mason."

"How much before?"

"A few minutes before."

"What are you doing here?"

Wenston interposed hastily, "She's calling on a matter of business. It's highly confidential. I don't want anything thaid about it."

Tragg pursed his lips. "Well, well, well," he said. "Now let's see. Wasn't there an ad in this morning's paper, an ad by someone who wanted to find the daughter of his dead partner?"

There was no sound in the room, save the rasping breathing of Elston A. Karr. As by common consent they turned to look at him.

"Your father's name was Wickford?" Tragg asked the girl, whirling abruptly back toward her.

"In China he went under the name of Dow Tucker."

"Wrote you about the partnership?"

"Yes."

"When? Exactly what date?"

159

"In the latter part of 1920."

"What happened after that?"

Karr said, "I can tell you. He . . ."

"Shut up, Karr," Tragg said without taking his eyes from the girl's face.

"I didn't hear anything more from my father after a letter written in the first part of 1921. I heard later on that he had died."

"How did he die?"

"I understood he was murdered."

"You don't know?"

"No."

"His body was never shipped home?"

"No."

"Ever get any property from his estate?"

"No. Not yet."

"Any other relatives living?"

"No."

"When did your mother die?"

"Around eighteen months before Dad went to China."

"With whom did you live after that? After your father left?"

"An aunt."

"Mother's sister or father's?"

"Mother's."

"Where's she?"

"Dead."

"How long?"

"Three years."

"And your father wrote about having a partnership arrangement with a man named Hocksley?"

"Yes."

"Didn't mention his first name?"

"I . . ."

"You didn't save that letter?"

"No."

"Mention the name of the other partner?"

She hesitated a moment, then said, "Well . . . yes."

"A man named Karr?"

"Yes."

"Remember the first name?"

After she had been silent for several seconds, Tragg said abruptly, "I asked you if you knew his first name?"

"I was trying to remember."

"Well, think fast."

She turned to Karr. "*Your* first name is Elston, isn't it?"

"Yes."

She said, "I have a haunting memory in the back of my mind that Karr's first name was Elston. I can't remember. Perhaps it's just the association of ideas, having met Mr. Elston Karr this afternoon. I . . . I may have confused his first name."

"With what?"

"With the name of my father's partner."

"What other Karrs do you know?"

"None who spell their names this way."

Tragg looked up at Karr. "Well?" he asked.

Karr said, "In the fall of 1920 and the spring of 1921 I was in partnership with three men in Shanghai. One of them was named Dow Tucker. I think he's this girl's father. The other one was a man named Hocksley."

"Indeed!" Lieutenant Tragg said, his voice showing only a courteous interest. "And what became of Hocksley?"

Karr said, choosing his words carefully, "Hocksley disappeared. He disappeared under suspicious circumstances. He carried away with him a very large sum of money in partnership funds. Fortunately, not all of the partnership funds, but a large amount."

"So," Tragg said, "naturally, you felt quite bitter toward Hocksley."

A gleam showed in Karr's eyes despite his attempt to

control his expression. He said, "The man was beneath contempt."

"And he took with him a large amount of partnership funds?"

"Yes."

"In other words, some of your money?"

"Yes."

"Naturally, you wanted that back."

"Yes."

"And naturally you made some attempt to trace him."

"That's right."

"And, in short, Karr, your efforts finally were successful. You located Hocksley in this flat below you. You took the flat above him and . . ."

"I did nothing of the sort," Karr interrupted. "I took this flat because I desired privacy. I believe the records will show that some ten days or two weeks after I moved in, the lower flat was rented to a man by the name of Hocksley. I can assure you that I didn't even know his name until this matter came up. I am confined to my house. I don't get out. I . . ."

"Your Chinaboy gets out?"

"He does the shopping."

Tragg pursed his lips, turned toward Gow Loong, then swung back toward Karr. "Well, let's finish this phase of the matter first. What was the first name of your partner in China?"

Karr hesitated.

"Come on," Tragg said. "Let's have it. Stalling around isn't going to get you anywhere."

Karr said, "We called him Red. I don't think I ever did know his first name. . . . If I did know it, I've forgotten it."

Miss Wickford said, "Perhaps I can help you there a little, Lieutenant. His name was Robindale E. Hocksley. I remember my father writing about him. I was just a child at the time, but names have always stuck in my

162

memory. I was going to tell you this before, but you interrupted me with another question."

Tragg said, without looking around, "You're not helping me a damn bit, Miss Wickford. I know what his name was. I knew all about that partnership before I came up here. I wasn't asking questions because I wanted information, but to find out who's trying to co-operate and who's trying to cover up. Karr, why didn't you tell me your partner had the same name as that of the man who was murdered?"

"I didn't know it until after the murder. Then it just didn't occur to me it was other than a similarity of surnames. I never knew Red Hocksley's first name was Robindale."

"How about you?" Tragg asked Gow Loong.

"What'samalla me?" Gow Loong demanded with the shrill rapidity of an excited Chinese.

"How long you been with Mr. Karr?"

"Maybe-so long time."

"In China?"

"Sure, in China."

"You remember the three men in the partnership Mr. Karr's spoken about?"

"Red Hocksley I heap savvy," Gow Loong said. "Him velly bad man. Heap no good. Alla time no can tlust."

Tragg said, "You've seen this man who lived downstairs?"

Gow Loong shook his head. "No see."

"You read his name on the door?"

"No read."

Tragg turned to Blaine. "How about you?"

Blaine said affably, "I have only been with Mr. Karr for a year."

"What's your job?"

"Well, I act as sort of nurse. You see, Mr. Karr is . . ."

"Ever do any nursing before?"

"Well . . ."

"Got a permit to carry that gun you're lugging around?" Tragg interrupted.

Blaine's hand moved automatically to his pocket. "Sure, I got a permit. I . . ." He stopped as he caught the triumphant gleam in Tragg's eye.

Tragg laughed. "What did you do before you became Karr's bodyguard?"

"I had a detective agency in Denver Colorado," Blaine blurted, red-faced. "I wasn't making very much money at it, and when I had this opportunity to draw steady wages and good wages, I jumped at it."

Tragg said, "That's better. If you want to keep that permit to carry that gun and if ever you want to go back into the detective business, you'll be wise to co-operate a little. Now what do you know about Hocksley?"

"Absolutely nothing."

"Ever see the man?"

Blaine said, "Look here, Lieutenant, I'm going to be frank with you. I was hired to act as Karr's bodyguard. I gathered that, because of some old feud in China, his life might be in danger. I've never heard him mention the name of Hocksley, and today is the first time I ever knew about that Shanghai partnership. Karr never told me what specific danger he feared. I had an idea he was still doing a little gun-running—getting stuff past the Japs. I won't go into details, but I think Karr's the brains of the works. I think it would raise the devil, not only with Karr, but with an underground grapevine by which munitions are being smuggled in, if Karr got any publicity. I don't know how the government would feel about it, but I presume that, at least unofficially, they'd have some interest in the matter. That's one of the reasons I've been keeping my mouth shut. I can't tell you a lot about methods, but, as I get the picture, there's quite a fleet of Chinese fishing junks that put out from all the coast villages. Those people have to live, and in order to live, they have to fish. The Japanese realize that. Occasionally, they search these junks. Some of them are considered above suspicion. Some aren't. They can't search them all. Therefore, you can see it's pretty important for Karr to keep under cover, and—well, that's been my job. I've been keeping him sewed up and out of circulation."

Tragg took a deep breath, looked across at Karr.

Karr said somewhat scornfully to Blaine, "You can keep your gossip to yourself. Your ideas of what I'm doing are crazy."

Blaine shrugged his shoulders, said, "I'm hired by you. I do a good job for you. I want to keep on doing a good job for you, but I know which side of the bread has the butter. I'm not going to tangle up with the police department."

"Where, may I ask, did you get your information?" Karr asked coldly. "Been snooping?"

Blaine said indignantly, "I haven't been snooping. I got it from you."

"What do you mean?"

"From little things you did, little hints you let drop, the expression on your face," Blaine said impatiently. "After all, I've been a private detective, and I was a cop before that. What the hell do you think? That I'm going to associate with someone for a year and then not know what I'm hired to protect him against? Nuts!"

Tragg got up, walked over to the window, stood looking out, his hands pushed down into his pockets; then he whirled to regard Perry Mason. "Personally, Mason, I think it's a runaround. I'm not saying anything—not yet. It's getting so that whenever we're working on a case and you come into the picture, the hot trail we're following develops a habit of running back to the starting point so that we're tearing around in circles. It's nothing except coincidence, yet—but it's a hell of a lot of coincidence."

"Speaking of running around in circles," Mason said, "did you come up here to pay this visit simply because you thought Miss Wickford was here and could give you some information on Karr's past connections?"

Miss Wickford said, "Don't be silly. Lieutenant Tragg couldn't have known I was going to be here, because I didn't know it myself until the moment I picked up the paper and . . ."

"I came up here to ask questions," Tragg interrupted.

"Exactly," Mason said, "and, I take it, they were rather important questions; and since this interesting information which has been uncovered about Karr's former partner has been purely fortuitous, I naturally am wondering just what really caused this visit. Or is Miss Wickford an undercover associate?"

Tragg said, "Well, I'll relieve your curiosity on that, Mason. I came up here to find out about a telephone."

"What telephone?" Mason asked.

"A telephone which seems to have been something more than a telephone, one in which I thought Karr might have some interest."

Karr said wearily, "I'm not interested in telephones. I'm a sick man, and the experiences of the afternoon haven't done me any good."

Gow Loong said, "Massah should have gone bed long time ago. Maybe-so go now."

Karr said, "All right, Gow Loong."

"Just a moment," Tragg ordered. "I want to ask a couple more questions."

"Massah sick," Gow Loong said. "No can talk."

"About that telephone," Tragg insisted, putting a hand on Karr's wheelchair.

"What about the telephone?" Karr asked, his voice gone flat with weariness.

Tragg said, "We have reason to believe that the person who committed that murder had a very definite reason for lifting the telephone receiver."

Mason avoided Tragg's eyes.

Karr said, "I suppose he wanted to call someone. You have to lift the receiver to do that, you know."

"When we first examined that telephone," Tragg went on, ignoring Karr's sarcasm, "we noticed only an ordinary desk telephone with two fingerprints which had been outlined in paint on the receiver. Then we made a more detailed investigation and found something which is very peculiar, to say the least."

Karr said, "Don't beat around the bush. If you're trying to accuse me of something, come out and say so."

Mason said, "He's just trying to surprise you into an admission of something, Mr. Karr. It's the way the police work. Apparently a person's poor health doesn't change their methods."

"I'm not accusing you of anything," Tragg said, ignoring Mason's interpolation, "but I'm telling you what we found."

"Well, what *did* you find?"

"Concealed in the base of that telephone in such a way that it would hardly be noticeable on a superficial examination was a small hole. The telephone was bolted to the desk, which was unusual. We further found that the desk was screwed to the floor so that the telephone and desk were held in one position. That aroused our suspicions. We made a careful examination and found that the base of the telephone contained a very ingenious burglar alarm, a ray of invisible light which could be switched on so that it played across the door of that room. The only way the connection could be broken was by throwing a switch which was on the far side of the light beam, or by picking up the telephone receiver and lifting it from its cradle, which automatically had the effect of cutting off the beam of light."

Karr said, "It doesn't mean a damned thing to me. I fail to see why you are telling me about it."

"Because," Tragg went on patiently, "when any person walked across this beam of light without first lifting the telephone receiver, it caused a buzzer on the screen porch of the lower flat to sound. And that buzzer, Mr. Karr, was fastened to the side of the house so that *it was directly below your bedroom window!*"

'Karr placed his thin, wasted hand on the arm of the chair, gripped it so that the cords stood out plainly under the skin of the back of his hand. "Buzzer—under my window. Then *that* explains it."

"Explains what?"

"That must have been what wakened me first, before I heard anything. I heard a peculiarly insistent sound which was like the buzzing of mosquitoes. It was high-pitched, distinctly audible, very irritating to a man of my nervous temperament. I kept listening, thinking at first it was a mosquito in the room, then realized that the sound was coming from outside of my window."

"How long did it continue?" Tragg asked.

"Some little time. I don't know how long it had been going before I woke up."

"How long before you heard the shots?"

Karr said firmly, "There was only one shot."

Tragg sighed. "I take it," he said, "I am indebted for the other shot to the versatile mind of Mr. Mason."

Karr said testily, "You are indebted for the extra shot to what I told Mr. Mason. At the time, I thought there might have been two shots. Since then, and on thinking it over, I have come to the conclusion that there was only one shot, and perhaps an echo from the side of the adjoining house."

"And how about the buzzing?" Tragg asked.

"The buzzing," Karr said, "continued for a few minutes after the sound of the shot, and then ceased."

"Think carefully. Did you hear it again?"

"No," Karr said positively. "I didn't hear it after that."

Tragg studied him for a moment, then said, "It would

168

have simplified matters if you'd told me this stuff when I first questioned you."

Karr, staring right back at him, said, "And it would have simplified matters if you'd told me about the telephone receiver."

"I didn't know about the burglar alarm then."

"And I didn't know that the buzzing of a mosquito was important."

"Then there was only one shot?"

"I've come to the conclusion now there was only one shot."

"Do you know what time it was?"

"I can't tell you exactly, no. It was sometime after midnight, and I would say before one o'clock. And now if you'll excuse me, Lieutenant, I'm going to retire. I'm not going to drive myself past the danger point for anyone. I've already put up with more than I should."

Without another word, Karr lowered his hands to the rubber tires of the wheelchair. But quick as he was, Gow Loong was the first to apply the pressure against the wheelchair which sent it into motion toward the rear of the house.

Doris Wickford said to Mason, "Apparently I'm to camp on your doorstep until this is cleaned up."

Rodney Wenston shook his head. "I know the guv'nor pretty well," he said. "Don't rush him. He won't do a thing if you crowd him."

Lieutenant Tragg said to Mason without any more expression in his voice than if he had been commenting on an unusual spell of weather, "Certainly is strange the number of coincidences there are in this case. And every time I come here I find you here."

Mason laughed. "I think of it as being the other way around. Every time I come to talk with my client, you manage to drop in. I was thinking that perhaps I was being followed."

"It might not be a bad idea at that."

Tragg started toward the stairway, then paused as he was near the first step, and beckoned Mason over to him.

"I see nothing for it but to arrest young Arthur Gentrie and charge him with murder."

"Whose murder?" Mason asked.

Tragg smiled amicably. "Thought you'd catch me on that one, didn't you? Well, just to put your mind at rest, when we discovered the body of Mrs. Perlin, we made a complete search of the premises. We went through everything, even cleaning out the ashes in the furnace, and in those ashes we found some interesting things, a few bits of charred cloth, some buttons, the remnants of a pair of shoes. On the portions that hadn't been completely destroyed by fire, we found dark stains. An analysis shows they were made by human blood. You might think that over, Mason. And now if you'll pardon me, I'll run along. I want to talk with young Gentrie as soon as he gets back from the hardware store."

■ 14 ■

Mason got Della Street on the telephone a few minutes after five o'clock.

"Closing up?" he asked.

"I was waiting for you. How's everything going?"

"Oh, so-so. Want to take a trip?"

"Where?"

"San Francisco."

"How?"

"Reservations on the six o'clock plane. I'll meet you at the airport."

Della Street said, "A dab of powder on my nose, and I'm headed for the elevator."

170

"Okay," Mason said, "make it snappy. I'll be aboard the plane. There'll be a ticket for you at the ticket window. Just pick it up and climb aboard."

"Be seeing you," she promised, and hung up.

The late afternoon rush was on at the airport. Speeding cars came dashing in or went roaring out. People milled around in little groups, saying farewells or greeting arriving passengers. The loud speaker blared forth the fact that the six P.M. plane for San Francisco was ready for departure, and Mason, giving one last look around, was starting for the gate when Della Street came sprinting through the door. She gave him a friendly wave of her hand, then ran over to the ticket window to pick up her transportation. She joined him as he was getting on the plane.

"Skin of my eyeteeth," she said. "A lot of traffic. Been here long?"

"Ten or fifteen minutes. Anything new at the office?"

"No. Drake's got a lot of men out and is picking up a few details. That must have been vile whiskey. He was taking his third Bromo-Seltzer when I ran in to tell him I was checking out for the night."

"Didn't tell him where you were going?"

"No."

They settled themselves in the comfortable reclining seats of the plane. A few moments later the sign flashed on requesting that passengers cease smoking, that seat belts be fastened, and then the motors, which had been clicking away at idling speed, roared into a deep-throated song of power. The plane taxied down the field, turned into the wind. The pilot applied brakes, tested first the port, then the starboard motor, then sent the plane skimming along the smooth runway.

"Always like to watch them take off," Mason said, looking out of the window at the ground speeding past.

"They do it so smoothly now you hardly know you've left the ground," she said.

Mason made no reply. He was watching the ground as it suddenly seemed to drop away. The plane was up in the air, smoothly gliding over the roofs of houses, across a railroad track, over a busy street congested with thousands of automobiles fighting their way foot by foot through the rush hour of traffic.

The sun had just set, turning a few streamers of western cloud into long bars of ruddy gold. Down below, lights on automobiles were being turned on. Neon signs began to gleam. Then suddenly all traces of civilization dropped behind. The plane was flying over mountains covered with chaparral and mesquite. The dark shadows of the valleys and canyons were in sharp contrast with the diffused gleam of sunset light which clung to the tops of the high mountains.

Far below, an automobile road wound and twisted its devious way up the mountains. Abruptly it drifted behind. There was a stretch of sagebrush-covered mesa, then more high mountains, this time crested with great pines. Slowly, twilight drew a curtain over the landscape, and lights within the plane blotted out what little view remained.

Mason settled back in his seat, said to Della, "I always like this trip."

"What's it all about?" she asked.

Mason said, "After I left you, I ran into Tragg. We had a talk, and then I went out and bought some San Francisco papers."

"What happened up at Karr's place?" Della Street asked curiously. "Did the girl make a good impression?"

"Apparently so. At least, on everyone except the Chinese houseboy."

"What about him?"

"I don't know," Mason said. "You can't exactly place him. Chinese are rather inscrutable at times."

"Did you find out anything of what it was all about?"

Mason said, "Evidently this man who was going under

the name of Dow Tucker and Elston Karr had a partnership sometime in 1920 and 1921. In the latter part of 1920 a third partner was taken in. He betrayed the outfit. Tucker was evidently captured, either executed or murdered. Karr managed to escape, and evidently he had a portion of the partnership funds with him."

"Who was the third partner?" she asked. "Anyone important?"

"Robindale E. Hocksley."

Della Street stared at Mason in surprise. "Surely Karr didn't admit that, did he?"

"Yes."

"But, good heavens, if that's the case—why, Karr's on the spot. They'll make him logical suspect number one."

"Don't overlook those fingerprints on the telephone," Mason said. "They're young Gentrie's fingerprints all right. Lieutenant Tragg's in something of a quandary."

"And this trip is to steal a march on him?" she asked.

Mason said, "Not exactly."

"What is it for?"

"Oh, just to look up a certain party," Mason said.

"I suppose that means I'm not to try to worm a more definite answer out of you?"

"Don't crowd me," he said, smiling. "If I'm right, I want to do something spectacular. If I'm wrong, I don't want to lose my reputation."

"How's Lieutenant Tragg coming?"

"Right on my tail. I'm not certain but what he may even be a couple of jumps ahead of me by morning, unless I take a short cut."

"And this is the short cut?"

"Yes."

Mason settled his head back against the chair cushions and closed his eyes. Della Street studied his profile for a few moments. Then she, too, settled back in her chair.

Mason's hand came over to fold over hers. "Good girl," he said, and drifted off into dozing slumber.

The plane settled swiftly down on the San Francisco field, gliding in just over the tops of coarse brush grass to settle on the runway and taxi up to the place where passengers were scheduled to disembark. A man in dark blue, wearing a chauffeur's cap, touched two fingers to the celluloid visor and said, "Mr. Mason?"

Mason nodded.

"The car's ready."

Mason said, "We'll get in it and wait right here. Be ready to start at any minute."

The man held the door open for them to get in.

Mason said to Della Street, "Well, I guess we have a while to wait."

"How long?"

"Perhaps an hour, perhaps longer."

"I suppose," she said, "this has something to do with our lisping aviator, Rodney Wenston."

Mason nodded.

"Did you gather the impression that he was pretty much disconcerted when that girl began to produce proofs that she was the daughter of Karr's former partner?"

"His expression didn't indicate that he was exactly pleased," Mason said with a grin.

"I was watching him closely. Would her showing up with the claim which she will probably make against Karr have some effect on Wenston?"

"It might affect the size of the estate he expects to inherit eventually. If there's any estate, and if he expects to inherit it," Mason said, smiling. "Come on, Della, let's move down toward this end of the field. Wait a minute. We may as well be comfortable. Here, driver. How about moving your car down toward this end of the field away from the lights, where we can sit and be comfortable?"

"Okay," the driver said, "I can move down as far as the edge of this fence."

"All right, go ahead. Got a radio?"

"Yes, sir. Any particular station you'd like?"

"Just a little organ music, if you can find any."

The driver moved the car. Mason settled back to the relaxation of a cigarette. The driver, after some dial twisting, found a program in which organ music was blended with that of a steel guitar. The furrows ironed themselves from Mason's forehead as he sat back and gave himself up to the music.

Half an hour passed. The program changed. The driver looked back at Mason for instructions. Mason said, "Try and find more organ music or some Hawaiian music. Perhaps . . . hold it."

A quick change came over the lawyer's face. He moved forward, dropping to one knee so that he could study the plane which was coming in from the south, a compact monoplane with retractable landing gear.

"Start your motor," Mason said to the driver as the lowered wheels of the plane slid smoothly on to the cement runway.

The driver obediently stepped on the starting switch. The motor purred into life.

"Switch off the radio," Mason said.

Della Street turned to look at Mason, then back to the plane again. The relaxation had vanished from Mason's face. He was as tense now as a runner awaiting the starting gun.

"Neat job that," the driver said, noticing Mason's interest in the plane.

The lawyer didn't even hear him.

The plane taxied up to a point almost directly opposite the place where Mason was seated in the parked automobile. A gate opened. A long gray-colored automobile with a red spotlight slid through the gates.

"An ambulance," Della Street said.

Mason, without taking his eyes from the ambulance, motioned her to silence.

The ambulance turned, backed up to the plane. The driver jumped out and opened the doors in the back. The body of the ambulance concealed what was taking place, and Mason frowned his annoyance.

"Get ready to go," he said to the driver, "and you're going to have to go fast. Never mind the speed laws. I'll stand good for fines."

The driver said dubiously, "You want that ambulance followed?"

"Yes."

"He'll use a siren and spotlight and go right through all the signals."

"Follow right along behind," Mason said.

"I'll get pinched."

"Not if you're close enough. Cops will think it's a member of the family rushing to the bedside of a dying relative."

"What'll the driver of the ambulance think?"

"I don't give a damn what he thinks, just so we find out where he goes. Okay, here we go."

The doors of the ambulance slammed shut. The driver ran around, jumped in behind the steering wheel, and the gates swung open once more as the big machine gathered momentum.

The driver of Mason's car started out in low gear, turned to say over his shoulder, "It might not be just a fine. Up here they . . ."

"Get over," Mason told him. "I'll take the wheel."

"I can't let you do that. I . . ."

"Look," Mason said. "If I threatened you with a monkey wrench, and made you get over, you'd do it, wouldn't you?"

"I don't know. I . . ."

"And then," Mason said, "if anything happened, you could say that you had been in fear of your life, that you thought I'd gone crazy, and that I took the automobile away from you by force. . . . Get over."

The man stopped the car, slid over in the seat, said dubiously, "I don't like this. You ain't even got a monkey wrench."

Mason swung his long legs over the back of the front seat, jackknifed his slim figure, slipped in behind the steering wheel, and snapped the car into second gear, easing back the clutch as he pressed the foot throttle. The car slid smoothly forward. Mason swung it into a sharp turn, snapped the gear shift into high, and fell in behind the ambulance.

The blood-red rays of the spotlight from the car ahead made a sinister pencil of light. A siren screamed. Mason, moving the wheel of the rented car with deft skill, kept the machine within a few feet of the rear of the ambulance, following through the traffic in the pathway cleared by the spotlight and siren.

The man who had been driving the car gripped the back of the front seat with his left hand, held to the edge of the door with his right. "Good Lord," he moaned. "I didn't know it would be like *this!*" His face was strained with nervous tension. Several times he instinctively pressed down with his feet against the floorboards as though trying to put on the brakes. Once when collision seemed imminent, he reached for the ignition switch. Mason, batting his hand away, stepped on the throttle and avoided the oncoming car.

"Don't be a fool," Mason said without taking his eyes from the road. "No chance to stop on that one. Using the throttle was our only chance. If you hesitate, you're licked."

Della Street, in the back of the car, hanging on to the robe rail, her heels braced against the foot rest, watched the kaleidoscope of traffic which flashed past the windows of the speeding automobile. Her lips were half parted; her eyes sparkling. The driver of the car, looking back to her for moral support to back up his demand for less speed, abruptly changed his mind and concentrated simply on hanging on.

The ambulance cut its way through traffic, to slow down in front of the red brick structure of a rambling hospital.

Mason left the ambulance as it turned into the emergency entrance. He swung his car around to the front of the hospital, parked it, and said to the driver, "Here's the monkey wrench I was holding over your head."

He handed him three ten-dollar bills.

The driver put the money in his pocket wordlessly.

"Okay?" Mason asked.

The driver tried to speak. His voice came as a throaty squeak. He coughed, cleared his throat, took a deep breath, and said, "Okay, but I wouldn't go through it again for a thousand."

Mason slid out of the car. "Come on, Della."

She followed him into the hospital. Mason said to the girl at the information desk, "I know something about this ambulance case that's just coming in the door now. I'm supposed to tell the doctor something about the patient."

"Yes?"

"Uh huh."

"What did you want to tell him?"

"Something he wants to know," Mason said.

She flushed. "I didn't mean it that way. Was it information about the patient?"

"Of course."

"He won't be able to see you right now. It may be an operative case. They telephoned the doctor from Los Angeles and again from the airport. He'd been waiting for the call."

"What's that doctor's name?" Mason asked. "I wasn't certain I caught it."

"Dr. Sawdey."

"His initials?"

178

"L. O."

"I'll be waiting here in the lobby. No. Perhaps I'd better go get in touch with the nurse. I think the information I have is something he wanted before he operated. Where will I find the patient?"

She said, "Just a moment," plugged in a telephone, consulted a memo, said, "What room will Carr Luceman be in? It's an ambulance case that just came in. Emergency operation. Dr. Sawdey. Oh, yes."

She pulled out the line, said, "The patient will be in room three-o-four. Dr. Sawdey is preparing to operate. Go to the third floor, tell the nurse in charge who you are, and ask her to get in touch with Dr. Sawdey's nurse."

Mason nodded, said to Della Street, "Come on," and walked across the lobby, down the corridor to the elevator.

"Third," he said to the attendant.

Once on the third floor, Mason motioned to Della Street, led her down to the end of the corridor where there was a solarium. Now the room was darkened, and the wicker furniture, spaced with the rectangular efficiency of a hospital rather than the careless informality of a private home, seemed in its stiff silence to be occupied by white-clad ghosts.

Mason looked at the door of 304 as they walked past, said, "We'll sit here for a while and watch."

A nurse garbed in a spotless, stiffly starched uniform walked by on rubber heels, rustling her way efficiently down the linoleum-covered corridor. She vanished in the door of 304. A few moments later, a man in the middle fifties, clothed in a dark business suit, pushed open the door and walked in. Shortly after that, the man left the room again.

Mason waited until this man had left the room. A few moments later the nurse bustled out, then Mason touched Della Street on the arm. "Okay," he said, "let's go."

They walked down the corridor, the faint smell of dis-

179

infectants in their nostrils. Mason paused before the door of 304, on which a sign said, "Dr. Sawdey," and below that a printed placard reading, "No Visitors."

Mason silently pushed open the door.

The man in the room lay in the hospital bed. The sheet-covered blankets were arranged with hospital efficiency over the thin figure. A dim night light made the shadows a backdrop against which the white, tired face on the pillow was sharply accented.

The man who lay motionless in the bed, his eyes closed, was Elston A. Karr.

In the hospital surroundings, with wax-like lids closed over the burning power of his hypnotic eyes, he seemed wasted, tired, as robbed of power as a burnt-out electric globe.

Mason stood in the doorway long enough to note that the bedclothes were rising and falling with the even respiration of a man who is sleeping under the quieting influence of a powerful narcotic. Then he closed the door, took Della Street's arm, and tiptoed down the corridor.

"What does that mean?" she asked, as Mason pressed the button for the elevator.

"Don't you know?" he asked.

She shook her head.

Mason said with a smile, "I'm still jealous of my reputation as a prophet. I don't dare risk it, but I think perhaps we'll drop around to Dr. Sawdey's residence for a little chat."

■ **15** ■

Mason's taxicab slid to a stop in front of one of the newspaper offices. A brightly lighted office on the ground floor marked the Want Ad Department. A separate door-

180

way to the street made it easy for persons desiring to place want ads to approach the long counter where two quick-moving young women waited on the persons who came in with ads to be placed in the classified column, or with answers to be delivered to advertisers.

Mason paid off the cab, said, "Might as well come in, Della, and help me look."

One of the young women behind the counter approached him. Alert eyes sized him up. She said, "What can I do for you?"

"I'd like back copies of your paper for the last week. I just want to look at them here."

She reached under the counter, took out a hinged stick through which had been filed copies of newspapers.

"Do you have two of these?" Mason asked. "I'd like to have my secretary assist me."

"You don't wish to remove them from the office?"

"No."

She walked down the counter a few feet, took out another file, and handed it to Della Street.

"What do we look for?" Della Street asked.

"We may not find it," he said, "but I rather think we will. A small paragraph somewhere on an inside page, an account of a Mr. Luceman who was cleaning a revolver when it accidentally dropped and exploded. It will probably be written in a somewhat humorous vein. Dr. L. O. Sawdey will have been called in to give emergency treatment."

Della Street, for the moment, did not look at the newspaper. Instead she looked at Mason, comprehension dawning on her face. "Then you mean that . . . ?"

Mason interrupted her. "Once more I am not risking my reputation as a prophet. Let's get the facts first, and make deductions afterwards."

Mason plunged at once into the pages of the paper, but it was Della Street who found the notice first. "Here it is," she said.

181

Mason moved over to look over her shoulder.
The article read:

"BURGLAR" DEMANDS MILK
SHOOTS HOUSEHOLDER IN LEG

It was an unlucky day for Carr Luceman who resides at 1309 Delington Avenue. It was nearly two o'clock in the morning when Luceman heard the noise made by a prowler trying to effect an entrance through the back screen door. Luceman sat up in bed to listen. The more he listened, the more certain he became that a prowler was cutting the screen.

Luceman, who despite his sixty-five years is a rugged individualist given to direct action, disdained to summon the police. He decided to teach the burglar a lesson he would not soon forget.

As Luceman expressed it, "I didn't intend to try to hit him, but I most certainly *did* intend to give him the scare of his life."

With this in mind, Luceman took a .38 caliber revolver from his bureau drawer, put on a pair of felt-soled bedroom slippers, and noiselessly tiptoed to the kitchen. As he opened the door from the dining room, he could distinctly hear the sounds of someone cutting through the screen on the back door.

Luceman cocked his revolver.

The doughty householder crept forward. Bearing in mind the admonition of a general who had exhorted his men to wait until the whites of the eyes were visible, Luceman tiptoed across the kitchen. He saw a dark form silhouetted against the screen of the back door—and promptly deposited his cocked revolver on the kitchen table—for the "burglar" was

182

Luceman's cat. Luceman had forgotten to give the animal its customary bowl of warm milk. The cat had sought to remind him by jumping to the screen. After hanging there for several seconds, it would drop back to the porch floor, then repeat the maneuver.

Luceman opened the back door, unlatched the screen, let in the irate cat, and approached the icebox in the kitchen. He had opened the door and was in the act of taking out a bottle of milk when the cat, purring in expectation of its deferred repast, jumped to the kitchen table and, in true feline manner, rolled over in squirming abandon. The cocked revolver teetered on the edge of the table. Luceman dropped the milk bottle, and tried to catch the weapon before it hit the floor. He was too late. The gun eluded his grasp. The bullet crashed into Luceman's right thigh, inflicting a painful wound. The cat, frightened by the noise of the explosion, dashed out of the back door, and Luceman, painfully wounded, tried to crawl to the telephone. The shock and pain, however, caused him to lose consciousness, and it was not until nearly four A.M. that he recovered sufficiently to call Dr. L. O. Sawdey who lives in the neighborhood.

Luceman will be on the inactive list for several days, but, aside from that, need expect no bad effects, as the bullet missed the principal arteries and only grazed the bone. The "burglar" at latest accounts had not returned. Perhaps it has decided it is less trouble to prowl the alleys in search of nocturnal quadrupeds, and forego its milk diet.

Mason glanced at Della Street, smiled, walked over to the counter, and said, "Could you let me have one of these papers of the fourteenth? I'd like to answer some of the ads in it." He deposited a nickel on the counter and after a few minutes the girl supplied him with a copy of the paper.

Mason thanked her and escorted Della Street back to the automobile. "We will now have a chat with Dr. Sawdey, who is doubtless back from the hospital by this time," he said.

Mason rang the bell of Dr. Sawdey's residence. After several moments, the man they had seen at the hospital opened the door.

"Dr. Sawdey?" Mason asked.

The doctor nodded, looking shrewdly from Mason to Della Street, then down to where the taxicab was waiting. He might have been making a diagnosis. "It's late," he said, "and except in matters of extreme emergency . . ."

Mason said, "I will detain you only a moment, Doctor. But I'm a friend of Carr Luceman. I knew him back East, and thought I'd look him up. I had his address, and drove down there as soon as I . . ."

Dr. Sawdey said, "He had an accident. He's at the Parker Memorial Hospital. Unfortunately, he can have no visitors."

Mason's face showed his concern. "I heard he'd had an accident," he said. "I want very much to see him, and I think he'd like to see me. I only expect to be here for another twenty-four hours. Would it be possible for me to see him in that time?"

"I'm afraid not. He has overtaxed himself. I warned him particularly against that very thing. As a result, he's weakened his resistance, and complications have set in. It's going to be necessary for him to be kept absolutely quiet for several days."

Mason said, "I *might* wait over if by day after tomorrow . . ."

Dr. Sawdey said positively, "I am certain that it will

184

be necessary to keep him quiet for at least three days."

Mason said, "Gosh, that's a shame. I'll send him a card. I'm awfully sorry I missed him. Have you known him long, Doctor?"

"I've seen him on several occasions," Dr. Sawdey said guardedly.

Mason said impulsively, "Well, I hope this doesn't affect his other condition too much. How *are* his legs now, Doctor?"

The doctor said gravely, "In a man of his age, one may expect progressive . . . however, I think it will be better if you correspond directly with Mr. Luceman. You can address him at the Parker Memorial Hospital, and I see no reason why he can't open mail within the next forty-eight hours. And now if you'll excuse me—I've had rather a hard day, and I have some operations to perform in the morning."

Mason bowed gravely. "I'm sorry I disturbed you, Doctor, but I was very much concerned. You see I was quite intimate with Mr. Luceman at one time."

"If you'd leave your name," the doctor said, "I might . . ."

Mason had already started down the stairs. "So sorry I disturbed you, Doctor. I can appreciate the demands that are made on your time." And to keep the doctor from realizing that he had failed to follow his suggestion, Mason went on, "What time do you operate in the morning?"

"Eight-thirty," Dr. Sawdey said and closed the door.

"Hungry, Della?" Mason asked as they approached the taxicab.

"I *could* use a little food," she admitted.

Mason said, "*I* don't feel particularly hungry, and I want to keep an eye on Dr. Sawdey. I want to see if he goes out within the next ten or fifteen minutes. Suppose you take the cab and go to Locarno's Grill. I'll be along in twenty minutes or half an hour."

She regarded him with that whimsical expression which a woman reserves for a man of whom she is very fond and who has been rather clumsy in seeking to outwit her.

"Something wrong with that?" Mason asked.

"Dr. Sawdey is a doctor. If he leaves, it will be on a call."

Mason nodded.

"And it would be on an urgent call. Therefore, he'll leave in an automobile. I suppose you're going to run after him on foot?"

Mason said, "No. I just want to know *if* he goes, not *where* he goes."

Della Street placed a hand on his arm. "Now, Perry, my lad, listen to me. You've got something up your sleeve. If there's going to be any housebreaking, I'm going to be just as deep in the mud as you are in the mire."

"What makes you think I'm going housebreaking?"

"Don't be silly!"

Mason said, "It's a felony. It's dangerous. In case we get caught, we can't very well make explanations."

"All the more reason, then, why you should have an accomplice."

"No. It's too dangerous. You go to the restaurant, and . . ."

"Bosh! I'm going to stay with you. Do we take the cab or . . ."

Mason said, "We get rid of the cab right here." He walked over to the driver, handed him a bill, and said, "The change is yours, buddy. We're supposed to be back in ten minutes. The doc's going to have a prescription ready by that time. So we'll just walk around."

"I could wait," the cabby said, "if it's only going to be ten minutes, and . . ."

"No, thanks. We're visiting friends in the neighborhood after that, so it won't pay to wait."

The cabby touched his hat and drove off.

Della Street said, "Here we go! Embarking on a career of crime! If I'm going to be an accomplice, I may as well learn crook jargon and talk out of one side of my mouth. What am I, a steerer?"

Mason said, "No. You're a moll. You're going to case the lay."

She walked with an exaggerated swing to her hips, said out of one side of her mouth, "Cripes, Chief, I'm the moll who can give you de office in case a harness bull tries to queer de act. I'll stroll on past an' give him de eye, an' . . ."

"And get yourself arrested for soliciting a self-respecting police officer on the street," Mason interposed.

"Well, what of it? Ain't you de mouthpiece that can spring me? Why should I take a rap when I got de swellest mouthpiece of 'em all on my string? Maybe you could slip the beak a grand an' square the pinch. But right now we got a crib to crack. We can't waste time. . . ."

She stopped as she heard a distinctly startled gasp behind her. Looking up, she saw Mason grinning broadly, saw an elderly gentleman who had noiselessly approached from behind on rubber-soled shoes, regarding her with shocked consternation. Then, with a muttered, "Pardon me," he had pushed on past, walking so rapidly that his feet seemed to be hardly touching the sidewalk.

Della Street muttered under her breath, "Good heavens, did *he* get an earful!"

"Did he get an earful!" Mason chuckled. "He acted as though he had two ears full."

"Where did he come from?"

"I don't know. I just happened to turn my head and caught a glimpse of him pussyfooting along behind. His face looked as though he'd suddenly received the bill for his new income tax."

"You don't think he could have been following us?"

Mason shook his head. "Not that chap. He's some mousy retired bird who lives somewhere in the neighborhood. You certainly gave him something to think about. The way he whisked himself around that corner, you'd have thought he was a puppet someone was jerking on a string."

Della Street said, "I thought I was putting on a swell act. My walk alone must have been enough to startle him. I felt like Fatima, the sideshow Turkish dancing girl."

"Well," Mason said, "he's got something to tell his friends now. He's really seen a moll in action. What's the number of this house where Luceman lived?"

"Thirteen-o-nine Delington."

"That's in the next block. Now listen, when I go in, you stand out by the curb. The minute you see anyone coming along the sidewalk, no matter who it is, walk up to the front door and ring the bell once. Don't seem to hurry. Don't act self-conscious, and, above all, don't look back over your shoulder. Simply walk up and ring the bell, making your action look as natural as possible."

"Ring it once?" she asked.

"That's right. Now, if that person should turn toward the house, ring the bell three times, three short, sharp rings. When you have done that, turn to walk back toward the street, and then apparently see this person for the first time. You can smile and say, 'There doesn't seem to be anyone home.' Then go to the next house and ring the bell. When someone comes to the door, ask them if they're taking the *Chronicle*. Tell them you're representing the newspaper and would like very much to take their subscription on a special introductory offer. Talk loudly enough so you can be heard across to the next house."

"Suppose he doesn't wait that long but goes right on in?"

"It's all right," Mason said, "just so you give me those

188

three short, sharp rings on the doorbell the minute you see he's heading toward the house. That'll give me time to get out."

"Not much time," she said, "particularly if you're on the second floor."

"It's all right," he told her. "It'll take a man a little while to get in, and it doesn't make any difference if I don't get out of the back door until he unlatches the front door—just so I get out. After all, there's not very much chance it will happen. We're just playing safe. That's all. Be absolutely certain the minute anyone shows up anywhere on the street, to give me a signal on the bell. I'll probably have to use the flashlight, and a person who happens to see the beam of light reflected against the window glass might call the police."

"And that's all I have to do?" she asked.

"That's enough."

"You're not trying to make things easy for me just to keep me out of it?"

"No."

"You take care of yourself?"

"I'll try to."

"How are you going to get in?"

"I'll try the back door and actually cut through the screen just to make Luceman's burglar come to life."

She placed her hand on his arm. "Take care of yourself, Chief," she said in a low voice.

"I intend to."

"There's no good telling you not to take any risks," she said, "because you aren't built that way. You could no more sit in your office, wait for business to come in, and handle it in an orthodox manner than a trout could live in stagnant water. But do keep an eye open."

"Okay, I will, and if you have to start back to town, meet me at . . ."

"Locarno's Grill," she interrupted. "Over the biggest, thickest filet mignon in the place."

Mason looked rapidly up and down the sidewalk, surveyed the dark outlines of the two-storied frame house, said, "Okay, Della, here we go. Keep your eyes open, and remember the signals."

He started as though headed for the front steps, then suddenly detoured to pass around between the houses. A small flashlight hardly larger than a fountain pen gave him sufficient illumination to show the cement walk which led around to the back of the house.

An inspection of the back door showed Mason that entering the place was not going to be as easy as he had anticipated. The screen door was unhooked, but behind it was a wooden door equipped with a formidable lock, a lock which had cost much more than the average back-door lock. A casual inspection of the windows showed that they were locked tightly, and there was something in the unshaking rigidity of the window frames which indicated the locks were more efficient than those a nocturnal prowler would ordinarily expect to find.

Puzzled, as well as interested, Mason returned to the back door. His small flashlight once more explored the lock. He turned the knob and tentatively pushed against the door. It was anchored as firmly as though it had been embedded in concrete.

Mason raised the flashlight to inspect the small square glass panels in the upper part of the door, and then suddenly realized that someone had been there ahead of him.

The putty which held one of the panes of thick glass in place had been neatly cut away, so that a pane some eleven by fifteen inches was now held in place only by four small brads which had been driven into the wood at the corners of the panel.

It took Mason but a few moments to get these brads removed. Then with the blade of his penknife, he was able to pull the glass toward him, so that it dropped gently into his extended palm. Thereafter, it was a simple matter to reach through the opening, find the knurled brass knob on the inside of the spring lock, turn it, and open the door.

When Mason had the door opened, he took the precaution of putting the square of glass back into place and inserting the small brads so that it was once more held in position. In doing this, the realization that someone had anticipated him in his entire procedure was a disquieting thought.

This person, Mason realized, had gone about his work with the cunning skill of a good technician. The putty had been carefully removed with a knife. The dried particles had been gathered up so that there would be no telltale clue left on the threshold or on the wooden floor of the back porch. Replacing the pane of glass with the four brads so neatly and precisely driven into the corners of the supports had made the door seem quite all right to a casual observer.

Mason was just closing the door when he heard the sharp sound of a buzzer cutting through the fog-swept silence of the night.

So explosive was the sound, and so engrossed had he been in the problem which confronted him, that Mason gave a convulsive start as the warning signal sounded. Then, tense with the effort to listen for every sound, Mason stood waiting. When nothing happened, he turned the knurled knob of the lock, and threw the catch which left the bolt held back. He slipped out to the porch, gently closing the door behind him. He could hear no steps, but as he neared the front of the house, he saw a dark form drifting past on the sidewalk, walking so rapidly that it seemed he must almost be running. Mason realized that it was the man who had passed them a few minutes earlier. Probably some neighboring householder, he reassured himself, who had gone down to mail a letter at the mailbox, or to a corner drugstore to replenish some toilet articles.

Moving silently, Mason walked around the house to re-assure Della. He gave a low whistle as he saw her standing on the front porch in the position of one ringing the bell.

She came over to the railing at the edge of the porch, and said in a hoarse whisper, "My same little man. He came around the corner as though he'd been shot out of a gun."

Mason said, "He probably lives here in the neighborhood. I've got the back door open, Della. I'm going in."

"Don't you think we'd better call it off, Chief?"

"No. I only want to give the place a quick once-over. That old man has probably forgotten all about you by this time."

She said in a whisper, "I don't forget that easily."

"Okay. Sit tight. You hadn't better go back to the curb. Your friend might have another errand to run. If he saw you crossing from the curb to the door for the second time, he'd get suspicious. Just stand here in the shadows of the porch. If anyone comes along, be ringing the bell. Remember the signals. I want to know when anyone comes along the street. Don't get rattled. I may even have to turn on the lights."

"Just what are you looking for?" she asked.

Mason dismissed the question with a wave of his hand, and once more retraced his steps to the rear of the house. Back inside the kitchen, he debated whether to leave the back door unlocked, but finally decided to release the catch and let the spring lock remain in position.

His flashlight showed him a conventional kitchen. Stale smells of ancient cooking clung to the woodwork. The linoleum was worn almost through in front of the kitchen sink and in front of the stove, the places which would naturally receive the most wear.

The icebox was electric, and the modern freshness of its white enamel stood out against the darker finishings of the kitchen. It gave the impression of having been recently installed.

Mindful of the story of the nocturnal cat, Mason opened the icebox door. As he did so, an electric light flashed on, illuminating the immaculate white of the interior.

Here was food such as a lone bachelor might cook for a quick repast, a saucer containing what evidently represented the half of a can of beans which had not been eaten. There was a full quart of milk, and a bottle which was half emptied. A dish contained a quarter-pound square of butter, still in its original tissue wrapping, and a smaller piece of irregular shape. There was a small bottle of whipping cream, a jar of mustard, some sliced boiled ham which had evidently been picked up at a delicatessen store, and a small pasteboard container holding macaroni salad of the type featured by virtually every delicatessen counter.

There were other odds and ends in the icebox, but Mason didn't stop to explore them. The quick inventory which he took told all he needed to know. He noticed that the milk and cream were still sweet. The temperature regulator on the icebox was set at a point which would hold the contents at a low temperature. The food smelled sweet and clean, but with an ice box of this efficiency, that meant absolutely nothing. The food might have been left there yesterday or last week.

Mason closed the door of the icebox, let his small flashlight cover the kitchen in a quick survey. Then he moved on into the dining room.

His flashlight gave him a general idea of the furniture, an old-fashioned assortment which had evidently been purchased years before. The dining-room rug was new and cheap. The surface of the table had been refinished. The chairs had evidently been gone over with furniture polish, but the incongruity of the new dining-room rug simply made it all the more apparent that someone, after

193

having lived in the house for years, had decided to rent it furnished, and had made an attempt to replace only the things which had been the most worn.

Mason moved on through the dining room and into the living room.

Here were bookcases built in on each side of a fireplace, wide windows fronting on the porch. The drapes on these windows seemed relatively new, and Mason realized with some apprehension that while these drapes had been pulled so that they entirely covered the front windows, the material was not heavy enough to shut out all light. The beam of Mason's flashlight would quite probably show through from the street, and the small rectangular windows placed high in the wall above the bookcases on each side of the fireplace were not curtained at all. Della Street could warn him of any approaching pedestrian, but persons in the adjoining houses would be apt to notice the traveling beam of the flashlight as it moved around the walls.

Mason's problem was not that of an ordinary prowler. He needed his flashlight for more than mere illumination to enable him to avoid furniture. He wanted to make a detailed study of the things in that room, to seggregate those things which had been furnished with the house, so that he could more fully appreciate the significance of those things which had been brought in by the tenant.

Mason hesitated only a moment. Then he walked across toward the front door and pressed the light switch.

Instantly the room was flooded with brilliance. Mason found several floor lamps, turned these on. He opened a book, placed it face down on the table. In case some curious neighbor might be peering in through those uncurtained windows above the fireplace, he removed his hat and slowed down his motions so that they would seem to be the casual moves of a legitimate tenant, rather than the hasty motions of a prowler.

194

An automobile driven at high speed slewed around the corner. Tires shrilled in protest as the car slid to an abrupt stop. The doorbell rang—once. Mason paused, motionless.

He heard the businesslike slam of a car door. The doorbell rang three short, sharp rings. Mason heard running steps as someone dashed past the living room, running along the cement walk toward the back of the house. Once more there were three rings, then the sound of heavy steps on the porch.

Mason, conscious of Della Street trapped on the front porch, reached an instant decision. He turned the brass knob which released the bolt on the front door, opened the door, said, "Good evening," to his white-faced secretary who was standing on the threshold. "Was there something I could do for you?" he asked, and then, apparently for the first time, became conscious of the police car at the curb and the broad-shouldered plain-clothes officer who was standing just behind Della Street.

"Good evening," Mason said cheerfully. "Are you together?"

Della Street said quickly, "No. I am soliciting subscriptions for the *Chronicle*. We have a very attractive—"

"Just a minute, sister. Jus-s-s-s-t a minute!" growled the officer.

Della Street turned to survey him with hostile eyes. "Thank you," she said acidly. "I'm trying to make a living at this, and I don't want to see any etchings. Just because I'm unescorted doesn't mean a thing—to you."

Mason said, "Won't you come in?" and to the officer, "And what can I do for *you*?"

The officer came pushing in on Della Street's heels.

"Really," Mason said with the polite indignation of an outraged householder, "My invitation was to . . ."

The officer threw back his coat, disclosing a badge. "What's going on here?" he asked.

Mason let his face show startled surprise. "Why! . . . That's what *I'd* like to know."

The officer said, "We're in a radio car. A man who lives a block down the street telephoned that he heard a couple of crooks planning on cracking a joint."

Mason looked at Della Street. "A couple," he said. "Have you seen any couple, Miss . . ."

"Miss Garland."

"Do sit down, Miss Garland. I take it you're covering the entire block. Perhaps you've seen . . ."

"Not a couple," she said. "But I did see a rather suspicious-looking woman. I thought she was just coming down off the porch. I was ringing the bell at the adjoining house, where there seems to be no one home, and I noticed her come up on this porch, pause for a moment, then turn around and go back down. There was a little old man walking past at the time, and I saw him looking at her as though he'd known her."

"Up on *this* porch?" Mason asked.

"That's right, but I don't think she rang the bell. She walked up on the porch, stood there for a moment, then turned around and went back down the stairs and walked rapidly down toward the corner."

"Which direction?" the officer asked.

"Down toward the cable car tracks," Della Street said.

"Did you get a good look at her?"

"She was rather—well, she looked rather—well cheap," Della Street said. "Something in the way she walked."

The radio officer frowned, said, "Guess I'll check up with my partner. How do you get through to the back of the house?"

"This way," Mason said, walking toward the dining room. "Sit down if you will please, Miss Garland. I'll be glad to talk with you."

The officer said, "I can find my way okay."

"I'll switch on the lights for you," Mason said, and

added apologetically, "I'm batching here. Engaged in some research work. Afraid I'm not much of a housekeeper when it comes to dusting."

The light Mason had switched on disclosed what his flashlight had failed to make plain—that the table and chairs were well covered with dust.

The officer, frowning at them, said, "You sure *aren't* much on housekeeping. Don't you eat here?"

Mason laughed. "I'm afraid I'm a typical scholar, the absent-minded sort. As a matter of fact, I do most of my eating in the kitchen. And my eating is rather sketchy at that."

The officer followed Mason on into the kitchen. As Mason switched on the lights, he could see the vague outlines of a burly figure standing on the back porch just outside the back door.

Mason said quite casually, apparently without noticing the man on the porch, "My diet is mostly milk, eggs, and things I can pick up at the delicatessen store. Incidentally, if you'd like a glass of milk, Officer, you'll find a cold bottle in the icebox." Mason laughed nervously and said, "I don't know what the etiquette of the situation calls for, but in view of the fact that you've come to protect my property, I . . ."

The officer who had been looking around the kitchen, walked over to the door of the icebox, jerked it open, looked inside, took a quick mental inventory of the contents, closed the door, and said, "My partner's out here," and went to the back door. He opened it, said, "See anything, Jack?"

"No."

"There was a jane up on the porch," the first officer said, "soliciting subscriptions. She saw a girl come off this porch and walk around the corner down by the cable car tracks. Guess that was the one the fellow saw."

"Get a description?"

197

"No. I'm going back to talk with her. Come on. This is my partner, Mr.—what's your name?"

"Tragg," Mason said. "George C. Tragg," and then added somewhat hopefully, "I have a brother who's on the police force in Los Angeles."

"That so?" the officer asked, his manner undergoing a subtle change.

Mason nodded. "Lieutenant Tragg on Homicide," he said. "You may have heard of him. He . . ."

"Sure I've heard of him," the radio officer said. "So you're Tragg's brother. Well, well! Say, you know I ran onto Tragg at the convention here a couple of months ago. He gave us a talk on examining witnesses who were at the scene of a crime. Bright chap."

Mason nodded eagerly. "Yes. He was up here a couple of months ago." He added, somewhat ruefully, "But I didn't see much of him. I had my work, and he was frightfully busy. I guess those police conventions are rather—well, I guess an officer has his time pretty well taken up."

The radio men exchanged grins. "We do for a fact."

Mason switched out the lights behind them. Della Street, making herself comfortable in a chair in the front room, unostentatiously glanced at her wristwatch as the trio entered the living room.

"What'd you say your name was?" the first officer asked.

"Miss Garland," she said, with somewhat aloof dignity.

"Getting subscriptions for the *Chronicle*," the first officer explained. "Now, Miss Garland, let's find out about this woman who went around the corner."

Della Street raised her eyes, looking at a far corner of the ceiling. She placed her gloved finger against her chin, and said meditatively, "Well, let me see. I couldn't tell how she was dressed, but there was something about her. Oh, yes, her walk. Rather an exaggerated swing to the . . . er . . . hips . . . I remember she had on a narrow-brimmed hat and . . . no, I don't think she wore any coat other than a jacket. Her skirts were rather short, and she was—well, leggy."

The radio officer laughed in high good humor. "Leggy," he said. "That's a good one. Damned if it doesn't describe that breed of cat."

"I don't think you could miss her if you happened to see her walking along the street," Della Street said.

The officers glanced at each other. "You didn't see any man with her?"

"No. She was alone."

"How close were you?"

"I was rather close," she admitted, "just up on the porch of that other house. But you know how it is when you're working. You have so many calls to make and such a limited time within which to make them. You don't dare to start too early or you break in on a family right after dinner, usually with the woman of the house doing dishes in the kitchen. Then after it gets just so late, you feel rather conspicuous, even when you know people are still up. Lots of times the ringing of a doorbell will waken a child, and that makes for a bad reception. So there's only a relatively short period of time in which you have to work."

The officer looked at his watch. "Pretty late now, isn't it?"

She nodded, bit her lip, lowered her eyes, and said in a halting voice, "But I had some emergencies—my kid sister—well, I just needed the extra money. I get paid so much a subscription, you see."

The officer said, "Okay, Miss Garland. Come on, Jack, let's take a run down the car track and see if we can't pick up this moll. Not that we've got anything against her. You're sure she wasn't prowling around up here on the porch?"

Della Street grew thoughtful. "She just came up here

199

for a few moments. I somehow had the impression that she might be just trying to avoid meeting the man who was walking along the street. That's why I noticed him more than I did her. You know how it is. Unescorted girls who have work which keeps them out in the evening quite frequently have—oh, well, you know."

"Guys make passes at you?" the officer asked, grinning.

"Uh huh," Della said casually. "I don't mind a nice clean pass at times, but it's this street-mashing, smirking pick-up stuff that gets you. And then you never know when someone may get really violent. You get fed up on it after a while."

The officers exchanged glances. "Well, we'll be on our way. We'll pick her up, and give her a shakedown. One thing's certain, she can't fool us if we once nab her. She talks tough. . . . So you're Lieutenant Tragg's brother. Well, well. I didn't know he had a brother here in San Francisco. He didn't say anything about it."

Mason beamed. "I'm very proud of him. I think he's making a splendid record from all I can hear. Occasionally he sends me some newspaper clippings."

"He's a good man," the officer agreed. "Well, so long. If you have any trouble, or see anybody prowling around, just give headquarters a ring. Probably nothing to it, but this guy said there was a couple talking about casing a lay in the neighborhood. He said he was trying to get past them on the sidewalk, and heard 'em distinctly. Well, good night, Tragg. Good night, Miss Garland."

"Good night," Della Street said graciously.

Perry Mason closed the front door, turned and bowed to Della Street. "It would be a pleasure to subscribe to a paper through such an attractive and poised young woman," he announced. "I can appreciate how badly you need the money on account of your sister, but really, you know, if I were to subscribe just through sympathy . . ."

"Don't mention it," Della Street interrupted. "I know

the approach already. We run into it *so* often. But I hardly expected that the brother of a police lieutenant would stoop to such a thing."

They both laughed. Mason switched out the big indirect light, leaving the room illuminated only by the floor lamps. "That was a close squeak," he announced.

"Are you telling me!" Della Street asked.

Mason got up from the chair, said, "Well, we'll take a look around."

"Think it's safe?"

"Oh, sure. Those officers will go on down the car tracks for three or four blocks, find no trace of the woman they're looking for, report to headquarters, and by that time have a call to investigate something else. But let's not stick around here any longer than we have to."

"Just what are you looking for?"

"I want to find out something about Karr's San Francisco personality."

"You think he's had this place as Carr Luceman?"

"I think so. Notice the fact that Luceman's first name is pronounced exactly the same as Karr's last name, although it's spelled differently. Notice that this place apparently hasn't been lived in except for short periods of time. Evidently, Karr is a marked man, probably in connection with some of his Chinese arms-smuggling ventures, or it may be because of that old partnership feud which dates back to 1921. When he came to San Francisco, he didn't want to stay at a hotel. Naturally, a person of his description is rather easy to spot."

"And that trouble with his legs?" Della Street asked. "The wheelchair?"

Mason said, "Figure it out for yourself. He had a bullet hole through one leg. Naturally, he didn't dare go to any doctor in Los Angeles, because a gunshot wound has to be satisfactorily explained. If Karr had given them his Los Angeles address and then the disappearance of Hocksley and his housekeeper had been duly noted . . ."

"I see," Della Street interrupted. "He had this identity already established in San Francisco. No one was missing from this place, so he could come here and invent that story of the accident. But who shot him?"

Mason grinned. "He shot himself. His cat knocked the gun off the table when he was . . ."

Della Street made a little grimace. "Save it for your brother the Lieutenant," she said.

Mason said, "We'll look this place over before we start speculating. There are better places to talk."

He started a slow circling survey of the living room, making comments out loud: "Pictures on the wall, regular stock stuff. Furniture the sort that would go with the house. Nothing very much to indicate a man's individuality. Books in the bookcase. Oh-oh, we've got something here. *The Struggle for the Pacific, Asia in Transition, The Economic Situation in Japan, The Strategic Effect on Singapore.* Here are fifteen or twenty books dealing with the situation in the Orient sandwiched in with books of the type that unquestionably went with the house, old favorites in frayed bindings. Well, that gives us something. Let's keep looking."

Della Street, with a woman's eye to the housekeeping end of things, said, "It looks as though someone comes in about once a week to do cleaning. Notice the ash tray over here."

"What about it?" Mason asked.

"It has a trap," she pointed out, "which opens into the bottom. Here's the stuff that's in the bottom, cigar bands, cigar butts, cigarette ends, matches, and . . ."

"Any lipstick on the cigarette ends?" Mason asked.

"Yes."

Mason said, "I'm going to take a quick look upstairs. I can probably tell more from the bedrooms and the stuff that's in the bedroom closets than I can down here."

"Just what are you looking for?"

"I don't know exactly. I'm trying to get the sketch. Karr's engaged in some peculiar activity. He's tied in with the Chinese in some way. He has a lot of money. Probably he's not a philanthropist. Hocksley was his partner, probably knows a good deal about his methods. Twenty years ago Hocksley betrayed him, and one of his partners met his death. Now Hocksley suddenly crops up again."

"You suppose he's trying to avenge the death of his partner and his old betrayal?" Della asked.

"That's just the point," Mason said, taking her elbow as he assisted her up the stairs, switching on a light in the hallway. "Twenty years is a long time to make an *unsuccessful* search for a man. The probabilities are that, following the episode in 1921, Karr didn't think very much about Hocksley until the present situation in the Orient started a renewal of his activities. Well, we'll take a look around and see what we can find. Take this bedroom on the left, Della. Switch on the lights, look through the bureau drawers. Find out everything you can about the person or persons who live here. I'll take this bedroom on the right."

Mason opened the door, switched on the lights, then suddenly stood stock still.

Della Street, looking back over her shoulder from the other bedroom, sensed the rigidity of his attitude. "What is it, Chief?" she asked.

Mason motioned her back. "Don't come in."

But she came to peer over his shoulder, then recoiled with a quick gasping intake of her breath.

A man's body lay sprawled half on and half off the bed, his head dangling limply downward, his face the greenish livid hue of death. From a bullet hole in his chest, blood had welled out to soak the bedspread and form in a pool on the floor. It was the body of the Gentrie's roomer, Delman Steele.

16

Della Street gripped Mason's arm. In her nervousness, she poured all of her strength into her fingers. "Don't—don't—"

Mason pried loose her cold fingers. "Stand there, Della. Don't come in the room. Don't touch anything."

"Chief, keep out of this! Don't. Please, don't! I . . ."

"I have to," he said. "We're in it now—all the way. Keep your chin up."

Mason moved cautiously into the room. He felt the blood on the bedspread, touched his finger to Steele's wrist, lifted the arm slightly, turned and left the room. With his handkerchief, he scrubbed off the metal plate and button on the light switch, then pushed out the lights with a forefinger padded with his handkerchief.

"Don't take chances on this," she said. "Call the police. You've got to do it now."

Mason's laugh was sardonic. "Yes. We're in a sweet position to call the police! I've told the radio squad that I live here, that my brother was Lieutenant Tragg of Homicide. You've taken the part of a young woman soliciting subscriptions for the *San Francisco Chronicle*. We can tell the police that we hadn't been in the house long enough to have discovered the body, that we didn't know the secret of this bedroom, that we stumbled onto the house as the result of some amateur detective work, that, as soon as we found the body, we decided we'd better cooperate and be good children. Then we'd have to tell it to a grand jury, and, perhaps even to a trial jury."

"But it's the only thing to do. We have to."

He shook his head emphatically. "They'd have us exactly where they wanted us. We'd be on the defensive not only for the rest of this case, but for the rest of our lives."

"It seems to me we will, anyway," she muttered. "As soon as the body is discovered, police will start an investigation. They'll ask Lieutenant Tragg about his brother. They'll give him a complete description of the pair they found in the house, and—well, you know the answer to that."

"Of course I know the answer to that," Mason said. "That's what I'm getting at."

"I don't get you."

"There's only one way to avoid being kept on the defensive. That's to attack."

"But how can we attack? We have no more hope of attacking than a rabbit that's being chased by a pack of greyhounds."

"That's just the point," Mason said. "Don't you get it? They aren't on our trail yet. They won't get on it until they find this body. They won't find it until some person comes to the house."

"Who?"

"Perhaps," Mason said, "it'll be Rodney Wenston—although I hardly think so. Even if he does come here, he's hardly in a better position to call the police than we are."

"Why?"

"Because of the purpose for which this house was used, and the deception Karr practiced on the officers. Karr evidently fears the police as much as we do. And Rodney Wenston, unless he has an iron-clad alibi, is more apt to have pulled the trigger than anyone else—remember, Wenston's been flying Karr back and forth to San Francisco, helping keep the secret of that wounded leg."

Della nodded, then, indicating the bedroom with a slight inclination of her head, asked, "How did he get there, and why was he killed?"

Mason said, "Let's get out of here. We'll talk in Locarno's Grill. Right now the big thing is a getaway."

They switched out lights in the corridor, went down

205

the stairs to the living room. Mason went around turning out lights. "No need to bother with fingerprints down here," he said. "Once they suspect us, the two police officers can make an absolute identification."

"Out the front door or the back?" she asked.

"The front door by all means. We stroll out arm in arm. Man-and-wife-going-to-the-movies stuff."

"It's late for a movie, and," she added, "my stomach says man-and-wife-should-go-to-restaurant."

"Okay," Mason said, "man and wife go to restaurant. Wait here while I turn out the lights in the dining room."

"Wait here nothing!" she protested. "What do you think I am? I stick to you like a foxtail to a dog's ear until we get out of this place."

Mason slipped his arm around her waist. "I know how you feel, Della," he said sympathetically.

"D-d-darn it," she said, his sympathy moving her almost to the point of tears. "Why couldn't we let Paul D-d-drake keep on f-f-f-finding our bodies for us?"

"We just led with our chins, that's all," Mason said. "Walked right into it, and, having walked right into it, we're going to keep our chins up and walk right out of it."

Della Street swung around to stand close to him. Her body pressed against his, her hands on his shoulders. "Don't get the idea my chin's down. I just got an awful jolt, that's all."

Mason finished switching out the lights. His small flashlight illuminated the way to the door. "All ready?" he asked.

"All ready," she told him.

"A stiff upper lip," he said, "and chin held high. We're on our way."

Mason flung the door open.

The fog-filled air stroked their faces with cool fingers. The street seemed deserted. Mason gave Della Street his

206

arm. "The next few seconds are the bad ones," he said. Together they walked down the stairs to the sidewalk. Halfway to the carline, Della Street said, "Lord, how I want to run. My feet seem to fly up at me. Do we take a car?"

"Yes. Remember, that radio patrol car is cruising around here, looking for two people who answer our description."

"But if they stop us, they'll recognize us."

"That's just the trouble. Seeing us together will make them realize how closely we check with the description given by the frightened party in the rubber-soled shoes."

"Oh-oh," Della Street said. "And even on the cable car we'll be conspicuous. If there were only a phone handy so we could call a cab!"

Mason laughed. "In any event, you have to admit our lives don't consist of a mere drab procession of uninteresting events."

"No," she admitted, chattering nervously to keep herself under control. "Life doesn't bother us at all that way. Do we wait here for the car?"

Mason said, "We walk a couple of blocks, find some place—No, here comes a car now. We take it."

The cable car which swung around the corner to the accompaniment of a jangling bell slowed at Mason's signal.

"Got mad money?" he asked.

"Yes, of course."

"All right, get on by yourself. Sit in back. I'll sit out in front. We're just two people who happened to have taken the car at the same corner."

The motorman pulled back on the big brake. Mason caught the hand grip and swung aboard a couple of seconds before the car came to a stop, permitting Della Street to board the enclosed section. The motorman released levers, pulled on a grip, and the car rattled forward.

After what seemed an interminable interval of twisting and turning, clanging across intersections, and being braked down steep hills, the cable car slowed in response to Mason's signal. The lawyer slid from his seat, swung his long legs out to the ground, and walked rapidly away. Della Street followed demurely a half block behind. Abruptly Mason turned, started back, caught Della Street's eye, and raised his hat. "Well, well, well," he exclaimed. "Fancy seeing *you* here!"

Her face lit in a glad smile. "Perry!" she exclaimed.

Two Marines who had been quite obviously interested in Della Street turned disappointedly away. Mason said, "This is indeed a pleasure. How about something to eat?"

"Do you know, that's a peculiar coincidence. I was just thinking of going to a restaurant."

"There's a very nice café in the next block," he told her. "Locarno's—noted for its broiled steaks."

"The way I feel right now, two cocktails and a steak would make a new woman of me."

"Going to trade in the old model?" Mason asked.

"I'm thinking of it. What am I offered?"

"Two cocktails and a steak."

"Sold."

' Laughing, she took his arm, and they started up the street together. She said, "My knees are wobbly. I've got the jitters. I need a drink, but I'm still hungry."

"You'll get accustomed to corpses after a while," he told her.

"Yes. Working for a man who isn't content to sit back and let a case develop, but has to go out and develop it, has its decided drawbacks."

Mason said, "One of the first rules of secretarial efficiency is never to find fault with the boss when he's about to buy a meal."

"Isn't a secretary entitled to her necessary traveling expenses?"

"Yes, but when she steps outside of her secretarial position and becomes an accessory, she loses her amateur status."

"What's an accessory?" she asked.

Mason said out of the corner of his mouth, "A moll who cases de joint."

"Stop it," she commanded. "I certainly led with my chin on that one. My face gets red every time I even think of it."

Mason piloted her through the doors of the grill. "I've got some telephoning to do," he said. "I'll seat you, order some cocktails, and run."

A headwaiter came smiling toward them. "Something near the . . ."

"A corner, somewhere far back," Mason said.

The headwaiter's smile became almost a smirk. "Yes, sir. I understand. This way, please."

When they were seated and had ordered cocktails, Mason went to the telephone booth. He first called the airport, found that two seats were available on the midnight plane, and engaged them. Then he called Paul Drake's office on long distance. Drake was not in, but Mason left instructions. "As nearly as possible," he said, "I want to find out where Rodney Wenston was during every minute of the day. Tell Paul to get a line on Delman Steele, a roomer at the Gentrie house on East Dorchester. Got that?"

"Yes. Paul will be in in an hour or so."

"Tell Paul to wait up for me," Mason said. "I'll be in his office about two-forty-five." He hung up, returned to the table where two full cocktail glasses were waiting.

He raised his eyebrows in surprise. "Getting formal and waiting for me?" he asked.

"I am not. This is my second. He just brought it. Here's to crime."

"Here's to crime," Mason said. They clicked glasses.

17

Paul Drake, seated at his office desk, a cup of black coffee in front of him, an electric percolator plugged into a socket and bubbling away, said, "How do you two do it? I've got my eyes propped open with toothpicks."

Mason said, "Excessive sleep is a habit, Paul. You must learn to control it. It will grow on you until you'll find you'll need two and three hours' sleep a night if you aren't careful."

"Well," Paul said, "I haven't got to that point yet. An hour or an hour and a half would seem like a swell break. Two hours would leave me doped. I suppose you two have been skylarking around in night clubs and just couldn't get here sooner because the orchestra didn't quit."

"That's right," Della Street said, holding out her arms straight from the shoulders and moving around the office in a waltz as she hummed a tune. "It was perfectly divine, Paul!"

Drake grinned and said, "Nuts to you. You're not kidding me any. You've been out committing a murder somewhere. Whose body have you turned up now?"

Della Street ceased waltzing, said scornfully, "That's the trouble with you, you have no romance. You've let life get you into a business rut, and just when I was beginning to tingle you start bringing up murders! Now the boss will talk shop—and we were having *such* a good time!"

Drake said, "I've been having a great time stalling Mrs. Gentrie for you folks. Tragg arrested her boy tonight. She's frantic. She called me around midnight. I told her you'd be in here around half past two or three o'clock. She said she'd wait up for you. I said I didn't think you'd see her tonight, but she said she'd wait up anyway."

Mason said, "I might see her, at that."

"She doesn't know anything new, Perry. She's just a frantic mother, trying to save her boy."

Mason slid over on the edge of Drake's desk. "Got any more coffee cups, Paul?"

Drake opened a drawer, pulled out some agateware mugs and said, "I can give you a couple of these. It's all I ever use."

Della Street said, "Don't talk so much. Just pour."

Drake turned the spigot on the percolator, drew out two big cups of golden brown coffee. "If you want cream or sugar," he said, "you get neither. This is a business office." He grinned.

Mason said, "What about Rodney Wenston, Paul?"

"I was trying to get you to tell you that he went to San Francisco right after Lieutenant Tragg's visit. This time they must have known my man was watching, because Karr's feet never touched the ground. They lifted him out of a car and into the plane as though he'd been a baby."

"What was Wenston doing before that?"

"He's been around off and on all day."

"Could he possibly have gone to San Francisco and back before he made that trip in the evening?" Mason asked.

Drake consulted his memo and said, "Not unless he went real early in the morning. Of course, we weren't keeping him shadowed. We've made a general check-up. He started for town about noon. That is, the caretaker at his place said that's when he left, and the man at the service station at the fork of the road, where he usually buys his gas, said he went past about one o'clock; but didn't stop to buy any gas."

"Driving his car?"

"Uh huh. Then he was in your office around three o'clock, I guess, wasn't it?"

Mason nodded. "Somewhere around there."

"Two-fifty-five he came in," Della Street said.

Drake looked at her. "You keep a memo of the time everyone comes in?"

"And when they leave. How do you suppose I can see that Perry charges for his time?"

Drake said, "It's a good idea. I guess I'll have my switchboard operator start doing the same thing. I should get double wages for overtime, shouldn't I, Perry?"

"You should," Mason said, "but I don't think you can make it stick. What about Delman Steele?"

"I don't get that bird," Drake said. "He's supposed to have a job in an architect's office, but when I checked up on him, it didn't pan out."

Mason gave Della a swift glance. "How do you mean?" he asked Paul.

"Well, he hangs around the office all right, but the architect says that Steele doesn't actually have any connection with the business. He rents desk room and comes and goes as he pleases."

"When was he in the office yesterday?" Mason asked.

"Came in about nine in the morning as usual, left about ten, and came back about two. He was in until around three o'clock, and then left for the evening. Funny thing, Perry. He has that room at Gentrie's house. It has an outside entrance so he can come and go as he pleases, but he's made himself one of the family and spends quite a bit of time there. Mrs. Gentrie thinks he's lonely and . . ."

"I know all that," Mason said. "What time did he get in last night?"

"I don't know," Drake said. "I got your call too late to ring him up on some excuse. In fact, she rather pointedly mentioned to one of my men that he didn't have the privilege of using their telephone. I found out about the arrangement in the architect's office more or less by chance. We didn't want to seem to be investigating him because you said to handle it in such a way no one would get the least bit suspicious. So we'd always taken it for granted that he was an architect. His name's on the door of the architect's office down in the lower righthand corner, and he certainly gave the Gentries to understand he was an architect. But around cocktail time this afternoon one of my men got acquainted with the architect and started asking casual questions. That's when he found out about Steele. Mrs. Gentrie may know something, in case you *do* go out there."

Mason said, "Well, I guess there's nothing to do tonight except sleep on it."

"Tonight!" Drake said, looking at his watch. "It's darn near daylight."

"It's always night until it's daylight," Mason said. "Go ahead. Finish your coffee, Della. Let's go."

Della Street tilted up her coffee cup. "Going to see Mrs. Gentrie?" she asked.

Mason nodded.

"How you folks do work," Drake said. "Personally, I'm going to get some shuteye."

Mason started for the door, then abruptly turned, stood with his hands pushed down in his pocket looking at Paul Drake with troubled eyes. "Paul," he said, "you've got to do something."

"Not until I get some sleep," Drake protested.

Mason simply kept looking at him.

"What is it?" Drake asked, at length.

"You've got to get a confession from Karr."

"A confession!" Drake exclaimed.

Mason nodded.

"I don't get you."

Mason said, "I'll give you the high spots. Hocksley wasn't killed. He was only wounded. I want to find out who shot him and why."

"How do you know he was only wounded?"

"Because I've seen him."

"You've *seen* him!" Drake echoed, startled.

"Yes."

"Where?"

"In the Parker Memorial Hospital in San Francisco."

"What did he say?"

"He didn't say anything. He had evidently been given a hypo. He's going to live, but the doctor's trying to keep him out of circulation."

"How did he get to San Francisco?"

"Wenston flew him up."

"Wenston! Then he's double-crossing Karr . . ."

Mason interrupted Drake to say, "No, he isn't. Karr and Hocksley are one and the same person."

Drake pushed back his chair and got to his feet. "Perhaps I've had too much coffee, Perry, or perhaps you have. One of us certainly is cockeyed. Hocksley is a red-headed man with a limp who . . ."

Mason said, "I'll put it this way. The one who *rented* the apartment was Johns Blaine dressed up with a red wig and purposely walking with a limp. In renting the apartment, however, under the name of Hocksley, he was acting as Karr's agent. Don't think for a minute that a man of Karr's shrewdness would establish a hide-out in a two-flat building without controlling the lower as well as the upper flat."

"That sounds reasonable," Drake admitted, "but what makes you think Karr's flat is a hide-out?"

"Karr's engaged in getting munitions over to China through a leak in the blockade. Naturally, he doesn't want publicity."

"Then the safe in the lower flat belongs to Karr?"

"Yes."

"Why didn't he keep that safe in the upper flat?"

"Probably because Johns Blaine keeps an eye on the safe, and sleeps in the lower flat."

"Then this housekeeper, Sarah Perlin, must have known."

"Of course."

"And Opal Sunley."

"Not necessarily," Mason said. "She may or may not have known. It doesn't make a great deal of difference. The housekeeper lived there. Opal Sunley came by the day."

"But you say Hocksley was wounded. Then if Hocksley is Karr, Karr must have a bullet hole . . ."

"In his leg," Mason interpolated. "That's why he's keeping his legs covered, so the bandage won't show."

"He doesn't have arthritis?"

"Probably, but not as bad as he wants us to believe now."

"Wait a minute, Perry," Drake said. "A doctor wouldn't treat a bullet wound unless he reported it to the police."

"That's right," Mason agreed, smiling.

"I don't get you."

"Karr," Mason said, "is a man of varied activities. He's very resourceful. Evidently, he carries on most of his activities under other roofs and under other names. Here in Hollywood, he's Robindale E. Hocksley when it comes to transacting business. Up in San Francisco, he's Carr Luceman, residing at thirteen-o-nine Delington Avenue."

"I don't give a damn how many names he's got, Perry. He still can't get a gunshot wound treated without . . ."

"Without making some explanation which would satisfy the doctor and the police," Mason said. "As Elston Karr who had the flat above a flat where a murder had been committed, he naturally couldn't have made any explanation in Los Angeles; but as Carr Luceman, living in San Francisco in a neighborhood where there hadn't been any murders, he had no difficulty in thinking up a story which would hold water with the police."

"What do you want me to do?"

"Make him admit the whole business. I'm hardly in a position to put the screws on him. You are."

"Where is he now?"

"In a hospital."

"Didn't the doctor send him to a hospital the first time he saw him?"

"Apparently not. It was a wound that wasn't particularly serious unless complications set in. The doctor probably advised him to keep quiet and call him in the event any unusual symptoms developed."

"Just what do you want me to get?" Drake asked.

"Dig up any information you can, find out his version of what happened the night of the shooting."

Drake said, "Won't I get into trouble, keeping this information from the police?"

"You haven't any information, have you?"

"You've told me a lot of stuff."

Mason grinned. "You don't think that it's incumbent on you to run to the police every time some lawyer gives you a goofy theory of a case, do you?"

Drake hesitated for a moment, then said, "Well . . . well, no."

Mason winked at him and said, "In all probability, it's just a crazy theory I have, but here's a newspaper clipping giving an account of how Carr Luceman happened to shoot himself in San Francisco. I'd like to have you make an investigation of the circumstances."

Drake said, "When do I leave?"

"Charter a plane. You can grab forty winks on the plane."

"Oh, not forty winks," Drake protested sarcastically. "Twenty would be all I could *possibly* use. I don't want to start getting too *much* sleep! Does Wenston know about this?"

"He must."

"About the bullet wound?"

"Probably. He flew Karr up there this afternoon. Karr was beginning to run a fever when I saw him last. His skin was dry and parched, and his face flushed."

"Who knows about what happened the night of the shooting?" Drake asked. "Anyone besides Karr?"

"Yes," Mason said. "One person anyway."

"Who?"

Mason grinned. "The one who pulled the trigger."

Drake reached for the telephone, said to the switchboard operator, his voice low-pitched from sheer physical fatigue, "Get me the airport. I want to rent a good cabin plane for a rush trip to San Francisco."

Mason nodded to Della Street. "Okay, Della, let's go tackle the other end of this case."

Driving out to Mrs. Gentrie's, Mason said, "I should have had Steele spotted a long time ago."

"I don't see how."

"Simple," Mason said. "Remember when we were talking over the case, I said that the person in the house who was getting the messages must have been someone who had easy access to the dictionary, and who, for some reason, couldn't very well be called to the telephone. Remember, Mrs. Gentrie told me right at the start that Steele had his room and was treated as one of the family, except that he didn't have the privilege of using the telephone. There were too many people using it already. She has three children, all of whom are at the age of making dates of one kind or another. Whenever the phone rings, there's a mad scramble to see which one gets there first. When anyone wants to call out, one of the children is nearly always using the phone. Remember what she said."

Della nodded.

"Here I was," Mason said whimsically, "looking for someone who couldn't use the telephone, and I was thinking in terms of some physical handicap, such as a man who was deaf or crippled. It never occurred to me

217

to consider the simplest possible solution—a man who was living at a place where he didn't have the privilege of the telephone, yet who couldn't put in a phone of his own without attracting too much attention."

"But why was Steele killed, if he was the one for whom the messages were intended?"

Mason said, "We're evidently dealing with the aftermath of an old feud. There's no other explanation which occurs to me at the moment. Of course, we haven't all of the facts as yet."

"Then Karr must have killed him."

"Karr's time's too well accounted for," Mason said. "And Wenston is out of it. Steele must have been killed at least two hours before we got there. There's no question but what Karr's been and still is a very sick man. That bullet hole in his leg, the loss of blood, the shot, and the general strain of events must have taken a lot out of him. He isn't physically robust. Then, in addition, he's had that arthritis in his legs. Evidently, he could walk, but it was a slow and painful process. We can leave him out so far as Steele is concerned."

"You think Karr went downstairs the night of the shooting?"

Mason said, "That's the only logical deduction. The burglar alarm was placed where he could hear it. He admits that he did hear it. He must have got up and walked slowly downstairs. He surprised someone at the safe, and got shot."

"Do you suppose Steele got the message you left in the tin before—before he was killed?"

Mason said, "I don't know. His death is going to complicate things somewhat."

"How do you mean?"

"There are two persons involved. One of them is the person who sent the message, and the other the person who received it. Now, if we assume that Steele is the person who was receiving the messages, the question arises,

Who was sending them? Let's suppose, for the sake of the argument, that it was Sarah Perlin. Steele sees a can placed on the shelf *after Sarah Perlin's death.* Therefore, he knows it must be a trap. For that reason, he won't touch the can. On the other hand, if Sarah Perlin wasn't the one who was sending the messages, Steele—conceding that he's the person who was receiving them—would undoubtedly have grabbed that decoy can the first chance he had."

Della said, "I'm getting all topsy-turvy. I thought the person who had sent the message, and the person for whom it had been intended were the murderers. It looks now as though they were the victims. Now, what are we going to do?"

Mason said, "While we're at the Gentrie residence, I'll make some excuse to get down in the cellar. If the can's still there, it will be significant."

Della Street's voice was filled with conviction as she declared, "The can will still be there. It's dead open and shut. Mrs. Perlin *must* have been the one who was sending the messages, and Steele the one who was receiving them. They've both been killed. Even if we didn't have an iron-clad case against those two, their deaths would prove it. You can see what happened. Mrs. Perlin was a spy. She was reporting to Steele. That was the reason Karr's attempt to trap the real Hocksley failed.

"Karr took the bullet in his leg, but that was all he needed to show him what was going on. With truly Oriental cunning, he tracked down the two persons who were responsible, and killed them."

Mason said, "There's another angle that puzzles me. What became of the real Hocksley?"

"The one who was in China?"

"Yes."

"Don't you suppose he's dead?"

"There's nothing to indicate it. Karr must have had some reason for taking that lower apartment under the name of Hocksley. He could have used any one of a thousand fictitious names, but instead of doing so, he has Johns Blaine make himself up so he *looks* like Hocksley, and then takes the name of Hocksley. That must be significant."

"Gosh, Chief, I wonder if Hocksley enters into the picture. After all, if he's anywhere around and saw his name in the papers—well, you can see what would happen. Karr has managed to hide his identity by taking the flat under the name of Rodney Wenston, but this case is getting a lot of newspaper publicity. If Hocksley is anywhere in the country, he'll see his name in the papers and—well, don't you see? It makes sort of a sieve that sifts out everything except one particular-sized article. Karr has hidden himself from everyone except Hocksley, but Hocksley will read about what happened and come to that apartment just as certain as—but what am I doing, rattling along this way? Paul Drake's coffee must have given me this talking jag."

Mason was frowning thoughtfully. He said, "Go ahead, Della, keep on talking. You're doing fine."

She shook her head. "I absolutely refuse to solve cases for you. It's a violation of my contract with the union."

"You're not trying to solve the cases," Mason said. "You're simply giving me ideas."

"You don't need anyone to give you ideas," she said. "Or do you?"

They laughed.

Abruptly, she settled down against his shoulder with a little wriggling motion. "I'm getting my wires crossed," she admitted. "In order to get anywhere in this world, a woman is supposed to be feminine and leave the thinking to the males. They like it better that way."

"You must have been taking lessons," Mason said.

She yawned sleepily. "I have. It's a swell book. *Sex Appeal for Secretaries,* in two volumes. It says a well-trained secretary never argues with her boss."

"Can't a boss argue with his secretary?"

"It takes two to make an argument. Go ahead, Chief, and solve your mysteries. I'm supposed to stand by and hold your coat. Here I was, forgetting myself and trying to put it on, and—somehow, I don't think it fits."

The rambling frame structure of the Gentrie residence was dark and somber, save for the dining room and kitchen, which were ablaze with light. Mason parked his car and climbed the long flight of stairs which led up from the street to the porch level.

"Remember now," he cautioned Della Street, "not to show too much interest in that can."

He tapped gently on the door with his knuckles.

They heard the sound of quick steps from the inside of the house, then Mrs. Gentrie flung open the door. She pressed her finger to her lips for silence. "Please don't make any more noise than possible," she said. "I would prefer not to have my sister-in-law in on this. She's never been very tolerant about the children."

Mason nodded.

"Come in," she invited.

They filed into the house, and Mrs. Gentrie escorted them through the living room into the dining room. "I hate to ask you to talk in here," she said in a low whisper, "but the living room is right under Rebecca's bedroom. She wants to know everything that's going on, and very definitely she isn't fair to Junior. What's more, that police lieutenant has been flattering her with a little attention, and it's turned her head. If we talked over anything where she could hear it, Lieutenant Tragg would know all about it before noon. He flatters her, and she thinks he's simply wonderful."

"What did she say when she knew Junior had been arrested?" Mason asked in a low voice.

"She doesn't know yet. I just didn't feel up to telling

her. I didn't know when you'd come, and I knew that she'd sit up and keep up an interminable chatter."

"What happened?" Mason asked. "Tell me in exact detail."

Mrs. Gentrie said, "Well, of course, I expected it. Lieutenant Tragg dropped in about dinner time. And Junior wasn't here. His father said Junior had complained of not feeling well about three o'clock in the afternoon, and he'd told the boy to go on home. Naturally, he was surprised and irritated to find Junior wasn't here."

Mason nodded.

"What did Tragg say to that?"

"I think Lieutenant Tragg was very angry—not with us exactly, but with himself. He thought he should have done something about Junior earlier. He put men on watch at the house, and instructed the telephone company to disconnect our telephone. We were held here during the evening as virtual prisoners. Of course, the other children had to learn about it."

"Was Steele here?"

"No. He's out several nights each week. I just can't size that boy up. He seems lonely. He's certainly attractive enough, but I don't think he has any girl friends. He just seems to enjoy sitting around with the family."

"How about Rebecca?" Mason asked.

"Fortunately, she didn't come in until after Tragg had left. There is only one thing she really cares for besides crossword puzzles and photography, and that's opera. She had a crossword-club dinner meeting, and it's also her opera night."

"What time did Junior finally arrive?"

"Almost eleven o'clock."

"Did Tragg ask him any questions?"

"No. He took him into custody. Then he took away the men who had been watching the place, and a short time after that the telephone rang. It was the telephone company to say that our telephone had been temporarily out of order, that service was now restored. I called your office right away. Of course, no one answered. I didn't think anyone would. Then I called Mr. Drake's agency, and it must have been nearly midnight when I got in touch with him. He told me he thought he'd be in touch with you later on, and if I'd wait up he'd pass the message on."

Mason said, "But if Tragg had men watching the house, Steele must have been stopped when he came in."

She said, "Yes—that's right, if he came in before Junior."

Mason said, "I'd like to know just where Tragg had his men stationed, and whether those men knew Steele by sight. I wonder if we could wake Steele up to ask him a couple of questions."

"Oh, I'd hesitate to do that," Mrs. Gentrie said. "After all, you know, he's a roomer."

"There's a door which leads to his room from here?"

She pointed toward a door which opened from the hallway leading from the dining room to the foot of the stairs. "He has his own private exit and his own bath," she said. "We rent him the room, then, of course, he can come in here whenever he wants to. We try to treat our roomers as one of the family—except on telephone service. We have so many telephone calls, because of the children and . . ."

"I understand," Mason said. "How about knocking on his door?"

"Oh, I wouldn't," Mrs. Gentrie said.

Mason said thoughtfully, "Well, after all, it's rather important."

Mrs. Gentrie said, "I'd rather you'd just take a peek inside. I'd prefer almost anything than to have Rebecca come down now with all of her questions and—you know, if she got the idea I knew Junior wasn't in his room when that shot was fired she'd tell Lieutenant Tragg. Oh, Mr. Mason, please tell me that Junior didn't do it. That's the thing that's been torturing me. You know how it is with a young boy, when he becomes infatuated with an older woman with more worldly experience. If she's inclined to play him along, she can make a terrible fool of him. And all through this thing, Junior has acted so queerly. He just drew himself up very straight and erect and white-faced when Lieutenant Tragg placed him under arrest. He didn't say a word."

Mason said, "I want to see if Steele keeps his door locked. That may have some bearing on the whole thing."

He crossed the dining room to the hallway, turned the knob of the door gently. It swung open on well-oiled, noiseless hinges. He looked inside, swung the door wider open so that light from the dining room illuminated the bedroom.

"There's no one here," he said.

Mrs. Gentrie got to her feet. "Why, good heavens, it's well after three o'clock. Of course, he *does* stay out rather late at times, but I never knew him to be as late as this."

Mason said, "However, because he has his own private exit and entrance, he could come and go very easily without you hearing him, couldn't he?"

She said, "Yes, I suppose so."

Mason swung the door tentatively back and forth. "These hinges," he said, "seem to have been freshly oiled."

"Well, I declare to goodness," Mrs. Gentrie observed, examining the hinges. "They certainly have!"

"*You* didn't oil them?"

She shook her head.

"Could they have been oiled for some time without you noticing it?"

"Rebecca does the dusting and cleaning up in here. She certainly should have noticed—but she didn't say anything. Hester cleans and dusts the outside. She might not have noticed. She isn't particularly perceptive."

Mason said, "Steele was in an admirable position then to leave this room, cross the kitchen, go down the cellar stairs, cross through the garage, and go over to the flat next door."

"Why . . . why, I guess he could have if he'd wanted to."

Mason went on, "There's a door leading from the cellar into the garage, then a door from the garage leading into the yard, and a few feet beyond that a side door to Hocksley's flat. Is that right?"

She nodded and said, "But I can't understand . . . Surely, Mr. Mason . . ."

Mason said, "Let's just step inside this room for a moment. I want to look around a bit."

"I'm afraid he wouldn't like it if he should come in."

"I think I can take the responsibility for that," Mason said. "It's rather important to find out why Mr. Steele isn't in now, why the hinges on his door have been oiled."

"You mean that he . . ."

"I'm not making any accusations just yet. If we're going to clear Junior, we must find out exactly what happened the night of the shooting."

They entered Steele's room, and Mason started a keen-eyed search.

Mrs. Gentrie said, "I thought I heard him come in about half-past two or three o'clock this afternoon. He seemed to be in very much of a hurry, rushing around. I'm quite sure it must have been Mr. Steele. He didn't say anything to us, however. Usually he looks in on us just to pass the time of day when he comes home in the afternoon that way."

"Does he come home frequently during the middle of the afternoon?"

"Sometimes. Very seldom during the morning, but occasionally he comes in the afternoon."

Mason opened a closet door, looked inside at the array of clothes. "Do you know how he was dressed?" he asked.

225

Mrs. Gentrie indicated a light gray checked suit. "Why, that's the suit he was wearing this morning."

"Is it indeed?"

"Yes, he must have come and changed to a heavier suit. I notice his tweed is missing."

Mason moved over to the light checked suit and calmly started going through the pockets.

"Oh," Mrs. Gentrie said, "I . . . do you think it's all right to do that?"

Mason said, "I think we've got to find out everything we can about him."

"I know, but isn't that rather—well . . ."

Mason said, "I think it will be all right." He glanced significantly at Della Street and said, "Get Mrs. Gentrie to show you where he keeps his linen, Della."

Della, distracting Mrs. Gentrie's attention, said, "I suppose in this drawer . . ." She stopped at the expression on Mason's face as the lawyer pulled a telegram from a side pocket of the coat Steele had discarded.

"Well, well, what's this?" Mason said.

"Really," Mrs. Gentrie protested as Mason unfolded the yellow oblong of paper. "I'd prefer that you didn't read that."

Mason, however, already had the telegram opened and was reading the message. "Well," he said, "this is something. It's a telegram sent to Steele at the office of the architect and says, 'Man named Carr Luceman accidentally shot self when cat knocked gun off table. Luceman's address thirteen-o-nine Delington Avenue, San Francisco. Grab plane investigate.' And it's signed K. Anamata."

Mrs. Gentrie, visibly perturbed, said, "I wish, Mr. Mason, you could handle this without prying into Mr. Steele's business."

Mason said, "Don't you see, Mrs. Gentrie? Steele got this room for a purpose. He must have made a habit of opening this door at night after you folks had retired, quietly sneaking down the cellar stairs, going through the garage door, and across to the flat next door. If he didn't go inside the flat, he at least snooped around the windows and got a line on what was going on inside the place."

"Why . . . why, I can't believe it."

"And," Mason went on, with a significant glance at Della Street, "he's very apt to be over there right now."

"But why should he want to spy on the people over there?"

Mason said, "He's evidently in the employ of some Japanese. I understand Lieutenant Tragg thinks some of the people over in that flat could tell something about the smuggling of arms into China."

"You mean Mr. Hocksley?"

Mason said, "There's evidence indicating that Hocksley has been engaged in Chinese gun-running for years."

"Well, good heavens!"

"And Steele evidently secured this room because it gave him such an excellent opportunity to keep an eye on what was going on next door."

"Well, I'll declare! Why, then he must have been—he must—why, Mr. Mason, that would make him . . ."

"Exactly," Mason said.

"Then don't you think we'd better communicate with the police, Mr. Mason?"

"Not yet," Mason said. "Just keep quiet so we don't disturb anyone. We'll do a little investigating on our own."

Mason led the way to the cellar door, opened it silently, tiptoed down the cellar stairs. Mrs. Gentrie clicked a light switch which flooded the cellar with brilliance.

Mason inched his way over toward the shelf where the preserves were kept, keeping his eyes, however, on the garage door. "Now, as I understand it, this is the door which was painted. Your husband painted it the evening of the murder. . . . Where is he, by the way?"

She said, "I made him go to bed. He couldn't have done any good by sitting up, and he's going to have a hard time at the store waiting on all of the customers without Junior to help him. That's one thing about my husband. No matter what happens, he can sleep like a log. I don't think he ever actually worries about anything. I don't mean by that he isn't concerned over the situation. He simply doesn't worry about it. If he knew he was going to be executed tomorrow, I don't think he'd lose a minute's sleep. He'd simply say, 'Well, if it's going to be that way and there's nothing I can do about it, there's no reason for losing any sleep over it.' "

Mason turned then, casually, so he could look at the shelf on which he had placed the can. Apparently, the can had not been disturbed. He noticed that Della Street was also looking at it. She turned, caught his eye, then looked hastily away.

Mason said, "Now, is there any chance that your son could have got his fingers in that paint in some other way than off the garage door? Your husband must have brought this paint home when he came from the hardware store."

"That's right, but he didn't mix it until after Junior had gone out."

"Now, this door, I take it," Mason said, "is not kept locked."

"No. It isn't. But the outer door to the garage is. There's a spring lock on that, and Mr. Hocksley has the keys to it. I believe he has three or four duplicate keys."

Mason said, "Let's take a look in his garage." He opened the door and stepped inside. "Is there a light in here?"

"Yes. There's a drop light somewhere, and a string that turns it on. Here it is."

She pulled the string and clicked a light on.

"There's no automobile here in the garage," Mason said.

"No. The police took the one that was here. There were bloodstains on the cushions, and they wanted to take fingerprints and things like that. They've never brought the car back."

"I see. Now this door on the side opens into the yard which communicates with the flat."

"That's right. But you've been over this before, Mr. Mason."

"I know," Mason said, "but I want to be sure I've got the thing correctly fixed in my mind. There's a spring lock on this door. It can be opened from the inside without a key. And by pressing that catch, the latch can be held back so the door isn't locked. Just as it is now."

Mrs. Gentrie looked at it and said, "Why, land sakes! That door *is* unlocked! We always keep that locked. I remember looking at it just this morning, and it was locked then. The latch was in position."

"Then," Mason said, "quite obviously, the lock must have been changed, either by someone who had a key, unlocked it from the outside and threw the catch into position, or by someone who entered the garage through the cellar of your home, Mrs. Gentrie. Now, of the people who live in the other house, Mr. Hocksley has either been killed, or has disappeared. His housekeeper has been murdered. Opal Sunley, who acted as stenographer, is the only one who remains. Was she there today, do you know?"

Mrs. Gentrie said, "I saw her going to the flat this morning—and I don't know why, for the life of me. There certainly couldn't have been any work for her to do."

"Well, of the people in your house, who could have been down here? Mr. Steele?"

"Well, he might have been. He does have the run of the house like a member of the family. When Mr. Gentrie is down here, Steele will come down to talk with him for a while; but it's in the same way he helps Rebecca with her crossword puzzles, just something to furnish an excuse for a visit."

"The children were here after school?"

"Yes, the younger children."

"Junior didn't get home until quite late, as you've mentioned?"

"Yes."

"Rebecca was here?"

Mrs. Gentrie shook her head. "No. Rebecca had that crossword-club meeting this afternoon, and then went to the opera from there."

"What time did she get in?"

"Around midnight. She was full of talk about the opera, and a lot of gossip that didn't interest me in the least."

"Now, she went upstairs to bed without coming down to the cellar?"

"Yes. She was all dressed up in her best bib and tucker. You couldn't have got *her* near the cellar."

"Who else was down here? Your husband?"

"Yes, Arthur was down here. He spends a good deal of time here in the evenings. But I'm quite sure Arthur would never have left that door unlocked. He's very methodical about those things."

Mason thought that over for several seconds. Abruptly, he turned away from the door. "I guess on second thought," he said, "there's no use making any further investigation at this end. Better lock that door now, hadn't you?"

Mrs. Gentrie snapped the catch on the door. "Yes, we'll leave it locked. I don't like the idea of having that door left unlocked. Anyone could come into the house without our knowing it—just walk right in."

Mason said, "That's right. Why don't you put a lock on that door that leads to the cellar? There's no necessity for anyone who uses the garage to use the cellar, is there?"

"No. There really isn't. I was telling Arthur sometime ago we should have a lock put on there, but after we'd rented it to Mr. Hocksley, it looked a little as though we might have been suspicious of him. Arthur said we should either have put it on at the time we first rented the garage to him, or else wait until after he'd moved out and we had another tenant."

"Yes, that sounds logical," Mason said, and yawned. "Well, it's time for me to turn in."

Della Street was watching him closely, her forehead puckered into a curious frown.

Mrs. Gentrie made no attempt to conceal her concern. She asked, "What am I going to do about Junior? I've got to do something for him. That's what I wanted to see you about. Isn't there something we can do? And what about Steele?"

"Let it go until noon," Mason said. "By that time, I'll have found out just what Tragg's planning to do. In all probability, he just wanted to make the boy talk and used that method to do it."

"Well, he won't talk, not as far as that woman is concerned."

Mason started for the cellar stairs. "Well, there's nothing more we can do tonight."

"You'll find out about Junior in the morning?"

Mason nodded. "First thing," he promised.

"Please be quiet going out," she requested. "I don't want anyone to know I was down in the cellar at this hour, or that I've been up so late."

At the front door, Mason whispered, "Try and get some sleep if you can. There's nothing you can do. I'll get busy just as soon as things open up. Good night."

He opened the car door for Della Street. She jumped in with a quick, lithe motion, then switched on the dome light and looked over behind the rear seat.

Mason laughed. "Why the precautions?"

She said, "I haven't felt easy in my mind since you set that trap and used yourself as bait."

"You noticed the can was still on the shelf?" Mason said.

"Uh huh. That must mean that it was Steele who was getting the messages."

Mason started the car. "There are one or two other possibilities."

"Such as what?"

"Tragg nabbed Junior before he had a chance to go down in the basement."

She thought that over, said, "That's right," then remained silent. Just before Mason turned into her street, she said, "I guess I haven't what you call a logical mind. The more I think of it, the dizzier I get."

Mason said, "Go to sleep and forget it."

She showed him that she was worried. "Look here, are you holding out on me?"

"What makes you think that?"

"Because when the police find Steele's body, we've got our necks in a noose, yet all of a sudden you're acting as though there was no particular hurry."

"There isn't," he said.

"Sometimes I could slap you!"

"Here's my cheek," he said. Then, after a moment, "If that's a slap, I'll turn the other cheek."

Della laughed lightly as she jumped from the car. "Don't forget to wipe off that lipstick. 'Night!"

" 'Night," Mason said, and stood watching her as she ran swiftly up the steps of her apartment house.

■ 18 ■

Mason was drifting into that warm lethargy which comes just before sleep when the telephone by the side of his bed rang with shrill insistence.

He groped for the receiver, said, "Hello," in a drowsy voice. "What is it?"

The voice which came over the wire was hysterical, the words intermingled with sobs. "This is Mrs. Gentrie. I

232

could see that you knew all the time. I can't last it out. Do what you can for Junior. I got into this for him. I suppose murder is never justified, but then a mother—that Opal Sunley was—Mr. Mason, I can't—please don't let Junior hold it too much against me. You've got my fingerprints. The message in the tin said so. Lieutenant Tragg switched tins. I had a pencil in my pocket and surreptitiously made a copy of the message. You were too clever for me. I knew there was no use fooling you. I know you'll try to stop me, but you can't do it. You're clever, Mr. Mason—too clever. Good-by. I . . ."

Mason interrupted her, his voice thick with the accents of a man who has been drinking heavily. "Thash a'right, sister. Go right ahead. Have you li'l fun. Betcha you don't know what I've been doin'. I've been shelebratin' a weddin' party. Rodney Wenshton got married. Li'l Doris Wickford. Nishe girl, too. Lotsh champagne! Ran onto 'em coupla blocks down street. Never dranksh sho much champagne 'n all my life. Now, don't try talk no bus'ness with me now. Tomorrow—tomorrow—I tol' you I'd try gettin' Junior out tomorrow—hic, yesh, tomorrow—tomorrow I be a'right. Goo'-by!"

Mason dropped the receiver into place, flung off the covers, stripped off his pajamas, wrapped a robe around him, pushed his feet into slippers, and raced down the corridor to where a pay telephone was ensconced. Mason dropped a coin, dialed Operator, and said, "Get me police headquarters just as quickly as you can. This is an emergency. Rush that call."

Almost at once, Mason heard a voice saying, "Yes, this is headquarters."

"Perry Mason. Is Lieutenant Tragg where I can get in touch with him?"

"No, Lieutenant Tragg's off duty. He . . . What's that? . . . Just a minute. . . . Oh, hello. They say he just came in from San Francisco. Want to talk with him?"

"Get him at once," Mason said. "It's important as the devil."

"Hold the line."

A few seconds elapsed, then Mason heard Tragg's crisply hostile voice saying, "Yes, Mason, this is Tragg."

"Lieutenant, don't stop to argue. Throw out a call for radio cars that are in the vicinity. Send them rushing to the Gentrie residence. No sirens. Handle it very quietly, but get into that house and hold every person there until you can get there. Don't let anyone have a chance to kill anyone else or to commit suicide."

"What's the idea?" Tragg asked.

"Dammit," Mason said irritably, "I told you not to argue. Do what I tell you to, and you'll be having the congratulations of the chief tomorrow. Fall down on it, and you'll be on the carpet right. I'll meet you there."

Mason didn't stop to give Tragg any further opportunity to argue, but slammed up the telephone receiver; then sprinted back down the corridor to his room. He flung off the robe and dressed in frenzied haste. When he had his clothes on, he paused long enough to dial the number of Della Street's apartment.

"Hello," he heard Della Street's sleep-drugged voice saying.

"Wake up," he told her. "The lid's blown off."

"Who? . . . What? . . . Oh, yes," she said, crisp wakefulness flowing into her voice. "Where are you?"

"Just leaving for the Gentrie house. Get a taxi and get up there as fast as you can. Bring a notebook. Better bring a portable typewriter. We might even get a confession out of it. You can't tell. The criminal seems properly repentant; but every second counts now. I've got to rush up there. Be seeing you."

Mason dropped the receiver, picked up his hat, and dashed out of the apartment without even taking time to switch off the light.

Through an arrangement with the garage attendant,

234

Mason's car was parked in a position where it was always ready to go, and Mason had only to fling open the door, jump into the seat, and step on the starter. The garageman watched him careen around the corner of the driveway, shook his head dubiously; then looked at his watch. It was five minutes past five in the morning.

"That guy should join a union," the attendant muttered to himself.

Two radio cars were already parked in front of the Gentrie residence when Mason arrived, and, as he was switching off the ignition to his car, Lieutenant Tragg, in one of the fast cars of the Homicide Squad, came skidding around the corner.

Mason paused at the foot of the front steps to beckon to Tragg. Tragg, running across to join him, said, "I certainly hope you're not giving me a bum steer on this, Mason."

"I hope so, too," Mason said. "Let's go."

Tragg tried the front door. It was unlocked. The men pushed their way into a strange gathering. Four radio officers were guarding the members of the Gentrie household: The younger children, huddled and frightened; Rebecca, swathed in a heavy robe, her hair in curlers, her face without make-up, her eyes glittering with indignation; Mrs. Gentrie, trying to take things philosophically; Arthur Gentrie, clad in pajamas and bathrobe, managing a prodigious yawn as Mason and Lieutenant Tragg entered the room.

"Perhaps," Rebecca snapped to Lieutenant Tragg, "you'll be good enough to tell me what this is about."

Tragg made a graceful little bow, turned to Mason, and said, "Perhaps, Counselor, *you'll* be good enough to tell *me* what this is about."

Mason grinned with relief as he saw the little household assembled under the eyes of the radio officers. "My telephone rang a few minutes ago," he said, "and Mrs.

Gentrie confessed to having committed the murders and said she was going to shoot herself."

Mrs. Gentrie said promptly, "Why, I never did any such thing. I absolutely deny it. You're crazy, Mr. Mason."

Mason grinned at her. "It was your voice all right. By pretending to be so drunk that I couldn't have been trusted to remember what happened or what was being said over the telephone, I threw the contemplated suicide out of schedule."

"I tell you I didn't telephone you," Mrs. Gentrie said indignantly. "If you say that I did, you're saying something that's not so."

"Of course," Mason went on, "your voice sounded somewhat strained, which was only natural in view of the fact that you were hysterical, but there were certain little mannerisms of expression which were undoubtedly yours."

"You're crazy," Mrs. Gentrie announced flatly.

"You also told me," Mason said, "something which came as a very valuable piece of information—that Lieutenant Tragg had found the can I had planted on the shelf, and removed the top, that he had then placed another decoy can there. That explained a feature of the case which had hitherto puzzled me."

Mrs. Gentrie said, "That's true about Lieutenant Tragg. He told me not to say anything about the tin; so I didn't. I didn't have any idea *you'd* put the tin there."

Tragg turned to Mason. "You planted that?" he asked.

Mason nodded. "To help clear up the case. I could have had it solved earlier if it hadn't been for your interference there."

"But I put a tin back to take its place," Tragg said, "and had the same code message copied and placed in the lid."

Mason smiled. "But don't you see that the person for whom the message was intended was present when you opened the tin, and so actually got the message without the necessity of having the can removed from the shelf. You crossed me up there, Lieutenant."

Tragg frowned, looked at Mrs. Gentrie, and said, "Mrs. Gentrie, I'm going to ask you . . ."

"You don't need to," she flared. "I've put up with a lot of official stupidity and a lot of bungling in this case. I realize that people can't be perfect, but I've never seen such utter ignorance as . . ."

Mason interrupted to say to Lieutenant Tragg, "Of course, she'll make all sorts of denials—now. She wanted to lure me down here so that she could kill me—probably not here in the house, but maybe as I left my apartment. You see, she'd got that message and believed what it said. And, in case you haven't as yet figured out the code . . ."

"I have," Tragg interposed.

"Then you understand what I was trying to do?"

Tragg nodded slowly. "I didn't realize it was a trap at the time," he said. "I thought you were holding out on me, and I was planning to do something about *that*."

Mason yawned, said, "Well, as soon as the telephone rang, I began to stall her along. I made her think I was pretty drunk. You see, Tragg, only two persons have the number of my private unlisted telephone. They are Paul Drake and Della Street; but, in an emergency the other night, we gave the number to the woman who was pretending to be Mrs. Sarah Perlin. That person must have murdered Mrs. Perlin. So when my telephone rang and it wasn't either Della Street or Paul Drake, I knew I was talking to the murderer. I pretended that the champagne I'd taken at Rodney Wenston's wedding had been too much for me."

"Wenston's wedding!" Tragg exclaimed in surprise. "Is he married?"

"You didn't know?" Mason asked.

Tragg shook his head.

Mason said, "He married Doris Wickford. You can rest assured Wenston would never have permitted Doris Wickford to have made a claim against a full half of Elston Karr's property without having seen to it that she couldn't give him the horselaugh afterwards."

"You mean Wenston was back of that?" Tragg asked.

"Of course, he was," Mason said with an amused smile. "Karr had some money that would have belonged to Tucker's heirs. He didn't know, however, his dead partner had left an heir until he found it out by accident. He advertised to try and find her.

"That, of course, was too good an opportunity for Wenston to miss. He knew that he had only to fake a few letters, putting in facts which he already knew from his intimate association with Karr in order to make a pretty good claim. If he could have the claimant produce a picture of her father which would tally with that of Dow Tucker, it would make the case absolutely ironclad.

"The probabilities are that Wenston stumbled on to the person he planted as the daughter by accident, and before he got the idea of palming her off as the heiress. In all probability, Doris Wickford's father actually did go to China, and wrote her a few letters. As a stamp collector, she had saved the envelopes. Wenston probably happened to be looking over her stamp album, and, seeing the entire envelope with its postmark and canceled stamp, got the idea. Well, Lieutenant, I'll leave you with your case. If you'll take Mrs. Gentrie into custody, I feel quite certain you'll be able to work out a good case against her. And now, if you'll pardon me, *I'll* go back and try to get some sleep."

Mason turned and started for the door.

"Look here," Tragg said, coming after him, "you can't walk out on me this way. I'm not certain you've even got a good case against Mrs. Gentrie. As far as that telephone business is concerned, it's your word against hers."

Mason said, "Well, I've given you enough stuff to work

on, Lieutenant. The obvious facts are now in your command. You can let them all go now, except Mrs. Gentrie."

One of the children began to cry. Mrs. Gentrie got slowly to her feet. "You're not going to do this in front of my children. You're not . . ."

One of the radio officers put a heavy hand on her shoulder. "Sit down," he said.

Arthur Gentrie pushed back his chair. "Now, you listen . . ."

Two officers held him.

Mason said, "That's all there is to it, Lieutenant. Good night."

He opened the door and ran rapidly down the steps.

Tragg shouted after him, "Hey, you! Mason! You're not leaving now!" He jerked open the door and ran down the steps after the lawyer.

Perry Mason paused by the curb. Tragg came running up to him, his manner bristling with indignation. "You look here," he said in a loud voice. "You've given me some ingenious theories, but . . ." He drew close to the lawyer, suddenly lowered his voice, said, "What is this, a trap?"

"Uh huh," Mason said. "Come on, Tragg. We should be in at the finish."

"Where?"

"This way."

Mason ran lightly around the corner by the garages. "Give me a boost up the fence, Tragg," he said, "and then I'll pull you up."

Tragg boosted Mason up the high board fence. Once on top, Mason reached down and gave Tragg a hand up. Together, the two men dropped silently into the dark yard between the Gentrie house and the two-flat building.

"Now what?" Tragg whispered.

"Wait," Mason said.

They waited in the darkness for almost a minute. Then

quietly the door in the garage opened, and a dark figure tiptoed silently across the yard to the side door of the Hocksley flat. A key clicked against the lock. The door was opened, and the figure slipped inside.

Mason and Tragg moved cautiously across the lot. The door was still ajar. Motioning for silence, Mason led the way into the warm darkness of the flat. Listening intently, they could hear the sound of the dial on a telephone; then, after a moment, a woman's voice sharp with emotion said, "What kind of a game do you think you're playing? What's this I heard about you marrying that little devil, that . . . Yes, you did, too! You were married to her this morning. Well, last night then. Don't lie to me! After all I've done for you, don't think I'm going to let you get away with that. The minute you try anything like that, you're all finished. . . . Well, he said so. . . . Mr. Mason. . . . I don't think it was a trap. No. I didn't say a word. . . . You wouldn't lie to me? You *dar*ling! No-o-o-o-o. I didn't really believe it, not down in my heart, but I wanted to find out. I—I must get back. The officers are over there. Mason is getting awfully close to what actually happened. You'll have to do something about him at once. Remember now, I've taken care of the others for you. You've got to do this for me. All right, lover."

The receiver clicked. There was the sound of rustling garments as a figure approached them.

"Okay," Mason said in a low whisper.

Lieutenant Tragg's flashlight sent a pencil of white brilliance through the darkness, a pencil which stabbed the white, frightened face of Rebecca Gentrie, and held it in a pitiless glare.

Morning sun was touching the tips of the tall buildings as Mason, emerging from the Gentrie residence, helped Della Street into his automobile and said, "Well, I guess we're entitled to play hookey today. Putting you on a day and night schedule and then having you type a confession afterwards is a little too much of a strain, isn't it?"

She said, "Wouldn't it be swell to take a plane over to Catalina, put on bathing suits, and just lie around in the sun, sleeping and eating hot dogs?"

"Temptress!" Mason charged.

She said, "If you'd drive right to the beach, we could catch the first plane over."

Mason turned the steering wheel of his automobile toward Wilmington. "I think," he said, "this is the direction of the office, isn't it?"

"That's right, keep going straight ahead," she said.

"I'm a little dopey this morning," Mason confessed, "so I'll have to rely on you. If we *should* get lost, we'd have to telephone the office and explain to Gertie."

"Gertie's a good sport. You don't have to explain things to her. She'll stall off any clients."

"You're acting as though we were going to get lost," Mason said.

"No, indeed. You're headed for the office right now. Listen, you've been holding out on me again."

"No. Honest I haven't."

"On Rebecca?"

Mason laughed. "Believe it or not," he said, "after having all of the factors for a solution in my hands, I couldn't put them together."

"What do you mean, all the factors of the solution?"

"Don't you remember?" Mason said. "We talked it over and decided that the two people who were involved must be persons who couldn't afford to be seen together, and who couldn't communicate by telephone, but who both had access to that basement. We thought about a person being deaf or being so crippled he couldn't get to a telephone, but the true solution never occurred to me."

"Which was?" she asked.

"Exceedingly simple. Rebecca could get to the telephone all right when she was called, but only after the children had answered the phone first, and she couldn't put through outside calls without arousing suspicions because she had lived so much as a recluse."

"But why couldn't Wenston simply have called and asked for—oh, I see,—that lisp of his. Anyone would have noticed it at once, and then after the case developed, it would have been commented on. His lisp is sufficiently pronounced so no one would ever forget it, once they had heard it."

Mason said, "That is it. And, having laid down all of the basic factors for a solution, I simply failed to apply them."

"But I thought you said the voice of the woman who called you was very cultured and . . ."

"Don't forget," Mason said, "Rebecca has remarkable powers of mimicry. Remember the way she imitated Opal Sunley's voice? She even tried to mimic Mrs. Gentrie's voice, but she was smart enough to know that she would have to make it sound as though she were in great agony, to cover up any little defects in impersonation. Read me her confession, Della. I want to check certain details."

Della Street said, "I'll have to read it from my shorthand notes."

"Go ahead."

She opened her notebook, read, "I, Rebecca Gentrie, make this voluntary confession so Lieutenant Tragg will see how stupid he was. He thought he could flatter me and pull the wool over my eyes. All the time I was laughing at him. I take the full responsibility for the murders. I don't want Rodney Wenston to be charged with them. He didn't have anything to do with them.

"Rodney and I met by accident after Karr took the flats next door. It was a case of love at first sight. I have always enjoyed fake photography. With a little practice, a person can transpose negatives in an enlarging camera so faces can be changed from one person to another. I had made a picture of myself and put Hedy LaMarr's face on it. I happened to have it in my hand when I stepped out in the yard between the flats. Mr. Wenston was there. I showed him the picture, and he became interested in my photography. I took him into my darkroom and showed him around and told him how skillful I'd become in switching faces around. I thought perhaps I could do something with it commercially because lots of times when a person is being photographed, he'll like one picture of his face, but not the pose of the body.

"Rodney told me afterwards he fell desperately in love with me then and there, although he didn't show it at all until three days later, when I saw him again. Then he couldn't conceal it.

"I have always hated my sister-in-law. I never wanted to live with her. I hated the children. I wanted a car. I could never even learn to drive while I was living there. I couldn't get a chance at the car. Then Rodney told me a scheme by which he could make enough money to marry me, and we could live in style, and go around the world taking pictures. All I had to do was to take an old photograph of Doris Wickford's family and place the head of another man on the body of the father in the picture. I told him I could do it if I could get both of the negatives. He gave me one of the negatives and explained that the other was kept in the safe over in Hocksley's flat. He said Hocksley was a blind, that his stepfather had rented that flat under the name of Hocksley. Rodney wasn't supposed to know this. They kept that lower flat so closely guarded he couldn't ever get in to the safe. There was a housekeeper who was really in on the secret, and a secretary who didn't know too much. There was also his stepfather's bodyguard, Johns Blaine, and Gow Loong, the Chinese. These people used the back stairs to go up and down from the lower flat. They claimed they were doing some business with this man Hocksley. Rodney found out that it was no such thing. Hocksley had been one of the partners in the gun-running business they'd had twenty years ago. Hocksley had sold out then. Afterwards, he'd done some gun-running and double-crossed his Chinese customers, tipping the Japs off to when and where the guns were going to be put on Chinese junks. As a result, the Japanese were letting all of Hocksley's business go through, so Karr simply took the name of Hocksley.

"Once, when Rodney flew his stepfather to San Francisco, Karr went very sound asleep and Rodney was able to get a notebook from his pocket. There was a string of figures in this notebook, and Rodney decided it was the combination of the safe. He told me to go over and try it. He said I'd better take a gun just in case anything happened. Rodney was the only one who could manufacture an emergency which would take everyone out of the house except the old cripple. In order to do that, he had to leave himself. It was going to take quite a little planning to make it work. He fixed the time as midnight and agreed that he'd leave an empty can on the shelf as a signal. If anything turned up, he'd scratch a code message on the inside of the tin. If there was no message it simply meant everything was fixed for midnight the night the tin was placed on the shelf.

"We had to communicate that way because I couldn't get to a telephone very well, and if Rodney called me, his voice would have been recognized.

"The yard between the Gentrie house and the flat was sort of common property. Rodney had access to that and had had a key made which would fit the door in the garage. Because the housekeeper didn't like him and was suspicious of him, Rodney thought it would be better if we were never seen together, so he arranged this signal and the code. Occasionally, when I'd see him in the yard, he'd bow and smile, and I'd also bow and smile very impersonally, although I could feel my heart pounding until I grew dizzy.

"The night of the shooting, everything went wrong. In the first place, my sister-in-law found the can Rodney had placed as a signal. This was before I had gone downstairs. I was afraid she'd be suspicious, but I kept commenting about the tin, and I saw she had no idea that it might be a signal. I intended to get down afterwards, find where she'd left the can, and see if there was a code message scratched in it. Then I found Arthur had used it for paint. Apparently, there wasn't any message. I got Steele to look at the can. Of course, Steele didn't know why. I simply told him that I wanted to find out about the can because I thought it was a very peculiar circumstance. I didn't know then Steele was a detective. I found that out later.

"Because of a mistake, I didn't get the message about disconnecting the burglar alarm. I went over shortly after midnight and got the safe open. I got a lot of papers out of the safe, and then I heard steps coming, slow, halting, ominous steps. I hid behind the safe. Karr entered the room and came directly toward me. At first, I thought he didn't know I was there; then he told me to come out. I shot. He fell over, and then I was completely paralyzed with fright. After a few moments, I started out of the house, and then I saw Junior coming in, lighting matches. I almost killed him. I kept backing away. He couldn't see me because the light of the matches was dazzling his eyes. I moved back and hid behind the safe. He telephoned that little floozy with the painted fingernails, wanting to know if she was all right. When he found she

245

was, he went back out. I was trapped in that room. Karr was lying there unconscious, but I didn't dare to go out, right on Junior's heels. I waited for several minutes. I took the negative I wanted out of the envelope and put the rest of the things back in the safe, closed and locked the safe; then I started out.

"I was near the door when I heard a key click in the lock. The door opened and the housekeeper came in. I should have shot her then, but I tried to rely on surprise and rush past her in the dark. She grabbed at me. I struck at her with the gun. She tore a piece of cloth from my dress, but I fought free and slammed the door. Then I sneaked in and went to bed. I didn't know a piece was gone from my dress until the next day. She'd seen that dress. Sooner or later she'd identify the piece she'd torn out.

"I heard people from next door take the car out of the garage. I knew they were driving the old man to a doctor. Rodney had told me about the housekeeper having her own place at East Hillgrade Avenue. I went out there the next night to try and make a deal with her. She knew she'd seen the pattern on the dress somewhere before, but couldn't remember where. That was all that had saved me. She'd have thought of it later. She was going to turn me in to the police. She pointed a gun at me. I struggled with her. The gun went off in the struggle. I really didn't intend to kill her.

"I wasn't the least bit panic-stricken. I thought I could ring up Mr. Mason and Opal Sunley and pretend to be the housekeeper, confessing to the murder, and then make it seem logical she'd committed suicide. It almost worked. I did intend to kill Steele, the snoop. He'd been prowling around. He knew too much. I found a telegram in his pocket sending him to San Francisco. I knew I had to kill him to save Rodney. I didn't care for myself, but I couldn't let Rodney be dragged into it. I love Rodney as I have never believed it possible for a woman to love.

246

"Afterwards, when the message in the second can said that Perry Mason had fingerprints, I thought of a marvelous scheme to clean up the whole business. I have always hated my sister-in-law. Lots of times I've thought I'd like to kill her. I rang up Mason, pretended to be Florence, confessed to the murders, and said I was going to kill myself. Then I only needed to go quietly to Florence's room, tell her that I had heard the phone ringing and had answered it, that Mason wanted to talk with her and was holding the line. Arthur sleeps so soundly I could have done this without waking him. When she came down to the telephone, I'd have shot her and then put the gun in her hand.

"You never would have got any of this if Mason hadn't lied to me about Rodney having married that creature. I couldn't go ahead with the scheme of killing Florence, because he sounded so drunk that he couldn't have remembered what I told him. I have no regrets. I did what I did for the man I love. . . ."

"That's enough," Mason said. "It will give Tragg everything he needs."

"How about the person who broke into her darkroom and lit a match?" Della Street asked.

Mason laughed. "Just a little more alibi stuff. Those films weren't fogged. She simply pretended to be trying to help. She was really manufacturing a lot of confusing details."

"And she flew to San Francisco?"

"Sure. She had a meeting of a crossword-puzzle club, and there was an opera afterwards, so she had a good excuse for one of her infrequent absences from the house."

"I never would have suspected her," Della said.

Mason was thoughtful. "I should have suspected her sooner than I did. Any person who has studied criminology recognizes in that type the most dangerous potential murderer. She was a creature of repressions, a sex-starved, disappointed female. By pretending to fall in love with her, Wenston had no trouble whatever in making her an accomplice. She'd have done anything for him. You have only to read any of the well-authenticated works on criminology to recognize her counterpart in dozens of murders."

"Did you have any idea the picture was faked?" Della asked.

Mason said, "Yes. Gow Loong tipped me off to that. He's Chinese. His eyes notice little details which we pass up, probably because the Chinese have such marvelous memories. He noticed that the picture of the Wickford family group showed a face on the father which was not only like the photograph of the picture of Tucker taken in Shanghai, but was *absolutely identical* with it in every line and shadow. Gow Loong didn't know enough about photography to realize what this meant, but, as is the case with Chinese the world over, being confronted with something he couldn't understand, he became suspicious."

"How about Opal Sunley?"

"Just a good kid," Mason said, "who knew something mysterious was going on. She knew she was being paid to keep her mouth shut, and she kept it shut. She was there to transcribe records. She transcribed them. She didn't ask any questions and didn't try to find out what was going on. Of course, Junior was in love with her. When he heard what he thought was a shot in the adjoining house, he dashed over there to investigate, because he was afraid Opal might have returned to the residence of her employer. He was in love. Her reticence about her job made him think she was having an affair with her boss. He was suspicious, and he was jealous. When he didn't find her there, he telephoned her. Notice her number was one that could be easily dialed in the dark. When she answered, he pretended he was calling from his own house. He then went back home, ashamed of himself. He never wanted her to know that he had suspected her to the extent of going over to the adjoining flat and

248

making a search. He's young and romantic. He would have even gone to jail before he'd have told the truth. Della, we actually *are* approaching the beach."

"Well, it does look like it," Della said. "You don't suppose that I got my directions mixed, do you? How about the charred remnants of the clothes Tragg found out at Mrs. Perlin's bungalow?"

Mason said, "That's simple. Karr went to San Francisco to be treated for his wound. According to the story he told the doctor there, he'd been shot after he'd retired. That left them with some bloodstained clothes to get rid of; trousers, underwear, shirt, possibly a coat, and most certainly a pair of shoes. When Karr came back, he gave those things to Mrs. Perlin, told her to keep out of sight for a while, and to dispose of those clothes. She burnt them in the furnace at her bungalow."

"Why did they have her disappear?" Della asked.

"Probably because she was the weak link in their organization. She couldn't have stood up to police questioning. Della, we definitely are headed toward the beach."

"Well—"

Mason said, "We'll have to telephone Gertie. Be kind of nice to cover up with warm sand and doze off to sleep, then plunge in the salt water."

"Uh huh. Ham and eggs and coffee would be nice, too."

"Stack of buckwheats on the side?" Mason asked.

"No. That's too heavy. I have to watch my figure, you know."

Mason grinned. "Not when you're on a beach in a bathing suit, you don't, baby. Plenty of other people are doing that for you."

She smiled across at him. "You're awfully nice," she said. "It wouldn't be so bad getting scared to death in murder cases if there were only longer interludes in between. Will we take a spin in the speedboat?"

"Will we go out in the speedboat!" Mason echoed.

"Well, I hope to tell you! After we've had a little sleep, we'll charter a speedboat and tear the ocean wide open. Speed, in case you haven't noticed it, is our middle name."

By way of illustration, Mason's foot pressed down on the foot throttle until the speedometer needle went quivering up into the high figures.

Della Street smiled, said, "Yes, I'd noticed," and then, adjusting the mirror on the sunshield of the car so she could apply powder to her nose, she added evenly, "And in case you're interested, there's a gentleman behind you on a motorcycle who seems also to have observed that trait in your character."

Mason slowed the car, started reaching for his wallet containing his driver's license. The siren wailed as the motorcycle officer putted alongside. "What's the idea?" he asked, as Mason sheepishly slowed the car to a stop.

Della Street leaned across the steering wheel. "What's the idea of stopping us?" she demanded indignantly. "We're rushing down to interrogate some witnesses in that Hocksley murder case."

"You one of the boys working on that?" the officer asked.

Della Street said, "Well, I hope to tell you. He's Lieutenant Tragg's brother!"

The officer grinned and waved them on. "Go to it," he said. "We just got a radio report Tragg had cracked that one."

As Mason eased the car into gear, Della Street smiled at him and said, "After all, there's no use having relatives if you can't get some good out of them once in a while."

250

x 7/1

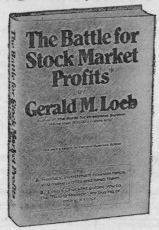